The
On
Earth

To Michelle,
who works me hard—
Thanks!
Tom Burby

Thomas Malcolm Burby
Illustrated by Brian Estes

1

THE LAST BOY ON EARTH
© 2011 by Thomas M. Burby
Library of Congress case no. 1-598762051

For information address:
Mindexcite Press, 333 French St., Bangor, Maine, 04401.
website: http://www.mindexcite.com
Interior artwork and design copyright 2011 by Brian Estes

ISBN-13:978-1460901229
ISBN-10:1460901223

DEDICATION
To my Wife, Victoria
If I was the last boy on Earth, and she was the last girl...

Thanks to my daughter, Megan, who loves monsters and mythology every bit as much as I do and whose good ideas are throughout this work. She continues to inspire me.

Thanks to my son, Jim, who was my model for Brady in a hundred different ways. Thanks for walking the cold winter streets of Bangor with me, putting up with a hundred different strange questions from your dad.

Thanks to my brother, Ray, who helped me get back on the path of writing and editing. Thanks for relighting the fire.

Thanks to my friend Frank Page, who has believed in me for as long as I can remember and whose good sense and humor has helped me make it through some very tough times. I do not know what I have done to deserve such a mentor. Thanks, Frank.

Thanks to my excellent collaborator, Brian Estes. Through your eyes, the world is always new and surprising.

Thanks to my friends, Sue and John McCallum, whose company and belief in the wonders of the world help me to believe in the strength of the human spirit and its tenacity.

Thanks to my Mother, whose love has always fed my belief in myself. Mothers are always right.

Thanks, Dad, for being the wizard of my youth. You are in this book – you are Joe and so much more. You are, and always have been, my hero.

Thanks to Brady and Kaileigh, who inspired the characters of this book. You are, and always will be, teenagers in my mind – amazing, courageous, kind and resourceful young people, no matter how old you grow. You taught me much.

Finally, thank you Mr. Ron Campbell, for letting me sit in your office that overlooks the Penobscot Narrows Bridge. You are a world champion, sir, in more ways than one.

4

Everything you can imagine is real.
-Picasso

Imagination is more important than knowledge.
-Einstein

Chapter 1
Awakenings

from the Journal of Brady Smith-

*"You see, there was this boy, and he ruled the world.
Everything belonged to him now. As far as his eyes could
see, he was the only one left alive. Now, you might think he
was pretty upset about the whole situation and, for awhile,
he was. There were dead bodies and nothing but desolation
and it's true that he sat around a lot and wished that he was
dead, too. For a long time he wondered why he remained
and all the others were taken. Then he thought, it doesn't
matter why. It just is and anyway, sitting around just got
boring. So he equipped himself with tools and weapons and
set out with his faithful sidekick so see what there was left to
see and do what there was left to do. He wasn't
disappointed, because since the fall of Humanity, the world
had changed in a thousand different ways too small to notice
at first and some so fantastic he couldn't believe it. As the
days passed into weeks, he discovered something amazing:
there really are monsters in the dark.*

I am that kid. My name is Brady Smith and I'm the last boy on earth.

I used to live on Holyoke Street, but I moved out a few weeks ago. I had to. There were too many ghosts. I'm fourteen and I lived with my mom in our apartment until the Abandonment. I don't know if she's dead or alive. My dad died two years ago in a hunting accident and I have no brothers or sisters and since my parents were only children, I have no cousins either. I had a lot of friends, but they're all gone. Sometimes I think I hear them when the Whisperers speak to me, but I know that must be my imagination. I'm alone in the world.

It's been five weeks since I awoke to the empty, silent world. No, that's not quite right because it isn't totally empty. The birds are everywhere and I see a lot of wild animals in the city: deer, raccoons, even a few bears. Everything is growing. The lawns that no one ever mows are all officially wild. Grass is growing in cracks in the streets and sidewalks and the trees are all leafed out. There are insects, more than I can remember. Everything seems bursting with life. Weredogs howl in the night. It's like the world hasn't even noticed that most of us are gone...

I don't know if anyone will ever read this, but if I don't write it, I know I'll go crazy. Since I can't talk to anyone else, I figure that I can talk to myself through this journal. So much has happened and there's no one else to talk to anyway, except my dog, Max. I knew that once I started talking out loud to myself, I was in trouble.

There's not much to do after the sun goes down. I can usually see the Flame of the North roaring against the complete blackness that night has now become. I can usually hear the howl of the weredogs in the forest, the darkest part of the Abandonment. If I let my imagination do what it wants, all kinds of things start looking into my windows and whispering into my ears. If anyone should ever find this journal, and I really hope someone does someday, I want you to know this: I didn't just sit around and wait to die. I made forward motion every day. Even if everyone else has gone, I'm moving on.

Right now it's 8 o'clock at night. My only companion is Max, my dog. The sun is just at the edge of the horizon, setting behind the hills over Bangor. Soon the world will go dark – so dark that I can see every star in the night sky. As far as I can tell I'm now living in the great second dark age, because when the sun finally does go down, my little light will be the only proof of human life on earth. I am a member of an endangered species – a species soon to be extinct, if I am truly the last. I will be a little speck of life in the middle of a vast cemetery. I haven't heard a real human voice in a long time, except for the Whisperers. I listen to music a lot and it helps because these are friendly voices, voices from the past. Right now, I'm listening to the Beatles. The song is "Nowhere Man." That just about says it all.

In a few minutes I'll turn off the music and the lantern and try to sleep. Usually, this is pretty weird because I know I'm alone and everything, but sometimes, I can't help but feel that I'm being watched and then I wonder, who's watching? That makes it hard to sleep. Some nights the Whisperers visit and I'll be damned if I can sleep at all. They won't leave me alone with their constant whispering in my ears. I wish I could tell them to shut up, but even though I can almost understand them, I don't think they can hear me.

I am the last boy on earth."

It wasn't yet morning and a silence had fallen over the world, a silence that once ruled it but hadn't prevailed against the constant grind of human machinations for centuries. Sunrise was near, so close you hear it just over the horizon, crawling up the wide rim of the planet. In the moist dew fall, a single bird began to sing its song, summoning the sun back into the world, heralding a beautiful day.

The earth turned and Brady opened his eyes. As he lay there, no urgency to get out of bed spurred him onward like when he had been a student in a school. In those days the alarm meant that he would throw himself out of bed, take his shower, quickly shove food down his throat and be off by 7:30. Now he could lie in bed all day if he wanted and no one would say a thing. No one would notice and no one

8

would care. There was no particular place to go and no one to mark his tardiness. As he lay there in the half-real world of morning, he thought back to the beginning of things, or the end of things, to the first day of the Abandonment.

He could see it in his mind's eye like a movie and he was the protagonist. Lying in bed in his mother's apartment, he was a boy sick with fever at a time when such a thing foreshadowed only one thing - death. The rumors were all over the Internet, television and the neighborhood. A new strain of the flu was killing people all over the world and it began with a fever. He had been ill for days, and a sore throat led to a high fever, body aches, vomiting and a sincere wish to do nothing but lie down and sleep. On that particular morning, Brady opened his eyes from a long sleep only to find the room in complete and utter darkness. As he remembered it, he pictured himself wet with sweat, shivering and uncomfortable. He searched for the familiar red L.E.D. of his clock-radio to tell him the time, but there was nothing but darkness in the thick and enveloping gloom and he was too tired to wonder. Instead, he rolled the covers off his body and closed his eyes. If the power had gone out, at least he was feeling a little better. Besides, there wasn't any school, not any more. The schools all over America, all over the world, had closed to help stem the growth of the pandemic.

As he lingered for the millisecond between sleep and waking, his mind wandered. Mom, fever, school closed, no medicine, bad news, worry, night sweats, sleeping, deep slumber. He remembered his mother mopping his head with a washcloth and he could see though the fever-haze that she was worried. No, it was more than that. She was frightened to a near panic. Words meshed together in a mephisto frenzy. What had she said to him?

"...must go to find help...be right back...stay right here...so hot...burning up..."

Then there was an image of her looking down on him with those big brown eyes, that wrinkled brow, and a hand upon his forehead. As he thought of her face now, he held it in his mind's eye like a treasure he was safeguarding. How long, he wondered, before he forgot what she looked like? He forgot what his dad looked like about three months ago and it bothered him then for weeks, making him feel unworthy and empty. Where do memories go, he wondered, when we lose them?

"...hospital might let me in...pharmacies closed...know a way in...must find ...something to help..."

Then there was darkness and quiet. Sleep.

In the swirling maelstrom that was his mind, he became aware that his mother had left him alone in the apartment in a desperate attempt to find something that might help him fight off this sickness, even though she knew there was no cure or vaccine for this new strain of influenza. What could she be thinking?

The world had stopped for most people. The Pandemic was running rampant throughout the continent of Asia and the Near East. So far, the northern United States and Canada had remained relatively clear of the contagion, but the news had been warning people for weeks to stay inside as much as possible and to be prepared for a long period of waiting for the clear signal from the World Health Organization and the Centers for Disease Control. They didn't really know how many had perished. No agency ever seemed to mention numbers or casualty rates and each day brought more dire news as the world went into lock-down. No one went anywhere. People stayed home unless their work was necessary to the functioning of the federal and state authorities in charge of the effort to isolate and manage the contagion. Schools closed and public gatherings were expressly forbidden. The world was waiting to exhale and the all-clear signal.

Then a small group of cases were reported in Canada, probably brought there by migratory birds as the weather warmed but it was unclear what actually caused the illness in the first place. Probably Brady would never know. Birds might be the carriers, or mosquitoes, or the wind. How were so many people coming down with it if they stayed inside and didn't mix? It had all happened so quickly that the united effort of all the health officials in the world were stymied in their efforts to discover the cause.

In the long wait, before he fell ill, he played video games, listened to music, and watched television while his mother worked as a nurse at the medical center in Bangor. Because her job was considered essential, she was allowed to travel.

"Brady," his mom would say before she went to work, "stay in the house, please. In here, you're safe. I know you're bored, but it's better to be bored than.....well, you know. If you stay in here, you'll be okay."

"I'll be okay," he said, trying to alleviate her fear. "I'll surf the web, I'll watch TV and text my friends. Really, I'm fine."

Since the world effectively shut down, the web was so slow as to be pointless. The cable was sketchy, going on and off randomly. Besides, most channels were 24/7 news, now that the world looked like it was ending.

"I know you will," she said, "I don't know what I'd do if," but she couldn't finish her sentence.

"What about you?" he would ask. "You work at the hospital. Aren't you in danger?"

She would smile a little, which Brady knew was for his edification. It didn't work. Then she would say something assuring like, "We take so many precautions. We keep everything clean and sterile. I shower before I come home every night. We wear masks and have clean rooms. We have protocols to keep the Pandemic from spreading."

But the problem wasn't the hospitals. Everyone seemed to get the illness, all ages, people who stayed inside, people who went outside – it didn't seem to matter.

He kept a strong interest in the development of the disease, checking the World Heath Organization's website every day for news releases. The idea that there might be something out there, uncontrollable, unavoidable, silent and lethal that could devastate entire populations of humans seemed as unlikely as zombies rising from the grave or a horde of orcs pillaging his village. Even a boy with a stalwart imagination had a difficult time imagining the effects of a severe worldwide pandemic. He spent many hours alone while his mom worked and his mind wandered to his small personal library, to his Norse mythology books in which even the gods faced an end at a time called Ragnarok. Those strong, tall northmen imagined an end to everything, even their gods. Thor and Odin, Freya and Balder all fell in the end, so why not lowly humans? Thor would tackle the Midgard Serpent and Fenris would rise and those were enemies worthy of gods. All people had was a virus of some sort, still largely unknown and invisible, tiny and imperceptible.

He never knew precisely why or how he had become sick, but his mother thought it might have been her fault. She might have brought it in on her shoes, she said. She might have brought it home on her clothing. However it arrived, she blamed herself. Brady was very tired and then the fever hit. His mother had seen it before. The illness hit very quickly and killed within a few days. He knew this when he took to his bed and stayed there. She called in sick so she could take care of him, spending hours of attention and nervous hovering over him, holding his hand. He couldn't seem to stay conscious. The few glimpses of his mother that he could remember were of a troubled woman, eyes red and tearful, lips pursed in a tense smile, her hand applying wet cloths to his forehead.

from the Journal of Brady Smith-

"There was this Pandemic thing going around and Mom thought that maybe I had it. I knew she was worried. There had been a lot of reports of people catching it and that's all that was on the TV or the Internet. I felt like crap. My mom made me go to bed and kept cooling me off with ice packs and wet towels and lots of pain killer. She kept muttering, and I can't remember what she said except that it sounded something like, "What good are doctors when you can't get one? What's going to happen to him?" Then she did something I hardly ever heard her do – she prayed.

To be honest, I thought she was a little crazy. I don't know how, but I knew I wasn't going to die. When you're really, really sick, but you aren't going to die, you kind of know it. I knew it and I kept saying, "Ma, I'm fine. I just have an infection. The leukocytes will save me!" But it didn't seem to stop her worrying and she was all over me, kissing me on the forehead and cooling me off. I kept throwing up, so she was really worried. I know enough about survival to know that you can go a lot longer without food than you can without water, so I really made an effort to drink. I could keep down sugar water, flat ginger ale, even suck on a popsicle, but that's about it. I just wanted to sleep. More than anything I just wanted to close my eyes."

Then the world went black again, a peaceful exit to the River of Dreams and the confluence of thoughts. The fever should have killed him, but it didn't. His mother left for the hospital and whatever desperate cure she could find.

She never returned. He wouldn't find that out for awhile. But he had survived, somehow. When he awoke that morning, the first morning of the new world, the sunlight filtered through the louvers onto the room, his bed and his face. Outside he could hear the song of a single bird. For a long time he listened to it and it seemed to fill his mind. How strange, he thought, that the whole world was out those windows but all he could hear was a single bird's song.

He looked for the clock-radio's telltale time, but its face was black. He fumbled for his watch and saw the time: five-thirty in the morning. He was going to put the watch back onto the side table when he pulled it quickly back to his view. It wasn't the time that concerned him; it was the date. The last time he remembered, it was June third. It was now June seventh. He had lost four days.

"Mom!" he yelled at the very top of his lungs. More a cry of panic than a summons, he called her again. She didn't respond.

"Mom!" he demanded to the silent room, the empty house, and the noiseless neighborhood. With no answer, he went to throw himself out of bed, but found himself unsure of his own legs. Weak and faltering, he had to steady himself by sitting on the edge of the bed for a moment. That was when Max sauntered into the room, oblivious to the intense fright in his master's mind.

"Max!" he said, as the dog rubbed up against his leg. The mongrel looked up at him with plaintive, hungry eyes. Hungry meant he hadn't been fed. Hungry meant that Mom hadn't fed him and Mom always took care of Max. Where was she?

He found the strength to make it to the kitchen where he could tell immediately that something was wrong and that in very small ways, the world had changed. He looked for his mother since calling for her seemed to do no good. She was gone. Glancing out of the kitchen window to the driveway below, he saw that her car was missing. Brady found his backpack and pulled out his cell phone, hoping that there was still some power in it. He dialed his Mom's number and waited for what seemed an eternity. Then his heart fluttered when someone picked up the line on the other end.

"Mom! Mom! Is that you? What's happened? The power's out....." but he was interrupted by the recorded voice of the cell phone provider saying, "*Message B12. Welcome to OneCell. The party you are trying to reach is not available. Our network is currently experiencing difficulties. Please try again later. We apologize for any inconvenience.*"

The message began repeating itself and Brady hung up the phone. Mom was gone, he had lost four days, the power and the phones were out. Still, what else was there?

For all of his panic, Brady did something remarkable. He forced himself to think, to observe, to calculate.

Observation Mode - a state of mind devoid of emotion to be used while gathering data. Observe and report to the brain and that is all. Use in cases where it is essential to maintain self-control. You are recorder. You are not thinking. You are watching.

When he was in the fifth grade he had consumed all the stories in *The Adventures of Sherlock Holmes* by Sir Arthur Conan Doyle. From the detective, Brady learned that in a time of uncertainty, one could piece together the clues or 'inferences' and come to some type of conclusion. Sherlock

14

Holmes had said *"Once you eliminate the impossible, whatever remains, no matter how improbable, must be the truth. "* Brady slowly began to realize that with a little concentration he could shut down his emotions for a short while and simply 'be' in the moment. It was strange, at first.

Brady stared out of the window towards Wilson Street for a very long time, analyzing the world, sorting out what he could eliminate. There were no cars rolling down the road. There were no people walking on the sidewalk. There were no airplane contrails in the sky.

He opened the window to listen. There was a quiet that covered everything, a silence in the midst of a world that was once buzzing with the sounds of movement and life. Here and there he could hear the barking of dogs in the distance, all muffled. No sound of civilization, no honking of horns, no sounds of jets landing or taking off from Bangor International Airport, no loud thumps and bangs from the eighteen-wheelers with their loads of wood chips and pulp logs as they hit the pothole by the Irving. One thought stabbed at his mind like a knife. It poked at him and he kept fending it off, but he knew in some small, strong place within him that he was right, even though he had not yet proven it.

It was the day after Ragnarok. The gods had fallen.

There were no people.

15

Chapter 2
The Abandonment

from the Journal of Brady Smith

"It's been three days to get strong enough to get out of this apartment and find someone else alive. I don't know why I'm not dead, but that doesn't really matter right now. I'm alive and that's what counts. I'm running out of food - no electricity for the fridge or to run the stove. There's been no sign of anyone else - nothing but quiet. I'm weak, but I can't just sit around not knowing what happened. I've been listening to my radio, searching the dial for any kind of signal, but there's nothing but static. Damn it!"

There was no running water but there were bottles of fruit juice, a case of soda and a few bottles of water. The food in the refrigerator had already gone bad so he lived on food from the pantry. He had his father's small butane camp stove and as dangerous as he knew it was, he set it on the table and cooked some ramen noodles. When darkness fell he lit candles and lay down on the coach, Max curling up on his feet. With the afghan that his grandmother had crocheted years ago to cover him, Brady stayed up as long as he could, keeping his mind busy, resisting the urge to panic. Whenever he felt like he couldn't stand his situation for one more second, he put his mind into *Observation Mode*. One of the benefits of this mode was the lack of emotion it required and therefore made suffering this eternity of waiting a little easier.

In this place inside his head, Brady imagined that he was Sherlock Holmes and he used the kind of logic that Holmes used, suspending his emotion. Oh, how those stories filled his mind that past summer after his father died and he needed something to make sense. He found a place in his mind where he could go and forget about the outside world that imposed itself so heavily upon him and this place became sanctuary, just as surely as Notre Dame was to Quasimodo. He was too tired to go far – his body wasn't cooperating with his mind, which was on fire.

He grew stronger and on the third day of the Abandonment he ventured outside, determined not to return until he had found out what had happened. He would have ridden his bike, but he found that the simple act of walking came only with slow, deliberate movements. With his backpack full of fruit juice and snacks and Max trotting slowly by his side, he ventured forth into a whole new world.

The screen door slammed shut, its loud report echoing through the neighborhood. A large brown form darted silently past them, sending Max in pursuit and it took him a moment to determine what had just rushed past them, his heart beating wildly. It was a deer, running up the middle of Wilson Street. A deer in the middle of a busy city in the middle of the morning? Brady wondered. Then he called and whistled until Max finally gave up his pursuit and came trotting back, happier than Brady had seen him in a long time.

His goal was the Shop-A-Lot Supermarket. The

government had closed all the stores and food was distributed at relief centers or even dropped at the curb, or at least that was his memory before he fell ill. If the supermarket was closed, then there would be someone on the road, someone at the Dunkin' Donuts or Tim Horton's. Every hour, hundreds of cars passed by the mall on the top of the hill in Brewer on their way to Ellsworth and the coast or into Bangor. Surely there would be someone there to answer his questions.

The long silent trek was causing his fear to mount with each passing step which was juxtaposed by the incredibly happy form of Max running ahead of him, his tail a crazy metronome in the air. His search for someone, anyone looked like a greater failure with every step. There were no people and it was then that a troubling thought slithered into his mind: everyone else might be alive and *he* might be dead, trapped in some strange afterlife, alone. Perhaps they are all still alive in the real world and he had died and been assigned to this place, bereft of any human company. It was the long moment of not knowing when anything might be possible and the world is uncertain, even foreign.

Abandoned, orphaned, lost and alone as the wind's slow lament whirled a candy wrapper across the road and made someone's wind chimes ring a strange dirge for an empty world, Brady urged himself forward. If this was the Land of Death, he wondered, why was it so much like the world he knew? Then his better sense, his Sherlockian logic, emerged. He found himself actually saying aloud, "The game's afoot, Watson!"

Once, as a young child, he had fallen and when he stood up, his hand was a bright crimson red. His index finger was cut deeply and he was bleeding profusely. Instead of crying or fainting, he stood silently and watched it bleed. Strangely, it didn't seem to hurt much, not anywhere near as much as it appeared it should. He bent his finger and saw the ivory white of bone beneath the blood and pulp and he might have stood there for another minute or hour, but his mother came running over. Brady never shed a tear, even when they stitched him up at the emergency room. He was fascinated

with the experience, if only because it wasn't any\
he expected. That was similar to what was happenir\
now. In the midst of a foreign world, something at tł\
end of things, he was full of its experience and
intrigued.

He returned to *Observation Mode*. He paid particular
attention to his senses. What was he looking at? What color
was it? Was anything out of place? Were there any sounds
that whispered to him? He would later be able to recall very
vivid details about the time he spent searching. It was like
stepping outside of himself for a moment and there were
times he swore, if he imagined hard enough, he could even
erase himself from the recording in his mind and zoom in on
details that he might have only glimpsed for a second in real
time. He might be able to pause a scene and examine the
visual for a long moment, closing his eyes and making a
little movie theater right there on the black screen that was
the back of his eyelids.

Scan the scene, he told his mind-camera. *What else is
there to see?* There were some cars stopped and only partly
on the road, their rear ends askew with the painted line of the
median. Some had their doors open. There were only a few,
perhaps four or five, in the entire stretch from his apartment
to the grocery store, but what might be lingering inside of
each of those cabs he didn't want to discover.

Not yet.

Avoiding them altogether, he continued toward his
original destination – the shopping center. He was on the
uphill slope of Wilson Street, near the Brewer Auditorium.
He walked into the parking lot and was encouraged because
there were cars parked in most of the spaces. He walked to
the entrance and tried the handle of the door but he couldn't
get into the building. There was a hastily scrawled sign
written in red ink taped to the inside of the glass of the main
entrance.

It read: *"Closed due to Contamination. DO NOT
ENTER!"*

Brady was sure by the way it had been written that there
were people inside. He imagined that it should have been

..nore official looking, with words like, "By the order of the Chief of Police..." but this hastily scrawled handwriting denoted a less sanctioned kind of message, a plea, a warning. "Contamination," meant sickness and that meant the Pandemic, or whatever they were calling it: the flu, the sickness, the shivers?

How old is the note? he wondered. *If there are people inside, are they alright? Are they...alive?*

He put his nose up to the glass and his hands around the sides of his head like he was holding binoculars and concentrated his vision, looking for movement, for anything. There was only darkness and the shadows as the light from the high windows filtered through. Peering for a long moment, he thought he saw the lower part of a leg lying on the floor just past the secondary entrance doors. It wasn't moving.

He banged on the glass door with his left hand and he shouted, "Hey, is anybody in there? Hello? Hello?"

There was no response, no matter how loudly he shouted. The thing that looked like a leg didn't move. After a moment that was his first slice of eternity, Brady left. He didn't have the energy or the inclination to break in. He was on a scouting mission. He kept walking.

He was near the Brewer Public Pool, what all of his friends jokingly called the 'Brewer Sewer.' That was when he saw his first dead body in the pool, face down: a man in a suit. He was lazily floating and Brady was shocked but at the same time found himself thinking, *"What do you call a man with no arms and no legs in a pool? Bob!"*

He found the hook that the pool cleaners used to grab items from the water and held it dangling over the body, snagging the collar of the man, nudging him to the edge. Later he might be lying quietly in bed and a shiver would cross his spine like a line of fingernails on a slate chalkboard, but now he simply pulled the man to the shallow end of the pool that gradually sloped upward to the edge. Using the end of the pole he carefully turned the corpse's head to the side.

He didn't know this man by name, but had seen him a

20

hundred times waiting for the BAT, the city bus that ran between Bangor and Brewer. His tongue was swollen and lolled out of his mouth like an engorged leech, his bulging gray eyes were wide open, staring into whatever world waited beyond this one. His white, puffy face was enough to make Brady pause his recorder for a moment before determining that there was nothing more to be gained here and that, in a very odd way, there was nothing to be afraid of in this dead man.

Really, this guy is no zombie who is going to stand up and chase me down and eat my brain, he thought. *He's just a bag of bones, what's left after you die. He's an empty potato chip bag. He's a candy wrapper or a plastic bag, blown on the wind.*

Later, after the events of this day, he would spend a considerable amount of time throwing up the contents of his stomach until there was nothing left but the heavy heaving of an empty thing.

Still, Death was not nearly as frightening as the prospect of being totally alone.

He tried to pull the body out of the water, but couldn't find the strength. He could have walked away immediately, but he persevered, managing to hold down his gorge and complete the task. He took a tarpaulin that was next to the pump house and covered the man's body, even though he was still floating. Forward motion needed to be maintained. There was nothing he could do for this man. Max jumped up and nearly pushed Brady over before running back to the street, waiting for his boy to continue.

If one were able to look down from above, from some high point in space and focus down upon the lone boy walking into the parking lot of a small shopping center, one would see a minuscule figure stop solidly in his tracks, frozen. One would see him as a statue for a long time except for the boy's head slowly swiveling as he surveyed the scene. There were cars with open doors and windows, empty plastic bags being played with by the wind. He perceived the flapping of the flags on the mall's roof. Perhaps twenty cars were haphazardly parked at angles in the lot. Upon closer

21

inspection, one had driven through one of the grocery store's massive plate glass windows.

A lone dog was loitering near the car and when it saw Brady, it froze. Max barked and ran towards it but Brady called him back, having to grab him by the collar. The other dog eyed them both for a long moment, sizing them up, regarding them in a curious fashion Brady had never witnessed in a dog before. It was as though it was studying them. Max wouldn't stop his tirade of barks and yips and it took all Brady had to hold him back. The other dog slowly turned away and ran, after a fashion, but not very far and not very hard.

When Brady discovered three other dead bodies, one in each of three cars, he determined that it did no good to gather more information about the contents of cars. He moved away from the vehicles and toward the grocery store. Perhaps someone was there, inside, alive.

As he stood in front of the locked door of the Shop-A-Lot, he understood why someone had driven through the window. They were looking for a way in. He stepped gingerly over the shards of glass and past the automobile. As he slithered past the car door, he looked inside to see a young woman draped over the steering wheel, still clutching it. Try as he might, he couldn't pull his vision from her. Did he know her? What drove her to do such a thing? He found himself wondering, in a detached kind of way, whether she was dead before she hit the glass or after. This grocery store had a pharmacy. Maybe she was looking for drugs. Maybe she was hungry.

The interior was very dark, like looking to the interior of a very deep cave. He had come to this shopping center looking for some sign of life and he had found nothing but this strange drapery of death covering the world. Now there was darkness.

The car that had smashed in through the window was the answer: the headlight switch! Hoping that there might be some power left in the battery, he reached down past the dead woman, over to her left, and flicked the lever that turned on the vehicle's lights. Instantly the supermarket was bathed in the bright halogen wash.

Answers were the first thing he sought. There was a set of shelves next to the checkout where a variety of daily and weekly newspapers were kept: *The Piscataquis Observer, The Ellsworth American* and *The Bangor Daily News*. *The Bangor Daily News*, or the BDN as his mother called it, was the only newspaper that Brady read on a daily basis. Like most kids, he started out reading the comics and the entertainment section, with a passing interest in the sports section. He had a habit now of trying to read the paper from cover to cover, at least for the headlines. He looked for the most recent edition. There, in the pile on the floor, was a copy of what must have been the final edition, four days old.

MYSTERY FLU DEVASTATES NATION AND GLOBE UNITED STATES GOVERNMENT RELEASES CONTROL OF ALL EMERGENCY AUTHORITY TO STATE AND LOCAL GOVERNMENTS. MILLIONS FEARED DEAD. MUTATED VIRUS SUSPECTED. WORLD COMMUNICATIONS FAIL.

Washington D.C.-The Centers for Disease control reports that a previously unknown strain of influenza has arisen out of the United States and has killed hundreds of thousands of people this week in Europe, Asia and the Americas, perhaps millions in Africa. Various public health authorities report that there is no way to accurately determine the number of casualties. The pandemic has stalled almost all air, land and sea traffic, work, and even communications as federal and local authorities wrestle with their abilities to handle the mass hysteria that is breaking out in cities and towns all across America, not to mention the diminished work force available to deal with the threat.

The World Health Organization has determined that this previously unknown virus has mutated much faster than any previously discovered virus and seems to be many times more contagious than the common rhinovirus, or common cold, making it the most virulent contagion known to modern science. Originally, authorities thought this virus similar to that of the Spanish Influenza of 1918 that killed over 50 million people worldwide. Unlike previous flu outbreaks, this new pandemic affects all ages equally. The mortality rate seems to be growing daily, from 50% last month to an unprecedented 90% in the past week. Hospitals in many major metropolitan areas have been turning people away, claiming that they are full and that they have no means to combat this killer. Antiviral drugs specifically designed to combat such strains as the H1N1 virus have consistently failed in treatment of this infection. The Center for Disease Control in Atlanta warns that the survival of civilization itself could be at risk.

Citizens are urged to stay inside and away from populated areas. If possible, the bodies of the deceased should be removed and either buried or burned within a few hours of death. People should stay well-hydrated and make strong steps to keep fevers down and consume anti-diarrheal medication to treat the symptoms.

The Centers for Disease Control have issued a few simple steps citizens may take to help ensure their own survival. If you are a healthy person, do everything you can to remain that way. The virus is passed from human to human and possibly from animal to human. The nature of the viral transmission is most probably airborne. Stay inside. Avoid any contact with others until notified. Wash your hands often. Make sure that you have emergency supplies including at least four weeks worth of nonperishable foods, water, and medical supplies, as well as emergency radios. All information will be issued through the emergency radio network.

Recent reports from around the world keep rolling in and the picture is grim. If the reports are correct, the World Health Organization predicts a 90% or greater mortality rate for this pandemic. Religious organizations are calling these the End-Times, referring to the pandemic as the "Wrath of God." Special religious services are being broadcast over

24

radio and television in the hope that people will stay in their homes until the crisis has passed.

Brady let the paper fall to the floor. The edition was very small, only a few pages, but he was thankful that someone at the newspaper saw it through and wrote it down. From what he was assessing, he had quietly slept through a horrific time, a time of rapid death and unimagined panic. Someone at a desk in the BDN's office decided to persevere through what must be the ultimate test of journalistic integrity and publish an edition that they must have suspected would be the story of the end of the world. It seemed that he alone had survived and it felt like they had published it just for him, their final subscriber.

As he stood there in the wash of light from the dead woman's auto, he heard the faintest sound, the quietest of whispers from somewhere to his left. There it was again, but this time it was to his right. Glancing quickly in either direction while in *Observer Mode*, he tried to discover the cause of the sound but there was nothing immediately evident. The lights of the car weren't bright enough to penetrate past several of the displays and aisle fronts. Quickly rolling the paper up, he held it like a sword and found his way to the hardware aisle, finding a flashlight with batteries pre-installed and then went searching the dark recesses of the Shop-A-Lot.

The pervasive odor of rotting flesh at the rear of the store stopped his progress, impelling him backwards, hitting him like a wave. The putrid smell of spoiled meat was overpowering. Still, he persevered in his search for the source of the whispers. There, past the meat aisle, was the deli, past the freezer cases which were mercifully sealed with magnetic catches, he slowly made his way, shining his light through the darkness, stopping and listening like a hunter seeking prey except that he had never hunted anything in his life and this was as much like being hunted as he could imagine. The feeling that he was being watched was preeminent. He couldn't shake it.

Then he thought, "*Why don't I just call out 'Hello'*?" and

25

a voice within him said, "*No way, moron. What if whoever is making that noise is crazy and wants to kill you and eat your brain or something? Just shut up and stay calm. Don't panic.*"

Don't panic.

That was the best advice he had ever read and he quietly thanked Douglas Adams for it, having read *The Hitchhiker's Guide to the Galaxy* just last year. *Don't panic.* The best advice in the world! He had seen his share of zombie movies and right now, a mindless slow-moving corpsicle could plunge out of the darkness of an aisle and take a bite right out of his skull.

Put that thought away, stupid.

Whispers in the darkness. What are they saying? Where is this sound coming from? Brady could not find the source of the sound and it bothered him greatly.

He took canned food, mostly, then a two-liter bottle of Dr. Pepper and some pretzels and he filled every pocket full with batteries and two flashlights and when he thought he couldn't carry anymore, he walked to the front of the store, never looking back. His backpack and pockets were full.

By the window was a display with paper and pens. Brady stopped and considered. He had always been a scribbler but now, more then ever, he thought that it might be a good idea to keep a record of happenings, thoughts and ideas. He felt for the first time the harsh tug at his heart that felt like hunger but would be more difficult to feed. It was the first vestige of loneliness. His heart was hungry for some company, any company at all. Maybe the words he would write could help stave off that growing hunger, if only for awhile. Maybe he would have to keep himself company.

Hey kid, why are talking to yourself? Oh, I only do it when I need intelligent conversation...

He looked carefully and considered. This might be an important decision, nearly as important as food. Finally, he chose one of the black and white composition books and a box of pencils, a manual sharpener, and a pack of fine point pens, stuffing them in his already overstuffed backpack.

Something caught his eye, at the very edge of the light's

illumination.

It was a person.

Max crouched down and hunkered his way toward the body, his nose to the ground, a low growl emitting from his throat. Brady was frozen in place as he watched Max creep closer, sniffing the ground. Max inched closer and the body remained stone-still. Then Max's nose touched the body slightly and the arm moved and a rattle of an empty bottle filled the store with sound.

"Max, here, now!"

Max turned and trotted back to his boy, his tongue happily lolling out of his mouth, barking his assent.

Brady made his way to the figure. Was he alive? He had moved, but perhaps it was the last involuntary movement of a corpse. Perhaps Max had caused the bottle the figure was holding in death to fall from his rigor-stiff hands. The old man was in the rear, in the wine aisle. Brady knew him as 'Rancid Randy,' the name given to him by a certain group of boys who never seemed to do their homework and who spent most of their time, as his mother said, *running the roads*. He was one of the homeless people who used to live behind the off-ramp for I-395 in a ramshackle hut made of tin and cardboard. He was sprawled on the floor like a rag doll. From the mass of empty bottles and puddle of vomit on the floor, Brady surmised what final activity Randy had spent his last waking moments pursuing. Brady thought that Randy must have found his way into the store, perhaps after everyone else had gone. Perhaps it was too much for Randy to bear and then there was an entire aisle of chablis and Port and chardonnay. There was little left to do except...

He drank and drank and drank.

Then he died. *At least he had a smile on his face*, thought Brady, feeling sorry for the old fellow. Then he thought, *Maybe he's the lucky one*. He would have given a lot to have a few final words with Mr. Randy.

As he looked at the old man, he tried to understand his own situation in this first crooked slice of time spent in the new world. This was the fifth dead body he had seen in the past ten minutes, to be followed, he was sure, by hundreds or thousands in the days to come. He left the store in a daze. A doctor might well have called it shock.

He did not know how long he wandered up and down the streets of his hometown. Time had no meaning anymore. The details were filed away in his mind neatly to be pondered in the small hours of night when sleep wouldn't come to him, no matter hard he tried to relax. He found that there were fewer dead people in the open than he thought there should be, so they must be in the houses. Perhaps the authorities had policed the area and forced people into their houses to contain the pandemic. Perhaps fear drove them inside. Every so often he would see a slumped form over the wheel of car and he would keep his eye on the form as he continued to walk, but they did not move. He heard dogs barking in some of the houses as he walked by but he did not intend to venture near and let them out. It was bad enough that he had to hold Max back by the collar and force him away from those places. Whatever lingered in those houses could stay there, for now.

The day was fading, losing color and erasing itself. He was walking back to his house when a curious thing happened. Brady heard a phone ringing. It was faint, distant, like something heard from a dream upon waking, but it was definitely there. He stopped and focused all of his concentration on listening. Sure enough, there it was again! A phone was ringing somewhere close enough to be heard, somewhere within one of these houses. Immediately he began to determine which house the sound came from. He tried to run but fatigue still dragged at his muscles from his recent illness and Brady had to push himself to a slow trot. Thank god, it was still ringing.

"Don't hang up!" he screamed and was surprised at the sound of his voice. "I'm coming!" he bellowed as he heard the ringing get louder and louder. Then it was a choice between two houses. It was ringing in Mrs. Novak's house, the elderly woman who lived a few houses away from his old apartment. She was the one who didn't like the children when they played in the park next to her house. She put up a fence to mask the sound of laughter and the shrill shrieks of delight as children slid down slides or swung so high they turned themselves inside out. Oh, not her house, he thought. Please, not this one. *She was scary enough when she was alive*, he thought. The ringing continued until his feverish need to hear another human voice overcame his fear of Mrs. Novak, the needle-thin, gray-haired woman who hated children.

The door was locked. No matter. He took a large stone from her garden and broke the glass on the door. In an instant, he carefully reached in and unlocked the latch. The phone was still persistently ringing. No time to look around, no time to wonder. Find the phone! Where was the phone? He heard it ringing upstairs. Bolting up the staircase, not sure where he was going, he stopped at the top of the landing. The phone was in the bedroom to the right. He also saw what was left of Mrs. Novak neatly covered by her blankets, slumbering in the sleep of death in her own very neatly made bed. He was horrified to look at her.

The phone! Just pick up the phone. Just lift it!

"Hello? Hello, please don't hang up. My name is Brady and I'm in Brewer, Maine. Can you hear me?"

A pause. A long pause. Then a gray voice, a ghost voice, a recorded voice said, "If you'd like to make a call, please hang up and try again or call your operator." It repeated itself several times. Brady wanted to throw it across the room, to rip it out of the wall. Then he thought, why not call the operator? He dialed zero and waited. The other end of the line rang and rang until that same voice, the recorded voice at the end of the line in some distant city said, "*We're sorry. All of our operators are busy helping other customers. Please hang on and we'll be with you shortly or hang up and try again later.*" Then the music started, that awful tinny elevator music that could numb anyone into unconsciousness. Brady pressed the speaker button on the phone and sat down on the chair Mrs. Novak had near her little phone table. He surveyed the room.

Mrs. Novak might have been a crotchety old woman who didn't like the sound of children playing at the park the city so ignominiously installed on the public land next to her

29

house, but now he could jump up and down shouting 'hallelujah' and not bother her at all. He had always avoided her gaze when he had been a younger patron of the playground. Now, he felt sorry for her. He cradled the phone on his shoulder and listened to the tinny elevator music emanating from some distant, unknown source. He waited for a minute, then two, and then an eternity. There was a slight chance that someone might answer on the other end, after a long time, if he could only be patient. A half-hour passed and still nothing. No sign of life.

He knew that the phone system ran on a different power supply than the rest of the grid and that a computer glitch may have randomly called Mrs. Novak's number, but the idea that someone, a living person, had dialed the house that he just happened to be near was troubling. Was someone trying to contact him? Did someone know he was alive? Who dialed that number? Suddenly he realized that there was such a thing as hunger for human contact, and it was far more debilitating than mere hunger for food. It was a need that demanded sustenance.

"Don't jump to conclusions. Base your hypothesis on the laws of nature and on data. Then investigate! Don't judge. Just question and seek answers. Then, when you have enough information, you can come to some real conclusions."

Mr. Page, his science teacher in the seventh grade, was one of the smartest men he had ever met, so he took these words to heart and recalled them now. Quite suddenly he was worried and he wondered what had happened to Mr. Page, to the other teachers, to the principal and he deduced that they were, to put it bluntly, no more.

As he stood there with the phone almost tenderly held next to his ear, something happened to him. He had done this thing so many times that now he wasn't even aware it was happening. For a moment, as the world became too inhospitable, degenerate and mean, he traveled somewhere else.

Observation Mode wasn't his only unique mental state. Since the death of his father, he became adept at creating *this*

30

place. There was a construction, a place in his head he went whenever things got to be too difficult to handle. He had tried to give it a name, but all he could come up with was his Fortress of Solitude and that was a rip off from Superman. Still, it was the best comparison he had. It was *his* place in *his* head and it was a place he controlled and no one, not a single soul, ever knew about. He had built it from bits of this and pieces of that until it met his needs.

When his father died, Brady spent nearly six months retreating into the Narnia books by C.S. Lewis, followed by a taste of Tolkien's *Hobbit*. He read from the piles of old Superman, Batman and Spiderman comics that were his inheritance from his father, collected when he had been a boy. He rented old movies for $1.00 at the local video store and found himself safely immersed in his own imagination. If his actual world became too much for him to bear, Brady had another mode his mind could switch to, very different from the *Observer Mode* he employed whenever he was in the midst of a crisis. He called it *Creator Mode*.

The rules of the Creator's game were simple – if the world is inexplicable, adapt it in your mind to something that you can understand. If the world is hellish, paint it over to look more like paradise, except instead of paint, Brady could use the mixed-media of elements from all the stories he had read, heard or seen. If his father had died, perhaps he was only visiting another realm and it remained his job to seek the doorway to the world where his father waited for him. If he couldn't sleep, it was for no other reason than the angels were whispering to him, telling him secrets in a language he didn't yet understand but one day, with study and perseverance, he would and then the secrets of the Universe would be his. If his friend suddenly decided that he no longer liked Brady and gave him the cold shoulder, it was because he had been possessed by an alien intelligence or perhaps because he was a pod-person, after all, devoid of human emotion. All of this was transitory and Brady always knew in another part of his brain that it wasn't real, except that *real* meant very little to a person of great and stalwart imagination. Einstein said that reality wasn't real, just

31

persistent. If Einstein believed it, well, Brady could too.

In *Creation Mode*, everything was open. If you wanted, you could create fun and interesting characters, give them difficult tasks and journeys to make and then, if it came to it, you could destroy those characters. You could make their suffering important so that they became better characters in the end. Even better, dead people could come to life again in the mind of the creator. Writers, filmmakers, songwriters, and artists – they were all creators. They were all responsible in some small part for the creation of worlds. So it was for Brady, in his mind.

Holding the phone in his hand with a dead woman in the bed next to him, we allowed himself to be transported. Now he was in this Fortress of Solitude, the place where answers were given and he was in charge. He had built it slowly over the years, furnishing it with items from his own imagination and from the books, movies and television shows he loved. He was sitting the Captain's chair from the starship Enterprise (the original series) and in front of that chair was Batman's wall of computer screens. Over in the corner he had a pinball machine copied from the one he liked to play at the Bangor-Brewer Bowling Lanes. The walls had AC/DC posters and there was a Gibson Les Paul electric guitar on a stand next to a whole wall of speakers that extended all the way to the ceiling. The place he had created was always changing. Things appeared when needed and disappeared when no longer required. This room was like *The Matrix* and he was Neo. It was his little room in between the worlds and no one else could go there. It was safe. As he sat in Captain Kirk's chair in front of the console of brightly lit red and green indicator lights, old-fashioned tube monitors mounted in an array, and a speaker grill above the keyboard, he thought about his question. The myriad lights were twinkling on the panel and he could hear the various system tones and beeps of the most advanced computer in the universe. He spoke to the system.

"Computer, analyze current situation on Earth, specifically Brewer, Maine, United States of America."

The machine whirred into a frenzy of action and sound

and after a few moments, a small strip of paper slowly printed out the computer's response.

He ripped it off the tape and read it aloud. "Human population nearly exterminated. Data indicates less than one percent of Humanity remains."

This was, of course, merely a recollection of something he had heard in the real world. In the days when the virus first began to spread, newscasters and scientists filled the airwaves forecasting scenarios of doom. How many times had he heard, "The government has this thing under control," only to have another talking head say, "This could be the worst pandemic the world has ever known." Numbers, percentages, and rates were thrown about and bandied while people waited in civic centers, hospitals, pharmacies and schools to receive what the government said was the vaccine that would save them all.

Except that it never arrived.

"Computer," he said, "determine what caused this event."

More whirring and flashing lights. The word *working* filled the screens in red, bold letters. A bell rang somewhere and this time a voice spoke. The computer changed from Batman's to another, even more sophisticated one. It was the voice of the computer of the Enterprise.

"Sensors indicate that there is a 99.998 percent chance that the mass extinction event was engineered specifically to destroy the human species."

Brady furrowed his brow in concentration. Where was Spock when he needed him? If this had been an engineered destruction of his species, it meant that someone, somewhere, had wanted the human race to go away. Perhaps aliens caused this in hopes of using Earth for their own without having to fight. Perhaps H.G. Wells' *War of the Worlds* strategy of destroying a species through infectious agents was a universal weapon used throughout the galaxy by more advanced species as their empires grew.

"Computer, speculate who or what was the cause of this engineered event. Who killed my species?"

The computer did not hesitate. "Data is insufficient to

determine at this time..."

He disconnected from the Matrix and found himself in the room once again. It was time to move on.

from the Journal of Brady Smith

'So there I was, just wandering around the streets of Brewer with no place to go that was better than any other place. I was in a daze, I guess. After hearing the phone ring, I realized how quiet everything had become. There must be someone else alive, but everywhere I went I saw bodies and heard silence and felt nothing – no anger, no fear, no sadness. The Pandemic did its job well. I think it killed my heart because I didn't feel a thing when I should have been falling apart.

And then I thought of my best friend, Noah, and nothing else mattered. I ran as fast as I could manage.

When I got to his house, the front door was open and like a hundred other times I walked in and said, "Hey? Anybody home?" There was no answer. I walked slowly up the stairs saying something like, "Hey, it's me, Brady. Are you guys okay?" See, Noah and his family treated me like family. I didn't know what to think. I mean, I knew what I was going to find, but I had to see it with my own eyes.

Noah's mom and dad were there in his room, slumped over the bed, as still as statues, obviously dead. I'd never eat another whoopie pie with Noah's mom or shoot baskets with Noah's dad. Who was that person under the covers? Was it Noah? Was he...? I didn't want to look, but I forced myself. I peeled the covers back from his face and looked down on the face of death. I could tell that Noah had been dead longer than his parents. How long they had lingered here near the body of their son I'd never know, but my best friend's body was already in a state of decay. I found my stomach rising to my mouth and I turned away and threw up. I ran out of that room and down to the front steps, sat down and cried. If the whole world was standing in front of me watching, I wouldn't have cared. I would've cried even more.

I sat there crying for a long time. I felt my emotions returning with a vengeance. I was Beowulf seeking Grendel.

I was King Arthur facing Mordred on the battlefield at the very end of Camelot. I was Frodo at the mouth of Mount Doom with the ring in his hand. I was Gilgamesh on the walls of Uruk and Thor guarding the rainbow bridge from the frost giants. Lex Luthor was holding a chunk of Kyptonite near my face and I was Kal-El, defeated and weak on the floor. But all of these heroes had someone or something to blame, a malevolent force that caused their troubles. All I wanted was someone I could blame for all of this death, loss and pain. Someone was to blame, somewhere. Someone had to be to blame. If I ever find the monster who did this..."

Brady stood on the doorstep of Noah's house letting the strangeness of the situation seep down into his mind, slowly leeching through to the little area where hope still sat quietly and waited. Noah must have died first and then his poor parents, knowing that they were dying, lingered there by the boy they loved so well until they, too, perished. He could picture it all so vividly in his mind and he profoundly wished he didn't have such a powerful imagination. Imagination was once his friend and kept him endlessly entertained. Harry Potter and Long John Silver, Ender, Ford Prefect, Percy Jackson and Artemis Fowl had been as real to him as any actual person. Once he had thought that this ability to conjure the reality of fictional characters was a gift but right now, at this moment, it was a curse. Counting Noah and his parents, he had encountered eight dead people. In the days to come, he knew the number would multiply exponentially. The truth was simple and harsh – they were all gone. Whatever systems were in place when everyone fell were still running, but not for long.   Soon the machineries of civilization would cease and for a very, very long time.

Brady wandered the lost world for the better part of two days. Everywhere he wandered he was met with the same sight repeatedly – the grisly and tired face of Death. He even imagined that Death was somehow a person, a being that had walked the earth, reaping a harvest of souls unlike any other in the long history of the world. A tall dark figure with a sickle or a scythe in a holocaust cloak who was very busy and, like Santa, able to travel with great rapidity. Perhaps Santa and Death were brothers? Except one was definitely real.

With each discovery he felt something building within him. A mother and her child, an old couple he had often seen walking the sidewalks to share a sunset in the spring, a whole family, and classmates from school: these were the denizens of his anger. No one had bothered to lock their doors, so entering their homes was easy. Many had preferred to perish outside and more than a few died sitting in their cars, forever going nowhere.

He called for someone, anyone, to answer him but time after time his shout was a mute witness to his solitude. Every time he found an unlocked car, he reached in and blasted the horn in an S-O-S fashion, three short blasts, three long blasts followed by three short blasts again. He listened intently, but no one within earshot answered his call. Then the angry tears would flow and add another set of bricks to the wall he was building inside of himself, one that would keep him safe from the hard light of the truth of things.

He wandered with no direction and when fatigue got the better of him, he simply collapsed on a lawn or inside an empty automobile.

Where have all the people gone? Why doesn't anyone answer me?

More than once he pulled out his dying cell phone and randomly dialed, hoping beyond hope that there was anyone left to answer. If he could have torn down the walls of the world, he would have.

He wandered to the Joshua Chamberlain Bridge between the two cities of Bangor and Brewer and sat down in the middle of the road. Never once did the idea flow into his mind, "I wish I were dead," but a thousand times came the longing wish, over and over, "I wish I'd never been born." He didn't know how long he sat there, his head bowed as if in prayer instead of desolation.

It was the sound of a bird that wakened him from his stupor, a prolonged squawk that compelled him to look up.

From the north side of the river he beheld a large black form of a raven flying alone in the air, gliding effortlessly above the incoming tide from the ocean. He watched as it flew lazily above him, circled his form two times and then flew beyond him, back towards Brewer. Exhausted though he was, he lifted his tired weight and with leaden tread he made his way back into the necropolis.

It was dark now, but the street lights still shone. He walked for hours with no release from the weight on his shoulders. There was the bowling alley where he had a birthday party five years ago and there were the fast food restaurants where he spent most of the allowance every week. What did that McDonald's hamburger taste like? He couldn't recall the flavor and it twisted in his mind like a knife. He thought of the ring and Frodo from *The Lord of the Rings* except the weight he carried was remorse, emptiness and loss. With every reminder of his new solitary state, the weight grew. He wanted revenge. He fantasized about traveling the wide world over until he found the person responsible for this devastation and when he found him, he imagined a hundred different ways to kill him.

Brady began to wreak havoc upon what was left of the world. His first act of terrorism was to break a window to a store front, which was harder than he thought it would be. He threw heavy stones that bounced off the windows and laughed at him as they fell to the ground. No matter how hard he threw them, it was no good.

He walked around the back of the bowling alley and in the back of the place in a rubbish pile he found a length of angle iron about three feet long rusting on the ground. Hefting it like Hercules would his club, swinging it like a Viking hammer, he began his rampage.

The store front window fell in a shattering rain of shards against the ground. Brady felt exhilarated. Car windows were smashed at the car dealership down the street and with every smashed windshield, another car alarm began to sound. One after another in a rising cacophony of angry noise, the world was filled with the sound of a hundred alarms blaring at once. Max ran wildly in circles, barking

37

and yelping, howling with a shared glee. As the sound intensified, so did Brady's anger. He thrashed at the cars with insane glee, the rusty angle iron suddenly Mjollnir or Excalibur and he was not breaking car windows but, like Don Quixote, he fought giants as tall as mountains who had come to destroy his world. If anyone else had been close enough to witness this spectacle of delicious abandon, they would have seen a frightening smile slithering on Brady's face. He let loose the dogs of the war from within and like Zeus, he freed the hundred-handed ones from Tartarus.

He saw a red camaro in the parking lot of the Burger King and a thought came to his mind.

No more walking for this boy.

He wasn't surprised to find the door unlocked and keys in the ignition. In the last moments, people simply stopped worrying about things and spent their last moments concerned about more pressing issues like life and death. Max sat in the passenger seat and Brady pressed the button that lowered the window for his dog. Twisting the key in the ignition, the engine roared to life! Stepping on the acceleration pedal, the growl of the motor swelled to a sound that filled his ears.

Flipping the visor down, he found several music CDs in a sleeve and carefully choose the loudest, angriest music he could find. The CD player sucked the disc in with a mechanical murmur and in a few seconds the rhythmic angry guitar of Angus Young blared back at him. Dropping the transmission into drive, he floored the Camaro and black smoke rose from the parking lot as the wheels spun frantically trying to gain a hold. When they did, he rocketed forth down U.S. Route 1A, his body pressed firmly against the seat, Max's head hanging out of the window, the wind forcing his eyes into slits as his tongue madly waggled in the breeze.

The idea that what he was doing might endanger his own life didn't enter his mind. He learned to drive in *Grand Theft Auto* and the roads were mostly clear and he imagined the strange digital world where he owned the only moving vehicle and the edges of the road were nothing more than a blur in his vision. He crossed the Penobscot Bridge and then stamped on the brakes hard, causing the car to skid and nearly tumble as he cranked the steering wheel hard to the left and the car's tires screamed against the ground. The Camaro stopped.

He sat there letting the rush of adrenalin course through him. It felt good! He was alive. He knew he was alive. He *felt* it. Still, he found no real solace. Only while he was in motion did he feel better. It occurred to him that the driving video games he had played for so many wasted hours had helped him. He could handle the machine surprisingly well.

He turned down State Street toward the medical center and cranked the volume on the CD player to maximum, opening all the windows, driving the wrong way down a one-way highway, holding the middle liked he owned both sides. He stopped when he saw the medical complex, the last place he knew for sure where his mother had been before he had lost contact with her. The song "Hells Bells" began blaring from the CD player with the doleful ringing and then the three-note riff repeating itself, growing louder and louder. As the song progressed, Brian Johnson finally started his guttural scream-song.

"I won't take no prisoners, won't spare no lives
Nobody's putting up a fight
I got my bell, I'm gonna take you to hell..."

From somewhere deep inside him a scream began to well. It gathered itself and reverberated like a dissonant chord. Rumbling like a roll of thunder, it roiled about inside of him, gathering strength. Looking up, he stared at the sky, eyes wide and red and he opened his mouth to release the fury. The thousand faces of every person who had ever caused him anger, pain or sorrow flashed in front of his eyes like an insane slide show. What had he done to deserve to live and what cursed him with life when everyone else was dead?

Oh, he longed for a name, a person, a thing to blame.

As he opened his throat, he imagined all the monsters

from all the books he had ever read, from the ancient myths to the modern novels, of all the villains from every movie, comic book or story. He called them forth, all of them, his mind morphing them into one creature, one fell, macabre, titanic beast whose sole purpose was the utter destruction of all humans. He imagined that this creature was *here,* walking the earth, savoring its carnage, this hater of humans. His scream was primal and utterly chaotic, with no recognizable syllable of any language ever spoken by humans. It mixed with the cacophony of the rhythmic roll of the guitar, distorted and tearing at the edges of the paper of the world. On a deeper level, his cry was a spell, a summoning. Max hunkered down in his seat and covered his eyes with his front legs, shivering.

It was a summoning spell from an ancient grimoire of magic, an alchemist's chant and a mystic's call to the great beyond. It was the scream of a lost soul named Brady and it etched itself against the hard side of the world. He was calling to the monster that caused all of this death. It was out there even as he had retreated to his Fortress of Solitude. Although he didn't hear it over his own scream, there was the sound of a crack opening between the worlds, a rift in the fabric of space-time and a quantum fluctuation that emanated from some other place to *this* place. The power of his deep and painful need to blame something contributed to the power of this spell, almost too much to bear, even for Batman or Captain Kirk.

But he was Brady Smith and he was real.

Somewhere nearby, the summons was heard. Music awoke him and rang in his head and the monster from the shadows stepped into this world and began to hate. He would stop all music everywhere.

The monster stared with bloodshot eyes from the top of the great building. A moment earlier he had not been there. He had no memory. He was new and the music rang in his ears and tore at his mind. How he had come to this place? It was a mystery to him, but he sensed his purpose. Somehow, his mind was clear and concise, even though his memory was nearly vacant. *Holding his great arms up to the yellow disk of the rising moon, he looked at fur and gangs of muscles and understood that he was not of this world, yet he was not alien. He was* other. *Great spasms of pain coursed through his unbalanced and heavy frame.*

In his mind he asked, "Who am I?" and in his mind he heard, "You are the Master of this World."

And the people? Who built this place. Where were they?

"They are gone, except for..."

He saw in his mind the answer to his question. His hungry glance fell toward the moving automobile and the source of all the noise. Was that a boy within, screaming?

"He is your nemesis. Beware this one, for he has power," came the whisper to his ugly ear.

He sat hunched as though ready to leap with Herculean effort over the wide waters and into the path of the object of his unsuspecting obsession. His long, greasy hair hung loosely into his eyes. The monster's heart beat with the anger and frustration of a thousand unfulfilled dreams.

As the monster's great heart beat savagely, he turned his vision away to some place within and wondered. Soon enough their paths would cross and then he would do that which he was meant to do since the beginning: he would kill the Renamer, the first hero, the one who had somehow survived the cataclysm. In this newest of worlds, the hero would fail: he would see to it. Before departing the rooftop of the great building to descend into his new home, the monster growled an angry curse into the air.

"I will meet you, Renamer. I will follow you and find you and draw you to me! Then we will see which world will remain: the old or the new..."

Perhaps the boy would come to him, after all. He had spent so much time in the darkness, planning, plotting. The monster cursed all life and as he did so, a stream of saliva dribbled out of his mouth as he snarled. A deep rumble of insane laughter sounded in the emptiness of the edifice. The creature knew how good it was to be alive...

Chapter 3
The Treasury

Brady drove around Bangor and Brewer in the Camaro until it ran out of gas. He left it where it rolled to a stop and didn't even bother to close the door as he walked away. The anger was finally purged. He had found absolutely no sign of life anywhere. Nothing stirred. Nothing seemed to breathe.

He found it puzzling but somewhat amusing to play with the idea of death so that he didn't have to say the word. If he could avoid the word, he could avoid the feelings that came with it. Therefore, he thought of all the people he had seen not as *dead* but as 'pushing up the daisies.' There were other euphemisms like, 'buying the farm, kicking the bucket, joining the choir invisible, shuffling off to Buffalo,' but he liked the phrase 'taking a dirt nap' the best. He thought of Monty Python's "Dead Parrot" sketch and thought that none of these people would 'voom' of you put 10,000 volts through them: these were ex-people. These corpses were not in the least bit funny and on a bone-deep level he had the instinct to avoid them. However, this was impossible. They were everywhere he went.

He devised a plan. Later he would return to all the places that housed the dead and mark them so that he would never make the mistake of entering them again. He would mark them with red paint on a window from the inside so that the weather would not wash the color away. It seemed necessary, even fitting, now that he owned the world. It was his right, his prerogative.

Death enveloped him and fear swirled in his mind every time he stepped out of a door. He was a needle in a haystack, a grain of black sand on a beach of white. The world clock ticked differently now. There was dawn, the day and then darkness again. No electricity, no movement except the movement of nature, and above all, the quiet. There were the birds, the barking of dogs, the roaring of the occasional wind and the rain. Elemental forces began to hunker down near him and taunt him with their energy. The world began to revert into the primeval state it had long endured before the arrival of humans and it did so very quickly, without so much as a whisper. Wounded by the judgment that he alone should live while all others perished, he laid his head down on his pillow every night and closed his eyes, hoping for the release that sleep could give him. Instead of the darkness in front of his eyes, he imagined throngs of people all around him, talking, murmuring, engaged in the everyday activities of life.

He could envision almost anything that his mind desired. His imagination was a mini-movie theater and he was the director, writer and principal actor in a series of ordinary, everyday scenes. There was the movie about buying groceries, the one about the restaurant and then, of course, the one about supper with Mom. There were his friends at the park playing catch and then at the movie theater: a mind-movie about a movie. All the small moments before sleep, while the soft caress calmed his mind, were the most precious ones of his day because he was not totally or wholly alone. Max cured up next to him and helped to keep the loneliness at bay.

The nearness of the dreamworld he entered was enticing, but he decided that he had to keep it at a distance. It was too tempting to dive into it. It was a cool, deep pool of water on a blisteringly hot day, but he did not know how deep he would sink before he would lose his breath and succumb to the pleasures of its depth, and then, inevitably, it would kill him. He didn't want to lose his mind and because he was young and because he had not lived enough to be weary of

43

the world. He wanted to live. He had to live because somewhere out there, for reasons unknown to him, his mother was waiting for him, unable to return. Maybe the government had closed down all the roads. Maybe she was sick. Maybe she was lost, but she wasn't dead. He knew this in an ancient and unforgiving way. She was alive and he needed to stay alive so that they could reunite. She was the light in the depths of his darkness.

The voices kept him company. He heard them everywhere. He couldn't help but wonder what they were, because he knew in his heart that he wasn't dead. They were. They must be. Everything around him was dead, or rather, everyone. All the other people in his apartment building, all the people in the cars on the side of and middle of the road, all of those left in the aisles of the stores he had visited. In the solitary silence of his mind, he heard them. *Whispers...whispers...*

The part that bothered him the most was that he found himself stopping, trying hard to bend his ear to the quiet air and hear what they were saying. It is only when one is denied something that one hungers for it, to the point of danger. He hoped to hear something familiar, another human voice, a conversation, even a passing phrase or a single word, perhaps a syllable. When he was walking down the street with Max by his side, he would hear a nearly silent sound and then he would stop, cock his head to the slight breeze and wait in eager anticipation.

What was that? Did someone say my name? Is someone trying to get my attention.

It was as though from a very far distance, someone was calling him. How strange, he thought. How many times had he been in a store or a classroom or a busy park and how many times did all the conversations blend into one long loud cacophony of sound, one voice indistinguishable from the next? Now, even when he should wonder if he was losing his mind, he found himself hoping for an echo of just one other human voice. Every time he had almost convinced himself that he was receiving the call from someone just around the corner, it proved elusive. When these whispers should perhaps be frightening him to the point of white-hot fear, he hungered instead for their companionship. Alone. Anything but alone...

Time passes, after all. For Brady, time became an intangible thing that didn't seem to matter much anymore. He was near his home, the apartment he had lived in since the death of his father. Mom couldn't live in the same house that she had shared with her husband, not after his death. Everything reminded her of him and so she sold it, rented this apartment and proceeded to raise her son alone. Brady understood his mother's need to move away from the house and into the apartment. Now he realized that it was time for him to move, as well.

The apartment was a place of power, a focal point. The whispers were louder in this place than in any other place he went. Still, he was lonely and home itself can seem like a person, providing a comforting, calming effect. Before he left, he determined to take some talisman with him, some reminder of the life before the Abandonment, of its truth. He knew he would need to remember that he was once one of billions who lived in communities and went about their daily lives without any regard for the end of things. He would take choice items and keep them safe, like a treasure. Then, like *Silas Marner*, he would count his gold coins in the silence of the fire, late a night, and remember.

He needed these items to remind him that such a time really happened and that he was anchored to something from before. This apartment would become his treasury. All the things close to his heart would be kept inside, stored for the day when he would need them, memories and photographs, small things that made his prior life seem real. He also knew that once he stepped out that door for the last time, he might never return. Events would dictate his return, not his own will, so he would need to take some small item with him as his anchor to the world of before.

The voices were whispering rather loudly, growing stronger every moment and every time he would close his eyes and focus on the nothingness underneath his eyelids, he would swear he could hear someone call his name. Out of

45

the indistinct mumbling of the voices his name rose above all, a clearly pronounced 'Brady' and then nothing more than incoherent mumbling.

Time to blow this popsicle stand. Time to haul ass out of here. This place is too safe, so safe it might trap me inside of it.

As he walked through the apartment, he could almost see her. There was his mother. Everywhere he looked he was reminded of her absence. Her coffee cups hung on the little brass hooks from the bottom of the cupboard shelf. In the living room, her photos hung placidly on the wall. Her name was on the mailbox. Her scent lingered in her closet. Her hair still populated the brush on the bathroom shelf.

He went to his mother's bedroom and sought for something to take, a keepsake that would remind him of her and bring her close to him when he was lonely. There was a photo of his mother and father in a small frame on her bed stand, a three by five in memory of a time that already seemed long ago and far away. Next to it was a small jewelry box. He opened it gingerly, somewhat ashamed to be peering into one of his mother's private domains.

She was very protective of *this* treasure. When he had been a much smaller boy he would lie on her bed and she would open it up and go through its contents with him, one piece at a time. This ring, Mom would point out, came from Grandmother Jalbert, while a pair of pearl earrings might have belonged to her husband's mother, Grandma Smith, a gift upon her tenth wedding anniversary. There were earring pairs, lampwork beads, necklaces, rings and bracelets. He knew what he was looking for. It was not in the top of the little chest, but in the small bottom drawer, a place set aside for only the most precious of things. He opened it and withdrew the item. It was her father's medal, awarded for bravery in Vietnam. Brady's grandfather, his mother's dad, had been a pilot in the United States Navy and had been shot down over the Ho Chi Minh trail. He had survived the parachute fall and for three weary weeks he kept himself alive in the jungles, all the time finding his way south, toward safety. He didn't know the name of the medal, but his mother often took it out and held it close when she was lonely. He died when she was nineteen when his plane had been shot down a second time.

This medal was her connection to him and it would be his connection to her. His grandfather had earned it with courage and perseverance. His mother has imbued it with love. Now it would serve as his talisman. He wondered how to carry it and decided that he would pin it to the inside of his shirt against his skin, so that he would always feel it next to him and remind him of his place in a family. Then he took the picture and slipped it from its frame, folded it carefully and put it into his wallet. As he did so, he looked at the three dollars in his wallet, laughed, and pulled them out, letting them fall haphazardly to the floor.

Worthless. No need for money. Not any more.

It was time to leave. Like a curator of a world-class museum, he shut the windows, locked them, made the beds, cleaned everything to within an inch of its life. Then he shut the door. In his imagination he heard the hiss of the hermetic seal sigh a final farewell. He took what he needed and said goodbye, perhaps forever. With no one to disturb its quiet stasis, it might last a hundred years.

"Come on, Max, ol' buddy! Let's go!"

He needed a place to live, but he also needed a place to spend the night. He might wander about the cities all day, but when the sun finally grew a bold orange-red at sunset, he preferred having four walls around him. This was today's problem.

Glancing at his watch, Brady saw that it was nearly lunch time. How he would have loved a hamburger or some fries from Jimmie's Restaurant. That would've been great. He would have murdered for a hamburger, but he hadn't had much meat except for canned tuna, chicken and some beef jerky for a while. He had food in his backpack and he took out some biscuits for Max and a Powerbar and a can of Dr. Pepper for himself. They ate as they did everything: quietly. Brady's music continued to flood his ears when the silence was too heavy to bear. Right now he was listening to Green

47

Day singing *Good Riddance*, and the irony wasn't lost on him. He was the world's number one rock musician, the world's best driver, the world's best thief.

I'm the best of the best 'cause I'm all that is left.

He surveyed the old neighborhood and decided that he no longer looked at the buildings as houses. They were something *other* now, no longer places to live. These buildings, with their windows all black and the doors either open or locked, these houses with their two car garages, their flowerbeds, their window-boxes, and their mailboxes all in a row, were no longer homes. They were tombs. Within each one, he thought, could be a body, a family of bodies, or nothing at all, just a place full of the artifacts of a life no longer being lived, each one a cave of disconnection. There might be photo albums full of pictures and each and every person in those photos was gone. The two cities of Bangor and Brewer were now what the ancient Etruscans called a *necropolis*, a city of the dead, and they deserved the quiet and the solitude that any tomb ought to have.

Max was still busy chewing on his biscuits, so Brady knew he had to wait until the dog was done before he could continue his journey for the day. He reached into his backpack and withdrew the black and white composition notebook and a black Pilot pen. Usually he wrote at night by the light of a battery-powered Coleman lantern, but from time to time he had a thought that required immediate recording or it would be lost. He wrote:

What I Need to Survive

Food - *This can be taken from various stores, restaurants and houses. Take cans and sealed food that keeps, like bags of chips, crackers, Spam, etc. Make sure to eat protein and carbs - Mom says we need a balance of both, to keep my strength. Food rules: canned goods are okay. Some dry goods are okay, like sugar and flour. I will have to learn to cook, so I need to make sure that I have a really good set of pots and pans and a cookbook. I still drink from canned and bottled sodas but only from small stores that have no bodies*

in them. Also, a really good lighter and tons of matches. I start small fires sometimes to cook my meals, even though I have really stocked up on Power Bars and granola.
A Place to Live *- This is a problem. I've thought about this a great deal and I know two things.*
 a.) I can't live in a house, a regular old house where people lived because of the Whisperers.
 b.) I don't want to stay in one place for too long.
First Aid Kit and Medicines *- I don't know what I'll need, so I should study up on it. I think a first aid kit is good for starters, with antibiotic ointments and band-aids and stuff like that, but if I get sick, I won't know what pills I'll need. There are pharmacies and hospitals I can break into, if I need to. I hope I don't get sick.*
Transportation *- I need to get from place to place. I left my bike at home because it will be too hard to take Max with me on it. He gets too tired running next to me. I need Max right now, too. He's my only company. I can drive any car I want. Still, how will I get gas into the gas tank? The gas stations must all have gas in their ground tanks, but the pumps run on electricity and there isn't any more of that. Still, there might be a way.*
A good set of tools and a map *- I'll need this because if anything breaks, I can't always rely on just going to the store and getting another one. I need a good tool set, maps, compass, and all those things. I wonder if GPS devices still work?*
***Music*-*this is to keep the Whisperers away. If I listen to my mp3 player, I can't hear the voices. I need music and that means power for my player. I have an mp3 player that uses a usb cable plugged into my laptop, but the laptop runs off electricity, so that means...*
A power source *like a solar charger or a generator. Oh, I need a way to play my xbox. This is really important. I don't even want to imagine a world without video games.*
A pair of binoculars. *You'll need these because you might want to see something far down the highway, or off in the distance. I haven't seen much yet, but sometimes I swear there's someone else out there, just in the distance, just far*

49

enough away for me to miss them.

A weapon. *I don't have any real weapons, not yet, but I'm going to find one today. I can hear the dogs in the distance and they are getting louder. I know that dogs will run in packs, even regular house pets will gang up together and run down a deer if they get a chance. It's not the deer I'm worried about. They might try to run me down.*

What I Need the Most: *People. I need to spend my time looking for other survivors. I can't be the only one. I need to find other people and then maybe together, we can find my mom. I need to know what happened to her and if she's okay. I need to talk to someone, just to know I'm not alone.*

He had been walking with Max for a couple of hours scouting out the lay of the land, beginning to fill his list of requirements for survival. There were several smaller stores in the area, as well as gas stations that held many of the items he would need. He marveled at how many little necessities of life could be crammed into a convenience store and wondered who had been responsible for planning the stocking of those shelves. His backpack was always full of bottled water, snacks and food for Max, but it was becoming painfully clear that Brady was going to need more than a backpack to organize his continued existence.

He entered the house just off Chamberlain Street on a whim. In the days and weeks to come, Brady would discover just how many roads we pass and never walk down, how many places are invisible to us even though we see them every day. This house was one such place, painted a nondescript white with red trim set back from the street a little further than most of the other homes and mostly hidden by the lush growth of low trees and bushes. Brady approached it with what he thought of as a strange delight. This house seemed a little different for another reason that he couldn't quite fathom. He must have passed this place a thousand times in his life and he couldn't remember ever seeing it before.

In the center of the front door was a metal knocker in the shape of a horse holding a brass ring in its mouth. Reaching up and unable to stop himself, he took the ring in his hand and banged it three times against the door. Although it was impossible, Brady could have sworn that he felt the earth shift the tiniest amount beneath his feet and from a distance, not from within but from somewhere else, he heard the long echo of a neigh.

He twisted the handle and found it unlocked. The door was heavy and when he opened it, it seemed to continue to open of its own volition. Inside, Brady found himself surrounded by a strange collection of artifacts, art and books. On the walls that weren't lined with books were paintings and photographs of horses and on the mantel of the stone fireplace were trophies with little golden-colored horses surmounting their tops. Whose home this was he did not know, but what remained told Brady enough to understand their passion for the noble steed.

From room to room he searched and in almost every nook and cranny there were the accoutrements of who must have been a person Brady would have loved to have known. *Too late*, he thought, *a real shame*. Brady liked this place, found it comfortable and welcoming and for the first time since waking to the Abandonment, he felt the small comfort of a home – not his home, but someone's home. Max explored every room, his tail wagging confidently behind him and then, after a thorough inspection, he jumped up on a worn leather sofa and curled up for a nap. Brady sat down in a leather chair next to the bay window with the green shades of sunlight straining through the trees and tried to think of nothing at all, for just a minute. He felt *welcomed*.

There, on the side table near a colorful stained-glass lamp were books. He ran his fingers over the titles in gold upon dark-brown bindings: *Moby Dick, The Scarlet Letter, Works of Shakespeare, Hard Times, David Copperfield, Little Dorrit* and *Don Quixote.*

He pulled the copy of *Don Quixote* out of the pile and opened it. It was the first time he had opened a book to read since he had awakened to the Abandonment. He read the tale for a long time, of an old nobleman in medieval Spain who spent his time reading his books about knights in shining armor and the destruction of monsters that no one but he could see. Accounted as a foolish man by most of the characters in the book, old Don Quixote didn't care what other people thought. The old nobleman looked at the world around him and saw treasures where other people saw trash. He surveyed the world and saw beauty where others saw ugliness and monsters where others saw nothing at all out of place. One day, realizing that sitting around and waiting to die of old age was a waste of his precious time, old Don Quixote put on a rusting suit of armor and took down his dull and timeworn sword and went forth into the world to fight evil and rescue the helpless. He rode an old bag of bones horse but to him and his imagination, Don Quixote saw a noble steed, strong of frame and able to carry his knight errant through the lands that held such promise. The noble steed's name was Rocinante.

Reading had always been his safe zone. Where other boys had baseball or hockey, he had books. They were portals, doorways to other places. Right now, in this quaint little edifice, a set of classic novels stirred his imagination and for the first time in a while, he lost himself in a book, a very large tome indeed.

In his mind, which was so adept at blending the real world with the world of imagination, Brady felt a strange kinship with the old nobleman from Spain. Don Quixote saw the world as it should be, not as others saw it. Even if it was the old man's imagination and even if he was insane, Brady thought that he could do worse than imagine a better world in place of the one outside the door. Then he fell asleep.

He awoke to the sound of birds singing in the bushes and the rustle of wind through the world. Glancing at his watch, he was surprised that he had slept so long and deeply. Max was sitting at his feet, his mouth open in that impossible canine smile. He needed to go outside and do his duty. Brady opened the door and felt the fresh, cool breeze and noticed a small garage behind still more greenery. It was a quaint little structure with more curves than straight lines. Instead of a standard overhead door, which never would have fit, there were two wooden doors with curved tops and colored glass. Brady had never seen anything like them. They were unlocked. Brady suspected that inside would be the standard garden implements and perhaps a mower like he had seen in a hundred other garages, but he was pleasantly surprised at what he found waiting for him within.

A red and black four-wheeled ATV sat quietly inside. Along the walls on either side were tools neatly arranged on pegs, their outlines traced against the old brown pegboard. Bottles of lubricant and cleaners lined the shelf above the tools. The faint smell of oil met his nostrils. Leaning up against the back wall next to three red gasoline cans was a small trailer.

The key was in the ignition. How could such things be? This house felt so familiar. This garage did, too. He could have closed his eyes and reached out and he would have known where everything was. It felt to Brady like this place had been set aside just for him, like this four-wheeler was maintained and kept in good condition so that someday, after the fall of civilization, a lone survivor might stumble upon it and use it for his own.

He mounted the seat and turned the key, opened the choke slightly and pressed the starter button with his thumb. The red Polaris surged to life, growling like a panther, rumbling like the thunder of hooves and with the fresh image of Don Quixote still mixing and lingering in his thoughts, Brady became the old nobleman and this four-wheeler became Rocinante, his noble steed. Squeezing the throttle, Rocinante roared out of the little building and into the world.

Max was barking and jumping up and down as Brady wheeled the machine out into the driveway, onto Chamberlain Street and sallied forth into the world of deeds and monsters. Burying the speedometer needle to the right, the wind rushing past his face, bringing tears to his eyes, exhilaration filled his heart. Here was his horse, his machine, his transportation. Immediately he began imagining how he could customize the four-wheeler to suit his needs and his mind was alive with a purpose other than simple survival.

Back at the garage, Brady took stock of his options with

the four-wheeler. It had a winch on the front, a second saddle in back of the driver with a black tube railing. There was a small hitch on the back that connected to the small trailer, which was big enough, he surmised, to carry a lot of supplies. There was a small can of white-glass enamel paint on the shelf of the little garage and some painter's fine brushes among the tools. By the time he was done, he had painted the word "Rocinante" on the front fenders.

"Come on, Max," he called, "get up on the back of this thing."

Max didn't quite understand so Brady gathered him up in his arms and sat the dog on the seat behind him. The steel tubing seemed to be tall enough to hold Max onto the machine as Brady slowly accelerated. Once moving, Max had no problem staying put. Brady hooked the trailer onto Rocinante and proceeded to find as many bungee cords, tie-downs and pieces of rope as he could to secure his vagabond caravan of supplies, as yet ungathered, to his mount.

That night he went through the checklist and next to the word 'transportation' he placed a big black checkmark. It was a beginning. He settled down on the big leather sofa with Max at his feet and by the light of a 3 L.E.D. battery-powered headlamp, he read more of *Don Quixote* until he fell deeply asleep.

As he slept, there were fair maidens and evil wizards, long highways upon which dwelt thieves and murderers. All of these denizens of his dreams waited for him and for the first time since he had awakened to the awful truth of the Abandonment, he slept without the whispers filling his ears.

Chapter 4
Mount Hope

from the Journal of Brady Smith

"I've been living at La Mancha now for a while. I call it "La Mancha" because that's the name of Don Quixote's home and I've been reading that book every night in a big old leather armchair next to the window that looks out onto the yard and the apple tree. The little house has everything I need. Whoever lived here kept oil lamps, batteries, a gas grill in the back yard, and a lot of the comforts of home. I have looked for evidence of a name, to figure out who lived here, but I can't find one item in the place that's personally identifiable. Max likes it, too. I'm beginning to worry. When I first stepped into this place, the Whisperers quieted down. They left me alone and I was truly able to sleep. But last night they found me again, like the house had a shield that kept them away, except they kept forcing themselves against it, weakening it. They're back. I may have to look for some other place. Maybe I have to give up on houses altogether.

I usually start my day at the Irving Gas Station on top of the hill by Wilson Street. It gives me an awesome view of the city of Bangor and the Penobscot River. Also, I have plenty of access to soda, candy and chips from the store, as well as gas. At the tractor supply store in Bangor I found a hand-cranked siphon pump with a long plastic tube that reaches down to the ground tanks at the station. I fill the tank with gas, check the oil, and then put some food and water for both Max and me into the tub, cover it and tie it down with bungie cords. Sometimes I hook on the trailer. Sometimes I don't. I drink a warm soda and eat a Twinkie, then open the DeLorme map I got from inside the Irving station and begin deciding where to go today.

I'm trying to figure out where my supplies are and what areas to avoid. Supplies are easy. I enter stores and businesses, empty cars, whatever. Treasure is what I'm after - food, fuel, tools, medicine, anything that might help me survive. I have some paintball guns. I took plenty of paintballs and a ton of CO_2 cartridges. Whenever I find a place that looks good, I leave it alone. If it's a bad place, for whatever reason, I shoot it with red: the doorway, the inside of the windows, whatever. It's my way of marking my territory. I also mark the DeLorme map with red and green dots to indicate where I can return and what places I ought to avoid.

Take yesterday, for example. I was in Bangor driving right down Main Street, right by the Penobscot Theatre and I decided to go down by the waterfront. It was a nice day and let me tell you, this is a quiet world now. I never hear much but the wind and the water. Yes, I can hear the river flowing if I listen really closely. I stopped Rocinante, turned him off and listened again really carefully. Max jumped off like he does all the time, even though he usually comes back with a whistle.

He wasn't gone a minute when there was a terrible commotion of sound coming from the river. There was a huge murder of crows all dive-bombing my dog. They were pecking at him and hounding him and I was sure they were going to kill him.

I started Rocinante and kicked him hard and off we sped, right down to the edge of the waterfront. The crows were so loud they didn't even hear me coming. I drove right into them, blaring loud and screaming at the top of my lungs. Max was still running as fast as he could, but a few of the birds kept at him. I took the paintball guns and started shooting with both hands. I knew the paintballs wouldn't kill them, but I thought that maybe I might scare them enough to give the little guy a chance. I took aim and hit one of them right on the back. He gave out quite a caw and screamed at me. They sounded like they were swearing at me.

"Get off him!" I screamed as they started diving at me.

That's when something weird happened, something amazing. I wasn't going to leave Max there, so just jumping on Rocinante and riding away wasn't an option. I guessed I had to stand and fight these dark creatures. I know they were only crows, but to me they seemed more than that, somehow smarter, more dangerous. They were like something out of The Lord of the Rings, some fell creatures of Sauron, modified for evil. I was looking at maybe twenty or more of these big, black, shiny birds all moving and hovering and diving at me when a much bigger black bird came into the picture, out of nowhere. He must have been twice their size, with a broader beak and a croaking voice. He dived at my attackers and one by one drove them off. They respected him, too. Most of them kept their distance and after attacking the largest of the crows, the Raven lowered his head near the ground and opened his wings to their full spread and croaked in defiance. One by one they took to the air and left us.

He landed on the top of the waterfront business building only a few feet from me and stood there, staring down. Then he croaked loudly, tipped his head, and looked me right in the eye for a long time. I think he was aware that he had helped me. I can tell a friend when I see one, even though he might be of a different species. I took out a Slim Jim from my vest, unwrapped it and threw it near him. He looked at it, looked away like he didn't care, then slowly moved towards it, played with it in his beak and picked at it. After a moment he flew away with it in his beak.

Sometimes something comes to you from somewhere deep inside. You don't even remember learning it or knowing it, but it surprises you and you wonder 'where the heck did that come from?'. Once I read a book about the Norse gods and goddesses. It was a scary book, full of brave deeds and

57

strong men and gods, all leading to Ragnarok and the Time of the Wolf, Fenris, who would devour the sun. The leader of the Viking gods was named Odin. He was a mighty, white-bearded strong man, like an old ex-wrestler. He had one eye because once, long ago, he had hung for a whole day from his neck to suffer and had given one of his eyes to the witch who presided over Hell, which was a cold place for Vikings. Anyway, he suffered as payment so he would be allowed to see the end of all things, the final destination that all of creation was heading towards. He saw it and left that awful place and took his throne in the palace of Asgard, high in the sky. He was a quiet and brooding person after that, and he didn't move far from his throne. But he needed a way to see the world of men and doings. He had two ravens, one perched on either shoulder. They were named Hugin and Munin, translation: "Thought" and "Memory." They flew over the earth all day and when they returned at night, they whispered in his ears, telling him what they had seen.

I named the Raven who saved Max, Hugin, because I suspect he is more than a Raven. From the tilt of his head and the intelligent look in his eye, I can tell that he's thinking.

For the past week, I've seen Hugin more and more often. I feed him from time to time, but I think he has plenty to eat. Anyway, I began to talk to him and he looks back at me and tilts his head like he can understand what I'm saying. He's never far away."

Hugin led him on a wild raven chase most of the afternoon. For the past three hours he led Brady and Max all over Brewer - down by the Great River, back toward the Depot, then back to the Great River again. It was as though the bird was searching for something. Brady had been surprised and then fascinated with Hugin's ability to lead him to places that he seemingly needed to go, as though he was able to anticipate Brady's needs. Today, however, seemed like the exception rather than the rule.

Brady had treasure-holds throughout the two cities and he had only just begun to investigate. There were hundreds, if not thousands, of other places he would need to break into and inventory before he was done. If he was going to survive for the long term, he would need a plethora of supplies. He would need to live off the detritus of the old world. He would need to be a scavenger. On his map, he had a color code and a few different colors of markers that he used to implement his own key.

It wasn't long before he decided that the old map he had been using was really of no use to him. There were just too many names to remember, too many places that begged to be renamed. There were empty places on the map that needed filling and places he had no use for, necessary for the world before The Abandonment. The nicely folded map had been refolded the wrong way too many times, anyway. It became clear to Brady that the world had moved in a new direction and that this was no longer a place where the old names applied. Indeed, this was a place more like Eden and he was Adam, naming all the animals and plants, all the buildings and roads. Street after street he made his way, increasing his knowledge of his kingdom, his domain. This was the land that would have to keep him alive and it was no good relying on the appellations of those who had now passed away.

He had broken into the middle school and found a large roll of tall white paper in the art room. He cut off a piece four feet by four feet and rolled it neatly, then placed it in a black plastic tube that was leaning against the wall. This would be his new map and he would be the cartographer of the new world that came after the Abandonment. He didn't know what he would name these places, pathways and roads, but in a bone-deep way, he knew that he would gain power over them by naming them. By naming the world, he would be claiming it as his own.

There were other kinds of symbols on the map. Some indicated food stores, some tools and raw materials. Some of these were stores and some were homes that were perfectly empty. The homes held some of the best items, things he could never find elsewhere. He visited a few of these each day, often having to break into them. It went like this: first he would check the doors to see if they were locked.

59

Because everyone was worried about contagion and plague, most were. Then he took out a five pound sledge hammer from one of the saddlebags and slammed it down upon the door handle. He didn't want to break any windows because even though he was breaking in, he held respect for these places. He didn't want to leave any entry holes for animals. Besides, he wasn't a thief. He was the sole survivor. These were his houses now.

When the door handle eventually gave way, as long as there was no deadbolt, he gained entrance. Then he did a walkthrough of the house looking for bodies. If he found any, he quickly went through closets, drawers, cupboards and if he found anything remarkable, he took it. Otherwise, he duct-taped the hole in the door where the handle used to be, pushed a heavy piece of furniture against the door and smeared red paint in the window next to the door on the inside so that he might never come back into this place. Then he would exit by the back or side door. Once outside he would mark it with a black X on his map and move on. If he found no bodies, he took his time searching. He didn't like seeing everyone's personal items, especially the pictures.

Sometimes he found himself inside of the homes of people he knew: kids at school, teachers, the people who worked at stores he used to visit. Sometimes he even found himself tearful when catching a sidelong glance at a picture of a face. Often he had to turn on his mp3 player to its loudest setting because the Whisperers seemed to be much louder inside the houses and it felt like they were screaming at him.

He carried a small pad and many pens and carefully noted things in the houses that might be of use to him someday. If the house was a good find, he closed it the same way, but shot it with green paint balls and noted it with a green dot on his map. There was no way he could carry off all of the canned food, tools, clothing and supplies that he might need later, but if he knew where to get them, he was one step ahead of death.

Brady stopped to top off Rocinante's gas tank, which he did twice a day. Max was thirsty, so Brady took out a small plastic bowl and opened a bottle of Poland Spring water, draining it. As Max drank, Brady opened another bottle and began to drink, too. Water was a problem. The faucets didn't work anymore and the water was probably undrinkable now that the sewage processing plants were no longer functioning. The Great River which ran between the two cities had long been undrinkable even before the Abandonment, so it didn't seem like a viable option for water now.   He had some filtering equipment, but he was lucky one afternoon when he discovered a water bottling company down by the river whose natural spring was still flowing. It was about a half mile outside of town, but worth the drive a few times a week to replenish his supply. It occurred to him that someday all the packages of food and bottles of water would run out. He would have to hunt and gather.

With Max finished, Brady looked up into the sky and saw Hugin circling above them, waiting for Brady to start Rocinante and follow. Max and Hugin kept the loneliness at bay and he found himself talking to them, asking them questions and imagining their answers.

Brady called, "Okay, old man, old Viking, I'm coming!" as he turned the key and the Polaris chugged to life. The bird was leading down to the Joshua Chamberlain Bridge and into Bangor.

The road to the medical center had been closed from the general public sometime during the last days of civilization. There were cement barricades on Hancock Street and State Street with yellow and black striped warnings stating, "Do not cross. Medical Emergency." He easily drove Rocinante over the lawn of a nearby house, by-passing the barricades altogether. In a moment, he was sitting on his four-wheeler staring at the medical center.

How had he avoided it for so long? It was the largest building complex in the area and would most certainly have been the center of activity during the Abandonment. Perhaps he knew instinctively that this would be more than a tomb. So many must have perished here that it would have been

61

transformed into a doorway to the Underworld. This great protector of the people must have fought valiantly, a citadel dark and strong, standing alone against the onslaught of a virus that even it, with all of its resources, could not contain. This place of life must most certainly have become a place of death in a dying world. Brady couldn't bring himself to go any nearer than this, on the roadway, far enough from the entrance and what lay within. It was the very mouth of Hell.

But my mother worked there...Maybe she's inside...

Brady went into *Observation Mode*. He became a recorder of images again, a detailer of things and all of his feelings were temporarily turned off. He saw the green national guard trucks and a great number of ambulances in the parking lot and the helicopter on the top of the parking garage. The large glass windows mirrored the blue sky and the clouds and all that was left. Hugin was perched on the power line just above him now and from time to time croaked down at him. Brady took out his map and pencils and took a moment to sketch, instead of the gray block tower, a great castle with a giant skull and crossbones over it. He drew slowly and deliberately. Then he wrote, "*Entrance to Hades: Beware*" next to a dark doorway that become the entrance in his mind. Hugin croaked approvingly and when Brady was done, he began to carefully roll the map into the tubular case he had duct-taped to Rocinante's fender.

About a mile down the road from the medical center, the turn to the area of the Bangor Mall and the Hogan Road forked. One way led to what used to be the busiest area of the two cities. The other led to a small town known as Veazie, the place his mother used to call the town of the living dead. This had been a joke at the time, but now it made the small candles in his mind jump and flicker from the wind of imagination. He decided to take the long way to the mall, through Veazie, on the off chance that there might be someone, anyone, alive there. Driving on, he saw the entrance to the cemetery on his left.

Mount Hope Cemetery. Brady had visited it with his mother a few times, not because they had any relatives there but because it was a vast repository of local history, a showcase of a white marble forest of graves and tombs that would rival anything made later in the history of cemeteries. Mount Hope had been built on the model of the Mount Auburn Cemetery in New York during the heyday of American free enterprise and before the First World War. It was a model of fine and high living even though it was built for the dead. Within the iron fencing and beyond the war memorials were the graves of the wealthy lumber barons of the 1840s and 1850s. In this place lay the honored and humble together under high elm trees, near babbling rivulets and high, green hills. It was a city of the dead with fine tombs made of imported Italian marble and pink granite from the coast of Maine paving many of the paths. There were all manner of tombstones, most somber and covered with simple, elegant epitaphs and moss, but some strange and remarkable in their macabre way.

Brady recalled his mother, who loved history and read biographies, as she led him on a tour from gravestone to gravestone saying, "See this one Brady? There's a lock of hair from the dearly departed behind this piece of glass, sealed forever from the weather. And this one, over here? It has an early photo, a *daguerreotype* of the person who lies below. Oh, and this one, it's made of Zinc, a metal that will last forever, never fading, always new in the passing of long, long years. Oh, Brady," she would say, "just imagine the stories below our feet, all lost and forgotten. What would these people tell us if only they could talk?"

Brady answered, "I know what they'd say. Get me the heck out of here! I want to live!"

His mother asked him, "Are you afraid of the cemetery, Brady?"

He answered, "No, I'm not afraid. I'm just...sad."

His mother smiled, cradling his young head in the cup of her hands, brought him close and kissed him gently on the forehead. "Me, too. I don't think anyone really understands Death."

Then he had asked her, "Mom, do you believe in Heaven?"

A small look of concern, a knotting of the brow and she answered, "Of course I do, honey. I hope you do, too. Because Dad is there, and he knows about us. He watches you growing up and he's proud of you, Brady. Oh, yes, there's a heaven all right."

"Does God love everyone?" he asked.

"Everyone. Saints and sinners alike."

He pondered for a moment and then asked quietly, "If there's a Heaven, then, is there a Hell?"

She hesitated. "I don't know, Honey. I was taught that there is, but I'm not so sure that this world might be hell enough for anyone." She paused, understanding in her way that she was confusing her child and that she ought to make this very easy for him to understand. She couldn't. Her own uncertainty stopped her.

Then Brady asked, "If there's a Hell, and God loves everyone, then how can anyone be in it? I mean, if Heaven is full of love, then how can people there be happy when they know that some of their family and friends are suffering in Hell?"

She gave no answer. Sometimes, silence was an answer. As he drove past the rows of stones, he thought that silence was the only answer left, now. The best he could do was to live where all these others had perished. He would have a story worth telling and where these other stories had been silenced, he was determined that he would make sure his story was told. The best he could do was to try to make a Heaven out of what must be his own little private corner of Hell. As he drove through the city, now merely an enormous graveyard, each house a tombstone, he wondered to whom his story might one day be told.

He took out his map and penciled in a rough drawing of the wrought-iron gate, followed by several square inches of gravestones, like trees in a forest on the whiteness of the paper. Then he labeled the place, "*Abandon All Hope, Ye Who Enter Here - City of the Dead.*"

The entrance to the cemetery was through a great wrought iron gate, one of only three openings in the fence that surrounded it. He brought Rocinante to a stop and dismounted the machine, whistling for Max to follow him. Hugin was sitting nonchalantly on a tombstone next to the side of the road. To his left was the World War II Memorial, a large angel rising heavenward holding in his arms the limp body of a dead soldier. Brady gazed up at the angel for a long time before moving along. He had a hard time taking his gaze from the soldier. He wondered aloud to no one in particular, "No more memorials for anyone, huh Max? No one's gonna build anymore of these things. No one to remember them but us."

From the corner of his eye, he saw a twitch, a slight movement that was impossible. Had the angel looked up from its perpetual gaze and met his eyes? No, it couldn't have been? Like something seen from the corner of his eye, he checked again to see the angel as it had been since it was mounted there by some artisan, so many years ago. Still, he could have sworn it moved.

He took his map out and began taking the lay of the land. Over the hill was Veazie, a sleepy little town even before the Abandonment where they rolled up the sidewalks precisely at ten o'clock every night. To the left and over another rise, beyond the mausoleum, was the area of the Bangor Mall and all the development that no one would ever need again. If he put this road on his map, it would cut a long way off the trek from this part of town to the mall area. He could avoid the river altogether and just cut straight through the cemetery.

As he laid the map out on the ground near the back of Rocinante, he heard a sound again. It was a whisper, a soft and nearly silent sigh of a sound such as a child might make in its sleep, different from the whispers that he had been hearing in his head, the ghosts of his imagination. There! He heard it again, distinctly. In *Observation Mode* again, he turned to the left and scanned the area, scrutinizing every inch of his vision.

A movement danced in the distance, a strange and disturbing motion that should not have been there.

"The world has changed," he whispered aloud.

There were many things now that should not be and

many things that should be that were not. No power in the universe could draw his vision from what he saw in the distance among a number of undersized headstones all grouped together, the final resting place of the Bangor's Children's Home, circa 1910. At least a hundred small white slabs were placed far more closely together than any other stones he could see.

Orphans. Dead orphans...

Although he had more reason than anyone to believe in ghosts, he was transfixed by the scene in front of him. His heart was beating a frenzied staccato and he struggled to catch short, faint breaths. This was fear, stone-cold paralyzing fear and he was a statue, unmoving, planted to the ground. Among the stones were the first human forms he had seen in weeks. People! No, these were not people as he knew them. These were shades, phantoms, ghosts.

There were the forms of children wandering, weaving their way among their own gravestones; the orphans, the children left behind, left alone, incorporeal and faint, like something seen through a fog. Any other boy on any other day might have run from that place. Any other boy might have doubted his vision, but not Brady.

The city was no longer a city. It was a graveyard, so this place was something more, something older. The graveyard was no longer a storage place for the beloved dead. The city, now devoid of people, was simply a mass of buildings and streets that reflected nothing but the darkness and the full-spectrum echo of a world that used to be. People made a city. Quiet made a graveyard. This graveyard was now the city. The city was now the graveyard.

As Brady watched, he saw them appearing all around him, white and faded like the old and chipping paint against the south side of a house. They faded into his vision, half there and in a minor key. They were memories of shadows, not shades, more missing than apparent, but he saw them, first a few and then more until the whole place seemed like it was city of ghosts, an invisible realm suddenly made visible now that so few were left to witness their presence.

Fear began to fade within him and he lost the urge to

scream. How strange, he thought, to miss the company of others so much, only to be surrounded by the ghosts of others, none of whom could hear him, see him, or acknowledge his presence.

The dearly departed were walking among the graves as though they were merely strolling through a park. Dressed in their finest funeral clothes, they smiled and greeted each other politely, these neighbors beneath the soil, these dwellers in the darkness. They didn't appear as Brady thought the dead should with fraying flesh and decay enveloping them like a shroud. Instead, they were arrayed in their finest apparel and though they were spectral in nature, he knew a happy smile when he saw one. There was a lovely elderly woman who reminded him of his downstairs neighbor, Mrs. Eldridge. Her long gown, gray and colorless, bespoke of a grandeur Brady had only seen in black and white films. She had a regal bearing and walked gracefully, waving with a mere flick of her wrist. She could never frighten anyone. She was beautiful.

He saw a young man, perhaps twenty-five, dressed in a woolen jacket and vest with shoes and spats waving to an elderly man across the way. The elderly man's ashen visage shone with a bright smile and he picked up his ancient pace until he was running right through the gravestones in his eagerness. They met in the middle of the road and embraced. Brady could discern the etherial tears washing both of their cheeks and he thought, these might be two long lost brothers or a father and a son, joyfully reunited, awake from the slumber of the long sleep of death.

He couldn't hear them, though he saw them clearly. Were these the ghosts he heard in the darkness in his bed just before falling asleep? The Whisperers? Where were their voices? He strained to hear them, to be an eavesdropper on their conversations. What were they talking about? Every fiber of his being yearned for the knowledge of which they spoke. Was he smiling? Was his solitary existence lifted only for a while as he stood there, in the midst of the resurrected dead?

He thought, "I'm the ghost in this world. They can't see

67

me but they can see each other. This is truly what it means to be a ghost." He was aware of the greater humanity surrounding him and he could take it no longer. He wanted to talk to them but what would he talk about? What did he have in common with them? They continued to greet each other and speak together, smiling and laughing and crying.

Unable to bear it any longer, he turned his eyes away as he was surrounded by them and he had no choice but to walk among and through them to reach Rocinante. He had parked near the plot of the Bangor Orphanage, and he was unable to avoid seeing the children running and jumping, rolling on the ground and laughing.

Most of them were very young and one of them had a small rubber ball that he was throwing to another child. It wasn't a real ball but the memory of a ball – a spectral ball. How did he get such a thing, this ghost child? Brady decided that he must have been buried with it and that somewhere underneath his feet in the grave of this small child there was a small rubber ball being clutched lovingly. Someone must have known that he loved it so much that they saw to it that he took it with him to Paradise.

That thought made a tear well up in Brady's eye for the first time since he woke up from his fever and delirium a few weeks ago. He had cried for Noah, but that was a moment of anger. He had not even cried in sorrow for any of the people whose bodies he had been encountering these past weeks. But now, he was crying. What was it about the thought of the orphan boy and his beloved toy, a person dead for over a hundred years, that stirred his heart when the death of the world hadn't moved him?

The little boy missed the ball and it landed soundless on the ground and rolled toward Brady, stopping at his feet. Brady froze to the spot, not moving, not frightened but hoping to avoid any contact with this child. The form of the boy ran over to the ball, bent over and plucked it from the ground next to Brady's feet. The boy was kneeling on one knee and as he looked up he did something that none of the other spirits did.

He made eye contact with Brady.

Brady stared back into the little boy's eyes and smiled. The child's surprised and wide-eyed face smiled back and spoke to Brady, and though Brady could not hear him, he could read his lips. The little boy asked, "Are you a ghost?"

For a long moment Brady stayed silent and still, a chill of realization freezing him to the spot. How could he answer that question? Was he a ghost? To the spirits now evident to him, walking and talking in their community, *he* was the ethereal one. To the children who all saw each other, running, laughing and playing, he was the one on the other side who couldn't interact with them, locked in a prison world that only one of them could see. Brady shook his head from side to side and smiled and said slowly so that the boy might read his lips, "No. I'm a friend..."

The boy nodded affirmatively, smiled and grasped the ball tightly in his hand as he rose and ran off towards the graves and his friends. Brady watched him go and began to understand why he was moved by the thought of an orphaned child, unclaimed and long gone. *He* was now the orphan. He wasn't a ghost, but he was living in a ghost world, lonely but still very real. He sat on Rocinante for a long time longingly watching the people, especially the children, taking them in. If this had happened a few weeks ago, before the Abandonment, when things ran according to science and logic, he would have thought he was crazy. There were no such things as ghosts in that world. In this world, a world that he now ruled, named and reinvented, ghosts were as real as a sunrise. He watched for at least an hour and the sun approached its zenith, indicating noon. He looked at his watch and as the sun reached its high point, the figures in the cemetery disappeared. He was alone again.

He wearily started Rocinante and scouted for Hugin in the air, but he was gone, He came and went at will, as wanderers do. Brady was exhausted from his vision and only wanted to go home and rest. As quietly as he could, he rolled out of the graveyard, back towards Brewer. The sun was a bright flaming chariot beginning its long fall from the sky and the wind was beginning to blow more fiercely. It whipped the trees into conversation as the silver and brown trunks and branches swayed like dancers in the breeze. It roared past his ears as he drove and it cooled his skin like ice. He drove past the old Bangor Water Works and down past the railroad tracks and then took State Street, which he had renamed The High Road, up to the hospital, the Entrance to Hades.

Feeling more tired than frightened, he stopped the four-wheeler on the road next to the emergency room entrance and took the edifice in from this angle. There were some liquid oxygen tanks that were spilling their contents in a white hissing cloud of ancient cold. He knew that this was a safety mechanism and that eventually they would stop when the pressure equalized. He also knew how dangerous these were. One spark would be all that was needed to ignite a tremendous explosion. This was yet another reason to avoid this place. There were a number of green army vehicles parked haphazardly around the area along with ambulances, trucks and humvees. He could only imagine the number of military people still left inside and he had a tremendous imagination.

Thoughts of his mother again arose in his mind and he couldn't help but wonder if she had made it. His love for her was so strong that if she had died, he thought, somehow he would feel it. He would know it in a bone-deep and heart-clenching way. Since he didn't feel this way, he hoped beyond hope that she had survived, somehow. He had made it. Maybe she did, too? Did he survive because he was sick at the time and somehow the sickness made him immune to the effects of the disease? Maybe it was a genetic thing. Maybe he had survived because he was born with a resistance to it and maybe his mother also had this resistance. All of this went through his mind like a dust devil in a wheat field, disturbing his already troubled thoughts.

He felt the burning grow on his chest, a slight warmth and then a hot flash. What was that? He put his hand into his shirt and felt his grandfather's medal glowing with heat, like a signal or a beacon against danger. Why would it glow hot, he wondered.

Is it like Harry Potter's scar? Is it like Bilbo's sword,

Sting? Does it get hot when I'm near danger?

That was when he heard the scream. Even though the wind filled his ears with its own muffling roar, he was certain that he had heard a piercing, bloodcurdling human scream. It came from the Entrance to Hades and it seemed both frightened and a plea for help. His blood was ice. His mind was stone. How long he sat on Rocinante and waited for another sound to confirm his wild imaginings he didn't know, but the sun was low in the western sky when he shook his head, started the four-wheeler and left.

I must be going insane. First the Whisperers and now a screamer. What am I going to do?

From the heights of the edifice, a foul and putrid smelling creature gazed down upon the lonely figure making its pathetic way back to its gypsy home. He hunkered down like the detestable creature he was and threw his head into the air, tasting the scent of the boy like a carrion beast might savor the stench of death itself. Long he sat there on his haunches, contemplating and considering his next move. How long would he have to wait for this boy to come to him? Why had he not investigated her scream? Perhaps he was deaf? Perhaps he was afraid? No, the monster knew better than that. Fear alone would not keep the boy away and loneliness should purge his fear, make him less careful and more curious. Perhaps his error was eliciting only one scream. Perhaps this boy was as intelligent and wily as he suspected and he doubted his own senses rather than enter the edifice.

His hardened heart asked him if he might venture into the night and overcome the boy on his own, outside of the safety of his sorcery. His answer to his heart was no, not yet. His own fear of the new world that might rise up and destroy him and consume him the moment he stepped foot out of his only sanctuary stopped him. He did not know this world yet. It called to him and yet, he was afraid. If it came to that, he might have to venture forth into the Abandonment, but before he would step out into the streets where the ghosts had risen and the Whisperers kept counsel, he would use all of his

71

powers to destroy the boy, before the boy destroyed him. The boy was his nemesis. The girl was his bait.

As the moon rose, he stood on his hind legs and threw his head into the air. Then he howled, long and loud. It was the call of the wild, the summoning song that beckoned the changed ones. These marauders would do his bidding. They were like him – made anew from something old. They had no choice but to answer his call for this was a relationship fashioned in the deep eons of Time, long before people and worlds. In his howl, though it might sound to anyone like a wolf's long lament to the endless night of the Universe, he spoke these words: "My brothers! Seek the boy and his creature. Kill them! End their existence so that I may come into my own. Gather yourselves and take counsel. I bid you! End his days!"

In the far distance of the woods and empty world, the weredogs began to howl, one by one.

Chapter 5
The Cave of Wonders

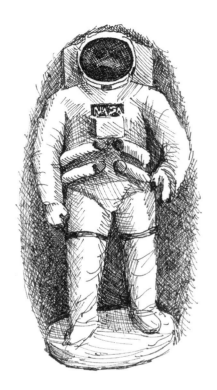

People made the rules and since the people were gone, the rules were gone, too. From now on there was nothing he absolutely *had* to do because of a rule someone else made. The thought occurred to Brady as he rode Rocinante down the empty streets that some rules might come in handy and be a good thing. For instance, it seemed like a good idea to never leave food uncovered because the rats would be attracted to it. Rats were a bad thing, and there were a lot of them in this new world so a good rule was to "cover the food." There were rules that were necessary, like never leave a fire unattended because all he needed was a bigger fire, one that could burn down the cities. He wasn't ready to survive in the wilderness all by himself, not yet.

But some rules were stupid. He knew it. Every kid knew it. He believed that every adult knew it. Some rules were there just to satisfy the sensibilities of grown-ups. When you belch, you say '*excuse me.*' That was out the door. Now he would burp long and loud and be happy he'd eaten. It was the same for farts. A fart meant that food was working through the digestive tract and that nutrients were being absorbed in his small intestine. A fart was a beautiful thing. It was the sound of survival.

So some rules make perfect sense. Some rules are actually cool. They set limits and life can be lived inside those limits. How many times did I stop myself trying something because I didn't want to look stupid? We don't try things because we're afraid to fail. We're afraid to fail because other people will know we failed and think we're stupid. But what about when there aren't any other people? That means I can try anything, do anything I want, as long as I follow the "safety rules" and not the "don't look stupid" rules. To hell with them.

He drove down the right side of the road because now that there was never anyone on the other side of the road, he decided that he *owned* the road.

Swearing was another thing. He had been told never to swear. His mother insisted that he *never* should curse in public so he tried not to, for her, but when he *did* swear, it felt good. When he was with his friends, now and then, he would utter a few interesting epithets and colorful metaphors. It was a bonding between friends. Of course, he was smart enough not to swear in front of any adults. That wouldn't be smart because there would be consequences. Now that he was alone, he could swear all he wanted. That's where the rules that help people survive veered away from the rules that helped make life worth surviving. He considered, as the analytical observer, that a life lived doing *anything* he wanted to do might lead to a short life that missed some of the significant things that a long life should encompass. He wanted to live a good life, not just any life, and it seemed to him that he should cling to *some* of the old rules even if they didn't help him simply survive. They made life more than bearable. He was used to them. They made life worthy. One of the rules he wanted to live by was simple and made the most sense:

Be prepared...

from the Journal of Brady Smith,

"I've been checking my survival list and think it's time to move on to the next thing. I have good transportation, but I still need a place to live and that's a problem. See, I've been staying at Don Quixote's house at night and it's been good – better there than anywhere else. The problem is the Whisperers. It's like they're following me. If I stay anywhere more than one or two nights in a row, they come at me with a vengeance. It's so bad that I can't sleep and I think they're driving me crazy. If I find another place to sleep than the place I was the night before, they still visit me, but only as background noise, like static on the radio. So as much as I like living here, I have to leave.

But how can I live anywhere going from place to place every night? I've thought about it a lot and I figured it out! Right now, as I write this in this little black composition book, I'm sitting at the table of my brand new recreational vehicle – a small motorhome. I remember seeing it parked next to a house off Grandview Avenue in Bangor when I was exploring, so I went back and after a little searching of the house, I found the keys in the sock drawer of the fellow who owned it – Mister Ouellette. He was a careful guy and pretty well-prepared. It's not one of those huge motorhome buses either. It's a little bigger and longer than a van, but it has all the comforts of home: a gas stove, a gas refrigerator, shower, toilet, sink for doing the dishes, heater, air conditioner and best of all – a generator for power. I can play my xbox, charge my mp3 player, have electrical light at night, everything! It's like camping every single day of the week and I can park it at a different place every night!

I have to say, I'll miss old Don Quixote's house. I never did figure out who lived there but I'm thankful I found the place. I'm going to write about this only once and not say a whole lot about it, but it was like that place came straight of out my head. Every place I looked for something – there it was. The books in the shelves were all books I had either wanted to read or had already read. All the artwork was stuff I personally loved. All the furniture was 'baby-bear' – just right. Everything was...perfect in every way. Sometimes,

75

just before falling asleep, it felt like I had lived there all of my life – and that I was the old man who had collected all this stuff and it was somehow mine, from a life I had already lived or was supposed to have lived but was interrupted.

*Oh, I almost forgot. I thought I'd better explain something. This motor home has the word FUNSEEKER painted in large letters on the side. I think it was put there at the factory like it's a model name or something. Anyway, I like fun as much as the next guy, but I'd feel stupid living in a place with the word FUN on the outside. I took some of the paint from Don Quixote's house and painted the word LIFE over the word FUN. I am now the proud owner and operator of the **LIFE**SEEKER. She's my home away from home, my gypsy caravan.*

"Max, we need to make a journey to the Cave of Wonders."

The Cave of Wonders was Brady's reference to the story of *Ali Baba and the Forty Thieves*, but it was also his way of letting go of the old names of things. Maine Army and Navy was a good enough name in the world of before, but in the present, the Cave of Wonders was by far more appropriate. The store had been one of Brady's favorites before the Abandonment. Once a month or so he could cajole his mother to drive him there, though she did not particularly think that a store with rifles in it was a fit place for an impressionable young man. To Brady, it was far more than a store. Besides the weaponry, it had a vast array of military surplus, survival equipment and a good supply of precisely those kinds of odds and ends that especially appeal to the sensibilities of a young man entering the world of men. There were guns, to be sure: rifles and pistols and replicas of some famous firepower from World War I all the way to Vietnam. There was so much more in the store that drove his imagination into flights of fancy. Time had a strange way of letting go in the store. Everywhere he looked there were Italian officer's helmets next to T-shirts with the Marine

76

Corps emblem: *Semper Fi!* There were dinner kits and water bags with straws, camouflaged duct-tape and meals in olive drab plastic pouches made for the military but also for the dining delight of the careful customer.

He had been to many places since he began mapping and scavenging for survival, but he had only visited this place once, early in his explorations. Of all the stores in this whole city, this was precisely the place that would have the supplies he would need to survive. As he pulled up to the front of the store, he was always a little taken aback by the fiberglass statue of an astronaut standing by the entrance. He had seen it many times before, an interesting conversation piece that was now a reminder of how far humans had gone and a relic of the world that had sent them. How long, he wondered, before humans would again walk upon the moon? Maybe never. What shook him a little was the sight of a standing human figure. It wasn't real or alive, but in some strange way it had the semblance of humanity.

Brady stopped the engine and waited until Max jumped out behind him before he approached the statue. It was larger than life, weathered in many a storm so that its colors were slightly fading and the weave of the fiberglass blanket was easily discernible. There had even been a patch job of khaki-colored plastic resin on the shoulder. The astronaut just stood there, a stalwart guard to the now abandoned store.

"Good morning, Neil Armstrong. How are you today?" he asked aloud. He didn't mean anything by it, but he found it amusing that he was talking to such a ridiculous, out-of-place 'thing.'

"Any problem with me just walking in and taking what I want? Yes? Oh, well, don't worry, I'll pay for everything...... *not*!" he said with a laugh. Too quickly, though, the silence that fell so heavily after every uttered word shut him up and left him feeling quite foolish.

Max jumped against the glass of the door and gave one brief bark. "Yeah, I know, boy. We got each other and I can talk to you all day long. Isn't that right, boy?" Another bark followed and the strange feeling erupted that he had stepped away from sanity for a moment by talking to a statue

77

evaporated.

There were security stickers proclaiming to the world that this was not a good place to break into. One of the signs was handwritten and said, "This store is protected by the most qualified and highly trained protection system ever devised: an American. Signed - the Management." There were signs like that all through the store and it was clear that the owners obviously thought of themselves as serious deterrents, but to Brady, especially now, they were empty threats. Besides, he was an American, wasn't he? Perhaps he was the *last* American. Somehow he believed that the people who had assembled such a useful collection of equipment and tools would not begrudge him their use. He was sure that they would say, "You need this stuff more than we do, buddy. Take what you need, and good luck to you."

Brady put his hand on the door and said aloud, "Cave of Wonders! It is I, Ali Baba, and I know the magic words! OPEN SESAME!" Brady could have sworn the reflection of the astronaut in the window tilted his head in a nod. No, that was impossible.

For an instant that lasted as a segment of forever, he waited. Then, it happened: the door opened. He didn't stop to question why or how this occurred. In the depths of his boyhood self, he simply accepted it as a strange coincidence and walked into his Cave of Wonders.

He took his time in the labyrinthine darkness, for the aisles were long and deep and there was no light. In a moment he had opened a plastic package containing a twelve L.E.D. headlamp and was moving forward through the darkness like a miner searching for glistening veins of coal, like Theseus in search of the Minotaur or Hercules in search of the Nemean Lion. Aisle after aisle was cataloged in his mind: military food rations, gloves, coats, boots of all kinds and types, heavy winter gear, and desert survival clothing. There were steel ammunition boxes, fishing tackle, some oddities like surplus gasoline cans from some defunct government in Eastern Europe and South American dress helmets complete with red feathery plumes. Aisle after aisle revealed a truly amazing assortment of tools he could use to help him stay alive in almost any situation. There were long johns that seemed absurd in their length and boots made for giants, canvas mittens that reached all the way to his elbow and green wool pants made for Gulliver. He began to gather his supplies, taking whatever he wanted in whatever amount he pleased.

He took several trips to the Lifeseeker, resupplying food, medical supplies, telescopes and binoculars, photographers' vests with superfluous pockets, and belts to which could be attached all manner of small containers, holsters and bags. Best of all, he thought, was a gas mask with replaceable activated carbon filters. Such a thing would be useful for entering places he was already forsworn never to enter again - the dead houses. The stench of decay seemed to fill some of the streets now that the really warm weather had begun to hit. This could make life more bearable.

The final aisle gave him pause. In the back of his mind he knew that there would be guns in the store. He had seen them when his mother had brought him in earlier days. He had always purposely avoided this particular aisle, for it was an entire wall of weaponry, an arsenal of guns. There were at least three hundred rifles all neatly and carefully leaning in their cases behind the counter. A long steel cable ran through and around all of them and they were equipped with trigger locks. They stood there at attention like sentinels, waiting for a rotation of the guard that would never come, never housing another cartridge, never hurtling another bullet through the air. In their way, they were dead now, too. They were all well maintained, their barrels bathed in the slightly fragrant oil used to maintain movement and repel rust. Brady knew that nothing could repel Time and its machinations. They would rust and crumble with the passing of the centuries.

His father died from a gunshot wound. He recalled it with the strength of loss that only yesterday might bring, especially here and now among such ordinance. How many times had his father cleaned that rifle of his at the kitchen table in the early fall, getting ready for hunting season? How many mornings had his father left them sleeping comfortably and warm in their beds while he rolled out in his old pickup so he could be there at dawn to take advantage of the quiet moments to take down his deer? Then every year he would proudly bring the kill home and call his son and wife out to see the deer, legs tied tightly and head morbidly lying in the back of the truck.

Brady stood in front of the glass case and ruminated over the vision of his eyes and the blending imagery of his mind. Rifles blended with photos of his father, boxes of bullets swirled together with the image of his mother sitting on the edge of her bed, hands cupping her face. Paper targets overlapped the long black hearse that carried his father's body to the grave. By now, Brady had seen hundreds of dead humans, all in various stages of decay. They had stopped frightening him, but the loss of his father still caused anguish he knew he would never lose, no matter how many tears he cried or how many years would go by.

Someone had left a pistol unlocked on top of the case. It was a large handgun, although Brady didn't know the caliber or the name of the manufacturer. Nearby was an open box of shells. Whoever had put it there must have had some idea in mind and then must have been drawn away from their original intention to some other future, some other fate. There it lay, an omen and a challenge. Brady found himself quietly bound by the grey gun's metal sheen and its perfect, hard lines. How might this weapon save his life in the coming days, weeks, months and years? Who knew when a wild creature might corner him in some future day and how might he simply pull the pistol from its holster and eliminate the problem? Who could say with any certainty that the future might require such a weapon to stay alive? The handgun was the simple solution, light and easily handled. It was as though the weapon had been prepared and laid there to await his arrival by some thoughtful prophet so that he, and only he, would claim it and take it for his own.

His heart was pounding a heavy metal rhythm in his chest as he slowly reached toward it. He picked it up and tested its weight. Heavy and dull, he found the need to hold it quickly vanishing and he dropped it back on the counter. Then, in a rush of memory, he recalled the late morning when his life had been so irrevocably changed as a single phone call and a scream from his mother tore the fabric of his happy, young life, revealing the harsh truth beneath: his father was dead.

A bullet straight through his heart. A single bullet. An occurrence with a weapon that accidentally discharged ended his world long before the advent of the Abandonment. He wouldn't succumb to the lure of the gun. It had already cost him too dearly. He would have to rely on other weapons and strategies to save himself.

That was when he heard the first voice, speaking from behind the case.

"Hey, kid, you need me. Yeah, that's right. Over here. I'm just the thing for the boy faced with a survival of the fittest situation. Let me tell you, I'm not too heavy. I have a built in scope and can take down a rabbit in three hundred feet, if you're a good shot."

Then another voice from further down the line of rifles said, *"Oh, don't waste your time. The boy's a sissy. Hey, kid, there's some toy guns over in the back. They ought to suit you fine. He's just too afraid of the big bang bang and the loud boom boom. Ha!"* Brady thought that the voice came from an M-1 carbine, standard issue, World War I. It was in excellent shape, but it's manners left a lot to be desired.

"Leave him alone, you jar-head," said a kinder voice from near the register. It was a hunting rifle, just like the one his father had owned.

"You don't want those, buddy. This place is full of big and shiny, but you need sensible and I'm just the right one for you. Your daddy had you with him the day he bought my brother, manufactured in the same factory on the same day. We're practically family. Hey, just take me. I'm free now, and I don't want to sit here and rust away. I'll serve you well, my boy, just like my brother served your dad."

"Shut up!" Brady yelled, breaking the silence that had fallen and nearly solidified in the store.

Had the voices been real? Were they in his head? He looked at the wall of guns in anger.

"Go to Hell!" he screamed. "Bastards! You killed him!"

He waited for a response, but either he was very persuasive or beginning to go out of his mind. He remembered the day he went with his dad to buy the hunting rifle. He remembered the first time they went to the gravel pit and shot at targets. He had wanted to shoot it so badly, but his father told him that it was too dangerous for a kid. In his ears still rang the loud report of the rifle and the acrid taste of fresh powder clouding the air whenever his father shot the rifle, echoing like a thunderbolt exploding in his mind. It always would, every day, and for the rest of his life.

Still, he thought, I will need a weapon. From what he knew of early man, who also faced the natural world alone, they always had weaponry. Had Theseus a gun? Or Hercules, or Jason? Did King Arthur face the armies that would tear down Camelot with a bazooka? A hero needed a better weapon, like Obi-Wan's light saber, a weapon of a nobler age.

What could serve to save him, to be of use, light enough to carry and easy to wield? He was drawn to the knife section of the store. Whoever had operated this establishment had a wondrous and fantastic taste in blades. There were swords and machetes, Bowie knives and pocket knives, knives that unfolded, locked open, or flicked easily with the quick wrist of the wielder. He liked the idea of a knife, even a collection of them. They would last a lifetime, needed no bullets and could be used for many different purposes, only one of which was killing. Boy Scouts had knives. It seemed logical to him that he might become proficient with a blade and that a man who knew how to properly use a knife might be a formidable opponent. In the end he took many, since they were light and easy to carry. He had one for his boot, two for his pockets, two for his belt, as well as a machete and for his own amusement, a replica of a Japanese samurai sword, which he strapped over his back for easy retrieval over his shoulder. He found a diamond sharpening kit that could be used to keep the blades seriously honed.

Before leaving, Brady felt a strange compulsion to return to the pistol on the gun counter. The way it had been

82

left there, unlocked and ready to use, haunted him. If there was some other person on earth and they happened into this place, they would have no problem arming themselves to the teeth, but they would not have this pistol at their disposal. He picked it up, along with the box of shells that lay near it and walked to the back of the store, switching his headlamp on to navigate through the channels of darkness that used to simply be the aisles. In the back he found what he was looking for – a large black gun safe, fortuitously left open. He placed the pistol and bullets into the safe and securely shut the door, spinning the combination lock after turning the handle to the locked position. There, he thought, it would stay until the seas went dry and the mountains crumbled into them.

Brady shooed Max out of the store and closed the door gently. He turned and looked at the astronaut, laying his hand upon its shoulder.

"Neil, old buddy, keep the cave safe until I return again. Remember, no one shall pass except if they utter the password." The astronaut's golden visor belied no movement or acknowledgment from within, but Brady turned back after a few steps and stared long at the astronaut. Had he just heard the slightest of sounds, a tinny radio voice saying, "Roger that"?

Brady walked away from the Cave of Wonders, toward an uncertain future.

Chapter 6
The Weredogs

Hugin was croaking in the sky, circling above Brady and Max in a widening gyre, persistent and vociferous. Brady had never seen him so agitated before. Every day for the past two weeks Brady and Max had followed the raven's lead and each day the bird had led them to places that would be of great use to them in their struggle to survive, bringing them to several unlikely looking places that had stores of food, water, tools, building supplies and even toilet paper. Brady renamed most of the streets and places to ones more suited to his knowledge and imagination. Hugin had become more than a bird. Brady determined that Hugin was an emissary from some unknown place whose purpose was to guide him throughout the vast Abandonment. How the raven knew where to go was a mystery, but with the bird's guidance, Brady's map grew ever more detailed and exacting.

Hugin swooped low and landed on the top of a telephone pole, spreading his black wings like a cloak and croaked, "Ragnarok! Ragnarok!" It was the only word he ever seemed to say.

Brady stopped Rocinante and dismounted, taking one of the three backpacks that were connected to the chassis with aluminum caribiner clips. Throwing it over his shoulder, he grabbed one of the paint ball guns, checking to make sure his knives were in place. He then took the gas mask in his other hand and walked into the yard of the house that Hugin obviously meant for him to explore when he heard Max whining behind him, still sitting dutifully on the back of the four-wheeler. Brady stopped and regarded him with amusement.

Before the Abandonment, Brady had enjoyed Max like any boy of fourteen years might appreciate his dog, with a passing pat on the head, a rare walk to the park, and late feedings after prolonged pleading. Since the Abandonment, Brady's feelings for his dog had intensified and refocused. He was Brady's boon companion, his buddy, his best friend. He was something from the world before the Abandonment - he was proof of continuation. Max had been an old puppy in Brady's eyes, but now he was a man's dog, a helper in a hard, dangerous world. In the days before the Abandonment he would never have sat there on the back of the four-wheeler. He would have jumped off and gone his own way and Brady would have had to call after him, swear a little, and then run off to find him. It seemed that Max understood his new role in the world and accepted it with courage and vitality.

Things had changed. The world had changed. Brady whistled and jerked his head to the side and said, "Come on, boy!" Max complied.

Like so many others, this house had nothing remarkable in it. There was no need for the gas mask because there were no bodies. Sometimes when Brady entered a house, even though there were no dead, he could feel someone's eyes watching him. Behind every door he could feel the presence of humans looking at him, only to find nothing but their absence. This was such a place: an empty shell that once housed people.

He stood outside of the house and withdrew a small red leather bound journal from his leg pocket and wrote down a few cryptic notes. "Forty-five Tamarack Street. Nothing special. NON-TOMB." He doubted if he would even put it on his map. It was unremarkable. Glancing up at Hugin who still called to him in his guttural tongue, he called, "What? What the heck do you want? What are you? Lassie? What am I supposed to find?"

Hugin croaked back, "Ragnarok!" He ruffled his feathers, tucked his beak underneath his left wing and picked at himself for a moment. Then he did the equivalent of a bird's shrug, took to the air and flew to the back yard of the house.

Brady followed. In a moment it was obvious why Hugin had summoned him.

The back yard was fenced in with heavy wire and there, in the back corner, was a small wooden building. On the ground, here and there, were several chickens. They didn't look particularly healthy or move with any great store of energy, but the fact couldn't be denied: they were chickens. Brady couldn't help but instantly recall the savory taste of fried chicken, chicken fingers, chicken nuggets, and chicken with stuffing, boiled eggs, fried eggs, scrambled eggs, eggs with ketchup. Fresh food!

After a visit to the feed store in Bangor and a rather nasty confrontation with a large rat that was obviously not afraid of him, he took care of the chickens like they were his pets and he was suddenly a farmer, not just a hunter-gatherer. This made sense because it meant continuity. He double-checked the chicken wire and made sure there were no breaks where any animal larger than a mouse could gain access. The coop needed a heavy cleaning, and then he spent at least an hour a night reading a book he had found in the house, a guide on how to raise poultry. More than anything he had done to improve his situation and standing in the world since the Abandonment, this raised his spirits the most.

Killing the chickens was out of the question. The first time he found eggs in the roost, he realized the new food source could be never-ending. Brady named each hen, picking them up and inspecting them, making sure that they were healthy, and spending no less then three hours scavenging the local houses for cookbooks on how to do anything with eggs besides fry them. In the end, his first omelet was a disaster, but the second one was better and the third one was definitely palatable. He decided that it was the absence of a little heavy cream in the mixture. He did find some early onions and there were some chunks of cheddar cheese he had in the Lifeseeker's cupboard. Within a week, he had added some precooked bacon from the Save-A-Lot and said aloud to Max, "Boy, I think this omelet is even better than the omelets from Dysarts Truck Stop!"

For the first time since he had become the lord of all he surveyed, Brady Smith felt like he had more than just luck on his side. All the problems he had, all the questions, all the unknowns that stood lurking in the corners of his immediate future were nothing compared to the feeling he had at that moment. Eggs were more than food to him. Eggs were independence from the grocery stores and cupboards of dead strangers. If he could keep the chickens laying he could ensure fresh food for the foreseeable future.

When night fell, Brady found himself entering the Lifeseeker and making sure the door was shut tight because he had heard them howling for the past few days. They had been in the distance and though he had seen the wandering dogs sniffing around the neighborhoods, he didn't know that weredogs existed until one day at dusk a week ago when he caught a faint glimpse of one.

He had been doing something crazy. Sometimes being the last boy on earth was fairly depressing, but there were moments when he could forget and the fact that he was a teenager was remembered. One thing that Brady had always loved to do was play guitar. He wasn't very good at finishing full songs yet, but he had a few licks memorized from some of his favorite tunes. When his mother had been working, he would crank his little amp up loud and on his one-hundred dollar electric guitar, he would let fly a cadence and panoply of notes that drove the neighbors mad. Since electricity had failed, he had played nothing and hadn't even thought about music except to drive away the sound of the Whisperers. Today, Brady took the time to *enjoy* himself.

Breaking into the music store near the bridge, Brady took care to choose his new guitar. There is was in its orange sunburst explosion – a Gibson Les Paul that would have cost thousands of dollars before the Abandonment, now it was his for the taking. He also managed a particularly heavy Marshall amp, cords, a tuner, several effect pedals and a whole rack of picks.

At the parking lot of the Brewer Shopping Center, Brady started the Lifeseeker's generator and plugged in his equipment. The Marshall buzzed and then hummed quietly, ready for him to strike a note and break the world in half with its loud report. The sun was setting by the time he had his concert ready.

For a moment, he was Angus Young, Jack White, The Edge or Jimmy Page as he cranked the amp up to ten and let his hand stroke the strings with a loud crashing strum. The trees melted, the sky changed shade, and the wind began to blow. The force of his playing was intense and he knew that at this moment, he was the *best* guitar player in the world, a boyhood dream finally realized because, he shamefully admitted, he was probably the *only* guitar player left on the planet. It didn't matter, though, because music can suspend the passage of time as surely as it can mark it, and Brady played every lick he knew, switching between effects pedals, building up to the only song he could play all the way through with any confidence: "Wild Thing" by The Troggs. In the mix of licks were Pearl Jam, the White Stripes, Alice in Chains, Rage Against the Machine, Van Halen and Green Day and he played from his heart and what was left of his soul, his mind migrating outside of himself to that place where songs go after they have been heard. He was encapsulated by a bubble of sound, effectively removed from the world and its vagaries. For a moment, at least, the music and the volume smoothed away the harsh edges of the world.

When he opened his eyes, the sun was nothing more than a memory and a red smear smudged across the edge of the horizon. Max was barking frenetically at something in the distance at the edge of the parking lot.

Brady stopped playing and narrowed his eyes to get a better look in the falling dark. It was a creature, larger than any dog he had ever seen, gray and fierce. He could have sworn it was walking on its hind legs like a human. When it caught sight of him, its red eyes flashed before it turned and fell on all fours. Frozen in place by fear, Brady changed into *Observation Mode* and studied it like it seemed to be studying him. It reminded him of a werewolf from the old horror movies that they showed on cable during October and Halloween time. Brady placed his finger on the high-e string and fretted it up high on the neck and began to play a long lick he invented on the spot. The creature seemed to cringe at the sound and in a moment, it turned away and bounded into the forest.

Late in the night, past midnight when the moon was high in the sky and all the world was as black as velvet, he would hear them, long lost brothers finally free from whatever human bonds that held them as mere animals. He wondered if they were humans who had turned into dogs or dogs that had turned into humans. Either way, they were caught somewhere halfway in between two worlds. Like a centaur or a minotaur from Greek mythology, these creatures seemed to have aspects of both man and animal and therefore could be doubly dangerous. With no humans to bind them, they had been set free and they were getting closer, taking their original shape from the depths of time, before the advent of civilization. He hoped that they would find enough wild deer to kill, but he knew that if that failed, these weredogs would hunt down, kill and eat anything that moved, including him.

They hunted at night, but with the loss of humans, they would quickly become less wary of the city environs and soon they would be sniffing around the Lifeseeker and the chickens. If he waited and did nothing, they would be on his doorstep in a week. Paintball guns did not seem like they would be enough, so he had to find another way to repel them. He didn't relish the thought of a knife fight with what he dubbed a 'weredog'. He didn't want to get that close.

When his mother had lost her job at the nursing home and before she found employment at the hospital, they had gone through some lean times. Ketchup soup and ramen noodles were not unknown in Brady's diet even two years ago. Still, his mother had made a friend in the Bangor area, a man who ran a pawn shop. She would bring in a piece of gold or silver jewelry and he would give her an amount of money for it and if she paid him that money back in thirty days, plus interest, she could have the jewelry back. Rick would hold the jewelry for much longer than he was legally required. Brady knew that though Rick looked rough around the edges that he was an honorable person and, more than that, a person with a good heart. However, he was no fool. The reason Brady was thinking of Rich right now was because he knew that Rich kept a taser in his office in his top desk drawer. Once, when his Mom had sent him in to pay Rich the money, Rich had showed Brady the taser when Brady asked him what he would do if anyone ever stopped to rob him.

"No problem," Rich said, opening his desk drawer. "I have a little something for them right here."

He withdrew a taser and said, "There's enough electricity in this little box to stop a man in his tracks. He'll fall down on the floor in so much pain that he won't be able to move away for a hell of a long time, which would give me plenty of time to call the cops. All you have to do is point this at the perp and press this button. The rest happens on its own."

Brady knew that he might need such a weapon to fight off the weredogs. They were intelligent and might be able to work together to take him down. He still didn't want to use a gun, as easy as that would have been. The death of his father left him forever wary of firearms, whose actions were undoable and from whose discharge came certain death. His problem was really very simple. Brady didn't want to kill anything, not even weredogs. He just wanted to be left alone. The taser wouldn't kill but it would render the creature incapable of attack and if they were smart enough to learn, they wouldn't come back for another taste of it.

It was just after three o'clock when Brady finally found his way into Rick's pawn shop. Going there was a last minute decision. He left Max at the Lifeseeker which was parked in the old Brewer Shopping Center parking lot. Max had become used to staying close to the Lifeseeker when Brady needed to take short trips and now, that's exactly what he did.

Like most of the shops he had entered since the Abandonment, the pawn shop was strangely hushed and lonesome. The items on the shelves and in the storage room and safe would rest there forever, never to be picked up by their previous owners. There were tools, mostly electrically powered, a few chainsaws, rifles and guitars, a drum set and a slew of video games and dvds. He paused and took a few of each. He wasn't stealing. They all belonged to him, now. The taser was in Rick's drawer, as well as two others in the back room. He had to check them to make sure that they were charged. He would have to read the manual that Rick had so fortuitously left next to the taser, hoping that he could charge them later using the small generator on the back of the Lifeseeker. If not, he had already mapped several generators around the area with full tanks of diesel. From what he could tell, only one taser was fully charged.

The sun was getting low in the sky and Brady sat in Rick's chair, watching the sky through the big windows. He used to really enjoy coming to this place. There were so many things here he wanted before the Abandonment that now seemed pointless and wasted. Anything that ran on electricity, including the tasers, had a limited lifespan. He needed things that would last and be of use without electricity.

As he was leaving the shop through the front door, he heard Hugin's raucous cry.

"Ragnarok! Ragnarok!"

Hugin was circling above Rocinante, continuing his

calling back toward the river and Brewer.

"What is it?" he asked.

Rocinante's wheels spun madly as he kicked the four-wheeler into gear, rolling past the casino and down to the riverfront and the bridge. Hugin was leading him back to the Lifeseeker. He took the center bridge over the Great River at full throttle.

The sun was setting when he saw them. At least six weredogs were surrounding the Lifeseeker and in the center of the pack was Max. He was so much smaller than they were and he was outnumbered, but he didn't seem to notice or particularly care. They had cornered him underneath the vehicle and they were on their knees, reaching underneath, growling and spitting, barking their anger and murderous intent. Max might be only just out of their reach, but when they reached beneath to grab at him, he bit them and tore their flesh, which served to aggravate their already intense frustration. They heard Rocinante and turned their attention to Brady.

Brady drove a circle around the Lifeseeker, trying to determine his best course of action. They were much bigger than he imagined when he had heard them breaking the night's silence with their guttural, monosyllabic calls. Grey, covered with coarse steel-wool hair, seeming to walk on all fours and then on two, they formed a circle and faced him as he drove around them at a distance. They glared at him with crimson eyes that followed his path. He didn't know if they were cunning or acting upon instinct. Max continued to growl from underneath the Lifeseeker and he knew that if Max sensed that he was in danger, he would leave his relatively safe haven and come to his aid, even if he was outnumbered and outsized.

Brady checked to see if his sword was unlatched from its scabbard on his back, then he pulled his paint ball rifles out of the twin holsters he had fashioned on either side of Rocinante's front axle. He stopped for a moment and took careful aim. His first shots hit the largest of the group, a particularly mangy, drooling fanged beast of questionable breed. It flinched and then cried out in pain but then growled more deeply. Its fur was no longer a dull and lifeless gray, but purple in the spots that had been hit. The next shot hit the same creature in the snout near the eye, and the creature howled to its companions as it moved erratically, blinded momentarily. It was disoriented enough to cause the other weredogs to stir into confusion. They milled about their purple-snouted companion, barking and growling.

"Now boys," called Brady, "I don't want any trouble. You all go on your merry way and I'll forget all about this little visit. If you stay, I'll shoot all of you in the face. I won't kill you, but you'll hurt like hell. Leave Max and me alone. We're not hurting anyone and we've got nothing here you want. Now go!"

Obviously, they weren't as intelligent as he imagined. Human speech seemed to have escaped them. He placed six quick shots from each weapon, hitting each of the weredogs. They were wild with anger, but they had new respect for the boy on the four-wheeler. They didn't come any closer, except for the big one. He was obviously the alpha male and needed to maintain his superiority in front of the others. Lowering his huge body to the ground in a coiled crouch, he was ready to fly through the distance and engage in combat.

Brady holstered both of the rifles and withdrew a baseball from one of the fender bags. Like a pitcher readying to throw the last ball at a shutout game, he stood on Rocinante and aimed, curling his body as he thrust the ball at the leader.

"Strike one!" he yelled, "The crowd cheers!" Brady made hissing and hurrah sounds and then took a paint ball pistol from his hip holster. It was a smaller weapon with limited range, but he needed one hand to maneuver Rocinante as he approached the Lifeseeker. Meanwhile, the last light of the setting sun was making this confrontation much more interesting that it would have been in the clear light of day.

The movement of the four-wheeler confused the pack of weredogs. Brady wondered who they had been before the change, before the Abandonment had forced them to transform into these fell creatures. Had he known any of

93

them? He didn't yet know the particulars of their origin or genesis, but he knew that they were not in the world before the Abandonment. The world had changed and in some ways, it had become a far more dangerous place. He had not yet given up trying to persuade them to leave. Besides, he had the taser, even if it had only one charge in it.

"What do you want here?" he called to them. Most of them barked and snarled, their circling motion aggravated by his question. Then the largest weredog said in a low and guttural grinding growl that sounded only vaguely like, "Kill!" He repeated himself. He spat it out with a vengeance. It was the only word in his vocabulary. He reared up on his two hind legs and used his forepaws to motion Brady to come closer.

"Not today!" shouted Brady and he gunned Rocinante, lifting the two front wheels off the ground. He fired a nonstop volley of paint balls at ever closer range as he moved quickly forward, veering at the last moment as the creature fell back whimpering and confused, blinded with color.

"Get away, all of you. Go!" Brady unclipped the sports horn from the hook on Rocinante's steering column and pressed the button. The sound was deafening. The weredogs' ears fell back flat on their heads and they cringed, falling back and away from the Lifeseeker. Brady stopped the four-wheeler and dismounted.

Strangely, he was unafraid of them even though he knew that he should be. He thought it would be otherwise, but the world had changed. He had changed. Walking towards them, he was their superior, though he was alone and young. More than that, he also had the taser in his right hand, ready to shoot the first weredog that got in his way. They moved one step back for each step he took toward them, their eyes all on their leader, who was dazed and confused on the ground, unable to see.

Brady pressed the button on the horn again and they began to flee into the darkness, all except the big one. As he got closer to it, he could hear it grumbling in a low growl, "Grrrendell! Grrrendell!" over and over again in frustration and, Brady thought, fear.

"Leave me alone. Never come back or you'll feel the bite of my weapon. I won't be so nice next time. Leave us alone!" Brady said emphatically.

"Graahh!" screamed the chief weredog. He lunged at Brady and hit him full on the body, pushing him down to the ground. Brady's grasp of the taser was lost and it clattered away on the pavement, rolling away. He was pinned beneath the creature, whose forepaws held each arm down to the pavement. He slavered over Brady as he sneered, revealing yellowed, calcified teeth, not like a dogs, but like a man's. Drops of spittle drooled down upon Brady's face as he fought to move the heavy creature from his own body.

"Kill! Ha! Grrrendell Ha!" His tongue shot out from his mouth and ran itself along its teeth, longingly. Brady's left leg was positioned perfectly and he lifted it with all of his strength, kicking squarely between the weredog's legs. Man or dog, this was going to hurt. It howled in agony and fell over, unable to move or think.

The other weredogs were approaching again. Max shot out from under the Lifeseeker and attacked the one closest to Brady, locking his jaws on the creature's lower leg. It fought back.

"Max! No!" Brady screamed, but it was too late. The weredog kicked at Max, and then in an impossible twisting of its own body, bent over backwards and bit Max on the neck. Max's body fell limp to the pavement. He moved no more.

Brady scrambled to find the taser but it was too far away. He had successfully defeated the biggest weredog, who was now limping from the parking lot and back into the fresh dark of night that, like a blanket, had just covered the planet. He ran at the weredog that had bitten Max, screaming at the top of his lungs and withdrew his sword from its scabbard on his back. It sang as it escaped its prison and felt the air. Holding it raised in his left hand, he took the paint ball gun in his right hand and emptied it at the creature, painting it with pain. It fled into the darkness with its master and brothers.

Brady stood there in the parking lot in near darkness and let loose a primal scream. It was the scream of early man as he hunted on the plains, it was the tribal scream of retribution, the soldier's bloody cry as he attacked his doomed foe, it was the release of tension and anger. It was his defiance.

When he checked Max, he feared the worst. The dog was still breathing, but he was losing blood. After a cursory check for broken bones, something he had never done before and was certainly unsure of, Brady gently picked him up and brought him to the Lifeseeker. He placed Max's shuddering body gently, tenderly on the floor. After applying a bandage, the thought occurred to him that Max might need stitches. Worse, he wondered if Max might die. The reading on first aid he had done told him to keep Max warm, stop the bleeding and administer antibiotics. Brady had anticipated a need for an emergency medical kit for himself, but he had never considered Max. It was imperative that Max survive. He had to. Brady couldn't bear the idea of losing his best, his only friend. If Max died, then the world would truly be dead and Brady would be lost. He would also be *alone*.

The Brewer Animal Clinic was unlocked when Brady entered, his headlight illuminating the waiting and examining rooms and the marble floor. He had been a visitor here with Max many times and had always liked Dr. Prayer. No matter what was wrong with Max, the fair-haired gentleman always reassured Brady that everything would be as it should be, not that everything would be all right. Brady liked that Dr. Prayer didn't talk down to him or make blanket statements that weren't true just to comfort him. Now, he wondered if things were as they should be and what that even meant.

The drugs were kept just outside the examining rooms. Brady had noticed them many times. Now he was looking for something - penicillin, amoxicillin, something that ended with -cillin. These were antibiotics and he knew Max needed some. He also looked for the supplies he would need to stitch Max's wounds. He relied so heavily on Max for companionship that he couldn't imagine a world without him. Strange, he thought, that I can live in a world I never could have imagined without any people, but without this old dog, I think I'll go crazy. He has to live.

Determining that it was better to be safe than sorry, Brady found suturing equipment and antiseptic. He brought Max into the operating theater and strapped him down, then he cleaned the wound soundly and carefully stitched it closed. He remembered that once, when Max had been very dehydrated, the doctor had given him a shot of water just under the skin to rehydrate him quickly. He knew Max needed fluids, but he didn't dare do any more than he had already done. Instead, he determined to nurse Max back to health if that meant one spoonful of water at a time.

The next three days were torture for Brady. Never leaving the Brewer Animal Clinic, he took care of Max and read all day from the manuals, lists of procedures and reference books. He learned a great deal in that time, enough to know that he had done almost everything that could be done for his friend. Max lingered quietly in a nearly motionless state, shuddering from time to time, making small whining noises and then falling into deep, deep slumber. Brady moved him into one of the cages in the back and closed it. He needed to resupply some of his own food and water. He wouldn't need to be out for very long, an hour or two at the most.

Chapter 7
The House of God

They began to whisper again. They always seemed louder near water and as he approached the middle bridge over the Great River, they started in. Not a whisper nor a murmur, but this time a moan and a cry permeated his hearing. The idea that the Whisperers were inside of his head, and therefore a figment of his imagination, was rapidly leaving him. The idea that they were remnants of the world before the Abandonment and they had something to tell him began to make sense to him. He couldn't tell one voice from another and he certainly couldn't understand their frenzied pleadings. To make matters worse, they spoke in strange cadences and rhythms, their volume rising and falling. They were not whispering now. They we screaming.

Before he knew it, he was out of the Lifeseeker on his knees with his hands covering his ears and he found himself screaming too. In the middle of the Joshua Chamberlain Bridge that spanned the Great River, with the wind blowing gently and the world in full bloom, the voices stabbed like icepicks in his mind.

"Stop! Stop it! Leave me alone!" he wailed, but they didn't stop. They intensified their attack, leaving not a millisecond of silence. There were a million voices all speaking at once but all saying something different. If they slowed down, he might understand them. If they were somehow more distinct he could comprehend them but to Brady it was as if they were speaking all the languages of the earth at once and he couldn't maintain any understanding beyond a word here and a phrase there.

He didn't know how long he lingered there in the middle of his pain over the flowing water that led to the sea and therefore the world. It was the water that connected everything and he understood that it was a good conductor of electricity and other things. Water always was. He knew he had to get off this bridge and away from the water, but he was immobilized with pain. Who were these people who now shouted so vehemently into his mind? What were they trying to tell him?

Then he heard another noise and somehow it broke the spell. It was Hugin, the great raven. He was only a foot from Brady, walking like a cowboy with two six-guns on his hip, itching for a fight. Dipping his head up and down in an exaggerated manner, he croaked and muttered like he was trying to talk. The world had changed, but Brady had the idea that his bird had always been more than just a bird. Hugin was a master of birds, a totem.

"Ragnarok! Ragnarok!" he croaked emphatically. Brady listened, but in his mind he heard, "Get up! Get back into that thing and drive! Go away from the river! I hear them, too."

He stretched himself upwards and arose, grabbed the

100

steering wheel and pulled himself into the Lifeseeker as the bird took wing and flew straight across the bridge toward the Bangor side. Brady followed, half aware of his own actions, driving by instinct, half-blind, an instrument of the bird's will. Miraculously, the Whisperers seemed to grow less vociferous as he reached the land again. Stopping the Lifeseeker a good distance from the bridge and the water, he gathered his breath and his thoughts.

For days and weeks he hadn't questioned his station in the world. For days and weeks he hadn't allowed anger to rise within him like the demon he knew it was. Beyond the idea that he might be the last boy on earth was the nagging question, "Why?" One three-letter word uttered at the right moment to the right person might give him the answer he needed to stop his meandering mind. Who would he ask? Who would answer?

St. Joseph's Catholic Church on York Street in Bangor had a black spire that rose toward heaven, reaching more majestically than any other building within Brady's view. It seemed like the tallest building in the city and even from a distance, the effect was that even after the very tip of the black spire culminated in a pinpoint, somehow the building continued to rise upward, toward its terminal connection. As a boy he had been inside at Christmas, Easter, Thanksgiving, and perhaps a few other times during the year when his mother felt the urge to be responsible about his spirituality. Brady had never been confirmed in the Catholic faith like his mother had, so he had always felt only partially at home within the massive stone walls built so long ago by Irish immigrants.

The placard on the front informed him that the services were held at 7 AM and 5 PM daily in the chapel, with a Saturday mass at 4 PM and again on Sunday morning at 7 and 10 AM. Brady's watch told him it was 9 o'clock in the morning. Since he would be the sole participant, he didn't think the owner of this building would mind if he was late. In fact, he hoped the owner would be ready to hear his words.

The inside of the church was serene, somehow

101

untouched by all that had happened. Brady walked up the center aisle and saw the crucified form of Christ in front of him, much larger than life, hanging behind the altar. The filigree woodwork from an earlier age rose from the altar to the vaults, belying the style of the Irish immigrants whose labor had built and financed its construction. The altar was still covered with a linen cloth and green embroidered cross. The lilies that had been left in the front of the church had withered, now only brown and crackling stems. Brady sat down. He didn't kneel as his mother had taught him. To Brady, it seemed like Judgment Day had passed and somehow, he had been left behind to carry on, an unlikely new Adam in an empty world.

For a long time he sat there in silence, the stillness strangely comforting, unlike the stillness that lay outside the massive wooden doors. As loudly as Whisperers had moaned their cacophony into his mind in the middle of bridge, they were strangely silent now – their voices hushed. He closed his eyes and tried to empty his mind. Questions came to him, things he wanted to ask, words he wanted to say. How does one speak to God when God seems so strangely inarticulate, even mute? How does one address God *after* the end of days? Thoughts of his mother, of his friends, his family, even his teachers came to him. Their faces flashed in front of his eyes and he was suddenly more lonely than he had been since the start of this macabre nightmare he now called *life*.

Brady said very quietly aloud, "I have some questions."

The sound of his voice was consumed by the vast space that this building enclosed. It was so quiet, even though he spoke, that he began to doubt if he had even said anything. He spoke again, somewhat louder this time.

"I know you can hear me. You know I'm here."

He looked at the figure on the cross and because he was a human figure, he was compelled to speak to it directly. Even a statue of the human form somehow made him feel less lonely and gave him comfort.

"They're all dead. Everyone I ever knew is gone. I've been worried about my mother. I hope...I think she's alive, but maybe that's just a wish. I've been working hard to keep myself alive. Every day I'm busy surviving. I've got lots of things to help me, but I'm beginning to think that..."

Brady stopped his confession. Somehow, he didn't quite dare to speak the next words, and then he thought that if he couldn't be honest with God, who already knew what he was thinking, there was no point in talking to anyone.

"I can't help but wonder...have you forgotten me? Did you leave me here as some kind of punishment? Because being the only one left is terrible! I don't know what I did, but I'm sorry for whatever it was that made you forget me here. Things are getting scary. The weredogs are getting braver, the dead walk the graveyards, and I can't take these voices in my head much longer."

After he spoke these words, Brady sat quietly and pondered the figure on the cross and said, "Why have you forgotten me?"

The words echoed through the cavernous space. In the silence, Brady heard a sound. Something was moving, but then it wasn't and he couldn't quite put his finger on it. Still, the question resonated in his head like an echo and he wouldn't let it rest. This question required an answer. It was essential and, as such, needed a direct and unequivocal answer.

But no answer came, or if it came, it was the faint whistle of the wind outside the church and that kind of sound was the noise of lonesomeness and forgetfulness. How could that be an answer? Perhaps the question wasn't sufficient. He'd read *The Hunchback of Notre Dame* and he knew that Quasimodo, the hunchback, had uttered only one word as he died, and that word still echoed in his mind. *Why?* He wondered, was the hunchback asking why he was dying, or why he had ever lived? He was the outcast now, lonely and wretched. He was the only living person, and that made him the odd man out. God had left him here, but Brady couldn't quite tell if God had abandoned him. Abandonment would have meant that God just said, "He doesn't die. He lives, but I have better things to do than worry about one boy. I'll just go on now and mind the Universe. Too late for this place, anyhow."

His face began to redden and his hands clenched into fists. In his Fortress of Solitude where visions turned into mind-movies, he reviewed every dead body he had seen since he had awakened and he recalled that each one had been a human being with hopes, fears, loves and desires. How many voices would never sing or speak again? How many of God's creations could no longer ask this ultimate question because they had no voice, no life? Brady decided to speak for them, his friends, his family, his...no..his mother? His voice rose as he continued, pleading into the ether of a church whose entire congregation had died.

"Why?" he shouted to the ceiling. He waited for a moment, because the world had changed and perhaps God would answer him or strike him dead instead of remaining silent. Then he continued, "Why? You sent the flood that killed everyone before, but then you promised never to do it again. You made a deal with Noah! Then you did it again! You let them all die? Even worse, is it possible? Did you *kill* them? Is this why you created them, so that you could just say "Okay, it's over. Everyone, you're toast?" Huh? Because if that's the case, *you* also left *me* here alone. Is this part of your master plan?"

Brady's frustration and anger did nothing to assuage his sense of pain and loss. He knew it was wrong to curse God, but he also knew that there was no one else left to blame. If the Maker of Heaven and Earth had planned all of this devastation at the beginning of days, why had he chosen to leave a lonely boy in the barrens to carry on?

"Answer me?"

Brady could sense no answer.

There was another possibility. Perhaps God had work for him to do. Perhaps his presence was necessary. What could God want him to do?

"Why?" he repeated. "Do you want me to do something?"

No answer. Long silence.

"I know. You need me around here to bury the dead. You need me to pick up the pieces. You need me to..." and his voice trailed off, faltering unexpectedly. What was it he had just thought.

No. Please, God, he thought, *the reason that just occurred to me, if that's the reason, then you must know something about me that I don't.*

He wondered in the silence if he was left here *to remember*. Every event needed someone to chronicle it or it would be like it had never happened in the first place. Every Trojan War needed a Homer. Every prophet required a testament. How could the world truly end if there was no one to tell the tale? It would be like people had never lived at all. But after he perished? What then?

When no answer was forthcoming and the silence had begun to solidify into stone, he exhaled a big breath and hunched his shoulders in a posture of surrender. It seemed there was no answer except what he had thought just a moment earlier - God needed someone to remember them.

He reached to the seat in the pew next to him and opened a book, what Catholics call a Missal, a book of verses, prayers and songs. It wasn't the Bible, but it was a bit of everything that one needed to know to make it through one's prayers and the form of almost any given mass. In front of him was a verse from the Bible, from the Book of Matthew, chapter five, verses three to twelve. He knew these words, had read and heard them before. These were the words from the Sermon on the Mount. Strangely comforting, he read through them slowly and patiently. Perhaps there was an answer in this book. Many people said that there were answers in the Bible. If there were answers, how did the Bible know which question was in your mind when you went searching for the answer? His question remained: "Why?"

There it was, in black and white, as plain as the nose on his face. It was as though Jesus had said this thing two thousand years ago just for him to read, here and now, in this quiet, empty building on the edge of forever. Was it possible that the Lord of Hosts saw this moment when he created the world? Did he know that a lonely boy would be sitting in an empty church in a world where everyone else had died seeking an answer in this book?

He read the lines over and over until he had to close the book quietly and shut his eyes. It made him angry. It made him positively furious but all he could manage were tears.

It read *"The meek shall inherit the earth."*

He stood up and walked toward the altar, then passed it and walked up to the giant crucifix that had so held his attention.

"I'll do my best to keep going. I wish you'd see to it that Max could get better. He's terribly sick and he's a good dog. He's better company that I could have hoped for, so I am asking you to save my dog. Please..."

Brady turned around and saw the church from a new angle. Over the foyer was the choir loft with its magnificent pipe organ. He remembered hearing it when a masterful hand played Bach on it and now the lack of sound seemed louder than anything he could imagine. It was a roaring silence. All the church pews were empty things. Long shafts of light came through the stained glass windows and each of them told a story. Each window was full of human figures. The high arched vault above him stopped in dark shadows, the faces of plaster cherubs gazed down at him, unblinking. He was seeing the church from the point of view of the parish priest, a place few parishioners ever stood. He looked over the emptiness and waited.

He walked away from the cross and the altar, turning his back on it in more than one way. There were some supplies he needed. This visit had been painful and now that he thought about it, it had been a mistake. Maybe churches and religion were only inventions made by people to help them make it through the hard times. Maybe he would have to go through his hard times alone. Maybe he would have to do it without any help.

He walked down the central aisle of the church focused on leaving this place, never to return. He scanned the place, as he always did, for anything he might be able to use to survive when he saw a newspaper sitting in one of the pews. It was a copy of the *New York Times*, and it was dated nearly five weeks ago. The headline caught his attention and as he read on, his heart sank in his chest.

FINAL ISSUE-Cause of World Pandemic Possibly Found

"The federal government has issued what may be one of its last communiques to the press. Reports have slowed or stopped from news agencies around the globe and an apparent end to our species is at hand. The Pandemic, originally thought to have originated in Mexico, weeks ago when thousands of birds fell dead from the sky in mid-flight, has spread dramatically to all corners of the globe. No one who has contracted the disease has survived. Government control has all but ceased in most major metropolitan areas and the federal government has issued a proclamation stating that those local authorities who have survived should take control and act in the federal government's stead.

The final communication to this newspaper from the Centers for Disease Control in Atlanta came from deputy director Lisa Stallman yesterday evening. She issued the following post on the website before contact with her was lost. This newspaper can neither deny nor confirm the validity of her claim, but in the interest of and hope for any humans who might survive this extinction event, we publish it here without further comment.

Dr. Stallman writes, "It is my belief that this pandemic is the result of the work of Dr. Peter Grindle, chief researcher for a little known agency called "Section 17" of the Homeland Security Administration. Dr. Grindle was working on a variety of methods to anticipate pandemic events and then create rapid responses to these events. If an event like a pandemic ever should occur, manmade or naturally occurring, Dr. Grindle's work would help to ensure a timely scientific response by the rapid creation, reproduction and application of vaccines using mass inhalant technology. The project sought to spread vaccines throughout the atmosphere from aircraft that would then disperse the vaccine in a suspension which could then be inhaled quickly by large numbers of people to help protect them from the ravages of a disease such as H1N1 virus.

However, it has come to our attention that about three

107

weeks prior to the first reported cases of the pandemic, Dr. Grindle and his associates released an experimental amount of vaccine into the air over West Texas. It was supposed to be a dead viral strain of last year's flu virus. However, it appears that the strain infected several of the birds in the area that then migrated south to Mexico, quickly becoming lethal to the bird population. It was there that I believe the Pandemic virus mutated into its lethal form. Therefore, I wish to state for the record that this pandemic is not a natural occurrence. It was man-made. I believe that this pandemic was caused by the release of an unstable vaccine candidate by the Homeland Security's Science Department in an effort to test the efficacy of airborne dispersal of inhalant vaccine technology as a way to counter biological warfare.

As a final note to your readers, I do not believe it would be right to blame Dr. Grindle or his team for this pandemic. He and his people were working to safeguard the American populous from a biological attack or natural disaster of unprecedented proportions. They had no way of knowing that the dead vaccine was still active and that somehow it would infect the birds who would then spread the disease so quickly and to such a deleterious effect. The Centers for Disease Control are working hard to lessen the severity of this pandemic, but it appears to me that Humanity, like the dinosaurs, has been targeted for extinction. All that we can hope for is that enough humans survive to begin again and perhaps this time, get things right."

Brady reread the article seven times. He hadn't known the extent of the Pandemic, but he had suspected. Every day he scanned the sky for high flying silver jets and every day the sky was clear. No one was traveling anymore because no one was alive.

He had just mouthed off to God in his own house, blaming him, styling him as a killer. God had caused the death of all humans, he had said aloud. He was ashamed and lost, perhaps for all eternity. He wished he could take the words back, but God has a good memory, he thought, and wouldn't forget his angry outburst.

As he sat there, letting the newspaper fall to the floor, we wondered about what man or woman had brought that final edition to this place, this final visit to the church before dying. Had the person been ill? Had they been alone in the church, much like he was now? Had this place been filled with those looking for solace and comfort in a time of dying or was the carrier of this newspaper as lost and alone as he was?

Then, Brady wept.

As he looked up his eyes widened in disbelief and wonder. The world had changed. Nothing had stayed quite the same. What he saw now didn't frighten him: it humbled him. There, in the windows around him with the sun illuminating them, he saw the figures in the stained glass windows slowly moving from their positions, looking soulfully at him with crystal eyes and he saw that they, too, were crying. Their tears fell from their faces onto the floor as small shimmering shards of crystal and tinkling glass. Brady watched as the figure of the shepherd made eye contact with him and nodded. In every window, he saw regret and mourning. The world had changed, even in this church. Perhaps they all had waited for the next supplicant to enter and pray and instead, an angry fourteen year old boy who blamed God for all his problems, for all the problems of the world, intruded.

Somehow, they understood. The Patriarchs and the children, the Roman soldiers and the angels, the Apostles and Saints, the figures halfway emerging from the Stations of the Cross and the Virgin Mary herself followed Brady with her eyes as he approached the altar again.

He knelt on the first step of the dais that led to the altar and bowed his head and then looked up at the figure on the cross. Whatever had happened to the world, he knew it wasn't God's doing. God wasn't to blame.

With bowed head, Brady spoke five words to the figure on the cross.

"I'm sorry. I didn't understand."

Brady stayed there for a few moments to gather his emotions, head bowed. There was much to do. He had to get his supplies, nurse Max back to health, and find a reason to keep moving forward, moving on. He walked away from the altar, down the center aisle of the church and out the door. When he left and all was silent again, each of the figures in the stained glass windows slowly maneuvered their way back into their original positions, glancing at each other before turning again to their still and quiet nature.

The creature growled in its dungeon. Long had he waited in the lower halls of this house of bones, his mind wrapped around a single thought – to complete the Transformation. He never thought of the Before Time, of the time when he did not exist. For the monster, Time was meaningless. He was a creature out of time. He had awakened in this world with a hatred like a hunger that would only be sated with the blood of the boy. He hated because he was made out of hate and for no other reason. It was reason enough. The boy was there, wandering about the world outside, claiming and renaming it like Adam in the Garden of Eden. She was here in the edifice with him, but she was evasive and cunning. He would find them both and erase them, thus ensuring his own world. As long as they existed, he could not be the One.

The cur prostrated itself on the ground before him. As the last light of the setting sun fell upon the Abandonment, Grendel spoke to the large creature that once was a German shepherd, but was now exhibiting the appearance and actions of a creature once known as Man. He had been summoned by the monster.

"Fenris," he spoke, "find the boy. Find the Renamer. Take your pack of deviants and kill him. He waits beyond the Great River, on the high hill by the statue of the warrior. He must not be allowed to live."

"But you, maasta...hum hum hummm, you could do this thing?"

Grendel slapped the weredog on the snout sending it backing away into the corner.

"You know I cannot leave this fortress. Not yet. I am still...incomplete. She waits and I must find her first. I am

not of this world. It tasks me. I must gather my strength before I venture forth. I will take care of her. You must find what courage you have in that minuscule heart of yours to do the deed. Besides, does not your pack of dogs grow as the long days pass?"

"Maasta," drooled the dog-like thing before him, "he hurts the brothers. He harms us and curses us. The brothers are still afraid..."

"Enough of this, sniveling dog! You don't need them," said Grendel, who spat on the ground in nervous frustration. "Do it yourself, then! He must not be here. He no longer belongs. I am the Master of this World now, not that....boy!" Grendel snarled at Fenris, leader of the weredog pack and the creature's fur rankled and bristled in antagonistic response. Yellow eyes gazed into yellow eyes and the two understood each other.

"Yesss. It ssshall be done," replied the weredog.

Fenris turned and skulked away into the falling dark. Grendel turned and began his nightly task of hunting she who could not be found, the female who haunted his dreams and stabbed at his mind with her cunning.

Chapter 8
Freedom Park

Brady lay in his bed inside of the Lifeseeker trying to drift off to sleep, thankful that Max was finally well. He spent most of his days keeping busy so his mind didn't wander to places where he might lose himself when evening fell and the pale moon rose on a chalkboard sky. He felt the stab of loneliness more acutely than anyone had ever felt before, or so he imagined. In the lonely light of the single battery-powered lamp, he prepared himself for the long battle that came every night: sleep. The shadows crept closer to him like tangible shades, moving patches of midnight that slithered and chattered their teeth, shaking their angry hands. Outside, the weredogs' howls grew louder and closer each night. Sometimes he would sit at the window of the Lifeseeker and look into the darkness for some sign of life, some movement on the edge of his vision. All that he could see were the uncountable stars, the moon, and the Flame of the North that still burned brightly. He called it the Flame of the North, but it was really the electrical generating plant in the small town of Veazie to the north of Bangor. It stood next to the river and was continually fed with a flow of natural gas from Canada. Before the Abandonment it was a large plume of steam filling the sky, but once people stopped monitoring it, the water stopped flowing and the natural gas was burned off at the top of the stack in a deliciously red, dancing flame. It was a safety mechanism and it had clicked in beautifully once the maintenance men failed to show up and keep the plant working. He knew that the flame wouldn't last forever. It had been made by the hand of man and all things made this way were failing much faster than he could have imagined. The grass was already growing in the cracks of the pavement in the two cities. All the lawns and shrubs were now overrun and for the last week he found himself encountering deer, moose, raccoons, skunks, groundhogs and muskrats in the city limits. It wouldn't be long before they claimed this place as their home and he would be the outsider. He witnessed isolated fires and plumes of smoke in the distance around the cities and he didn't like to think of what would happen if the cities themselves went up in flames.

The worst part of trying to get to sleep was the sound of the Whisperers. He found that if he didn't go too close to the river or streams and parked the Lifeseeker in a different place every night, he could keep their discordant cacophony to a tolerable level, but he couldn't manage to ignore them once the hour of midnight came upon him. In the daytime he could easily put on his headphones and turn the volume up but such sound only served to keep him wide awake long into the primeval pitch that was the nonelectrical night of the Abandonment. That was when they hammered at his eardrums and pounded on his mind.

When he closed his eyes, the blackness behind his lids often would light up with flashes of his mother, his friends, and of people he had seen dead in their cars or their homes. All of these faces were seen as flying photographs coming from a distance, zooming into focus and then quickly receding into the vast sea of darkness that lay behind his eyes, the mad screensaver of his mind. Then the Whisperers would raise their voices and sometimes Max would sense his fear and snuggle his warm body closer into his master's side, as if to say, "You aren't alone. I'm here, too." Brady would lie there often for hours before he mercifully fell asleep and away from this world. If he was lucky, he didn't dream.

He awoke to the blackness and looked at his watch. It was three o'clock in the morning. Why had he awakened? Then he heard it, a scratching sound in the darkness and a

113

strange feeling gripped him like a vise. His heart hammering in his chest, his breath shallow, he tried to determine what could be making such a sound. He heard Max growling and he put his hand on the dog's snout, holding it there so he wouldn't bark.

There it was again, against the side of the Lifeseeker. Something was scratching against the side of the camper, punctuated by an occasional thud and pounding. Brady didn't dare to move, frozen in his bed like a statue. He was ice. He was stone. Whatever was making that noise sounded deliberate and intelligent. In a moment that seemed like an eternity, the sound ceased. He didn't dare to look at his watch. For a very long time, he didn't shift from his position.

In all, he waited a little over an hour, when the first light of the new day began to edge its way over the ridge of the eastern sky. Arming himself with his full array of weaponry, he threw open the aluminum door of the Lifeseeker and quickly surveyed the world outside. There was nothing unusual or out of place. Max shot out from behind him and ran to the far side of the camper and began to bark. Holding his sword in one hand and his paint ball gun in the other, he rounded the corner and saw what had occurred during the hours of darkness.

Someone or something had painted words on the driver's side of the Lifeseeker in red paint. It read, "*Leeve or dye.*"

It was signed "*Grendel...*"

On the ground were the painted paw prints of a large dog leading away and into the city.

Brady let the significance of the words sink into his mind before reacting. Someone or something had written a warning to him in the darkest hour of the night. They didn't break in upon him while he slept, kill him or find cause to drive him from his home. They had simply issued a warning. What troubled him the most was that this message had been written not in red paint but in blood - chicken blood. The body of a limp bird lay on the ground by his feet. It was Hermione, his favorite hen.

"The weredogs paid us a visit last night, Max."

With all the speed he owned Brady threw himself on

114

Rocinante and turned the key, but Rocinante didn't respond. There on the ground was a stream of gasoline that was already evaporating in the morning sun. The rubber gas line had been torn from the tank to the carburetor. Someone had not wanted him to follow where they may have led him.

"Come on, boy," Brady yelled as he held open the door to the Lifeseeker. Brady stamped on the gas of the camper.

When they rounded the corner to the house, he could see that the gate to the chicken yard had been ripped from its hinges, the chicken wire shredded and ripped. All of his birds lay scattered, their necks wrung and their limp bodies lying.in the throes of death.

Brady sat down on the back step of the house and put his head in his hands. He had placed so much of his hope in these birds. For the last week he had thought of little else. The evidence was clear: the weredogs were getting more intelligent, lending credence to his idea that these creatures were not people who had turned, like werewolves, into animals, but quite the opposite. They were dogs who were turning into humans, gaining intelligence, becoming less cautious and he knew this development might describe his own end. He had been quite alone before. Now he had enemies. For some reason that he didn't understand, they were hunting him. Who was Grendel? Surely not the monster slain by the hero Beowulf, from Anglo-Saxon myth.

Observation mode: Brady entered his Fortress of Solitude and called up his data file on Grendel. It read as follows:

"Grendel: monster from Anglo-Saxon mythology. One of three monsters that were slain by the hero Beowulf, along with Grendel's mother and the Dragon. Grendel was terrible to look upon. Descendants of the Biblical Cain, the first murderer, Grendel attacked Heorot Hall, killing and feasting upon the men he encountered. The noise of the drunken revelers in the mead hall roused his anger and drove him to madness. After a prolonged struggle, the hero Beowulf rips Grendel's arm off. The monster retreats to his underground cave and dies there."

115

In the silent glow of his wall-sized computer screen in his mind, he sat and pondered the idea of sharing the planet with another being who wanted nothing more than to kill and eat him.

Brady gathered the chicken's bodies and placed them in a hole he had quickly dug near the chicken house. He was troubled that the weredogs hadn't eaten that which they had killed. Killing for food was as natural as breathing, he thought, but indiscriminately killing for the sake of bringing death into the world was a human quality. It was murder. It was clear to him the he had to change how he had been living.

For a long while he simply drove around the city, but his restless mind could find no ease. He knew he couldn't keep living as he had been, a vagabond moving from place to place, never settling in or down. He wasn't surprised that he eventually parked the Lifeseeker where he had started that day. Rocinante needed repair. There were decisions to make.

Freedom Park was just to the left of the Irving gas station. He tended to put his hands in his pockets and slowly saunter, looking at the ground, when he needed to really have a good think, shuffling around. He soon found himself sitting at the foot of the bronze statue of General Joshua Chamberlain, Civil War hero of the Battle of Gettysburg and Little Round Top, savior of the Union because he didn't surrender or retreat. Every Brewer student knew the stories of this illustrious man whose courage, tenacity and spirit made him the city's most favored son. Brady liked the statue's look. It seemed like it was thinking, contemplating something with its arms crossed in stern consideration of some unknown stratagem. For some reason, Brady's head was always a little clearer up here, on the high ground. The makers of the little park had gone to great pains to make it an accurate replica of Little Round Top, that hilltop in Pennsylvania that Colonel Chamberlain so gallantly held against the rebel onslaught. Brady liked the effect, somehow feeling that this artificial place had more realism than all the real world that surrounded him.

For a long time he sat there lost in thought. For reasons he didn't understand, the weredogs never came out for long in the light of day. What troubled him was their message and the reason behind it. This was an empty world, but a big one nonetheless. There was plenty of room for all of them – boy, weredogs, and all the other creatures now emerging from the great forest. Why did his presence disturb them? More than anything he puzzled over the signature in blood on the side of the Lifeseeker.

Grendel.

Leave or die...

As he sometimes did when he needed to hear a human voice, Brady spoke aloud. "We're in a bit of a pickle, Max. I sure wish I knew what to do."

Brady was stunned when he heard a reply to his statement.

"Yes, that seems about right. You, sir, are on the precipice, the very edge of a dilemma. Your next move could determine the fate of your life. Choose wisely."

He hadn't heard another human voice for a very long time outside of his own sweet and somewhat fanciful imagination. Who was speaking? He scanned the area and saw no one, his heart pounding like a ten-pound hammer in his chest.

"Up here, cadet. Look up."

General Joshua Chamberlain of the Twentieth Maine was looking down at him with a calm demeanor on his bronze face. Brady couldn't muster a word or movement: he was the statue now and the form of Chamberlain was the only thing moving. It seemed that all he could do was move his head. The rest of his form was paralyzed in metal, but he looked down at Brady, blinked and smiled.

"Sorry to frighten you, lad. I only just realized I could talk. It has been awhile coming, but I must say that now that I can utter a sound, it is a great relief."

Seeing that Brady was still stunned, the Colonel looked away to the Bangor side of the river and up the Penobscot toward the bay. He was waiting for Brady to respond, which he finally did a few moments later.

"You...you can speak? You're alive?" Brady asked.

"I think the answer to the first question is obvious. As to the second question, I have my doubts," answered the colonel.

"But if you're not alive, what are you?" Brady asked, still incredulous and dumbfounded.

"Make no mistake. I am not the actual General Joshua Chamberlain. That would be quite impossible. He passed on long ago and went to his final reward. No, I am not the real thing. I am something similar," replied the statue.

"Something similar?" Brady couldn't hide his astonishment.

The form of the Colonel seemed to muse upon the idea for a moment before replying.

"A facsimile. I believe that I am animated by all the thoughts, ideas, knowledge and opinions of General Joshua Chamberlain that once were housed in the minds of people. Memory kept the General alive. Since there is no one left to remember him, except for you, of course, I believe I am the amassed memory of the man. All of those thoughts have coalesced. Somehow I have been made more than a hunk of fashioned metal. I am not at all sure that the real Colonel would approve of this situation. He would find this an abomination of nature, I am sure."

Brady felt the bonds of sanity gripping him. He knew this was impossible, but he also was smart enough to understand that the world had changed, was changing still. If, without humans, dogs could turn into human-like creatures, perhaps talking statues might be something to consider.

Or he was insane.

"How long have you been...aware of things?" asked Brady.

"I do not know, exactly. The passage of time is a human thing and I am not human. I have counted daylight and darkness and I would say about three weeks. However, I have not been able to utter a sound until just now. Perhaps I could speak all the while, but you are the first person I have

118

had the chance to engage in conversation."

"Do you know what happened, to the people?" inquired Brady.

The colonel shook his head. "Not precisely. I can surmise that some terrible contagion may have taken them all suddenly, but I must confess that it seems like the Wrath of God for such a number to perish so quickly. Like the Angel of Death over the armies of Sennacherib."

"Nope. It was a scientific mistake. People did this to themselves," answered Brady.

"Is that so? Then this is truly desperate. May I inquire, how is it that you survived?"

"I don't know. Just lucky I guess."

"Yes sir, I suppose that's one way of looking at it," answered the Colonel. Then he said after a long pause, "We have not been introduced. I am he who represents all that was once held in the minds of people as Joshua Chamberlain. And you are...?"

"Brady Smith. I'm just Brady Smith."

The colonel looked up at the river again and then, after a pause said, "Not *just* Brady Smith. From what I have observed, you are *the* Brady Smith."

"Sir?" Brady asked.

"I have had little else to do up here on this pedestal but watch the world go by and a large part of that has been watching you. You are a resourceful fellow, Mr. Smith, and one I would have been proud to have served with if circumstances allowed. You are a survivor of the first order. I'd daresay that if the very survival of the species relied on your actions, Humanity stands at least a fighting chance."

Brady smiled and said nothing in reply.

"Still, Mr. Smith, nothing is certain. You are not without your adversaries."

"I know," agreed Brady, "the weredogs."

"Weredogs? Do you mean the curs and mongrels that are gathering into packs around the cities?"

"Yes, they're the ones. They're getting smarter."

"And more dangerous. Their leader seems a particularly vile beast. You should know that their numbers are growing.

119

As you sleep, they stir among themselves and gather. Something is happening to them. They are forming into something more cunning than a pack of dogs. They are organized. They have direction and superior numbers."

Brady stooped his shoulders in frustration.

"No sir," said Joshua Chamberlain, once governor of the state of Maine, chancellor of Bowdoin College and Civil War hero, "far be it from me to offer any advice. A man has to make his own decisions."

"What? No, I would like some advice. Really. I mean, I haven't heard another human voice in so long."

"I am not technically a human. But I take your meaning. And if you would like my thoughts on your predicament, I would be happy to oblige."

"Yes, please," answered Brady, "I don't know what I'm supposed to do."

"Strategy is in order, Mr. Smith. You need to find the high ground or some place of strength that these creatures cannot intrude upon. A fortress of some sort is in order. These creatures are still animals – they are afraid of such things as fire, loud noises and the bravery of a human. They will, however, take advantage of the foolishness of a boy. You must think like a warrior."

"A fortress?"

"Yes, a place of strength whose walls can withstand their onslaught. I know just the place."

"Where?" asked Brady. He anticipated that the statue might suggest the Armory or Air National Guard Base in Bangor.

"The Bangor Public Library," answered the statue.

"The Library? What? Are you joking?" asked an incredulous Brady.

"I am perfectly serious, young man: the library. Your prior strategy of moving from place to place has worked so far, but these creatures will follow you to your death eventually. It occurs to me, sir, that your continued existence will absolutely rely not on your ability to run but upon your ability to *learn*. You have been a scavenger. Now you need to be a builder. You are but a boy, although a resilient and capable one at that. Your education has been interrupted and must continue. The library has the best repository of human knowledge you will find. It is a veritable armory of facts and instructions for survival. There is also the heavy stone of which the building is constructed to consider. The edifice is all stone and glass and metal. The doors are heavy and thick. It is as safe a castle as you will find in the two cities. Inside you can safely rest while the creatures outside walk circles in frustration around you. You've much to learn before you can overcome your opponents."

"Opponents? You mean the weredogs?"

"Yes, and another..."

Brady was intrigued. Was there another? Who?

"Another?" he asked.

"In that direction, behind me" he gestured by turning his head to the north as far as his could turn, the metal screaming as he twisted, rending and grinding. "I have not seen him, but he is in that direction, toward the hospital. He is angry and determined. I have heard his screams in the darkness, even though you, apparently, have not."

"Is he...human?" asked Brady, not sure whether to be hopeful or afraid.

"I cannot tell. But humans can be monsters, Brady. They can destroy the world, kill millions, even billions, from what you have told me. They can conspire to commit acts of atrocity and all because of selfishness and greed, anger and revenge.Humans deal in darkness. So you see, your question has no answer. He may be human, he may be a monster, or he may be both."

"*Grendel*," whispered Brady.

Brady sat in silence for a long while, sitting on the pedestal in the shadow of the General. He wasn't sure what to call the statue – General or Colonel. Joshua Chamberlain has been a Colonel when he defended Little Round Top on the outskirts of Gettysburg, but he had been a made a general after his actions. He decided that as long as the statue didn't care, neither did he.

They both looked out upon the great river, like a father

and his child. Brady's mind had quickly acclimated to a talking statue and the advice that the statue gave seemed prudent, even profound. To move into a place of shelter and security seemed like the only way he would survive. They had warned him last night when they could have killed him.

At that moment, Hugin swooped in and settled on the General's shoulder and began to croak and caw. The General seemed to be listening intently and then said, "Your scout here returns with news. The main pack of dogs is headed this way. I suggest a retreat is in order, Mr. Smith."

"You mean I should run away?" Brady asked.

"Bravely run away, I should think. You know where to go. They cannot open heavy doors that have been bolted shut."

"What do I do once I'm there? I can't just wait inside while they prowl outside. I'll starve to death. It will be like a prison."

"Nonsense," sputtered Joshua Chamberlain. "You will have an arsenal of thoughts and ideas at your disposal. These creatures are little more than dumb brutes, but you will have all the amassed thought of the ages at your hand. I would start with books that deal with tactics – perhaps some military histories, and from what I can tell, a smattering of mythology could not hurt. The world seems to have changed."

Brady could hear the howling and baying of dogs in the distance. He knew time was of the essence and that the Colonel's advice was sound. However, he was loathe to leave his companion, even if he was a statue. He had many questions to ask and answers he needed.

"Go on now," said Joshua Chamberlain, "make your move."

"But I...it's just that..." Brady faltered. He didn't quite know how to say what he was feeling.

The Colonel seemed to understand Brady's reticence. "I'll be right here. Once you've thwarted their plan, come back and speak with me. They usually keep to the darkness of the forest during the day. I'll help you as much as I can. And always remember, you have a weapon stronger than any that those creatures could ever possess. Used wisely, it will always bring you home safely."

"I do? What weapon. I don't even carry a real gun."

"Your weapon is even stronger than a gun, my boy. Your weapon is called '*Imagination*.'"

Chapter 9

The Library of Alexandria

from the Journal of Brady Smith:

"For the past week I've lived inside the Bangor Public Library. When the weredogs howl at the moon, I know that even though they know I'm here, I'm safe. It wasn't easy setting up my fortress. I had to break in! Who would have ever thought that anyone would be breaking into a library?

Anyway, I looked things over and found ways to make things more secure. The outer doors were already locked and made of steel, so I left those alone. The main doors, which are huge and made of wood, were also locked. I put a couple of iron bars through the handles on the inside for added security. I know the weredogs can't open doors; not yet. I can't take any chances. I've put plywood over the windows on the ground level to keep them out.

The Lifeseeker is parked to the side of the library. I filled the main room with supplies like a few boxes of food, water jugs, some tools - you know - the whole load of stuff I need to survive a siege, if I have to. There's a big generator on the side of the building and I figured out how to turn it on, which I do for a little while every day to charge my batteries and cook some food on the electric stove in the little kitchen in the basement. I miss the fresh eggs.

I still go out every day, but I come back before darkness falls. I'm still mapping the new world, checking places for supplies and keeping my mind busy. It's really important to keep busy. Maybe the best part of this whole remapping of the world is a kind of remapping of my mind. If I spent the day thinking of nothing else but death and loss the world has known, I'd go crazy. Besides, the more I look around, the more I can tell that the world is different. The line between the real world and the world of my imagination has gotten thin.

Normally, if there were other people around, this kind of thinking might make me think that I'm insane, but since I'm it, I can think whatever I want. I'm not hurting anybody and by seeing the world as I want to see it, and not as I was always told it was, I've been able to survive. Is my imagination creating reality or has reality been there all along and no one could see things as they really were? I really want to write this part carefully so you, reader, will know that I'm not just going crazy. It's like seeing something from the corner of your eye and then turning quickly to double-check and you know what? Nothing's there, but you're certain that something was there just a second ago. Now that I'm alone, some of the things I double-check are still there: the weredogs, a raven that talks, not to mention a statue that gives advice - all of these things are impossible. I know it. But they're real to me, and since I'm the only one around, I guess they're as real as I need them to be. I wonder if my mind is playing tricks on me to help me cope with all the trauma that's come my way, but then Hugin leads me to a place he shouldn't have known about, full of food, or the Whisperers come at me with a vengeance and then I know it's real. I've visited the general and told him what I've done and he seems happy. He is a good...man...statue...whatever. I bet the real Joshua Chamberlain was even better - he's educated, wise and even funny - in a dry way. He knows a

125

thing or two about survival, as well. We talk - well, he talks and mostly I listen. He's a smart...I was going to say person, but he insists he is not a person, just an "assemblage of all the thoughts, ideas and memories evident in the minds of humans before suddenly they all perished." I think that means he was the magnet for everything anyone ever knew about Joshua Chamberlain and when everyone died, their ideas and thoughts didn't die with them - they all sort of migrated to the statue in Freedom Park and that's how he 'became aware,' as he puts it. I'll say it again - the world is changing. In the general's case, it's for the better. In the case of weredogs, it's for the worse.

I've been having more and more trouble getting to sleep: the Whisperers. I worry a lot more about my future, now that I lie awake at night unable to sleep. I think that maybe I might just go to sleep some night and never wake up and that this is all just a nightmare. Then I wake up in the morning and it's the same old me. I wonder what would be better.

Then there's the other one - the one who General Chamberlain says is watching me. He tells me to be very careful not to go near his lair, which I have determined to be the Entrance to the Underworld, Hades, what people used to call the medical center. The general insists that this is not just a person - that it's an enemy "more formidable than you can imagine," he says. I don't want to be alone, but even worse is to be nearly alone in the world and have the only other person on earth want to hurt you.

Still, I can't get over the feeling that I am going to have to face this Grendel character sooner or later. The general tells me that this enemy wants to see me dead. He hasn't shown me his face yet."

As the day began to fall down before him and the pink tinge of twilight painted the edge of the world, Brady stared out of the windows of the reading room of his new home. The colonel had been right, of course. The Bangor Public Library was now his castle keep, his Mount Olympus, his Asgard and temple, all rolled into one. Made from the bones

126

of the coast of Maine, the granite was impermeable and tolerant to the passage of time. It was overbuilt to last the ages. Brady had seen a few fires already on the outskirts of the cities to appreciate the nearly permanent nature of stone. Castles in Europe lasted hundreds of years and this place was made the same way they were. It would stand the seasons, or at least as long as he needed it.

For the last week he had haunted the library in the evenings. The weredogs were conspicuously absent in the daylight, though they could be heard in the distance. When evening began to fall, Brady returned to the library.

It was the biggest home he had ever known. He knew about another library from the ancient world that ignorant crowds had burned to the ground: the Library at Alexandria in Egypt. It was the gathering place of all the ideas known to Humanity in the ancient world, before the dark ages – like the Internet was to modern man. An angry crowd just put it to the torch and all of a sudden, it was gone, like the Internet was now. All of that scholarly work just extinguished in the blink of an eye made Brady remember and long for his old friend, the World Wide Web. He used to spend at least three hours a day online, especially when his mom was at work and he was home alone. His favorite place had been Wikipedia where he researched classic hard rock bands and their histories, UFOs and the gods and goddesses of Greek, Roman and Norse mythology. He was ashamed to think about how much time he had spent watching monkeys throw poo or cats performing acts of feline foolishness. With all the knowledge in the world at his fingertips, he could have been learning about things he would need to know to survive, but he played with the knowledge like a toy instead of using it like a tool. It was the safe playground where he didn't have to think or even imagine. It became a place to go to when he was alone and along with millions of other people sitting in solitary rooms, he could be alone with them. Brady was as alone as anyone had ever been before and right now, in the gathering gloom of night in the library, he regretted his childish use of such a philosophers' stone.

Those were the days. If he wanted to know anything at

all, all he had to do was point and click and somehow the information that he was seeking was there, like magic. That kind of magic was gone the minute the electrical generating stations shut down. Brady imagined that bit by bit, the Internet slowed down and eventually stopped and, like the Library at Alexandria, all the massed knowledge of Humanity was gone, forever.

But there were books and he was thankful for them. When he first took up refuge in the library, he wandered for hours. It was an old building with a new addition. He liked the place, except for two rooms. He avoided them. One of the rooms was the computer room with all the empty workstations, bereft of power, all black mirrors staring back at him, unblinking and unseeing eyes – dead Cyclopes in their caves. The reminder that he would have to work for his knowledge and pour over pages and pages of words to find what he was looking for seemed like such a waste of his time, especially in this room. He would have given a lot to have access to the Internet for an hour.

The other room that bothered him was the Periodicals Room. It was the largest room, its ceiling vaulting up two stories and even though it had very comfortable chairs in which to sit or sleep, something about the room made him very uneasy. At first he thought that it might be the pictures of happy people on the covers, or the newest automobiles, or maybe the latest newsmaker and the scandal that went along with their picture. He tried ignoring the feeling of unease, but it didn't work. He couldn't spend more than a few minutes in this beautiful room.

He had been in the building for two days when he realized what bothered him about it. The books on the shelves didn't bother him. They were comforting in their own way. Someone had taken the time to write them and so these books still held a little of the life of the writers - at least they recorded the words and ideas of peoples' minds, though all the people were dead. The books were essentially *timeless* things. A book that was written a year ago lived in the time and space it was written in: a year ago. A book that was considerably older, say, two hundred years old, was another thing to Brady altogether. A book that was published any time before his own birth and knowledge of the world was in a category he referred to as "pre-Brady" and as such, it was suspended in time.

In the magazine room, however, the covers all stared back at him reminding him that the next issue would never arrive in the mail. There would never be another *National Geographic*, *Smithsonian*, *Time, Electronic Gaming Monthly* and sadly, no more covers of the *Rolling Stone*. It was unacceptable. More than anything else, his eyes were always drawn to the date stamped innocently on each issue. Of all the works of Humanity he had encountered during the last few weeks, the knowledge that nothing new from the mind of other humans would be coming his way saddened him. He had seen more death than anyone in the history of the world, but here in this white, sunlit room, he felt the weight of the darkness that had settled.

He could have removed the magazines from the shelves and had the room to himself, but this was the magazine room and in his mind, it always would be. It was now a museum - a photograph of the world just before it ended. He would not touch it. He avoided it.

from the Journal of Brady Smith
"It's eight o'clock and I'm sitting in the Library of Alexandria II. That's what I've renamed the Library after the old one in Egypt. I can see the city well from the big windows on the second story in front of the fiction stacks. Max and I sometimes come up here to watch the sunset.

Damn it! The weredogs know where I live. I've seen them a lot of times sniffing around the front of the building, over by the Lifeseeker, and they like to walk circles around the building. I know they're trying to figure out how to get in here, but for the time being, they're mostly just dogs. They don't have any thumbs! They can't grab a doorknob or handle. I figure I'm pretty safe in Alexandria at night and in the daytime, they make themselves pretty scarce. I wonder why. I think they're different in the daytime - more like dogs than humans. I hope they stay that way.

129

The day is usually interesting and I find things that make me wonder. Yesterday I found a really cool world band radio that runs on a hand-powered generator. All I have to do is crank the handle for two minutes and then I get about an hours worth of static. I use the static sound to help me get to sleep because it's better than just the silence and it seems to keep the Whisperers in the background of my mind. They're always there and it still frightens me, but I keep going. Even a crazy person has to eat and drink and take care of himself. Anyway, I sat up here last night and very, very slowly worked the tuning knob on the radio through its bands. I turned it really slowly, like the speed of a minute hand on a clock. I tried every single band on the radio and there were a lot. I found some signals, but they were just dots and dashes that kept repeating over and over, like automatic signals. I think they might be from airports that still have power to broadcast their positions. Are they significant? I need to find out. They come and go. After two hours of trying to connect to something out there in the world, I gave up. I'll try again, later.

I think it's time that I did something good for my mind. I think I'd like to read a book. I read some of 'Don Quixote' and it made me feel better. A person can't always be thinking about his situation. Sometimes its good to think about something else and that way, underneath it all, your mind goes to work figuring things out. Tomorrow night, after supper, I'm going to find another good book and read it. The General tells me that every book is like a world in and of itself and it might be nice to do a little 'escape' reading."

He cruised around the library for a long time, acclimating himself to the lay of the land. He had never really spent much time in any library simply because his mother had kept him well-supplied with books for his own personal library. He had never bothered to organize his books, either, so that he might find *Harry Potter* right next to *Tom Sawyer*, or *The Lion, the Witch and the Wardrobe* next to the *Guinness Book of World Records* or a dog-eared copy of *Ripley's Believe it or Not!*

This was a library with three stories of books all neatly arranged and clearly marked. The bronze placard on the marble steps on the front exclaimed that the library was almost a hundred years old and there were books here a lot older than that. He found himself strangely spellbound by the tomes lining shelf after shelf. Because he had all the time in the world, he lingered with them.

Aisle after aisle of bound volumes reminded him of people. For the past weeks he had been lonely for the company of another human being, the sound of another voice, or even simply the words of another person. Here, lining the shelves, were literally millions of words from the voices of thousands. Any time he wanted he could simply take a book in his hands, open it and partake of the words and thoughts of another human being. It was that easy. People might die, he thought, but if they write their words down, they preserve some part of their minds, perhaps even part of their souls. He didn't have to feel so alone if he could, for some part of his day, open one of these books and forget his imposed state of solitude.

The third floor of the library had a large central room with two massive oak tables in the center. There were green-glass library lamps and bankers' chairs and plenty of light from the great windows. The walls of this room held history books and though he loved the ambiance of this room.

There was something wrong with the history books. He discovered it when he was casually thumbing through them in passing on his way to the fiction section. As one so often does in a library or bookstore, he was running his hand over the spines of the books as he walked by them. He stopped for a moment when he heard the voice. It spoke clearly to him in a plaintive tone.

"Read me! I happened! I still matter! Don't walk by. Pick me up! You will need me!"

The imperative tone of *The History of the German Nation, circa 1890,* caught him off guard. It commanded him to read it. It ordered him into a sense of obedience. He refused. When he removed his hand, he could still hear it, whispering to him, but as from a distance. It was frustrated that it might never be read again. Then he touched *The History of Greece* and another voice began to speak aloud to him.

"Empires rise, empires fall. It has all happened before. It will happen again. At least, I think it will. I might be of use to you. Pick me up, open me. Read me and I will attempt to assist you in your situation. I am a message from the distant past, but I might also point toward what will be."

Book after book, *History* continued to speak to him. These voices were not the ones he heard and called Whisperers. These were no indistinct whispers at the edge of the darkness that could easily be hushed with his mp3 player at the medium volume setting. These were distinct voices, clearly pronouncing and enunciating their terms. All of them in some way commanded, pleaded or begged for his indulgence so that they might be opened again and consumed, experienced, and pondered. Because he had already heard the Whisperers, these more strident voices didn't frighten him. He had spoken to statues. He had followed ravens. He was not afraid. The problem was that these weren't human voices; they were the voices of books and only slightly human in their nature and intonation. They spoke of binders' tape and glue, thread and leather, carbon ink and aged paper. He could tell that only part of their message was human. Books were only books, after all. They were no substitute for people.

He could stop, leaving this room and never enter it again, but the fascination was too strong. In a way, it was like watching a train wreck-too horrible to wish to see but once the eyesight has a purchase upon it, too rare and strange to look away. Besides, he wondered, was he crazy or was the whole world changing because people were now absent? He wondered if what was happening to him now was because it was the natural order of things, now that he was the only one to see, hear, taste, smell and feel. Perhaps the world had a finite amount of sensory input and, like the little HAM radio, he was the last receiver on earth.

The next book that spoke to him was *The Autobiography of Benjamin Franklin*. He touched it and it didn't say

132

anything except, "Yes?"

It had actually asked *him* a question. The other books were all expository in nature, but this one was interrogative.

Brady found himself speaking back to the book, "Oh, sorry. Nothing. I was just passing by." He felt a bit foolish until the book answered him, which meant that there could be a conversation, something books didn't always do all that readily.

"Young man, I sense that you and I could be of service to each other. While I am perfectly content to sit here until the end of days, I would rather be of use. If for no other reason, than to gain my own understanding of what has happened to the world."

Brady gawked. "You know what's happened? How can that be?"

"To be clear, I am not certain about the state of things in the world in your day. I cannot say that I was even quite clear about the state of the world in my own day, but I have made it a habit in my time on earth to listen and observe much more than I speak. I can tell from the vast quiet that has befallen creation that something has happened to Humanity. I am intrigued."

Brady, his hand still touching the spine of the book, withdrew it from the shelf. The cover showed old Ben Franklin. He half expected the painting to be animated, but it wasn't.

"Are...are you alive?" Brady asked.

The book hesitated and then said, "Not strictly speaking. No. I am merely a representation of the human person who was known to the world as Benjamin Franklin, postmaster, diplomatic envoy, inventor, scientist and most important, printer. Like most books, I am partly real, partly imagined. However, I am usually read by tens of thousands of people at the same time, so I only have the energy to whisper to them. However, I can sense that at this moment, you are the only human on earth who is reading me. This means that all of my power is, in a way, lent to you while you are engaged with me. While we are together, young man, I am as alive as books ever get."

Brady found himself smiling even though he was a little frightened.

"Are you really the voice of Ben Franklin? I mean, are you a book or a person?"

The book replied after a long hesitation, "Some books make better friends than some people. While both may lie to you, a book will never borrow money."

Brady considered his words. Money was a non-issue, but good advice was in short supply.

"Would you mind if I took you along with me. I've been a little lonely."

"Happy to oblige, young man. I will think of you as my ship upon the ocean. Carry me wherever you will. But I cannot keep calling you 'young man.' What is your name?"

Brady shook his head in disbelief and then, for the first time in his life, introduced himself to a book.

"I am Brady Smith, Mr. Franklin."

"And what is it that you do, Mr. Smith?" asked the book.

"Do? Well, I'm a survivor of the great falling of

Humankind. I live in the Abandonment. I survive. That's what I do."

"A pleasure you make your acquaintance, Brady. Let us depart this room."

Brady carried the book with both hands, reverentially. As he reached the top of the stairs to descend to the nonfiction section, he heard the history books he had touched begin to shout at him. They were angry that he had not chosen them and were making their bitterness known through their vociferousness.

"What's wrong with them?" asked Brady aloud.

"They're worried that they'll be forgotten, or worse, go unread. A book that remains forever unread might as well be good as dead. They, too, sense the change in the world."

"Yes, but why are they so angry. I mean, you seem pleasant enough."

"Oh, that's because they are histories. I, sir, am an autobiography..."

Chapter 10
The Whisperers

The Beast stood on top of the edifice and looked out upon the world nearly devoid of human life, desolate of intelligence and design, except for *them*. The first quarter moon was rising and night was well upon the land. He had been chasing her for the last week through the labyrinthine tunnels and hallways of this strange edifice and she had evaded his grasp and because she was human, he hated her with every thread and sinew of his being. Each breath was a curse leaning towards her death. He mused, "How does she elude me so? I chase her and she tasks me, seeing only a glance of her as she moves away and I am vexed. I shall find her, if not tonight, then tomorrow."

He liked the darkness and would have given much to leave the safety of this sanctuary, but he was afraid of the world that waited for his first footfall, the world *outside*. He saw the Abandonment as 'other' and he would set foot upon it only after he had shed her blood or his own, as payment for the world. He would buy the land below with blood, one way or another. Somewhere in his own personal darkness, he understood that while they drew breath, he was in danger. In this place, his birthing place, he was safe.

The wind blew a cool breeze over his face as twilight's last gleaming fell from the edge of the world. The beast found himself strangely silent, even reflective. The entangled and confused mind that predominated his actions fell quiet and Grendel found himself making his way down the stairs, to the place that had been the emergency offices set up by the government health agents as they fought their final battle against the pandemic. There, underneath a pile of papers that lay scattered on a desk he deliberately searched for an item: a photograph of a woman and a child. In a moment, he had it in his taloned claw. He quietly gazed at it. The woman and child in the picture were smiling, sitting on a wharf near a body of water. She had long, blond hair that cascaded in curls over her shoulders. Her arm clutched a young boy to her side and both were absolutely beaming at the photographer. Feelings of tenderness,kindness,even of love, briefly made themselves evident to the creature. Was that a wrinkled brow on his face? Was that a single tear appearing out of the corner of his eye? He looked up from the photograph and scanned the room in which he stood, full of disorder, dead bodies, rack and ruin. Then, slowly, he let his glance fall back upon the picture, now nothing more than a lost world. He put the picture back on the desk and turned toward the stairwell.

If the boy and girl remained, then nothing was fair. Why had they survived when those two in the photo had not? What magical power, what provenance of grace, held their lives more dear than these two? How had they survived?

He would never speak it, but he was afraid of them. They were *'other'* and from before. For the Beast, it was like something from the time of the beginning of things had somehow survived and even thrived in this new universe. If those in the photo had to die, then so did all of Humanity! If the boy and the girl lived then he could be destroyed and the Beast feared his own destruction more than anything else and because he had no god, he consoled himself with the idea that their deaths would ensure his life.

She might be his undoing. She was strong and resourceful. She should have perished. She had been surrounded by the dead and dying. Indeed, had been locked up with them and yet, she survived. Had something gone wrong with his plan? Was she immune to the disease? It was the only explanation. In the weredogs, he had found an army. He had not expected such a thing but this world was new and delicious to him, full of surprises. They were still more dog than human, fearful,even submissive. Something held them back, but as they grew increasingly human in their thoughts, their deeds would follow course. With any luck and some prodding, they could eventually subdue and kill the boy. But her?

So far, he mused, the weredogs had proven ineffective against the boy's cunning. What concerned Grendel even more was that it seemed to him that the boy was receiving advice, perhaps even aid, from others. Also, the boy had already stood against the weredogs. Courage? He did not run from them; he fought back. His choice of weaponry would be his undoing, thought Grendel. A weapon that shoots paint will soon not deter the growing intelligence of the weredogs. In a matter of a week, perhaps, they will persevere and attack with dire consequences and surely the boy would perish.

She was another matter altogether: cunning, brave resourceful. Since the beginning of the great falling she had survived in his charnel house while he pursued her, floor to floor, stairwells and heat ducts, and though he was the lord of this new world, she had continued to elude capture and destruction. Surrounded by the decaying and putrefying corpses of hundreds of people, she continued to live. How did she manage?

To thrive in this place, she must have a more than natural constitution, a courage of hardened steel. She lived in the topmost part of the old building, farthest away from the dead, in what was once the nursery. At first it had been her cunning that kept him from that floor for she had been the one to blockade the entrances. Over the weeks he had begun to think that it had been his doing and that he had successfully imprisoned her, but he had been unable to capture and kill her.

She had found an alternate way out of the top floor down to the lower levels, a way he had been unable to determine. Twice she had faced him briefly before escaping. He suspected that she was more than a human and that she had somehow changed when the world fell down and died. Perhaps both she and the boy had survived because they had changed while all the rest of Humanity hadn't.

She was his Nemesis.

Dark thoughts fed inside the creature's mind while the stars came out and wheeled overhead. His latest reconnaissance from Fenris informed him that the boy was safely inside the Library. He cursed the boy's choice of lair. The monster abhorred knowledge because it was *human* knowledge and therefore was a charm against his own power of ignorance and fear. Given enough time, human knowledge had always destroyed him before. How many times during human history had he arisen, teeth bared and fangs dripping, only to be smashed down by human knowledge? In the old world, he had fed with delight upon millions in all of his myriad forms, but when science arose, he finally found an enemy capable of stopping him. He had been reduced to exerting his influence in the poorer quarters of the world, the part forgotten by the West with all its riches. He knew that given enough time, humans would always push him back down, detain him, even destroy him. Speed was his weapon this time. It had all happened so quickly that even science was blinded by it. So close this time! So close! Yet, two survived.

Two could rebuild a world.

He heard the howl from below and knew it to be the call from Fenris, the largest and brightest of the weredogs. Grendel had summoned him earlier and was eager to speak with him. It took him a few moments to descend the seven floors to the hallway that was now the entrance to his realm. Opening the great glass door, Grendel ordered the animal in.

"What isss it you want...master?" asked the weredog as he walked in circles around Grendel's feet, shoulders crouched low to the ground, never meeting his master's gaze.

"I want the boy dead, but you have failed in that achievement."

"Masssstaa...the boy is in the stone building. We cannot force him out," answered Fenris.

"Your pathetic minions could follow him and trap him during his daylight treks throughout the cities. He is plainly out of the library then," growled Grendel.

The weredog shrank back, his ears laying back upon his head. "You know we are only dogs in the daylight. Only the moon calls out our true selves."

"Even a group of dogs should be able to kill the boy in broad daylight!" answered Grendel.

"Massstaa...we are wary of the boy. He stings us with his weapon. He outruns us with his machine. If this he can do while we are changed, then in the daytime how much more might he hurt us?"

"Oh, shut up, you pathetic dog!" Grendel mused for a long time and then said, "I will make it possible for you to set upon him."

The part of Fenris that was forming into a human more and more each day was clearly confused. "Massstaa...why do you not go to the stone building and kill him yourself? It is only a short walk away."

Grendel sprang forward and grabbed the weredog by the throat, lifting him high off the ground. Fenris whined and whimpered, his breath coming in short gasps.

"I told you once! He is what remains of the old world, *before* my time. As long as he lives, I cannot come to my full power. So I fear his power because it may *equal* my own! Fear! Do you understand fear? Everything understands fear..." he growled as he backed the creature's body up against a cement wall. The weredog's limbs flailed helplessly.

"Fear is a language everything understands!" said Fenris through his twisted throat.

That was when a realization came to Grendel's mind that showed him the way like a lit candle in the darkness. Fear. He would use it as a weapon. He had done this before, but this time, in this new incarnation, he could do so much more.

He dropped the weredog on the floor and Fenris backed away into the darkness, his teeth bared, a low growl emanating from this lupine throat.

His master's demeanor had changed. Grendel was no longer angry but almost convivial, a wry smile cracking on the side of his face. For the first time, the weredog began to question the call of his master. He had been a good dog, once, before all memory ceased and his first master died. Hiding somewhere deep inside of his mind the weredog remembered a boy and an afternoon, a walk and a grassy place and a ball he would fetch. He remembered, ever so vaguely, the feeling of having a master he loved and who loved him back. When all the people went away, this new master called him from somewhere deep in his mind and he answered the call and he had tried to please him. But this master was temperamental and difficult to please. The things he wanted him to do were not right, but he was the master and they must be done. That was the way of things. Lately, though, ideas came to him in the darkness, dreams and images neither canine nor human but a strange mixture of both. Killing for food was canine and felt natural. Killing for the pleasure of a master was beginning to trouble his mind.

"Bring your people to the Library tomorrow, just as the sun sets. We shall see how long he can wait inside while the elements rage without."

The weredog padded to the door and the monster opened it for him, planting his foot squarely on Fenris' haunches. The dog turned and growled.

"That was for nothing! Now...do something!" growled Grendel as he shut the door and dissolved back into the darkness within darkness.

A day passed before the monster called Grendel climbed to the top of his high tower and began to summon the elements. He raised his hands to the angry skies and toward the southern horizon in the West he called, "Come now!

Show me your powers! Towards me! Mount your dark horses and make your way to the new master of this world! I call you forth from the nether regions, from the edge of things, from the world beneath the world, from the high heaven beyond all view. Break down the cities! Crumble into the dust the remnants of the world of before. Cleanse the lands with your rain and fire! Show me your strength or forever let it be said that you were nothing, weak and insignificant! Hear me now!"

As he shouted his imperatives to the skies, one might have discerned a blackness growing at the edge of the world, crouching and slouching toward him and answering his call. Like reluctant armies, the powers that lay hidden from modern man for ages arose from their slumber and took their place in the old order of things. Thunder married lightning, power and rain. Cold shook hands with the flooding rains and the hail and together, like Valkyries riding to gather up the bodies of the slain upon some forgotten, lost battlefield of old, they rode forth to wreak their long pent anger upon an almost empty world.

Grendel stood atop his ramparts for a long time before he was appeased and retired to his darkness below. As he stood in the doorway that led to the labyrinthine world of the old medical center, he could be heard muttering, "This will flush him out of his castle of books and stone. Then that miserable excuse for an ally, Fenris, can kill him. But I must be the one who takes care of her. Tonight..."

Today Brady would be Don Quixote riding his noble steed, Rocinante. They would travel the roads in search of injustice, righting wrongs as they went. Today he would see giants, not in the form of windmills like in Cervantes' book, but in the giant form of the statue of Paul Bunyan on the Bangor side of the river. He would be a knight errant today, because today that is what he felt like being. Yesterday he was Hawkeye from *The Last of the Mohicans*, scouting the deep forest for Mohawks. Tomorrow he was already planning on being Frodo Baggins, approaching Mt. Doom as he wove his way through the hidden paths of Mordor. Had there been other people around he would have only imagined but because he was so utterly alone, he decided to do more than imagine: he would become. He had been happy to imagine when other people were watching, but he had discovered something wonderful after all the people were gone. When no one was watching, you could be anyone. You could do anything. With no one to judge you, you could be anything at all and the world was like a blank piece of white drawing paper, only you were the pencil.

All the books he loved to read and reread were suddenly more than books. They were doorways to other worlds. Somehow they had more meaning than they had before the Abandonment. A string of words before were now an incantation of power. Where before he might have imagined a tall white tower on top of which dwelt a princess, he saw the Thomas Hill Standpipe, tall and white and no longer a water tower for the city. Instead, its usefulness gone because those who had built it were gone, it fit *his* needs. The whole world had begun to fit his needs. It was as though he was playing a game that he was designing as he went and somehow, it made this empty world more bearable. He was in a real life role-playing game and he didn't need an xBox. It made this empty world less empty. If the Standpipe was no longer a standpipe but The White Tower, who would care? Who would judge? If the hospital was no longer the hospital but the Entrance to Hades, who would chide him for it? No one, except perhaps for Joshua Chamberlain.

Brady stood at the foot of the statue of General Joshua Lawrence Chamberlain and saluted. The figure moved its gaze from the sky to the lower ground and acknowledged the boy.

"Good afternoon, General."

"Smith," said the General.

"I've come for some...advice, if that's alright with you, sir."

The General smiled for a second and then let his face fall back to its normal distant, pensive look.

"Certainly, Smith. Say it plain."

"As you know, I took your advice. I moved into the Library and secured it against the enemy."

"Good."

"Well, sir, I've made a new friend. It seems that you are not the only image of a human to take on a personality."

"Go on..."

"Benjamin Franklin, Printer, sends his regards, sir."

The General's head creaked and shivered as he moved his gaze to look down at Brady and maintain it.

"How is this possible? Is he a statue, like me?"

"He's a book. I found him in his autobiography."

"Fascinating," the General said. "This begins to make some sense. I, too, made autobiographical writings. Perhaps this action caused a portion of my personality to remain bound to this place, this time. This is cause for further speculation. Still, Benjamin Franklin! You've outdone yourself, Smith. A better ally you could not possibly make."

"Yes, Thank you, sir."

"Your question, Brady?"

"Sir, what's your advice on my next step. Ben asked me to ask you. He made me write it down. Here, let me see," Brady pulled out a folded square of paper from his pocket and unfolded it gingerly, reading it.

"Why didn't you bring him...I mean, the book, Smith?"

"I wanted to, sir, but he gets tired from time to time. He claims he needs his sleep, so I put him back on his shelf and leave him there and he comes back to me after awhile. I think he's quite an old man, now. He's shelved at the moment."

"So he sleeps? Very human of him..." mused Joshua Chamberlain. "I do not sleep. I wonder if he dreams?"

Brady did not know.

"He says, 'What is the nature of the enemy of which you speak? Do you know anything about the enemy that can aid our young friend?' "

The general did not speak for a moment, as though gathering his words carefully.

"I have been listening and observing, but my conjectures must be taken with a grain of salt. I speak from incomplete

144

reconnaissance. But I do know this much. The enemy of which we speak is both monstrous and human. He is in residence in the hospital. He does not leave it, but he sends out his ranks in the form of these creatures you so strangely name 'weredogs.' He is not alone: someone is with him who evades him and he screams in the darkness as he pursues this elusive one. I am surprised you have not heard him."

"I think a might have, a couple of weeks ago," answered Brady. "Wait, did you say he isn't alone?"

"Precisely. He screams at this other...person, I would warrant."

Brady was stunned. Another person!

"I think I might have heard a scream from the medical center, days ago."

"Really? Interesting. Still, he commands forces beyond the control of an ordinary human being. I have heard him summon storm clouds and winds, and black clouds formed moments later. Such an adversary is difficult to comprehend, afraid to leave a building but capable of summoning the elements themselves, like Prospero in Shakespeare's *Tempest*. I do know this: he is restless and determined to kill you, Smith. He is also bent on destroying this other one I have spoken of."

"Do you know who it is?" Brady asked, suddenly awestricken by the idea that there was another survivor.

"I know only that this person faces the wrath and anger of the enemy daily, whereas you have been surprisingly free of trouble from him. Whoever it is does not leave the building, I assume, because all the exits are secured or guarded. This person could be an ally to you, Smith. Why, together you would both double your numbers!"

No thought since he awoke from his fevered sleep to the Abandonment had filled his mind with such surprise or concern.

"Should I...try to break in and save this person?" asked Brady.

The General pondered this, his face showing the slightest agitation of thought.

"*The inspiration of a noble cause enables men to do*

145

things they did not dream themselves capable of before," was his only answer.

Brady was confused. "Sir?" he asked.

"Oh, something I wrote a long time ago, Smith. Tell Dr. Franklin that I cannot advise action without more information. You have no reinforcements, Smith. If you attack and fail, there is no second charge, no second chance."

Brady walked up to the hill behind the General and looked up the river, to the hospital and the lair of the monster. He waited a long while before he spoke to the general again.

"Sir, isn't saving this person a noble cause?"

The general nodded slowly in agreement as his gaze settled off into the distance again.

"Doubtless you are correct, Smith, but fools rush in...We, that is, you, shall have to act before long, anyway. Send your raven to the place. He will come back with the information we seek."

"What? Hugin? He doesn't understand me and I don't understand him."

One eyebrow raised, the general replied, "Oh no? Have you tried asking him?"

"Well, no, but..."

"How do you know you can't understand? Perhaps it is because you haven't been listening."

The bird, who had been sitting on the General's shoulder, turned his head and looked away at nothing in particular in the distance.

"Send him. I can understand his speech. I would warrant that Dr. Franklin can understand him, as well. One day soon, if you learn to listen properly, you might also understand the raven's speech. He is a cunning creature endowed with a strong intellect, and something more..."

Brady saluted the General and, facing him before he left, said, "I'll take it under advisement, sir."

"Yes, see that you do, Smith."

Hugin, who had been sitting on the General's shoulder, seemed to understand the meaning of their conversation. He croaked at both the General and Brady before taking flight,

146

seeking the topmost towers of the old hospital to spy among its spires.

Hugin did not return. For the past two hours Brady had been waiting near the water's edge by the Great River's bank, but to no avail. He closed his black composition book just as a drop of rain left a wet circle on the page. As he was sitting up on the bench watching the Great River flow by, in the distance Brady heard the rumble of thunder and the black clouds began to roll in from the West revealing a heavy thunderstorm on its way. As the dark clouds began to cover the landscape he felt a strange change in the air, almost electrical but also something more, something...*other.*

He whistled for Max who dutifully appeared from around the shack at the edge of the river.

"Come on boy! It's time to get back home. It's going to rain really hard."

By the time he reached the library it was raining hammers and nails and the thunder had begun to crash more loudly showing its approach as fast and furious. He unbolted the heavy lock on the door in the back of the library and entered. Once inside, he quickly latched another bolt and padlock into place. Secure inside his castle, Brady sought out dry clothes and his friend, Benjamin Franklin.

"Weather's acting up, Dr. Franklin," Brady said as he took off his T-shirt.

"Really?" inquired the book known as Ben Franklin. "Oh, I do enjoy a good thunderstorm. Did I ever tell you about the time I discovered that lightning was electricity?"

Pulling on a dry T-shirt, Brady answered, "Oh, um, no, not really."

"Oh, that was a time, let me tell you. I postulated that the friction of the particles in the air created a charge and so I determined to see if that charge, like a flowing river, could move from one place to another. Has there been lightning?"

"Not yet, but it's coming. I spoke with the General. He's certain that whoever is in the old hospital is out for my blood, but he insists that someone else is in there, as well. He told me to send Hugin to check the place out. The

General thinks we need more information before we can make our move. I guess all we can do now is wait and be patient," answered Brady.

"He that can have patience can have what he will," answered Ben.

As the minutes turned to an hour, the thunderstorm continued to grow. The sky, which normally would still have been sunlit with the early rays of dusk was now black and the rain descended in sheets against the large panes of glass along the front of the library. The lightning was striking with great regularity, crashing like nothing Brady had ever heard before. Thor was hammering the earth with Mjollnir and the mighty Zeus himself was hurling Hephaestus' thunderbolts one after the other into the thirsty ground, surrounding him as they continually closed in. This was more than a mere thunderstorm.

Crash after crash shook the walls of the library, rattling the windows and making Brady fear for his life. He took Ben and called Max and together they ascended to the topmost part of the library- the copper cupola.

"Brady," asked Ben, "why up here? Why not the basement? It would be safer."

Something intuitively told Brady to seek the highest point nearest the storm. Brady only answered, "I don't know why, but I *think* this is what I'm supposed to do."

"What's that you say? Supposed to? I don't understand," said Ben.

"Me neither. Call it a hunch."

This was the worst storm Brady had ever known. He sat down in the center of the floor directly under the cupola and gazed upwards. The only windows up here were those circling the dome itself and he could see the flashes of light but not the actual lightning strikes that were currently drumming their frenzy outside. Max huddled on Brady's lap, shivering and whining like an overly large puppy, each successive lightning strike and thunderclap driving his head farther into Brady's armpit.

For a long time they sat there hoping the storm might abate so that they might live to see another day, but after an hour the storm showed no sign of lessening its attack. One thunderbolt struck so close to the building that Brady heard the snap of a tree and could smell the sharp, pungent ozone produced by the static discharge. It was apparent to him that he was now in the center of the whirlwind and that was also precisely the moment when he began to hear the Whisperers again.

In the center of the thunderstorm, they were no longer Whisperers.

They were Screamers. He could hear them clearly now. They were crying, screaming, moaning, calling his name. They were plaintive and urgent in their need for some sort of answer. Brady could hear them all clearly for the first time since he awoke to the Abandonment. There were so many and if he closed his eyes, he could envision them all around him – above, around and below. He didn't know what he should do and he knew that if he continued to listen, he might break with reality altogether. He began to hold his head and moan in confusion and pain.

"Brady, my boy, are you quite alright?" inquired the kind old Philadelphian.

"No, not really," was Brady's answer.

"Is it the storm, lad? It will pass, you know. They always do," said Ben Franklin.

"No, it's the Whisperers. They're in my head. I can't stand it. They're screaming at me..."

Ben had no eyes and was only a book and the idea of a man long dead, but even that personification could understand the fear inherent in Brady's voice.

Ben then asked the probing question, "What are they saying? Brady...talk to me," said Ben.

"I can't quite figure out anything they're saying. It's like they're saying *everything.*"

Once Brady had read that while drilling a test hole during the Soviet Era in Siberia, some geologists drilled the deepest hole on earth. It seemed like they hit an air pocket deep down beyond any place humans had ever drilled. The scientists lowered a microphone into the hole and recorded the sounds from far below. The story was that they had

149

found not just a hole in the earth but Hell itself. The subsequent recording, released on various Internet sites, was supposed to be the sounds of millions of damned souls crying out in anguish and torment. Of course, Brady knew that this was foolish. The deepest hole in the world is in South Africa and it is a diamond mine. Brady also wondered why the scientists sent down a microphone instead of a camera. The sound file on the Internet was probably just a recording of a middle school dance. Of course, Brady knew that the story was pure fabrication, but he couldn't help but think that this sound he heard now sounded like...Hell.

He struggled to hold on to his mind, but each time he made a strong effort to focus on something other than the voices of the Screamers, the storm outside rose in intensity as though in answer to his effort. He sat cross-legged under the center of the cupola, his hands covering his ears, his head bowed in concentration and effort.

"Brady!" screamed Ben as loudly as a book could scream. "Brady!" he shouted again.

Brady opened one eye and said, "What! What do you want!"

"Son, you have to stop resisting the voices. Stop trying to shut them out. Just imagine what would have happened if you had never listened to the General or to me? I think they're trying to make contact. They want to speak with you.

"They're angry! Ben, they hate me! I'm afraid of them!" shouted Brady.

"Just so! Face your fear, my boy. They're only voices. They only have words and words can't destroy you. Try to understand instead of giving in to your fear. Investigate, observe, listen. Listen to them! Don't work against the world. Work with it. There are forces all over the place that we can't see or hear or understand until we pay attention to them-like electricity! Perhaps they are invisible but they are still present!"

Brady hesitated. He was almost as afraid to admit his true feelings about the voices as he was about the voices themselves. He imagined the Whisperers to be the last words of all the people on earth who had perished, streamed at him, flooding him and possibly overwhelming him until finally he would crumble beneath their sheer persistence.

"Damn it, Ben, I'm scared," Brady said quietly.

Ben replied calmly, "Scared? Well, of course you are. You'd be foolish not to be. But to let that stop you would be a shame. I understand fear, Brady. When I signed the Declaration of Independence, when I sailed to Europe and dealt with kings, when I sought to understand the fire in the skies, I was concerned for my safety, too. But I did it anyway. That's courage, Brady. Courage is being afraid but doing the thing anyway. Anything else is running away."

Brady understood, finally. It wasn't so much a submission to his fear as a sudden understanding - he couldn't successfully hold these voices apart from himself. However strong he might be, he was nothing compared to their inexorable onslaught. He settled back against the marble column that supported a carved figure on a pedestal called "Thought" and opened his mind.

He closed his eyes and waited. Whenever a bolt of lightning hit nearby, his mind's eye was illuminated with the vision of another world, another reality, another way to be. In front of his mind's eye he saw flashes of thousands upon thousands of human forms, writhing, grasping, mouthing anger toward him. Then the darkness resumed until the next lightning bolt found ground and lit the ethereal place he was now witnessing. Brady didn't flinch or open his eyes and all the while, Ben spoke calmly to him saying, "Keep going, Brady, my boy. You are the pilot of your own soul. You have nothing to be afraid of."

As the storm raged about him, it lit his view erratically, like he was on a journey towards or away from something and each illumination showed him a different scene. The tense and tortured scenes he witnessed upon first surrendering himself to this dreamworld had been gradually replaced by scenes of less violence and far less anger. There were happy people, families, those who even began to look vaguely familiar, as though he had seen them before. There were people of all races and colors, heights, and builds, all turning in a maelstrom choreographed by one rampant need:

to make contact with the being known as Brady Smith.

In the center of his mind a face came into view and a face that went with a voice. At first it flickered and evaporated, wavered and faltered, but the moment lingered and the face took definite form. The voices that sounded like so many tortured souls lessened in intensity and faded into the background. All he could see was a girl's face and all he could hear was her voice.

"Hi Brady," she said.

Brady knew her. He would know her face at another time, in another life. She was Susan, the girl he had thought about, on and off, for the last four years. She had been in his class since the third grade and he had never so much as spoken to her privately. Sometimes they had to work together in class and at those moments, Brady was fascinated to the point of distraction. Susan played the trumpet in the band. Susan was a straight-A student who had been to Europe. Susan read Jane Austen books when other girls read Twilight books. She was golden-haired and beautiful, quiet and strong. As she appeared to him now, he barely had the courage to speak in return.

"Hi Sue," he answered.

She smiled at him. "I've been trying to talk to you for awhile now. We all have. I am so glad you're finally listening."

Brady could not look away from a vision in his mind, so he demurely answered, "Sorry, Sue. I...was afraid."

She continued to smile but her eyes, always the prettiest things in the world to him, took on a compassionate look and she said, "We all have been watching you. We only want to help you."

"Help me?" Brady asked.

He couldn't stop staring into her eyes. They were so perfect and he felt like he could look into them for an eternity and still not even begin to plumb their depths. She was so beautiful, so perfect.

"Yes. Is that so strange to you? It shouldn't be."

"What do you want to help me do?" he asked plaintively.

"We want you to survive. You have to survive. You're the

One."

Brady was confused. "I don't know what you mean. I'm the last boy on earth."

"No. There are others. But you are the one who sees things as they really are and not as they seem. You are the one with the Power. You need to carry on so you can lead the others. There are so few left."

"Others? How many?" he asked urgently.

She didn't seem to hear him. Like one of the fading ghosts from Dicken's Christmases, she was of the moment and couldn't linger long upon this plane. She continued to tell what she could.

"You must rescue her. She's in the hospital, on the top floor, where we were born. He has her trapped there. She's been able to escape him so far, but tonight the world will take another step toward changing and he'll capture her. Then he'll kill her. You must rescue her before he does this, for if she doesn't survive, neither will you."

"She? She? Who is she? Is it...my mother? Is my mother in the hospital? Who is this person who has her trapped?"

"Brady, if I had lived, we might have been better friends...maybe even more. I always liked you best. I'm sorry I can't be there to help you. As we speak, we're fading from you. Because you listened, we'll trouble you no more. All you needed to do to stop us was...listen."

She smiled. He was Dante and she was Beatrice.

"I'm sorry, Susan. If I knew I could have talked to you, I would have listened sooner, but I was scared. Sorry..."

"You're the bravest person on earth. You're frightened, but it's the other who should be frightened by you. You're only beginning to see things as they are. Soon you'll understand more of what you see. Once you understand, you'll be even stronger. He's the one who should be afraid. As you gain knowledge and see things as they truly are, he weakens. Even now, he's afraid of you. "

She began to fade, to rock in and out of focus and to become silent. Brady was not ready to let go - not yet.

"Susan, is it my mother? Is she the one there?"

"Goodbye, Brady. Remember - in whatever way you

153

may, seek her out in the hospital tonight and rescue her. If not, she'll perish and then all hope will be lost. Save her and you save everything good that all people ever stood for."

Brady watched as first one, then two, then ten, then a hundred, a thousand, a million visages of departed souls appeared behind her. They were all smiling now, looking at him, some nodding, most simply content that he had listened, finally.

Brady opened his eyes. Though the thunder still rolled and the lighting played an infernal dance upon the night sky, they were gone. The Whisperers were gone.

And she, whoever she was, needed his help...now.

Grendel stood upon the roof of the hospital and watched the storm he had summoned with great satisfaction. One might even see a hint of glee upon his face, albeit a wild and undisciplined glee. One by one the lighting strikes set the great city on fire, so much so that even the rain could not undo what the wind whipped into a fury. The great city, once known as Bangor, was burning. Plumes and pillars of smoke could be seen against the stark white of the lightning's staccato strikes. Soon the boy would have no place to run and when the fire completely devastated the city, the boy would be dead. He would have to go out into the open, out of that infernal hall of knowledge and there his weredogs would finally fall upon him and tear him to shreds.

She was on the top floor, in the ward where Brady and half of the children in the area were born. The Maternity ward seemed to be flooded with an energy that weakened Grendel. All of those souls ushered into the world created a field that gave her power and sapped it from him. She was one floor below him. Though she had locked him out of her area, he had found the blueprints. He had studied the floor plan and he knew of a way in that he was certain she did not know. With dread purpose, he slipped over to a ventilation cover and ripped it from its base, exposing a pathway to the top floor and the air return system. He concentrated his energy into shrinking his form. Bone collapsed onto bone, cartilage twisted and folded against itself, muscles held unnatural positions so that he could fit into the shaft. As he began to slither into the hole that would lead him to her, he smiled a crooked grin. With great effort and concentration, he caused his body to contract. His feral senses would lead him to her.

He could sense the truth of things, for he was attuned to the underpinnings of the world. The boy was strong, but she was stronger because she represented a force he could not overcome with all the power of the cosmos – she was not merely a human. She was the embodiment, the very personification of his most hated enemy.

Chapter 11

The Entrance to the Underworld

"You must be swift and decisive, Brady. Don't linger anywhere. Make your way to the hospital, find her and return here as quickly as you can," Ben counseled as Brady donned his various belts, vests, and weaponry. Well-equipped with all manner of tools and assistive devices, he looked like a post-apocalyptic poster-child. He was the Batman setting out to prowl Gotham, bent on finding the Joker's lair. He was Beowulf setting out to find a particular cave wherein dwelt a foul beast.

"Both eyes open, Ben," he said, pointing to his own eyes with the horns symbol he made with this left hand that he had seen a thousand times on music television.

"And one foot in front of the other. That's the spirit, Brady. Find her and liberate her. Remember, don't engage the enemy unless you must."

"Got it," replied Brady.

Just as he opened the door, the great black form of Hugin flew into the library. He had never been in the building before and he was visibly flustered. He flew around the main room for a moment before settling on the circulation desk, croaking and flexing his satin wings back and forth.

"Hugin! Did you see her? Did you find out anything?" Brady inquired.

The great raven crackled and croaked what seemed to be a positive response. He had done as he had been asked. He had been to the monster's den.

"I wish I could understand you," Brady said in frustration. *The Autobiography of Benjamin Franklin* spoke. "I can understand him, Brady. He has information that will help you."

Rushing to the main table at the front of the main room, Brady put both hands on the book and asked, "What does he say?"

The bird began to remonstrate and flutter its wings in agitation. After a moment of noise and motion, he settled back into his usual proud raven stance and began preening his feathers casually.

Ben translated, "She is on the high, in the high part of the building. I think he means the top floor. The man-thing has trapped her there, but he cannot get to her. He said that the man-thing has left the doorway to the building unguarded. You can walk right in. No dog-things, either. But he says that the city is red and hot, full of smoke. Brady, the city...it's burning!"

Brady walked to the window, cracked it open and took a deep breath. "You're right. Why do I have this feeling that he's trying to smoke me out?"

"You're worried that this might be a trap?" Ben asked.

"Could be," answered Brady. "But I have to go anyway. Hey, you," Brady said, pointing to the great raven, "wanna fly over there with me and be my eyes in the sky?"

Hugin made himself big and opened his wings, letting out a long, complicated crackle.

Again, Ben translated. "He says, 'It's what he does.'"

The bird flew to his shoulder and settled there. Brady turned to leave when Ben said, "Brady, if I should, well...if

157

the library should burn down, would you do me a favor?"

Brady had not thought about the library and its fate in the fire that now was raging through the city, unchecked and feeding on the untended real estate.

"Yeah, Ben. Anything," answered Brady.

"Find another library and make contact with me again. Will you do that?" asked Ben.

"Can I do that?" replied Brady.

"I certainly hope so, my boy. Now, off with you..."

With that, Brady and Hugin ventured into the coal-red night.

Hugin took flight as Brady brought Rocinante to a full roar down the road towards State Street. Before taking to the road, Brady had donned the gas mask that he had used so often when investigating the houses of the dead. In those circumstances, he hadn't wished to smell the odor or death. Tonight it filtered the smoke from his nostrils but also limited his vision. Rocinante's headlight had a strong halogen bulb, but the smoke was filling the city, wafting in waves through the skies, down the streets and up into an ever-reddening night. When he made it to the intersection of State and Broadway, he saw the devastation from the top of the hill. Wind and rain, fire and smoke animated the entire view with motion. Flickers of fires combined with flashes of lightning and the smoke, like dark nebulae, obscured the fires at the very edges of the city. Brady hoped that the fuel storage tanks down by the river would escape the conflagration.

It seemed like Brady's world was quickly destroying itself. All of his carefully mapped caches of food, his supply depots, his map full of renamed places and things; all were being erased and consumed by flames. Bangor was burning as it had done a hundred years ago. All he could so was hope that Brewer would escape the fire and remain a safe haven on the opposite side of the Great River.

Brady had Rocinante held at full throttle down the center of State Street toward the Entrance to the Underworld. Hugin was barely a yard in front of him the entire way, pumping his wings and struggling to maintain his lead.

158

There it was -the medical center. In its day, more people worked in that building than in any other building for two hundred miles. It had been the place that held out the longest against the virus. Brady recalled vaguely that central Maine had been one of the last places in the country to be stricken with the virus. One day his mother had come home and told him that the 'bigwigs from the Centers for Disease Control' had just set up shop there. Accompanied by a military contingent of the Maine National Guard, all measures to stop the spread of the virus were now centered out of this building. The whole of the United States Health system was reduced to the control center in the eastern part of the nation, a small dot on map in the middle of a vast forest that is, or was, Maine.

Hugin swooped down and caught his attention as if to say, "This way, boy. The doorway is this way..." Brady turned Rocinante down the street and into the main entrance of the complex. The road was blocked by large concrete barriers, behind which lingered the forgotten dark green hulks that were troop carriers and supply vehicles from the Maine National Guard and the Centers for Disease Control. Brady was used to entering the facility the way he always had when his mother brought him to work to do such things as collect her check or eat in the cafeteria. Hugin was leading him in another direction, however. He was flying to the right, near the river and away from the main complex. It was the Parke Building, a large addition to the hospital with seven floors of doctors offices, laboratories and meeting rooms. Brady vaguely recalled the main lobby, accessible by its own set of glass doors. Hugin had settled on a railing near the doors and made a raucous cry, lowering and raising his head in a signal of urgency.

"This is the door," he seemed to say.

Was Brady beginning to understand him? Was be beginning to read Hugin's actions and motions, his intonations of sound?

Brady turned on the headlamp he wore on his forehead. He still donned the gas-mask and with the headlamp he looked like sort of alien astronaut, freshly landed on a

159

strange new world, unsure what he would encounter. He had another long black flashlight mounted on his paintball rifle. Around his waist was a belt with knives, ammunition, other flashlights, a first aid kit, a coil of rope, and a variety of tools he might need in a pinch. Over his shoulder was slung the katana he had taken from the Maine Army and Navy company. He didn't know how to fight with a sword, but he thought that, like so many things he had learned lately, he might be forced to learn on the job.

He stopped in his tracks when he saw his reflection in the windowed door. Who was this warrior descending into the belly of the beast? Who was this Childe Roland mounting the million steps toward the Dark Tower? Who donned this war-gear and walked the path of danger toward an uncertain end? Frozen by how much he had changed in the last weeks, he considered that he was unsure of his own personality. There, in the glass, was a post-apocalyptic freak, a figure from a Tim Burton stop-motion animation, a comic-book hero. Who was he to face the Beast and save the maiden? In that moment, Brady aged a lifetime and passed from one stage of his existence into the next. Eventually, he knew, one had to step over the threshold and face the monster. Otherwise, the monster would win by default.

The hallway was a large space. Chairs and couches that served as waiting areas were clumped in groups against the walls, in favor of beds, cots, and makeshift emergency medical stations. Everywhere he looked he saw evidence of the great falling, the dying, the Abandonment. There were no bodies that he could see, which perplexed him, but there were discarded medical supplies, syringes, drips, bedpans - in short, all the accoutrements of a medical disaster. Everything was in disarray.

The long hallway was mostly glass and it faced the Great River just below. His own light sources, along with the ambient glow of the fires in the distance caused shadows to suddenly flicker, illuminating different sections of the place and causing Brady to work diligently to find his way to the stairwell. His plan to find 'her', whoever she was, and get her out of this place was not sophisticated. Like Beowulf

160

descending into Grendel's cave, he went with one purpose and that was to put one foot in front of the other until he faced the creature. He had little time to prepare his rescue plan, especially after Susan's plaintive plea to make haste. He would find his way to the highest floor in this building. Since the two buildings were connected, he would make his way to her vicariously, from the side. He only hoped he wasn't too late.

There was the doorway clearly marked with the words "Stairs." Brady realized that this must be how the monster navigated through this place. Brady had to use the stairs, too. He couldn't fly to the top floor. He couldn't climb on the outside of the building. The elevators didn't work. There was only one way.

He ascended each step with caution, his eyes scanning in *Observation Mode*, investigating each shadow and shape, attending to every sound. Higher and higher, past the first three floors. On the fourth floor he saw evidence of a struggle. Broken glass littered the landing from the small window in the heavy steel door that led to the main floor. The door handle had been sheared off, probably with a heavy hammer and from Brady's perspective, it seemed as though whoever had done this was seeking a way onto the floor and not away from it. Was this his first evidence of the monster?

As he approached the topmost landing, he heard a growl and a shout of frustration. The sound was coming from behind the doorway that led from the stairwell. Brady turned off his flashlights and stopped as he listened to a series of thrashing sounds, of items being thrown and smashed muffling their way through the heavy steel door. He crept to the steel-wire reinforced window and looked through, seeking the cause of all of this sound.

The creature behind the door worked in nearly total darkness. Brady surmised that the Beast must have night vision, like a cat. He took off his gas mask meaning to don his own night-vision goggles when the odor of death, so concentrated and intense, hit him, causing him to gasp and stagger. He scrambled to put the gas mask back on his face, to regain his wits. The odor was so powerful it seemed alive and he wondered, is this smell of dead bodies or of the monster? While he regained his senses, the monster on the other side of the door continued its shouting and cursing. Brady assessed the situation. If he was supposed to save her, he'd better do it soon, even though he had no clear idea how this was to be accomplished or even who she was. He didn't dare look for long through the window in the door, but from several furtive glances, he could picture the beast in his mind.

It was very tall, perhaps nine feet, perhaps more. Its limbs were massive, with what Brady thought of as comic-book proportions, shaggy, not furry, and it had a massive head. Bony spikes protruded from its spine and clicked against each other as it moved. He couldn't see the creature's face, yet. Truly, it was the largest, most frightening living thing he had ever seen, like a vision from a nightmare or a scene from a horror movie, taking its frustration out on a wall which it hammered with two closed fists.

"I am coming for you!" shouted the creature.

There has to come a time, Brady thought to himself, when you just have to go one way or the other. Either move forward now and risk everything or skulk back down the stairs, out into the fire and the darkness and forever wonder what would have happened if...

There has to come a time, Brady.

He removed his mask and took in a deep breath, steeling himself for the battle that was sure to come. He didn't flinch from the fetid odor of death that permeated everything in this place.

Brady opened the door and quietly slipped through as the creature hammered its anger upon the wall, its back still to him.

The Beast hadn't heard Brady as he entered the room over the sound of his own frustrated pounding. If the creature succeeded in breaking down the wall, Brady knew that he would have access to his prey. Susan had been emphatic in her plea: he had to save her, now, on this night, at this moment, or the creature would succeed and all that

162

had been the world would end. The history and future of all Humanity hung in the balance.

Brady holstered his paint ball gun and slipped the paint ball rifle to the floor, realizing the futility of his weapons against such a fearful opponent. From his leg sheath he withdrew a long knife. In his other hand he had a canister of pepper spray. He knew that he couldn't kill this creature - not here, not now, but he might hamper its progress long enough to save her. He kept hoping that she was his mother, the person he wanted to see more than anyone else. She had worked here in this building. It could be her.

The creature sensed Brady's presence. It stopped its anger against the wall and Brady heard from the hulking form a deep but nearly silent laugh. Bracing himself for the fight of his life, Brady watched intently as the creature slowly turned to face him.

Beyond all reason, the creature faced the boy, towering over him as a colossus. Brady's eyes grew wide when he beheld the face of Grendel. The monster's head was enormous and surprisingly amorphous, his face ever-changing. The dimly lit room was bathed in splashes of electric light emanating from the fierce storm outside and Brady could see first one face and then another form and dissolve. First there was a face that looked like Adolph Hitler with fangs, then Darth Vader, Emperor Palpatine, Marilyn Manson, the Alien from Alien 1,2 and 3, Predator, the Terminator, Lord Voldemort, and the substitute teacher he had in fourth grade. There was a succession of visages that lingered but a moment and then morphed into something else.

"You!" said the creature quietly, as though pleased. His voice sounded like a discordant chorus of reverberating tones. He was a hundred broken bells, a thousand shattered mirrors, a million stars about to die.

The Beast spoke with a small amount of amusement in his otherwise anger-filled voice. "I did not think *you* would ever come to *me*! Renamer! I am your *death*," mouthed the monster.

A small seed of bravery germinated in Brady when he

said, "No. I came to destroy you." Brady was surprised by his own words. Did they emanate from him or from Jack the Giant Killer? Was this the giant that Don Quixote met on the plain before he toppled off his horse so ignominiously?

The deepest of laughs from the belly of the beast came to his lips and he laughed again, this time truly bemused by Brady's words.

"We shall see, boy. We shall see..."

They stood face to face for a long moment, each measuring the other. An onlooker might have thought that the boy could not stand a chance against such insurmountable odds. Brady moved his index finger over the top of the pepper spray and felt a little foolish to think that something that was a mix between a mutant rhinoceros and a superhuman alien monster from an eighties era DC comic could ever be affected by something so inane. In one fluid moment he threw the can at the creature and reached far over his head to withdraw the katana from its sheath on his back.

He raised it as high as he could and brought it down at the monster's face.

Grendel dodged the blade's swift flight with the agility of a feral creature and quickly moved behind Brady, grappling him with his enormous clawed paw.

"So easy, then, after all," mouthed Grendel in satisfaction. "One little moment of excitement and it's all over! So unfortunate!"

Brady brought the knife he had been holding in his other hand down onto the leg of his assailant. The blade only went into the flesh of the muscle a few millimeters, but it was enough to cause the creature to cry out in anger and what Brady could only assume was shame. He let Brady go for an instant, but it was long enough for Brady to slip away.

Brady had never been an "A" student in P.E. class, but he was strangely agile tonight. In fact, he found himself to be as agile as he wanted to be, almost like he could summon prowess at will. As he ran down the hallway and away from Grendel, he could sense the monster close behind. Over gurneys and counters, behind rolling carts and past scenes of previous disarray obviously caused by Grendel on previous

164

attempts to find her, they buckled and grappled. Brady was slippery and lithe and his blade made many cuts in the flesh of the creature but they only seemed to draw more strength and speed from Grendel.

Brady hoped to draw attention away from her long enough to aid in her escape. He could see the monster gaining on him, almost at his throat with his swinging, pendulous arms, sharp claws like Bowie knives, scorpion tails brushing his back as he moved away from the creature. Grendel was Medusa and Brady was Perseus; Grendel was the Minotaur and Brady was Theseus. Grendel was Darth Vader and Brady was Luke Skywalker.

"Run, run, as fast as you can! You can't catch me! I'm the gingerbread man!" shouted Brady, taunting the creature as he slid underneath a bed and then out the other side. He had little time to assess, but he was now in a new mode he had never experienced before in his life. He was in Observational Mode, but he was moving with speed and determination.

Engagement mode.

Come on! he thought. *Wherever you are! Run for it. Get out of here!* With Grendel at his back, Brady found himself at the end of a corridor with nowhere left to run. The monster's bulk slammed into the floor with each footfall as he approached Brady, whose sword was already held out perpendicular to his body, grasped with both hands, legs apart, ready.

As the monster was within arm's reach, Brady brought the blade down as hard as he could. Grendel's elephantine fist blocked the blow and in one movement caused the blade to fly from Brady's hands onto the hallway floor far behind them. Brady was pinned against the cement wall, crushed by the force of the creature's body against his. His lungs barely able to gather enough breath to stay conscious, Brady turned his head away from the stink of the creature's foul breath and the glowing red glare of its amorphous eyes. They were both very quiet for a moment, each attuned to the other's breathing and awaiting the next movement.

Outside the window to his right, in the direction his head

165

was turned, Brady could clearly see most of the city was on fire. Huge sheets of flame roared and licked their tongues upward to the darkness of space just as Grendel's own tongue began to slide from one side of its gaping maw to the other. Finally, the face started to take shape and gain solidity. It was a human face, except that its features were overstated and outgrown, like a mutant, stretched from a normal sized skull to cover one twice or three times its original size.

"Why?" Brady managed to gasp a question. "Why do

you want to kill me? How can I be of any trouble to you?"

"You are human. You remain when the others have all fallen. You are a son of the light and I would tear down the Sun. That is all," was Grendel's response.

"Haven't enough people died already?" asked Brady through his grimace of pain.

"Not until you both are gone. Then enough will have died," responded Grendel.

"I'm not afraid of you," Brady asserted simply.

"You should be. I know who you have come here for. You want your mother, don't you? I knew her. Did you know that? She was one of those unfortunates who worked in this house of death. Before she died, she suffered, like you will. She was brave, boy. You should be proud of her."

Brady looked deeply into the eyes of the creature seeking the truth of things.

"You're a liar!" Brady screamed. "She isn't dead! She's alive and I'm here to save her!"

The monster laughed. "You've put up a good fight, boy, but you're too late. She died weeks ago, along with the others. I should know. I killed them all, every last one of them."

"No!" Brady screamed, but the beast had already begun making its final move upon the struggling body of Brady Smith.

"I know you don't believe me," the monster continued, "but to prove it to you, I will let you hear her final words."

Then, nearing the doorway of Death himself as the monster pressed hard against his throat, he heard his mother's voice coming from Grendel's mouth. She was saying, "What about Brady? God help him. Oh, my boy, Brady..." Her voice broke into a weak stream of cries and whimpers.

The beast spoke again in its own sandpaper and gravel voice, "I am many things, but I am not a liar."

The creature took its massive hand and began to raise Brady by the throat high up against the wall, tightening its grip. Brady found one hand free and thrust it into his trouser pocket.

167

"Finally!" said Grendel through self-satisfied, gritted teeth.

"No so fast, asshole!" shouted a voice from behind the monster. Brady couldn't see who had spoken, but he felt the creature loosen its grip on his throat and then, ultimately, Brady fell slumped against the floor.

Grendel screamed in pain. He had been wounded. The darkness was heavy, but the lightning storm, which had been reaching a frenzied level, revealed a form to Brady that would remain forever in his mind's eye. The monster had whirled to face his attacker but had also fallen on one knee. From his vantage point Brady could see one long three foot gash deeply cut into the monster's back, blood seeping and flowing from the wound and spurting onto the spiky protrusions.

There she stood, the mighty Athena, goddess of wisdom and war, her gray eyes and black hair falling down upon her shoulders. She held the katana in front of her and perpendicular to her frame like a veteran warrior and she was advancing upon the monster, all the anger and hatred of the world concentrated in her powerful gaze. She didn't speak. Her actions spoke louder than words.

Brady could see that the creature would only be down for a moment. Withdrawing the item from his pocket, he pointed it at Grendel and fired! The taser hit the creature and released its electrical fury into the body of the beast, causing it to rear up and then fall to the ground shivering and twitching. For a moment, the Beast was down!

Brady arose and ran at the girl. He grabbed her by the arm and said firmly, "Let's go! Now! Before he gets up again!"

Strangely, she didn't want to leave. Brady could see the determination in her eyes, feel the firm tense muscle of her arm as she clutched the sword with an almost desperate firmness of purpose. He squeezed her arm more tightly and she turned to look at him. If looks could kill, Brady would have been a dead man.

"This ends now!" she said.

She sliced down at Grendel's right hand, cleanly slicing

168

off the monsters fingers. Still immobilized by the taser, she could see the pain welling in the monster's eyes. She raised the sword for another strike, but Brady held her arm and looked into her eyes. She wasn't his mother. The disappointment he felt over her loss was intense but was countered by his curiosity. Who was this mysterious, powerful, angry girl?

"Please, you have to listen to me. I know. I just know. We have to leave, now, before he recovers. He gets stronger every time we wound him! He get's knocked down, but he get's up again! Come on! Run!"

She looked at him and in a second that lasted longer than a hundred years, she lowered the sword and nodded in assent. The girl was the first one into the stairwell. Before following her, Brady took one last look at the monster. Already he was beginning to rise from the floor and pursue them. They had to be the essence of speed to escape him. They held to the handrail and jumped down the stairs, nearly falling down to each of the landings.

The creature was only one floor above them. He called out in grief and pain with each step he took, but even with his bulk and wound, he was gaining on them. The girl was like a bird. Her feet barely touched the floor as she held the sword carefully at her side moving like flowing water. She was water, Brady thought. *How could she be water*?

Brady was less lithe now, and found himself less adept than he had been only moments before. The speed and agility he had summoned were leaking out of him and he was slowing down. Brady followed the girl into the main lobby toward the glass door that led out into the conflagration of the burning city but away from this prison. That was when he realized that he was bleeding. There was a gash in his leg, about four inches long. He didn't remember receiving the wound. It must have happened in the struggle with Grendel. He was feeling dizzy and the world around him began to slow down into a smaller and smaller spiral.

"Come on," the girl said. She held out her hand, sensing that Brady was having some trouble navigating.

He took her hand and they made their way to the

doorway as Grendel exploded through the stairwell door and began to lope towards them, running on all fours. Each time he put weight on what remained of his right hand, he screamed. Once he stumbled and crashed into a pile of medical supply boxes and wheelchairs, which gave the fleeing pair just enough time to reach the doorway. Brady was barely able to walk but the girl seemed to have superhuman strength and put her shoulder under his, nearly carrying him out. As she ran up the walk and away from the building, the last thing Brady saw was the angry form of Grendel pressed up against the glass of the doorway, his anger as tangible as the rain and as hateful as the fire that now consumed the city around them.

Chapter 12
Kaileigh

The first thing Brady saw when he opened his eyes was the face of the goddess, Athena. Her steel gray eyes, tinged with blue, looked down seriously upon him, studying him. Her face didn't betray any emotion beyond a vague concern. When she saw that he was conscious, she dabbed a wet washcloth to his forehead and put a thermometer in his mouth.

"You've been out for ten hours," she said.

When he tried to respond, she shushed him, "Don't talk while I'm taking your temperature."

The silence was awkward for Brady. He had so many questions to ask. His heartbeat was quickening. She was alive! They had escaped!

The thermometer emitted a beeping sound and the girl withdrew it, examining the results.

"Well, that's better. Fever's down. Now, we need to look at those stitches..." she said as she removed the blanket and looked at his leg.

He was surprised to look down and see six well-sewn stitches on his right thigh, closing a jagged tear in his flesh.

"What? Where did that happen?" he asked.

"You don't remember?" asked the girl quizzically, measuring his response.

Brady thought aloud. "I remember everything that happened at the hospital, I think. I went there to save you, but in the end, you saved me. That monster must have slashed my leg with his claws."

The girl evaluated his statement for a moment and then answered, "Yes, that's right. I guess we could call him a monster, certainly. As for claws, well..."

"Are you okay?" asked Brady urgently.

She didn't respond easily, taking her time to not betray too much too soon.

"I'm in good health, but I don't think I'm okay. Neither are you, not in our current situation."

"What do you mean?" asked Brady, "We're alive. We've escaped. That's pretty good."

"You're wounded and possibly infected. I cleaned your wound thoroughly and I've given you penicillin. I'm pleased to see that you are not allergic to it. I'm afraid that while you were out, most of Bangor burned to the ground. Everyone else is dead and there's just us, huh? This is good?"

Brady answered simply, "Yeah, see, it's that last thing you said that matters the most to me. We're still alive."

She looked away from him. Her raven black hair followed her face over her shoulder, hiding her image from Brady's view.

"It's one of those blessing or curse things, I guess," was her answer.

172

Brady waited for her to continue but he could sense that she was caught up in a perplexity of her own, a private one she didn't wish to share with someone she didn't know. Brady realized then that they were still strangers.

"I'm Brady," he said.

"Brady?" she answered, turning back to face him. "You went to Brewer High, too. I'm...or was...a junior there."

Brady was puzzled. "I know. I recognize you."

"You do?" she asked, her interest piqued.

Brady sheepishly responded, " I saw you in the hallways. You're Kaileigh Tremble."

"Impressive," answered Kaileigh, a small hint of smile in crisis on the edge of her mouth.

"It's hard not to have heard of you. I mean, you had a reputation," Brady explained.

She just looked at him, her head tilted to one side.

Brady immediately tried to correct his original statement.

"I mean, it was a good reputation. You're really smart and creative and everything, but you didn't always do what people expected, right. I mean, I heard you a couple of times arguing with a teacher in the hallway."

She didn't respond to him. Instead, she wiped his head again with the wet washcloth but let her hand rest on his forehead for a moment longer than Brady thought was necessary.

"Well, anyway, I'm really happy to meet you," Brady said.

"Me, too," was her answer.

"Where are we?" he asked.

"My house, in Brewer. I didn't know where else to go."

Brady wondered about the Library, about Max and Benjamin Franklin.

"How'd we get here? I can't remember anything once we left the Entrance to the Underworld."

Kaileigh tilted her head, giving Brady a long, considered look. Then, without changing her expression, she answered his question.

"You were hurt, so I helped you out. You began to black

out on me, but I'd seen you before, driving around the city from the top floor, and I knew you owned a four-wheeler. I saw it there in the parking lot. I threw you over the gas tank and took off. The whole city was on fire and the rain was falling and I could barely see anything, but I went down State Street, over the new bridge and then I was out of danger. I knew he was too frightened to leave the hospital and follow us, goddamn freak."

She had a way with words, Brady thought.

"Yeah...freak," he responded, "I can't believe we got away. He was massive! I don't even remember getting this wound. I feel like an idiot, passing out like that."

She looked at him, considering. How amazing! Just as she was about to give up all hope of surviving another day in that house of death, he arrives just in time and puts his life in the balance so that she could escape. How did he even know she was there?

"I don't know why you passed out, Brady. Maybe you were in shock."

Brady answered, "I bet it was because Grendel's poison infected me."

"You know Dr. Grindle?" she asked in astonishment.

"Who?" asked Brady, not sure what she meant. "Doctor who?"

"Yeah, and he has a tardis and everything. Dr. Grindle is the man we were fighting. Dr. Grindle..."

At that moment, Brady tried to tie together the strings of their two minds. He had fought a monstrous beast, an amalgam of a thousand lucid nightmares and she claimed that the monster was a doctor? She had been in the medical center for weeks being hunted by him. Perhaps she was suffering from some sort of psychosis.

"No, I don't know Dr. Grindle. I'm talking about the beast who calls himself Grendel. His name was written in blood on the side of the Lifeseeker."

Kaileigh asked, "What the heck is the Lifeseeker?"

"Oh, sorry," answered Brady, "it's my modified motorhome. I lived in it until it wasn't safe anymore. Now I live in the Bangor Public Library with my dog, Max, and the books, of course."

"Of course," answered Kaileigh, clearly bewildered but still willing to thread her way through this odd boy's language.

"Dr. Grindle's name was written in blood on the side of your motor home? That doesn't make any sense."

"Oh, it wasn't Dr. Grindle's name. No, it was Grendel, like in Beowulf. You know, the monster."

"G-R-E-N-D-E-L?" she spelled aloud.

"Yes, that's right. That's when I knew it was time to find a safer place. So the library became my fortress. We need to go there, and soon," Brady said emphatically.

No words passed between them for a few moments. Kaileigh was looking out the window, over the river towards Bangor. How marvelous to be with her! he thought. How wonderful to see and speak to another human. He had seen her a hundred times in school, but they had never spoken because he suffered from the common malady of the underclassmen: he was shy and intimidated. Pretty girls always made him nervous and foolish and on the edge of bolting the moment they looked his way.

He remembered her. She often walked alone in the halls of the high school, even though she was heavily involved in theater, forensics, and track. He also remembered seeing her in the office from time to time, but he wasn't sure why. He got the feeling that things weren't always easy for her. Looking at her now, he wondered if she had trouble fitting in, just like him. She wasn't any taller than he was, was athletically built and, Brady thought for the briefest of moments, very beautiful. He had a hundred-thousand questions to ask her, but he found that forming even one question right now seemed impossible. He waited for her to speak.

"How did you survive?" she asked him, still looking out at the burning city across the river.

Brady moved to a sitting position on the couch and, through a brief spasm of pain, replied, "I don't know. I was sick, but I survived. I woke up and everyone was dead."

She nodded.

175

"And you?" he asked.

She turned and made eye contact with him. Her gaze was so intense that Brady found it took all of his attention just to meet it, her eyes boring a hole into his own.

She's so intense, he thought.

Brady could see that her eyes, the color of burnished blue steel, were deep with loss. Immediately he knew that he was pushing too hard, that it was none of his business, even though she had asked first. He didn't want this first conversation to end badly, so he tried to counter his own question.

"Oh, I'm really sorry. I didn't mean to...I mean, you don't have to tell me. It's none of my business."

Kaileigh's stern look changed. The smallest of smiles crept across her face, and she shook her head gently. "No, it's okay. I asked first. Really, we need to know a lot about each other if we're going to survive."

Brady nodded.

She said, "My mother worked in the hospital. She was an administrator and I was a candy-striper. When the order came down from the National Guard for a quarantine, I was already there with my mom. The candy-stripers weren't really supposed to be there, but they needed all the help they could get and Mom wouldn't let me out of her sight. She told me I was safer with her and so we lived in her office. Things deteriorated over the next few days. The hospital had to turn people away because it was already full and there was nothing we could do to help. The National Centers for Disease Control had set up a headquarters in the Parke Building and for awhile, they were the last functioning field center in the country. Everyone was pretty freaked out, including me."

Kaileigh stood up and walked over to the shelf by the television, picked up a photograph of her family and then slowly sat it back down before continuing.

"The plague traveled everywhere. It was a true pandemic, worse than any other virus previously known, worse than the bubonic plague of the Middle Ages. It was even worse than the Spanish Influenza of 1918. The scientists just couldn't get a handle on it, couldn't understand how it had mutated so quickly. They didn't even know for sure how it spread. When the birds began falling from the sky all over the world, it only made the mystery deeper. The leader of all the scientists to arrive at the medical center with the national guard was Dr. Grindle, all the way from Atlanta.

"It was pretty bad when we realized that there weren't any safeguards. Dr. Grindle told us that everyone was going to get this disease, doctors, nurses, everyone, and there we were under our own quarantine order. Over the course of a week almost everyone died. Those who were living tried just to survive in that...awful, insane, hopeless place."

She stopped and looked at him for a long moment before continuing. She showed no emotion except for stony silence.

"I watched everyone die, one right after another and I..." she stopped and took a deep breath, looked away to break eye contact with Brady, and completed her thought, "I was with my mom when she died. I didn't get sick! Not one little symptom! How could that be? I should have been sick just because I was surrounded by so many infected bodies, but I didn't. I can't figure out why."

Brady asked quietly, "So why didn't you leave?"

Her expression changed from one of regret and loss to one of frustration when she answered, "I would have, but he wouldn't let me go."

"Grendel?"

"*Dr. Grindle.*" she corrected, "Amazingly, the man who was in charge of the whole rescue operation, Humanity's last hero, whose job it was to save us all, survived to watch everyone else die. Just like me, he didn't get sick and when he found out that I was still alive, it sent him over the edge. He tried to kill me. He just kept trying to kill me, over and over again, until you showed up. Then he tried to kill you."

Brady said nothing, knowing that she was working through an emotional pressure ridge within herself, not wanting to distract or deter her. Eventually, she stopped staring straight ahead into her memory and spoke again.

177

"I ran from him, hid in all kinds of places, but it was like he never slept. He kept finding me, shouting at me, throwing things, hitting me. But I was too quick for him. I ran. I hid. He almost caught me, time and again, but I knew the place a lot better than he did. I practically grew up in that hospital. I went higher and higher until I found that the top floor was the one place he seemed to fear."

"The top floor," said Brady.

"The Maternity Ward. I don't know why, but he just couldn't bring himself to enter it. I think it hurt him to be on that ward. So I lived there these past few weeks, eating from the refrigerator, breaking into the vending machines, sleeping when I could. Fortunately, it was the one floor that was nearly empty of bodies. But whenever I tried to leave, he was there."

Brady said, "He was on the top floor when I found him."

"Yes, he was," she said, a tinge of wonder lingering in her voice. Then she asked inquisitively, "How did you know about me?"

Brady was unsure how to respond. Already he was beginning to suspect that she didn't see the world as he did, that she couldn't detect the subtle and not-so-subtle changes that already were resounding throughout creation. *Maybe, he thought, I should be more careful with my words, so that she doesn't think I'm totally crazy, off my rocker, a few pounds short of a load...*

"Call it a hunch," he said. "I knew someone was in there. I could hear him screaming from outside. I thought maybe someone needed my help and, hey, I was right."

She looked at him doubtfully and only said, "You should know right away that I'm really good at finding the truth. In fact, I rock at it. So don't lie to me, ever. We can't make friends that way. Now...how did you know I was there?" she demanded.

Brady succumbed, knowing that he was about to appear foolish, stupid and crazy, like he always did in front of girls. He hadn't missed the judgment of others during his isolation and time in the Abandonment and now it came back with a vengeance. She was judging him.

"A dead girl told me," he answered simply.

"A dead girl?" she asked, her mouth agape.

"Yes. Her name is...I mean was, Susan."

"A dead girl named Susan told you that I was being held captive in the hospital?"

Brady shook his head affirmatively. An eternity of silence encompassed them, her steel eyes boring into his soul, inspecting him and judging him. Amazingly, her next words both lightened and worried Brady.

"I believe you," she said. "I mean, I believe you think that's what happened and I don't care if it's real or not, Brady. You came to the hospital and fought to save me and for that, I'm very grateful." She took his hands into hers and looked him in the eye. "Thanks."

His face beamed and he met her gaze, saying simply, "No problem. Rescuing damsels in distress is one of my specialties."

She smiled. "Don't get too cocky. I believe *I* was the one who dragged *you* out of that hospital."

He returned her smile and didn't say another thing for a long while.

The strange thing was that even though he had faced death, gone into the monster's lair and borne a wound that might have been laced with the angry virulence of Grendel's hatred, it really had been nothing compared to having someone to talk with, someone to just *be* with. It seemed like a fair price to pay.

As the day passed, Kaileigh and Brady talked. With every passing hour, Brady felt his strength returning. He could swear that as he engaged in conversation, the pain seemed to diminish. It was as though simply being with Kaileigh was a kind of healing, a tonic to his soul. He hadn't realized how lonely he had been until now. They ate crackers and canned ham, cheese and some fruit jerky from Brady's stash of food on Rocinante. After lunch, Kaileigh seemed refreshed, less distant and she was full of questions.

"How did you survive? What did you eat?" she asked.

"Oh, food's not a problem, not at all. Fresh food can be

hard to get, but there's a ton of canned and preserved foods in supermarkets and houses, peoples' pantries, you know. I made a map of the places with food and I even created a few stashes around the two cities in case of emergencies. I found a good spring with fresh water."

"And you say you lived in a motorhome? That sounds like a good idea. Nice," she commented.

"Thanks, but I had to move when the dogs became a problem." He made sure not to say *weredogs*. "They run in packs and anything is food to them. They're dangerous at night."

"So you live in the Library?"

"That's right. Max and I live there," he said, and when he mentioned the dog's name, he suddenly realized that in his haste to leave last night, he had locked the dog inside. Images of the burning city flooded his mind as his heart began to race and he imagined the worst, that the library and all the books had burned down, with his boon companion inside.

"We have to go!" said Brady emphatically as he rose from the couch and found his gloves and jacket.

"Whoa, you're not going anywhere," she said, "Not until your leg is better. I can go."

"No, I need to go. You don't understand," Brady insisted. "Besides, my leg feels much better. Perfect, in fact."

He pulled up his pant leg and showed Kaileigh the wound. Inexplicably, it was gone. All that was apparent were the stitches that she had sewn there a few hours ago.

"What? How did that heal so fast?" she asked. Her voice intoned a hint of incredulity.

Brady was so intent upon leaving that he simply said what he thought was responsible for his rapid healing. He knew it wouldn't make sense to her, but he felt the truth of it in a bone-deep way.

"The wound was full of hate. At least, a kind of viral hate, the kind that covers Grendel. It entered my body, but you drove it out. The penicillin wasn't my cure. You were. You did the trick. Now, can we go? I need to check on Max."

180

Kaileigh's mind couldn't grasp the idea that was thrust upon her, but she tried as hard as she could to maintain a grip on the leadership in this situation. The boy had no injury that she could see. He should still be seeping blood. To her memory the cut was at least four inches long and about half an inch deep. It shouldn't have caused him such immediate trouble, which also puzzled her. Either he was some sort of evolutionary freak blessed with the ability to rapidly heal himself, some kind of latter-day Wolverine, or she was having her own break with reality. It was a feeling she would come to know very often in the next few weeks.

Much of the city was in ruins. Plumes of smoke still spiraled into high columns across the landscape. The smell of charcoal and smoke permeated everything, but the rain that had followed the violence of the lightning storm had successfully put out most of what it had ignited. The monochromatic ruins made Brady's heart sink as he navigated Rocinante towards downtown, towards the library and what awaited him there.

Kaileigh held onto his waist and felt the enormity of the situation settling on her shoulders: such destruction, such decimation, such loss. Running through her mind were the events from the last few hours. She hadn't slept in so long. She was weary and soul-battered. After escaping with Brady from the clutches of Dr. Grindle's insane attack, she found herself rescuing her own rescuer, tending to his wounds. Once that was completed, she had done something she hadn't disclosed to Brady.

He was passed out on her couch and she was full of dread and concern. She had to see for herself, so while Brady slept, she left him there, taking Rocinante on an errand of her own. She drove the four-wheeler to Bob's house. They had last seen each other just before the quarantine had been implemented but she had managed to talk with him on her cell phone for a few days after that. Then she lost contact. She didn't know what she would find inside his house. She had every expectation to find something there she didn't truly want to see, but she knew that she could not live with herself a moment longer without knowing what had happened to Bob. Any hope that he might have survived lived only in the quietest, smallest portion of her heart, a flame barely burning in the wind of change.

At the house on Parker Street, as at every other house in the city, there was nothing but silence and stillness. The door was locked, but she knew where the family kept the spare key. Strangely, there was a red blotch of paint spattered all over the inside of the window, which looked frighteningly like blood spatter. A paint ball, perhaps? Once inside, there was no longer any doubt of what she would find. After only the briefest of explorations, perhaps a minute, she knew the final fate of her boyfriend, his mother and father.

All of them were dead in their beds, in various states of moulder and decay. She was sorry she had come here. As she sat on the front steps, her face buried in her hands, she realized the awesome definition that the word 'alone' now held for her. Her mother had died in her arms. There was no one left, unless her brother had managed to survive somewhere in the Washington, D.C., area where he attended college. With the communication systems down, there was no way of telling. What of Bob? Oh, she had loved him. She had told him so, even before the beginning of the end. She had truly liked him, as well. Bob, who she'd even imagined spending the rest of her life with, and whose strong arms and deep eyes might have carried her through even the hardest of times, was nothing against the onslaught of the viral pandemic.

She thought about Brady. He had managed to survive when no one else had. How had he known she was there, imprisoned by that madman? How did he know exactly when to appear, just as her defenses were failing and Dr. Grindle's eagerness to destroy her was nearing its zenith? She wondered as the tears fell down her dirty, roughened cheeks. She cried for a long time because she was alone and crying was something she absolutely never did if even one other human being was around. She was not secretive so much as solitary, able to walk alone, if she had to. Sometimes she even preferred her 'alone' time to time spent with others, but as she broke down she remembered every person's face in her life as it flashed into her mind and she would have given much just to see them one more time and tell them the truth: that she loved them, needed their company and desperately didn't wish to be without them for the rest of her life. Now, as she held on to him and surveyed the damage done to this city, she wondered if anything would ever even begin to resemble the idea of *normal*, if there was a place for either of them in this new, empty, falling-down world.

When Brady saw that the library remained untouched, he let out a yell and twisted the throttle on Rocinante so that Kaileigh had to squeeze him hard to remain seated. He parked right in front of the building and there, on the main steps, was Hugin the raven, sitting placidly on the quarried stone, looking calm and cool. Brady called to him as he raced around the corner to the side entrance.

"Hey, you crazy bird! It's good to see you! Thanks for your help last night!"

"Ragnarok!" croaked the raven.

Brady unlocked the padlock and entered the library. Meeting him at the door was Max, jumping on him, walking on his hind legs, barking and licking Brady's face.

"Hey boy! Am I happy to see you!" shouted Brady.

Kaileigh entered behind Brady and when Max saw her, he immediately abandoned Brady and began lavishing all of his affection upon this new person, whoever she was. It was clear to Brady, from watching Kaileigh's reaction, that she was happy to be greeted in such a fashion.

"Hey, Max, give her some room. Come on boy, let her be," Brady said.

"Oh, he's so...friendly! Aren't you, boy. Yes, you are! Oh," she laughed, " I'm pleased to make your acquaintance, too."

Brady watched with a smile on his face as Max and Kaileigh began what he hoped would be a long friendship. The library had been spared. Ben Franklin had been spared. His immediate impulse was to pick up the volume and explain everything to the good doctor, but he fought against this idea because, again, he didn't know what Kaileigh would think of him. He could only lie about the way he saw things, knew things, for so long before the truth slipped out. For now, he would try to keep things as normal as possible for this strange chance at not being alone.

"Let me feed Max and then I'll show you around," Brady said.

"Mind if I look around a little on my own," she asked.

"Nope. Make yourself at home. I did."

Kaileigh saw Brady's stashes of food, his piles of tools, supplies and items whose purpose eluded her. She walked into the computer room and sat in front of one of the terminals, put her fingers on the keyboard longingly and gazed into the black eye of the monitor that stared at her. *This feels stupid*, she thought. No more Youtube, no more Google, no more Facebook, no more instant messaging. Nothing but the outward appearance of technology that no longer worked; a husk, a shed skin.

After touring the main floor, Brady found her and said, "Hey, wanna see something I've been working on. It might make you feel better."

"That would be good," she replied.

He led her up to the room at the very top of the library: the cupola. It was a wide open space with some items of historical significance, some statuary and paintings, and to the side, a large room with a stage. There, taped to a rolling blackboard, was Brady's handmade map of the area.

She was drawn to it. A smile crossed her face, as it often did when she was engaged in an academic or intellectual pursuit.

"So this is the hospital, The Entrance to Hades, and what are these green dots?"

"Food and supplies. Sometimes they're houses, garages, stores, warehouses."

"What are the red dots?" she asked.

"Tombs. I went to these places and marked them with red paint if they were 'occupied' by dead bodies. I've seen enough of those to last me a thousand lifetimes."

Kaileigh was adept at putting two and two together and realized that Brady had already been to Bob's house and had

184

marked it as such. How many places had he scoped out and marked? The map seemed to indicate hundreds of red and green dots.

"This is amazing!" she said after tracing the routes Brady had drawn in three-dimensional fashion, almost like a cartoon, with her index finger.

"You've really been busy!"

"Well, to tell the truth, there wasn't much else to do. If I just sat around and waited to die, I probably would have," was his reply.

"So this is how you spend your days – exploring?"

"No, not every day. I never go out at night if I can help it, but sometimes I have to. The dog packs, remember? I explore, plan, prepare, and then I come back here and read...you know, talk to the books?"

"Talk to the books?" she asked, raising one eyebrow.

Knowing he had misspoken, he quickly corrected himself. "Oh, a metaphor. The books kind of talk to me, if you know what I mean."

"Sure..."

"I listen to music, and I run the generators a couple of hours every day. I have a bank of batteries all charged up and I can even cook on the electric stove in the basement. I wish this place had a washer and a dryer, but it does have an electric water heater and the water is still running, so I can offer you a hot shower and a good meal."

Kaileigh stared at him and said nothing, for no words could even begin to express the surprise she felt at his words. How had this boy achieved so much? A hot shower? A hot meal? The ideas seemed as foreign to her as walking on the moon.

"Are you hungry? Give me about an hour and I'll cook you some pasta with meat sauce and some canned peaches. We can go out and pick raspberries tomorrow. I know a place right in the city. People planted gardens out there before the Abandonment. We can harvest some of the early vegetables, too."

"The Abandonment?" she asked,

"Oh, sorry. I have a habit of naming and renaming

185

things. I don't know why I do it, but after I do, things seem to make more sense. It's like the old world doesn't exist anymore and the new one kind of *needs* these new names. I mean, I think it's my *job* to rename things. I hope that's okay with you," he said hopefully.

She cocked her head back and forth and said, "Why not? It makes as much sense to call things by new names as old ones. The people who knew all the old names are gone anyway. We might as well take ownership. That's what you've begun to do, isn't it?"

"What?"

"Take ownership. You've drawn a new map. You've given things new names. You're planning to survive, aren't you?" she asked.

Brady considered her question carefully. Of course he was planning to survive. Who wouldn't?

"Well, aren't *you*? Don't you want to *live*?" he asked in response.

She looked out of the window toward the smoke columns still rising in the distance.

"I'm not so sure we have a choice."

Brady didn't understand her answer and thought it was the better part of valor to simply ignore it.

"I plan to live. In fact, I plan to live well and for a long, long time," was his reply.

Brady started the diesel generator outside of the library. He dutifully checked the oil and fluid levels, as written in the manual he had found in the head librarian's file cabinet. He set the timer for two hours and pressed the starter switch. It was a very large generator encased in a large yellow metal enclosure the size of a truck capable of fully powering the library in case of power loss. He had been using it for a while now and the fuel level had hardly moved. Then he went back inside, tripped the circuit breaker to the hot water heater so she could shower and began to prepare a meal for them both.

He spent a furious hour in the kitchen creating a feast for them both from his personal store of provisions. It would be *their* store of provisions from now on and he was glad that he had toiled so diligently to be selective as he had. He had taken special care to choose foodstuffs that would last the seasons. He had as much canned food as anyone could ever eat in a year, but already he was getting tired of them. He kept dried goods like flour, yeast, sugar, pasta, powdered milk and eggs in great sealed plastic tubs. He also had three twenty-five pound bags of potatoes leaning against the wall. He found himself eating lot of dried fruits and found that a dried prune was a delicacy if he just gave it half a chance. Initially Brady didn't take the time to cook anything, but he did know how to cook. He rather enjoyed it, especially now that there was someone else to eat with. He could imagine using the Dutch ovens over a slow fire cooking things like stews and monkey bread. He knew that he needed fresh fruits and vegetables, but these were seasonal things and he knew that the gardens he had found would suffice for this year, but next year he would have to till the ground, plant the seeds and then hope that those seeds would sprout. He would have to begin living the old way. He would have to learn how.

Kaileigh emerged from the shower, thankful that someone had the foresight to put a shower in a library. It was not used by the general public, of course. It was in the basement, as was the kitchen and some general purpose rooms. Recently the place had been renovated, bringing it into the next century and beyond and she was impressed that some well-meaning engineer thought of adding a shower to a library. It was lucky that she was about the same physical size as Brady, if a little less muscular. He had given her a pair of jeans with a belt, a T-shirt and a flannel long sleeve shirt to wear over the T-shirt, for which she was grateful. He was good with details, she thought.

Night was already falling when Brady served the meal on the library table in the recent acquisitions room. He took the trouble to serve her and she let him. Although she was hungry, she found that she had to eat slowly and deliberately, having survived on very meager rations for the last month. Where she had been surrounded by death and danger, she

187

was now safe, sated and to her great surprise, very tired. She began to nod as Brady tried to make conversation about what they needed to do tomorrow, pondering what their next steps should be.

Unable to focus any longer, she said, simply, "If I don't get some sleep right away, my face is going to end up in the spaghetti. I'm exhausted."

Brady looked up, trying to be accommodating. "Oh, no problem. You can sleep on my mat. It's really comfortable. It's one of those mattresses that automatically inflates when you unroll it. Its baby-bear, you know?"

"Baby bear?" Kaileigh was tired.

"You know, not too hard, not too soft. It's just right."

She laughed. It was a small thing, but in his world, it filled the empty spaces and made him feel strangely content. Kaileigh was also surprised at her gaiety. There had been moments in the last few weeks when she thought that she would never laugh again.

"No, Brady. I can't take your bed. You've done enough. I'll camp out somewhere else. Right now, I think I could sleep on a bed of nails."

Brady knew of one place. "Follow me," he said. "There's another place where you can get a good night's sleep. There's a leather couch upstairs."

They walked up the marble stairs, past the gargoyle given to the library by one of its benefactors. It sat there squatting, immobile and protective. Brady had spoken to it before, fearing it might need to be 'moved' outside, but he discovered, much to his surprise, that its name was Gregoire and although it looked medieval, it was made in Hoboken. Brady gave the gargoyle a dirty look and it blinked back at him, giving the slightest hint of a peeved expression. The last thing Brady needed right now was a talking gargoyle.

The top floor of the Bangor Public library was surmounted by a large, circular glass and copper cupola, a kind of round skylight. Around the inner rim were fine plaster castings, twelve ornate plaques with names, some of which Brady knew and some of which were unknown to him. He knew Hawthorne to be Nathaniel Hawthorne and

188

Longfellow to be Henry Wadsworth Longfellow, a fellow Mainer. He was unsure of some of the others, like Holmes, who he imagined to be Sherlock Holmes but in fact was Oliver Wendell Holmes.

There, against the wall, was a wooden couch covered with red leather. It sat behind a red velvet rope held up by two brass stands. On a sign next to the couch were written the words, "Please Only Look. This couch is an important historical artifact to be preserved. Over time, the simple act of sitting on it would wear, and compromise the integrity of the original surface. The library staff thanks you for your cooperation."

Kaileigh smirked and said wryly, "Now there's something you don't see every day. A couch of historical significance."

Brady laughed and then walked over to the couch, pointing to a small brass plaque screwed to the back of it. It read, "Last used by HANNIBAL HAMLIN, U.S. Vice President, Tarratine Club President, July 4, 1891."

"I still don't get why this is historical. I mean, how many vice-presidents sit down and then have the chair put behind a rope so no one can ever sit in it, ever again?" Kaileigh wondered aloud.

"I think he died on it," answered Brady.

"Oh? I can't sleep on that! Besides, maybe I shouldn't"

"Oh, I don't think anyone would mind, not anymore. After all, this whole library is an 'important historical artifact to be preserved."

"Quite right," said a man's voice, audible only to Brady's ear. He had heard some of the books speaking to him since he returned, but he had never heard a painting talk to him before. There, behind and to the left of the couch, was the portrait of Hannibal Hamlin, vice president under Abraham Lincoln during his first term as president. Had Lincoln been assassinated during his first term, as many people in the South would have liked, Hamlin would have been the next president of the United States, not Johnson. He was an imposing presence, and Brady was sad that Kaileigh was unable to hear him and he wondered why she couldn't.

189

Maybe it would just take some time. He would have to speak in such a way so that she might not suspect he was having a conversation with the painting.

"I don't think Vice-president Hamlin would mind if you slept on this couch." said Brady.

"Of course I wouldn't" muttered the old statesman, "silly thing, to preserve a couch someone sat on before he died. I mean, if they preserved that, why not the pot I last pissed in. The audacity of people!"

"I don't know," Kaileigh said, "I mean, it looks kind of stuffy and I bet it smells."

"Like cigars," said Hamlin, "and probably whiskey, too. But it is a fine leather couch, if I do say so myself. I would be honored to have the young lady sleep on it."

"I bet it's comfortable, though. Go on, try it. The vice-president won't mind," Brady said.

"Of course he wouldn't. He's dead," Kaileigh answered.

"Well, there's no need to state the obvious!" muttered Hannibal curtly. "Still, she's got a good point and there's no disputing it. A dead man needs no couch."

Brady moved the velvet rope and she sat down on it. It wasn't the most comfortable thing she ever sat upon, and it was a little stiff, but she lay down and closed her eyes.

"I think I could sleep on this," she said.

Brady looked up at the painting, who nodded slightly, the corner of his mouth turning up in a weak smile.

"A damn sight better than me dying on it. Things should be put to use."

"I'll go get you a pillow and some blankets."

When he got back, he saw that Max had curled on the floor next to Kaileigh. She was already asleep. Brady brought her bedding, a battery-powered lantern and a bottle of water.

Before he left, she awoke.

"Brady, thanks for coming for me. He was almost there, nearly killed me. He would have, too. I wasn't safe on the ward any longer. If you hadn't come along, I'd be dead right now."

Brady shrugged and said, "No problem. If it's any

190

consolation, Grendel was very strong. I'm impressed that you kept away from him as long as you did."

"Brady," she said wonderingly, "are you okay? I mean," she said through tired eyes, "How have you been able to keep your spirits up in this...dead world?"

"Oh, keeping spirits doesn't seem to be a problem for me," he answered. "Besides, the world's not dead. Just the people. The world is full of things. Things kind of come to life when there aren't any people around."

"I'm sorry. What do you mean?" she asked, her eyelids getting lower with each breath.

Brady searched for a way to explain it to her simply. "Before the virus, did you ever spend any time alone somewhere?"

"Our house...oh, and our camp up at the lake."

"At the camp, when no one else was around, did the world seem a little more like it was...there? Did the sun shine a little brighter? Did the wind feel a little fresher when you were all alone? Did the birds sing a little louder and did every little sound spook you a little?"

She mused. "Sometimes at the lake, when mom left me there because she had to work, time kind of disappeared and I loved it there. Everything slowed down. Even the little things seemed better; a can of coke, an ice cream cone, a rerun on television. Sometimes as night, every little sound seemed like someone was trying to break into the camp," she said.

"Exactly! The world is still here. That's why I survived. I concentrated on what remained, not what was missing."

"Good," she said, drifting off to sleep. "That's good. Night..."

Brady found himself looking at her longer than he should have. There was more than a slight fascination with her, apart from the obvious fact that he was no longer alone. Back when they walked the hallways of the high school, he had always thought that she was the slightest bit distant. Now, in this world and time, he saw strength, intelligence, and he dared admit it to himself, beauty. Since the Abandonment, beauty wasn't something Brady had spent any time contemplating. Was there something here that hadn't been here before? If all the other things were somehow in his mind, she, at least, was real. She was more than real and he didn't mean she was drop-dead gorgeous, either. He imagined that she was the most precious part of his life now- a friend.

The picture of Hannibal Hamlin simply said, "Stop staring at her, young man. It isn't seemly."

"Oh, sorry," he said quietly in response. He patted Max on the head and went back downstairs to clean up the remains of the feast.

Kaileigh dreamed. She was no longer in the hospital. Instead, she wandered the world alone, looking for things, seeking human contact. Everywhere she looked there were the empty places where people used to dwell, long paths that no one but she walked, and vistas of sky that only she beheld. In her dream, she had the strange feeling that she was being watched, as though from every window in every house, sets of hollow eyes followed her. Occasionally she would feel the hairs on the back of her neck rise and she would quickly turn and see a human form fade from her sight.

She moved from street to street in a strange town she had never visited before yet she *knew* where she was, somehow. This was a town of the dream world, a town that only partially existed because it was inside of her mind, but she knew it existed elsewhere, too. While she investigated, the feeling that she wasn't alone grew and intensified until she knew she was somehow on the road that led *homeward*. With each step, the sky seemed to grow more blue, the clouds seemed more brilliantly white and the wind caressed her skin while birdsong filled her ears. It was as though the world was coming into focus for the first time in her life.

There was a small cottage on the edge of a meadow surrounded by flowers, rock gardens and weeping willow trees bending down to earth, their tendril branches waving at her in the breeze. What was this place? Surely she had never been here before, but why did it feel so welcoming. The pebbled path beneath her feet led to the doorway and as she moved closer, she saw a person. It was a woman, tall and long-haired, wearing a long brown dress. Kaileigh moved more quickly and began running towards this woman and as she did, the woman opened her arms and they embraced.

"Welcome back," whispered the woman in brown into Kaileigh's ear.

"Where am I?" asked Kaileigh.

The woman let her embrace slacken and she gestured to the wide world around them. As she did so, it seemed to expand to infinite proportions. Kaileigh tuned and took in the view, the mountains in the distance, the long, green valleys in between. It was beautiful.

"You, my dear, have come home. You always do," said the woman in brown.

That was when Kaileigh realized something was wrong. This world, those mountains, valleys and this cottage – they were all under water.

Kaileigh awoke to the sound of Brady talking to someone. She quietly arose, not even rousing Max, and tiptoed down the marble stairs in near darkness. She glanced at her watch to find that it was three o'clock in the morning.

"I don't know if she sees things the way I do," she heard him say.

"Give her some time. She might begin to view things as they are, by and by," said another voice. She kept creeping closer. Was there another person in the library besides Brady?

"I think we might need to fortify the lower levels. The weredogs are getting smarter. Soon they'll figure out a way to pry off the plywood I nailed over the lower windows. It'll be a lot easier with her help."

"Life will be a lot more interesting now that you have someone to share it with. A word of advice?"

"Sure."

"Listen to her. She is obviously resourceful. She may not see things as you do, but she sees things in her own light, a light you might need as the darkness continues to fall."

Brady glanced up and saw her standing there in the shadows and quickly closed the book.

"Oh, hi!" he said, "Sorry. Did I wake you?"

"I heard you talking and I...is there someone else here?" she asked plainly.

"Oh...I was reading out loud. Sometimes I do that. You know, I read dramatically. It helps me when I can't sleep. I do different voices for different characters, that sort of thing."

She nodded in understanding.

"Sure, Brady. I understand. I mean, you haven't heard another human voice for a long time. I used to talk to myself once in a while, too. It's okay."

"Right," he said, obviously relieved.

"So, I guess I'll go back to bed, then," she said.

"Okay then," he said, "I think I will too. The sunrise is only a couple of hours away. I'll make us a mean breakfast in the morning, and then...we can see how much of the city has burned down."

After she climbed the stairs back to her 'room' Brady opened *The Autobiography of Benjamin Franklin* and said, "That was close."

"Undoubtedly. She obviously has heightened senses. I would warrant a guess that with the amount of marble, stone, plaster and iron in this building, the chances of her hearing our conversation from all the way in the cupola was small. Perhaps she has changed in ways different from the ways you have changed. Perhaps she has developed a more acute sense of hearing, like a hunter. Watch her for any out of the ordinary abilities. She may be even more remarkable than you already think, Brady."

Kaileigh lay her head back down on the pillow and closed her eyes, relieved that all was well. She could feel the weight of the last few weeks lifting from her chest. She had managed to survive and she knew that it was nothing short of miraculous. She hadn't known she had it in her to be so intuitive, so able to outguess Dr. Grindle's moves and traps. Suddenly she was here, safe, quiet, even peaceful. She let the thoughts she hadn't allowed herself to think roil and arise

194

in her mind randomly as sleep began to visit her again. Her mother's face, her last conversation with Bob, the face of Dr. Grindle, the general dread in the hospital when the quarantine had been established. She remembered her bedroom, the color of the wallpaper, and of all things, the last time she watched Spongebob Squarepants.

As the blessed silence of sleep began to cover her like a blanket, she opened her eyes once more and as the earliest ray of dawn came through the windows at the top of the cupola she could have sworn that the alabaster statue, a Grecian woman arrayed in a chiton with the word "Truth" on a brass plaque on her pedestal turned its head slightly and looked at her.

Then she fell into the darkness and slept.

Chapter 13
The Quantum Theory of Fiction

Kaileigh slept more deeply than she had since the great falling of the Abandonment. She slept the sleep of the dead. She journeyed into the depths of the darkness behind her eyelids until she was a million miles away and safe, at last. How she had been rescued, this strange boy, and the unlikeliness of their situation made it all the more difficult to imagine that she hadn't been dreaming all along. When she awoke, it was to a new day, the sun filtering down from the light of the library's cupola filling the white marbled space with a soft wash of warmth. When she opened her eyes, she felt like she might have just awakened on some goddess's couch on Mount Olympus. The statue of Thought seemed to be looking back at her with alabaster eyes, and Kaileigh could have sworn that it blinked.

She put her feet on the cold floor and ran her fingers through her hair, taking in a deep breath. This was safety, she thought, when she didn't need to be on her guard, always aware that a madman was actively seeking her death. She listened carefully to the sounds around her. Was that Brady's voice she heard from downstairs? Was he talking to himself again? Hadn't he told her that they were the only survivors?

Would he have awakened her if, somehow in the night, another survivor showed up on the library's doorstep? She slipped on her shoes and began to descend the rounded marble staircase down to the main lobby.

She could distinctly hear Brady speaking again, although she could only hear his voice. Poor boy, she thought, he's been alone so long and seen so much death that he's gone a little crazy, talking to himself. She wondered why she hadn't gone around the bend herself when she heard a voice with a distinctly French accent speak to her.

"Allo, mademoiselle! You 'ave slept well, eh?" said the voice in a low and somewhat suave timbre.

Startled, she scanned the area but couldn't see anyone.

"Who said that?" she asked nervously.

"Eh? I did! Gregoire! No,no,no,down 'ere, mademoiselle!" replied the voice.

She looked down to see the squatting stone figure of a concrete reproduction gargoyle licking his hand and slicking back his invisible hair. A grin that could have melted glass stretched across his face.

He reached his stubby arms forward and flexed his stony fingers, his first experiment with his new found digits. "Zat feels so refreshing, eh?"

Kaileigh stared at him in disbelief. Then the gargoyle looked her up and down and said, "I see you 'ave given me a reason for living, eh? A beauty you are, too, no? Mademoiselle, I am Gregoire and I keep watch over ze upper reaches. I watch. I don't do a zing, but zat is my bizness. If somezing 'appens, I scream. You will 'ear," he had said in an instructive, scolding tone. "You feel like I am giving you the creepy look? Ah, but you would be mistaken. I am a gargoyle - we give ze creepy looks to everyone. Zat is what we were made to do!"

He grimaced and added, "My bowels are like crushed rock. Oh, I need a laxative! Do you 'ave any limestone?"

Kaileigh wanted to scream but when she opened her mouth, she found she couldn't draw breath. Stymied by the idea of a talking, moving piece of stone, she became stone herself, unable to talk or move.

197

"I know. I 'ave this effect on all women. I cannot 'elp it. You are marveled at me, yes?"

Finally, after a long moment passed, she forced words from out of her throat.

"What the hell are you?" she said, trying to catch her breath.

"I am ze guardian of zis place. I protected you last night from all ze world. You slept well, no?"

"But...but you can talk..." she uttered.

"Oui, and zat is not all I can do, ha ha ha...I am a Frenchman, after all..." said Gregoire with a snicker in his demon throat.

"Brady!" she shouted at the top of her lungs, "Brady!"

In a matter of seconds, Brady arrived at the foot of the stairs and took stock of the situation. It was as clear as a bell to him that perhaps he should have been more up front with Kaileigh about the state of things before she went to sleep last night.

"Yes?" he asked innocently.

"What? What do you mean 'yes'? This...thing...is talking to me!"

"It is?" He was pleasantly surprised, even relieved. If she heard statues talk, then either they were both insane or neither of them were.

He continued."Oh! Yes,it is! Has he been appropriate? Sometimes he's a little mouthy."

"Eh? Me?" replied the gargoyle. "I am ze soul of 'onor and respectability! I never..." sputtered the squatting stone guardian. He crossed his well-muscled arms and turned his head, staring a hole through the wall.

Brady smiled bravely at Kaileigh's frightened and confused face. How was he to explain all of this, he wondered? How could he make sense of how the world had changed?

"I know. He's a talking statue. I see a lot of that lately."

Kaileigh's eyes widened even more. "You mean there are more talking statues?"

"Well...yeah, a couple," he managed.

"I don't see what ze problem is. I was merely being

198

polite to 'er. 'Zere is no reason to be so huffy! Humph!" he said, and he crossed his little stone arms and turned his head away indignantly.

"Oh, I see," Brady said quietly, a smirk washing over his face. "He likes you."

Kaileigh walked past Gregoire's squatting form, hugging the wall tightly as she did so.

"Who were you talking to, just now?" she asked directly.

"What? Me? Just now?" asked Brady with false innocence.

"Don't lie to me! I know you're hiding something from me!"

Brady saw clearly that he had no choice but to tell her the truth, however improbable and insane it might sound.

"Okay, just hear me out. This is gonna sound weird, but it's the truth, at least as I see it, okay? The world's changed. We've changed. There are monsters, now. There are also statues that can talk. That person you heard me talking to just now? You heard me talking to a book," he began.

"A book? How can you talk to a book?" she asked.

"Oh, it's easy. Just take it in your hands and open it up," he replied.

"No doubt. That's what my English teachers always told me except, it's wrong. The book talks to *you*," she replied.

"Yes," he answered, "but sometimes you have to wake it up."

From his back pocket the paperback edition of the *The Autobiography of Benjamin Franklin* began to speak. "She is shrewd and cunning, this one. No beating about the bush. Tell her the truth, Brady, but say it well. Don't stumble over your words. From a slip of the foot you may soon recover, but a slip of the tongue you may never get over."

Brady anticipated that she couldn't hear Ben, at least not yet, but he considered his next words well. Kaileigh was a force to be reckoned with and even though he didn't want to admit it, he couldn't take his gaze from her. She was something more than a mere girl, but what?

"But how can books talk? How can statues come to life and walk the earth? Brady? Are you seriously listening to me? None of this makes sense."

"I know it seems wrong and that it doesn't make any sense," Brady replied, "but I've been thinking about it for a long, long time, trying to make a theory where everything works. I think I get it."

Wide-eyed and still spooked by the words of the gargoyle, Kaileigh said, "Really? Enlighten me! Explain it. I'm all ears."

Brady offered her his hand and smiled. "Come on, follow me. I think this will make more sense in another room."

Impatiently, she moved toward him and only inches from his face she urged, "Another room? What's wrong with this one, Brady?"

"We're on the stairs," Brady replied, "but it might make more sense if we were surrounded by books."

She glared at him but he just kept smiling, awaiting her reply. Realizing that this was his game and his place, she had little choice. She slapped her hand angrily into his and led him away into the new fiction room.

There was a long handmade ash table in the center with eight handmade chairs surrounding it. Lining the walls ten feet high, with accompanying rolling ladders, were the newest and final works of fiction that this library would ever acquire, all arranged alphabetically according to the authors' last name. An *objet d'art* resembling a steam-punked airplane was suspended over the table.

Kaileigh pulled out a chair and sat down at the head of the table, crossing her arms and pursing her lips in frustration. Brady sat at the far end, as far away from her as he could manage.

"Everything I'm about to tell you is going to sound crazy, but you've got to remember the monster we fought in the hospital. I know you think it was a human, a doctor, but I saw a *monster*. It was real and it wasn't *human*. In the world of *before,* monsters were things in books and movies, from the imagination. In the Abandonment, monsters walk the earth. I don't know why, but the world has changed. Statues move and some talk. Books can speak to us in words we can hear, not just in words we read, and there are other things, like ghosts that whisper to me when I sleep and a whole graveyard full of spectres waiting around like they need to go on a journey except that the train is late."

She felt in her heart that Brady was creating a scenario that made sense to him, however unlikely, but there had been a small talking Frenchman in the form of a gargoyle hitting on her just a minute ago on the stairs. This turn of events changed her perspective.

"I know you're not crazy, but I was shut up in a building for the last few weeks trying to stay one step ahead of Dr. Grindle. I watched everyone die. I didn't sleep through it, so if any one of us ought to be crazy, it's me and I'm not crazy. These things we are seeing don't make any sense. They simply *can't* be real."

"But they *are*," he said simply, letting the idea slowly sink in. "Everything we see is real," Brady said, beginning his explanation. "Everything that can be imagined is also real."

Kaileigh shook her head. "No, Brady, it isn't. I can imagine that you're a white rabbit and that my name is Alice, but that doesn't make it real."

Brady continued to smile at her and she thought to herself, *I'm gonna wipe that grin right off your face, buddy, if you don't stop talking like an idiot.*

"Let me explain. You promise not to get angry if I explain?" he asked.

"Yes, but only if you keep it quick."

"Promise."

"Good."

Brady walked around the table, every so often pulling out a book from the shelf and setting it down. He found a few and set them up in a straight line in front of Kaileigh.

He began. "Each one of these books is a story that came from the mind of its author. Each of them takes place somewhere. Each one has a setting. We were taught in school that a story is fiction, unless it was a work of nonfiction. If the author does a good job, when we read the book, our imaginations bring that world to life. We go to Wonderland. We travel to Mordor with Sam and Frodo. Hogwarts is a real castle in the Scottish highlands, at least while we're reading the book."

Kaileigh nodded. She understood what he was talking about. Books did have a life of their own, but it was a lower form of life than the real world. Their reality was tempered by the imperfections of their author's imaginations. Imagined worlds were incomplete – no author could imagine a world wholly.

"See, I figured this out a while ago, even before the Abandonment....oh, sorry, I keep renaming things. Anyway, before the Pandemic, I had an idea. Are you familiar with the quantum theory of multiple universes?"

"Yes...no...sorta," was her response.

Nodding his head, Brady continued, "I don't really understand it, either, but I know that the best minds on earth had a theory about our universe being one of an infinite number of other universes. We can't see them or touch them, but they exist. Astrophysicists could even show you the math to prove it. See, the theory came about because of quantum mechanics."

"What? How do you know about quantum mechanics?" she asked incredulously. She was at the top of her class in both math and science and what she knew about quantum mechanics could be written down on the back of a ticket stub.

Brady shrugged, "Wikipedia?"

A look of acknowledgment came over her face and she answered simply, "Oh..."

"Anyway, these astrophysicists claimed that there is an infinity of universes out there. Some of them have life in them, some of them don't. Some of them have the same laws of physics we do and others have different laws. One idea is that all of these universes are like leaves on a tree, all sprouting from the same branch."

Kaileigh had no idea where this was going, but she was intrigued.

"Infinite universes, huh? That means there's a universe out there where everyone else is still alive?" The idea held some promise for her even if it seemed far-fetched.

Brady nodded. "Yes, probably, but we can't get there. We're here – in this room, this universe. There aren't any doorways."

"Keep going," she said, this time averting her eyes from Brady's gaze.

"So the idea that caught my imagination was this: one of those astrophysicists I read about said that there are an infinite number of these other universes. Infinite, right? That's hard to imagine, isn't it? How much is infinity? So I thought about it, and I thought about it, and I thought some more. Finally, it came to me. Infinite means never ending, forever growing, always more. I thought, anything that can be imagined can exist in another one of these other universes. Anything. All the books I've read and loved weren't just figments of the authors' imaginations. They were real! The authors imagined and anything that can be imagined can be real in one of these infinite universes. They could exist in another universe. Middle-Earth could be real. Mount Olympus could truly exist! In some other universe, Spongebob Squarepants lives in a pineapple under the sea and he's real!"

Kaileigh wanted to give him the look of death, roll her eyes and laugh in his face with a single, "Yeah, right..." but she didn't. She couldn't. She had witnessed impossibilities with her own eyes. She had fought a man with a katana and sliced off his fingers. She had watched as the world fell around her and here she was, in the Bangor Public Library's fiction room listening to a boy younger than her explain why books and statues can talk.

"Books are more than stories to keep us entertained. Remember that I said that there aren't any doorways to these other universes in the multiverse? That's what the scientists told us, but they were wrong. They didn't use their imagination like they should have."

"You mean there are ways to access these other universes?" asked Kaileigh.

"Yes! *Books* are portals. They're doorways to other universes. These stories are the only ways we can visit them We can't go to them with our *bodies* but we can voyage to them with our *minds*. Without realizing it, authors figured out a way to travel through the multiverse. People just didn't realize these places were *real*, in a quantum kind of way."

Kaileigh looked at Brady for a long moment, considering his words. Full of surprises, this boy claimed that the world has changed. What a world, she thought, when a fourteen year old boy could piece together a quantum theory of fiction: books as doorways to other universes similar and yet different from our own?

"Okay," Kaileigh said, looking at the books on the table in front of her, "how does this explain how you can hear Benjamin Franklin and that little gargoyle wants to look up my dress?"

Brady laughed. It was the first laugh he had uttered for a very long time.

"It's like this, anything that can be imagined is real, somewhere, in another universe. Anything that can be *imagined,* except that there's no one around to imagine anymore, is there, except for you and me? All the possible universes - do they still exist if we're not there to *imagine* them?"

Kaileigh waited for the idea to sink in. She waited a long time, pondering it, tasting it in her mind, ruminating. He had an interesting point.

She asked, "So you think that by imagining these other realities, we make them real? And if we don't imagine them, they aren't?"

Brady couldn't meet her eyes for long, but he said quietly, "I don't know. Is there a universe out there where everyone is still alive? If I imagine it, does it become real or was it always there, a universe right next to our own? Right now, if I imagine it, does it pop into existence, or has it always been there? I don't know."

"If no one is left to imagine, does the other universe cease to exist?" she asked.

They looked at each other for a long time without speaking, each hoping the other would venture an answer.

Brady finally replied, "I don't know, but I think that the books, the statues, everything, is responding to imagination. I think that we're it. Here's the big secret. Here's the thing that Einstein and Stephen Hawking probably knew but weren't foolish enough to reveal to the world: the multiverse *requires* imagination. It runs on it. It's the fuel that powers everything and there's no one left to dream, to think, to make things up. Just us. I think the world is waking up, responding to our imaginations. Someone is imagining things alive..."

A palpable silence fell across the length of the reading room, but Kaileigh could have sworn she heard the whispering of a thousand voices chiming like tinkling bells in the distant wind, as though the books were calling out to her from unimaginable distances.

"Who is imagining these things to life? Could be it someone here...or in another universe, imagining us? Is there some writer in another universe who is putting our story down on paper, imagining us?" asked Kaileigh.

Brady shook his head. "There could be a writer or

perhaps it's a reader reading the book he wrote. Maybe it's a kid in middle school reading a book titled, *The Last Boy on Earth*. I don't know."

Kaileigh saw a movement from the corner of her eye in the new acquisitions room. It was Gregoire, looking at her from a distance with eyes the size of silver dollars and a dreamy smile smeared across his rugged face.

"What do you want?" she asked.

"Did you just ask a statue a question?" asked Brady.

"No, of course not...wait a second. Oh my god, I did. Am I going crazy?"

"It doesn't take long to get used to," he answered.

"Oh, she is so...'ow do you say...delicious! Oh, Monsieur Brady, you 'ave made 'zis place a palace! She is our queen! He..he..hee..."

"Oh, shut up!" she said sternly.

Gregoire smiled, for he had been addressed by Kaileigh. He winked at Brady and turned, waddling back to the main room of the library to continue his vigil, reaching his long clawed hand behind him to scratch his left buttock.

They sat in silence for a few moments. Kaileigh began to notice small movements in the paintings hanging on the wall. Did the painting of Molly Molasses, tribal elder of the Penobscot Nation, painted so long ago, just smile slightly and nod to her? When she concentrated, she could hear the faint whisperings of the books on the shelves. She thought to herself, 'This can't be real! I know better. This is impossible.'

Her logical voice replied to her wondering side, 'If you were crazy, you wouldn't know it, would you? And if you knew it, that would mean you weren't crazy, only that you *thought* you were. If you *thought* you were crazy, you wouldn't be, would you?"

Brady could see the look in her light blue eyes and he understood.

"I have someone I'd like you to meet," he said. "He might be able to shed some light on this weird new world."

"It's *Brave New World*, you know, a book by Huxley and a line from Shakespeare?" she replied.

"Oh, yeah sure," he answered, somewhat annoyed.

206

"There's someone else?" she asked.

"In a manner of speaking," he replied hopefully.

"He's not real, is he?"

"He's as real as we are. He's just not quite...human."

She stared at him for a moment and then looked away, shook her head and replied, "Oh, what the hell..."

The statue of General Joshua Chamberlain stood as a sentinel overlooking the Penobscot River on its course down to the bay and therefore, the ocean and the world. He stood with his sword dangling from his belt, his hat tucked neatly into his belt and his arms crossed. An expression of stony silence covered his face and belied no suspicion that this was a talking statue. Brady parked the Lifeseeker in the parking lot of the old Irving at the entrance to the small park dominated by the statue of the general. She had said little to Brady on the short drive over the bridge. There was so much of *nothing* to look at, so much of what should be and wasn't. It was like looking at a picture of your family except everyone but you has been cut away by some madman with a pair of insane scissors.

"I want you to have an open mind about what you're going to see and hear," Brady said in low tones as they approached the base of the statue. "He's been like my advisor. He was the first thing in the world that came alive to me. He's pretty cool, too. He's wise *and* he has a boss sword."

Kaileigh nodded and followed him down the path. She stood behind Brady and he told her to stand a short distance away so that the General could get a good look at her.

"General," Brady began, "I have someone I'd like you to meet. Her name is Kaileigh Tremble."

She was surprised even though a stone gargoyle from New Jersey had just hit on her in the library. She knew this statue. She knew Joshua Chamberlain from the two different reports she had written on him for fifth and eighth grade. She had driven by him a thousand times and barely ever looked his way. He was something, some *thing,* put there by well-meaning historically minded citizens intent on keeping him forever linked with his boyhood home of Brewer.

Her eyes were frozen wide as the statue slowly tipped its head down for a better look and the metal eyes rolled in the metal head while the metal mouth opened and a human voice came forth saying, "Pleased to make your acquaintance, young lady. I am at your service."

Later she would marvel at her actions because she didn't know from what hidden well of courtesy she lowered her gaze and replied, "Sir, I am at *your* service."

The metal man smiled and said nothing.

"Sir, I'm sorry to bother you this morning, but we have some questions, and since you seem to know so much about the way things are now, I wonder if you wouldn't mind?"

"Brady, I am at your service, too. I have little else to do, it seems."

Kaileigh and Brady sat down on the ground in front of the statue as the warmth of a summer morning began to fall upon them.

She was thunderstruck but went right to the source of her conundrum. "How is it that you can talk? How is it that anything that looks remotely human, or has a connection with humans, seems to be able to talk or even move about? It doesn't make sense to me."

Chamberlain tilted his head a little to the left and then to the right before bringing his gaze back to the pair below him.

"I am uncertain as to the means of my awakening. I am not Joshua Chamberlain, not *the* Chamberlain I represent. He passed away years ago and left this place. I seem to remember things he wrote, events he may have seen, even conversations he may have had. I think in his way, as though I possess his engrams...is that right? *Engrams?* Do I know this word? I am puzzled and troubled by all of this, as well, Kaileigh."

"Can you remember specific details? Can you recall your actions at Little Round Top?"

The General paused and looked away for a moment, accessing some deep idea from wherever his seat of memory and thought lived.

"Do you know my history?" he asked plainly.

"I've done my research. I know something about Chamberlain."

"Do you? Can you tell me...did I like birds? Did I enjoy the outdoors? I can't remember that..."

"You did," she replied. "You were a scholar. You taught yourself Greek in a year. You were bookish before the war. After the war, you spent a lot of time on the coast, when you weren't being called on to stop a riot or travel to France, or even attend Grant's funeral."

The General nodded as memories were created where they had not existed before.

"I do not know how I came to be. I am much like you, I suppose. Who knows how they were given the power of thought and memory? Consciousness is such a strange thing. Is it so hard to imagine that when all have been taken away, by contagion or war, that part of them remains? Perhaps I am part of *what remains...*"

Brady had heard something akin to this before from the General, but Kaileigh was weighing this for the first time and her mind was more logical than his, less likely to believe in chimeras of the imagination.

"Nothing remains. I'm insane. I'm living in a dream, a nightmare. None of this is real. I'm still in the hospital and the doctor is still after me or worse," she said in anger and frustration.

"No, Kaileigh. You're wrong. You deny your own senses and these may be the only things that you can trust. Think about your own true self. That person the world knew as Kaileigh still exists, even though she is confused. I exist, even though people no longer walk the earth, except for you. I wrote about it once, or rather, *he* did."

"What could he have possibly have said about the situation we are in?" asked Kaileigh, still sure she was tipping toward the brink of insanity.

The General spoke the words from some deeper well of understanding that neither Kaileigh or Brady possessed. He spoke from the mind of a man long dead, yet whose words were still lingering in his consciousness. She looked off into the distance and Brady was stunned to see him move his hand from his side and raise it over his heart, in gratitude and remembrance of deeds long past.

"In great deeds, something abides. On great fields, something stays. Forms change and pass: bodies disappear: but spirits linger, to consecrate ground for the vision-place of souls. And reverent men and women from afar, and generations that know us not and that we know not of, heart-drawn to see where and by whom great things were suffered and done for them, shall come to this deathless field, to ponder and dream. And lo! the shadow of a mighty presence shall wrap them in its bosom, and the power of the vision pass into their souls."

The pair let the words fall over them and settle down deep into their pores before saying a thing. The General had spoken words written to remember the Battle of Gettysburg, but somehow, these words seemed to apply to them.

Brady wondered aloud, "Forms change and pass: bodies disappear: but spirits linger, to consecrate ground for the vision-place of souls?"

As if reading his thoughts, he heard Kaileigh mutter, "Vision-place of souls?"

"It is my belief that I have come to life, so to speak, so that those who still walk this earth will not forget Joshua Chamberlain. All of the other *homunculi* also seem to be focal points for a kind of memorial energy. Even if all the people have passed, somehow the world itself refuses to forget what has passed and longs for the presence of its people. Perhaps these are the musings of a foolish old scholar looking for an easy answer, but I am certain of one thing. You two have been spared for a reason. You have been brought together by forces beyond your control. Your survival is not less miraculous than my own awakening."

Kaileigh moved directly in front of the statue so that he could not tip his head down to see her. Instead, he looked again out over the long Penobscot River.

"What about the killer in that hospital? What is he?" she asked simply.

The General did not reply immediately. Then he said, "I

do not know. That is for you to determine, as you stand and face him. Your enemy is often less strange to you than you might think. The monster we slay today may be the brother we mourn tomorrow..."

Kaileigh screamed a short burst of frustration and walked away, arms crossed. She stood at the edge of the hill and gazed out over the city beyond her.

Brady watched her in fascination. She was wonderful, he thought. How could he help her understand and even *accept* some of the things he had come to live with so easily? It was going to be an uphill battle.

"I am sorry, Brady," said the General in a quiet tone, "I am as puzzled as you, but I believe that, such as I am, I was put here for a purpose. We are all here for a purpose and it is our duty to determine what that purpose might be. She is angry, and rightfully so. Give her some time and she will begin to accept the way things have come to be."

"I hope so, Sir. I sure hope so."

Chapter 14
The White Tower

The monster sat in the very depths of what had become his prison. The escape of the two survivors left Grendel full of a new emotion. Where hate and the spit of anger had roiled in his gut before their escape, the backwash of loss and futility rose in his gullet. The sense of sheer helplessness began to whisper into his ear that, alone, he too was vulnerable.

He had met her before, a thousand times in other times and places, in this world and countless others. She was his antithesis and arose alongside him, the antiparticle to his particle. He could exist for awhile, conquer nations and devour worlds, but she was always looming on the horizon. Through her flowed the energy that could destroy him. She was the *conduit* through which all change would flow and if she was free to work with the Renamer, he would need to redouble his efforts to destroy them both, before they rose to the apex of their power, before they understood how they might work together to destroy him.

How was it that he could not bring himself to leave this place and seek them on his own with so much hanging in the balance? If he would move forward and step out into the world, it could be his. Was his role that of holdfast? Was he supposed to stay inside? Was that his destiny? What inhibition kept him bound with invisible and adamantine chains from the world that had been created for him? He held his wounded hand and in his crouched position on the cold concrete floor, contemplated his failure to destroy the Renamer and she who seemed to know his every movement. She could anticipate his every thought, too implacable for a creature of the quantum state.

If summoning the ancient powers of the earth and sky was not enough to destroy them, things were dire, he thought. Nearly everyone on earth had succumbed except for a few survivors. He knew that the boy and the girl were not alone. Across the globe a few others had also survived, against all of his planning and morphing throughout the long span of ages through which he had formed. He had been so certain that this time he had coalesced into something entirely deadly to the human race and he would carry out the purpose for which he was summoned. Now his plan, like a poorly woven cloth, was unraveling in front of his eyes.

There was a part of him, deeply buried and pushed aside, that kept saying, "*This is wrong. You are wrong. I should have destroyed you. All those people. You truly are a monster, and if I ever escape, I will hunt you down...*"

Who was the owner of this inner voice that never lasted for long and was soon extinguished by other inner voices that whispered other observations? He did not know.

Another inner voice said, "*You are powerful, lord, but you should seek aid from the others. They are waiting for you. They, too, are hungry...*"

Another voice interrupted, "*If your bite cannot forestall and destroy these two, then surely an army of ones such as yourself would do the trick. Imagine, you as their leader...*"

Still another voice from within the depths of his

213

darkness said, quietly, *"Or even better, lord, assimilate them. Make them become part of you. Absorb them as they arrive, make their weapons your weapons, their strategies your strategies. You have lost fingers, but you can take their hands, their limbs, their strength and combine it with your own, deep within yourself. Then you will have the courage to leave this building, to seek them out on your own. Then you can proceed to wander the wide world over, hunting the few who have survived."*

Grendel listened closely to this final voice. Whose voice was it? Was it a doctor's voice? No. A lawyer's voice? Possibly. A politician's voice? Yes, most certainly! A voice suave in the use of power, a slick and sickeningly sweet voice whose dulcet tones predicted success. Grendel liked being told what he wanted to hear.

He arose from the floor in some discomfort. His hand still throbbed and his wound bound him to his pain, but nothing would could stop the juggernaut that he was about to create. Nothing could. He was an inexorable force and had been since the dawn of time, lingering just below the fringe of things, waiting and watching. He was the fulcrum upon which all life balanced, a leveler, a gardener who weeded the crops and ripped the weeds from the fertile earth. Tonight, the weeds were two young people hiding from him. Soon, perhaps in a week or a month, he would have the strength to emerge and confront them.

He made his way to the medical library on the second floor of the hospital, a place used primarily by the staff before the Abandonment. He avoided any place where the ideas and thoughts of humans lingered in books. Books were almost alive with the presence of their human authors and he could not stand them. It also housed the names of a thousand other monsters whose sustenance had dried up, suddenly. They would be hungry, even desperate. He stood in the center of the room and closed his eyes. His mind imagined tunneling downward, ever downward by powers of ten. There just below the surface of things was a realm of infinite space and time, an entire universe in the space of an atom and there, even smaller things dwelt, popping into and out of

214

existence. In his mind he journeyed to that minuscule Ultima Thule underneath and between all things where dwelt his siblings from long ages ago.

He called to them, summoning. "Brothers! Sisters! From the depths of my hatred, I summon you. From the desolation of the world, I cry out to you! Heed my call! I offer you new life!"

He waited for a reply. Long minutes passed before Grendel began to hear their muffled whispers among themselves, invisible incarnate voices drifting upon the air between the quantum fluctuations.

"He calls us? The pig? He has summoned us?"

"Hungry ass. He survives while we wither. How shall we survive now?"

"Ignore the summons! He will trick you!" screamed a high-pitched female voice, ancient beyond years from a great distance.

"No, no. He is strong. He solely accomplished what we together could not. And I am hungry...He is all we have, now."

"Yes, yes, yes," said a hundred thousand insolvent voices from beyond.

Grendel waited but the cacophony grew until even he could stand it no longer.

"Enough!" he shouted. "I offer you life and continued existence. Without my offer, you will wither and crumble. No humans to imagine you or nightmares for you to inhabit. What will you do? Your food supply is gone, save for a few and they are not enough to sate your raging hunger. So I offer you something, which is better than nothing."

There was a hissing of static and a long moment.

"What is your offer?"

"A simple plan. Join me or perish."

The voices of demons, of vampires and trolls, of Jenny Greenteeth and Redcap all arose in anger. They were thoughts, imagined by people throughout the ages and now, they were living in the borderland, almost totally forgotten except for the weak bonds of those few humans who survived. If those humans all perished, so too would these

215

bogies and ghosts and things that go bump in the night, these infections and diseases and bringers of death.

"Join you? How is this possible? Do you mean to fight side by side? There is nothing left to attack. You dare invite us to feast and yet you have already eaten all the food! Ha!"

"I mean," Grendel said, "precisely what I said. Bond with me! Become one with me. Meld with me, melt my flesh into your flesh, my spirit into yours. Separately you will perish. Only I can survive. Without this last chance, you will perish. The humans are dead."

"He speaks the truth," said a saddened voice, coughing and hacking. "Perhaps we should consider this joining he speaks of. Perhaps it is all that is left."

Another voice, gasping for breath, muttered, "I will submit. I will submit. I do not want to perish. I want to live."

"As do I," said another, and then another. Not all agreed and many of the voices pronounced their opposition to his plan, but before the hour was done, the majority of his brothers and sisters agreed to this strange bonding he had proposed. Though such combinations had happened before, this was the first time so many had agreed to such a thing.

"You are an abomination!" shouted the old female voice from a distance. "I know you! I bore you! I am your mother and you will stop! I call you what you are. You descendant of Cain – first of all murderers! You are unnatural and should not exist. The boy summoned you in a moment of weakness! He does not know the truth of this and I would rather perish like all the people of the world than submit to your will. You are a failure! The boy will beat you. He is better than you!"

"I can do this with or without you, hag," answered Grendel. "Any who do not join with me, know this. I am the undisputed master of this new world, this new order. If you are not with me, you are against me."

"So be it," said the old female voice from a distance. "You sicken me," she said.

Grendel smiled. "Yes, that's what I do..."

"I will have no part of this violation of nature. Those of you who join this creature will rue the day you gave away

216

your souls! It will be a sordid boon, indeed!" screeched the voice of the Hag as it receded into the distance and disappeared. The other voices mingled, indeterminate and confused.

"Good. So it begins," said Grendel aloud as he nodded his massive head.

The plans were made for the unification of Grendel to his airy brothers and sisters. Their essences would return within a fortnight for the bonding. Grendel needed to gather his own strength to heal before such a thing could be attempted. He knew in the black pit of his own soul that this unification might destroy him, but he was certain that he would perish anyway if he did not attempt it.

He left the realm where nightmares go before they dissipate into oblivion and arose back to the world of the Renamer. Alone, his fear of the world was too powerful and made him vulnerable. With the combined strength of all who would join him he would be able to leave the sanctuary of this place, hunt down the survivors and bring a new world finally into play.

Brady and Kaileigh stood at the foot of the Thomas Hill Standpipe, a huge white shingled water tower. Inside of the wooden structure, which was by far the tallest structure on the highest point in the area, was a tank that held nearly two million gallons of water. The bottom part of the structure was made of quarried stone and was impenetrable. A thick wooden door barred the entrance. It was a solid, defensible tower except that it was made of wood on the outside and that wood could burn. Brady was pleased to see that it hadn't burned down. This tower and its placement so high above the rest of the city was the reason Brady still had running water in the library, feeding the city on gravity alone. Because of its high position in the city, it was the most visible structure.

"So, how do we get up there?" asked Kaileigh.

"There's a winding stairwell all the way to the top. I went up there once with my mom, a few years ago. It was pretty impressive. I bet you can see half the state from up there. I saw Mount Katahdin."

"Should be a good place to check out how damaging the fire has been to the city," Kaileigh agreed. "How are we going to get in?"

Brady pulled a ring of keys from the lanyard that was attached to his belt and searched for the right one. He found it and held it aloft to her like a musketeer pledging allegiance to his lady.

"I have the key," he simply said.

She was amused. "How in the world did you get that," she asked.

Brady smiled and looked off in the distance. "I'm a thief. You don't want to know."

"Yes, I do," she declared.

"Well, I had a lot of time on my hands. I explored everywhere. The water tower was run by the Bangor Water Company so I broke into their offices a few weeks ago looking for...stuff, and I found this. It was clearly labeled "Thomas Hill Standpipe," and it was in the top drawer of the counter in their main office. I shoved it into my backpack and kept moving on. I've become pretty good at breaking in to places, but I prefer to use keys, if they're around."

"Smart. Let's see how much of the city is left."

The door opened easily, revealing a dark and dusty interior. Light from a few small windows lit the narrow wooden stairwell as it wound its serpentine path above them, leading to the promenade deck at the top. There were small benches built into the sides of the stairwell from place to place.

"They used to leave this place open all the time, way back when, before a little boy fell and died. Then they closed it and only opened it under a lot of supervision a couple of times a year. People used to come up here, picnic at the park, walk up here to take the air. It's pretty cool. Wait until you see."

Brady was excited to share this experience with Kaileigh, like a boy allowed to wander free at the fair for the first time. Near the top of the ascent, a glass panel showed them the level of the water and the sheer circumference of the massive iron tank. Kaileigh found herself drawn to the water, getting closer and closer to the glass panel, now putting her hands on the surface, and then leaning against it.

So much water in one place, so concentrated. So placid and cold...

Brady watched her for a moment, wondering what she was thinking but she said nothing. She seemed to be concentrating, lost in thought, but what was that? Did the water slosh towards them? Did something move in the water? No, impossible, he thought, but the closer she leaned into the window, the more the water lapped to the side, towards her, like she was some kind of magnet. Brady quickly grabbed her by the waist and found that she didn't struggle against him. She was transfixed.

"Hey, don't do that. We don't know if that glass will hold, and if you fell in, I don't even want to think about what could happen," he protested.

She withdrew and looked at him like she had never seen him before. Slowly her memory returned and she regained her composure.

"Sorry, Brady. I don't know what came over me. It's just that the water, it sounds...interesting."

Brady had to think about what she had just said. Water sounding interesting? What did that mean? He listened and couldn't hear a thing except for the reverberations of their own movements and voices in this artificial mountainous cistern. Perhaps all the days of imprisonment had a cumulative effect on her. Brady was nothing if he wasn't patient.

"Come on," he said. "Wait until you see the view. We're nearly there."

The door at the top of the stairwell opened to reveal a beautiful early sunny afternoon. The sense that they were suspended in the air, like ethereal spirits, immediately seized them both. They had both been in high structures before, but this one was open to the winds and the birds. The rim around the circumference was chest high, maintaining at least a modicum of safety for any casual bystander who might loose his or her balance. No one could fall off this structure without a great deal of effort.

They looked out upon a strange landscape. From up here, it was obvious to anyone that Bangor and Brewer were cities set in the middle of a huge, seemingly endless forest reminiscent of the earliest days, before the advent of the hand of Man. Usually the majority of the city hid beneath a green plume of trees, with only the largest of structures peeking out from the canopy.

The fire had taken its toll. Downtown Bangor was gone. Both the eastern and western parts of the city had taken heavy damage, but there were pockets that survived. The Bangor Mall area was untouched. Brewer, protected by the deep flowing Penobscot River, was totally unscathed. Broadway was a cinder. Union Street and most of the houses clustered on that side of the city were also gone, smoke still rising in pockets. Every now and then small explosions could still be heard from oil tanks and gas lines, and with no human hand to tend to them, they continued to burn. This city was still in danger.

"Oh my god," began Kaileigh, "this is what happens to cities when there are no more people."

"Well, no time like the present," Brady said, taking a long black cylinder that he had carried with him on his back

220

and unscrewing the top. He withdrew his map and laid it out on the floor of the deck. A black Sharpie in hand, he began to make adjustments to the lay of the land as pictured on the paper.

Working together, they began to remake the world.

"That's gone," Kaileigh said, as she watched Brady work. Brady carefully marked each section of the city as burned or safe. He paid particular attention to the green spots on the map where food and supplies had been found.

As Brady began nearing the boundaries of the map, he got up often to visually check places in the distance with his binoculars. He was about to delete a depot in the distance when Kaileigh said, "No, that's still there."

Brady looked up and said, "I just checked. I can't see it. It must have burned down. Here, check it yourself with the binoculars."

Kaileigh said simply, "I don't need binoculars. I can see it perfectly well. See, it's still there. It's kind of hidden behind some trees, but it's still there."

Brady looked without the binoculars, but it was simply too far. Then he tried again with the binoculars. Sure enough, the building he was about to cross off the map that held at least a year's worth of canned food was, in fact, still standing. She had seen it with her naked eye.

Brady lowered the binoculars and slowly turned his head to look at her.

"Did you see it," she asked.

"Yes," said in a low tone, "but the question is, how did you see it?"

Kaileigh wondered silently in her own private thoughts. If he could speak with books and she could see things with the eye of an eagle, something besides the world had changed. She heard water speaking to her. No, that wasn't right. She heard water *chanting* to her, *singing* to her like a chorus of worshipers. Brady had changed but so had she. Somehow their powers of perception were growing to include new characteristics and that frightened her, because deep down, she also felt strangely excited about it.

"Brady, how did it feel when you first heard the general

221

speak? Did it make you feel...like a freak?"

Brady kept surveying the greensward as far as his eyes could see and answered, "Yup, definitely freak time in Strangerville. But you know what? It didn't take long before it seemed perfectly normal. I think books and statues were always able to speak."

"What? No way! That's definitely new. Books and statues could never speak," she said resolutely.

Brady turned from surveying his new realm to look her straight in the eye. "How do you know? Was it just because they never spoke to you?"

Chapter 15
The Signal from Beyond

from the Journal of Brady Smith

"It's late and Kaileigh is asleep upstairs under the watchful eyes of Vice-president Hannibal Hamlin, although she doesn't have a clue. I don't dare to tell her that paintings sometimes talk, as well. My life has changed so much since my battle with the monster, Grendel. In a lot of ways, there are more questions now than answers. Kaileigh insists on calling Grendel 'Dr. Grindle'. I don't think she sees him as he really is.

However, I don't think she's come through the Abandonment without some changes, other than the obvious ones. I know for a fact that she can see at least twice as far as I can, even with binoculars. Her sight is amazingly sharp, like a falcon's! She's also fascinated with the sound of water. I know that's really weird, but it's true. Today in the White Tower she was drawn to the water. I had to pull her away from the glass, worried that she'd break it and fall into almost two million gallons. It was weird because I swear the water moved toward her, in ripples and waves.

We took a drive down by the river to survey the damage down there and the minute I stopped Rocinante, she rushed to the edge of the water and thrust her hands into it. She knelt like that for a couple of minutes and I didn't think anything of it. I mean, I thought she was just cooling off. But when she didn't come back from the edge of the river, I went down to see what was up. She was staring off into the distance like she wasn't looking at anything in particular but something far, far away. I asked her, "What are you doing?" and she said in a weird quiet voice, "Looking downriver, to the sea. I don't know, Brady. It's weird, like the water is a living thing and it's kind of talking to me. It connects things. It's like a telescope - I can see through it to other places..."

That would have made any normal person think, "Whoa, this girl is crazier than...well, you know – add your own ideas here."

I know better. It's the Abandonment.

After we got away from the river, she was a lot better, back to her old self. Her senses, her sight, hearing, intuition - they're very sharp. I mean, how did she manage to avoid Grendel for so long in that hospital ward? I have two thoughts about that. First, she was on the Maternity Ward, where all the babies around here are born. Heck, I was born there. We both were. I bet that all of that birthing and bringing life into the world has a power that still hangs on. Because he is so preoccupied with death, the power of life causes him pain and suffering - it's matter and he's antimatter. It's life and he's antilife. He avoided the ward where so much living began and contained himself in the rest of the place, where all of the death occurred.

Secondly, I think she has a sixth sense. She knew when he was coming for her a minute or two before he arrived. That's precognition -classic ESP - extrasensory perception. It's like she could tap into his mind for a moment when she was in danger. She could easily move away from the area where he was going. She could anticipate him.

As for the city, it's quiet again. I think it's going to rain again tonight so that should put an end to most of the few small fires left smoking here and there. I lost about three-quarters of my food and supply depots, but I'll survive. Thank God that the Brewer side of the river was left untouched.

I miss my mom. I really miss her."

After they had surveyed the damage to the city, it was time to kit Kaileigh out for what Brady called, "Survival

101."

At Maine Army and Navy, the astronaut waited for them like a sentinel by the front door. Kaileigh was about to cross the threshold into the store when his golden-gloved hand moved to halt her and he asked through a million miles of space, "Password?"

Kaileigh looked back at Brady and shot him a quizzical look.

"Open Sesame!" said Brady, smiling.

"Roger that," was the astronaut's reply as he took the handle of the glass door and opened it.

As first, she found nothing that she liked, but she made do with a few weapons that seemed to suit her. When Brady watched her face as she surveyed the weapons, he was impressed and a little taken aback. She lingered over the knives, choosing four blades in all plus a Japanese katana of her own that she slung over her back in an improvised sheath.

Then she found the guns.

Where Brady had an aversion to them because of the manner in which his own father died, Kaileigh had no such scruples. Most of the rifles were locked and secured, nearly impossible for her to take down and examine. Brady watched with mixed emotions as she broke the glass display cases and reached in, removing and handling several handguns before finding the one that she liked the best. She eventually chose a .45 automatic. He was fascinated as he watched her break into the cash register and retrieve the keys to the gun locks on the pistols. It took her a few minutes, but by the time she was done, she had a shoulder holster, several boxes of ammunition and a cleaning kit.

"Um," Brady ventured, "What are you gonna do with that pistol?"

"Oh, I don't know...knock down a few walls?"

"Oh," he answered.

"Hey, why don't you take a pistol? I know how to use one of these. I can show you."

"How do you know how to use a pistol?"

"Easy. I'm a hunter. My dad taught me. It was a kind of

father-daughter bonding thing after the divorce. You know, get together and kill a living thing for the release of tension. Really – get a gun. They work well against monsters and wild dogs. You can sleep with one under your pillow. Keeps the monsters away."

"Oh," he said. "No, that's okay. I'd rather not use a gun."

"Why not?" she inquired, "You use a paintball gun."

"Yeah," he answered, "it's not the gun so much as the bullets I have a problem with."

"Okay. Why?"

Brady swallowed hard and fought with the idea. Should he tell her? He barely knew her and to share something so close to his heart meant a lot to him. Still, he thought, if I don't tell her, she'll think I'm even weirder than she already does. A guy from Maine who doesn't like guns? He pictured a stereotyped hunter standing at the Gun Shop shaking his head, saying under his breath, "There's something wrong with that boy."

"My dad was a hunter, too. He died in a hunting accident. He was shot and killed. It put me off the idea of guns," he explained.

That was odd – she felt it more deeply than she usually did. Tears rapidly rose to her eyes and she felt her heart quicken. Was she receiving something from him?

"Is it okay with you if I have a gun?" she asked simply.

Brady shrugged nonchalantly. "I guess. I mean, just be careful where you point it. Don't expect me to use it."

"Oh, I won't. It's just that it's a crazy world out there now and until I know that Dr. Grindle is going to leave us alone, I'll sleep better at night with this."

By the time they returned to the Library for their evening meal, they had also acquired another valuable item: another four-wheeler. Brady had a list of available recreational vehicles, from dirt bikes to other motor homes that he had discovered in his travels, but for Kaileigh he went directly to the dealer. He chose a display model.

Kaileigh was visibly pleased with the choice. She would have preferred a car, having just received her license last

226

fall, but she understood how a car would limit her access to many kinds of places.

"Here," Brady said, handing her a helmet.

"What do I want with that?" she asked.

"To keep your brain in your skull."

"Real women don't wear helmets," she said. "I didn't survive the plague so I could be careful now..."

Brady looked at her in surprise.

"Look, if you get in an accident on this thing, I'm going to be your doctor. I'm fourteen years old. I mean, I think of myself as a pretty smart guy, but I'm no brain surgeon."

He held the helmet with outstretched hand, looking at her patronizingly.

She took it from him grudgingly. "Don't say anything. Just give me the damned helmet."

Kaileigh was in the small kitchen in the basement helping Brady make their evening meal of canned beef stew, homemade biscuits in the oven and canned carrots, followed by peaches in heavy syrup. She would have preferred a Big Mac, but those days were gone.

"I'm going to go out to check the generator. I have to write in the maintenance log. It helps me remember to keep the fluids topped."

As he checked the gauges and fluid levels, Brady watched as Hugin arrived from his daily ramblings. He called to the bird. The great satin-feathered raven descended from the power line in front of the library and croaked a greeting. Brady produced some beef jerky from his pocket and put it on the ground next to the raven. He was still amazed at how the bird didn't shy away from him. Deep down, he wanted to speak with him.

"Hugin, can you understand me?"

The bird looked up and croaked, "Ragnarok..."

There was that one word, *Ragnarok*, the end of things, the fall of the gods and rise of the frost giants from Norse mythology. What did it mean? Was the bird reminding him of the state of things on earth now or was it just a random sound.

"I don't understand you, but I'm trying. I think you understand me, so help me out. I'm going to ask you a question and hope you answer so I get it. Okay?"

"Ragnarok," replied Hugin.

"Okay. I need to know if you've you seen any weredogs in the city since the fire?"

The bird's head began to bob up and down like someone wriggling a water hose in an odd serpentine rhythm. He croaked, "RAGnarok!"

Brady watched and a small lightbulb could have appeared over his head when he realized he *understood* the raven's response.

"That's a *yes*, isn't it?"

The bird settled back to giving its attention to the beef jerky.

That was something! thought Brady.

"Hugin, buddy, are there more of them than before? Is the pack growing?"

The bird took his time, consuming the entire piece of beef before replying, "RAGnarok!"

The accented first syllable means 'yes', thought Brady. He would ask him a question that he thought would have no for an answer to check.

"Hugin, do you like crows?"

"RagnaROKKKK!" was his reply and as he spoke he also walked back and forth like a wild west gunfighter with heavy holsters at his hips.

Success! thought Brady. At least he could elicit yes and no answers from the bird, and that could help him immensely. Hugin croaked and pecked at the ground assertively.

"Oh, sorry," answered Brady, "I forgot. Here's another," he said as he threw the final bit of beef jerky to the ground in front of the bird. He pondered why this amazing bird had chosen him. He knew that without Hugin, he would probably never have rescued Kaileigh in time. He may never have survived at all.

He said goodbye to the bird as Hugin took to the sky again and went off on his nightly flight.

Kaileigh had set the table. Eating w̲
they had both taken for granted in the wo̲
Abandonment, but now it took on a ver̲ ̲that
significance. It meant another day, another chance: ̲
purposeful and something they paid more attention to th̲
they ever did before. It was a time to just talk.

"How did you make friends with that raven?" she asked
casually as they ate.

"I didn't. He made friends with me. Hugin helps me. I
follow him on his flights sometimes. He knows where things
are."

"Don't you think that's kind of strange?"

"There's all kinds of strange out there right now,"
answered Brady.

"Yeah, I guess there is."

When darkness came that night, the empty spaces in the
library seemed to expand to infinite proportions. Just as
anyone in a totally lightless room might only know the
boundaries of his prison by the sense of touch alone, so it
was for Kaileigh and Brady. When the generators were
switched off, their light was isolated and small. Kaileigh
used a battery-powered lantern to examine the contents of
the piles of supplies that Brady had so assiduously stacked
all over the main floor. She wondered at Brady's planning
skills and the reasons he might have for considering many of
the items he chose to save and treasure. Here there was a
pack of ball point pens, there a set of coffee cups, a brass
yardstick, a violin in a case, a half-full plastic container of
red licorice whips. There were piles of things she saw no
rhyme or reason for keeping, but she let them pass as the
brainchildren of Brady's imagination.

He was good company. She could follow his reasoning
with the cases of ropes, bungee cords, a variety of tools and
foodstuffs, blankets, first aid supplies and the like, but if
Brady thought to group these essentials with the likes of a
paint set or a case of yarn, who was she to question him?
Wading through the piles of supplies, she found the small
brown portable world band radio. She knew enough about
world band radio to understand that it essentially worked the

                    ⹁pt that you could hear stations
                  ⹁, especially at night when the earth's

 same as⹁⹁ed it on.
  from ⹁'⹁as no sound at all.
    io⹁ ⹁ ⹁as no sound at all.
      Brady, where do you keep the batteries?" she called.
    "In the gray plastic tub clearly marked 'Batteries' Why?"
    She didn't want to tell him that she just wanted to try,
even though it was a foolish notion, to see if anyone was
broadcasting. Brady rounded the corner with his headlamp
on high and saw what she had in her hand.
    "Oh, that. You don't need batteries. It's hand-powered.
See that crank? There's a little generator inside hooked to a
rechargeable battery. Crank it for a minute or two and
you've got about forty minutes of power. There's a little
lamp on the front, too. Go ahead, give it a crank."
    She flipped the crank from the side, put the radio on a
library table and began to turn it. She counted to three-
hundred and stopped. When she flipped the switch, the radio
sent static roaring through the cavernous darkness of the
room.
    Brady sat down next to her and they both stared at the
radio in wonder.
    He said, " I can already tell you you'll find nothing on
the air locally. Try the world band. There are a few different
radio bands to choose from. Be careful! It's really touchy.
See? If you go through the bands really, really slowly, you
might catch some sounds, but all I ever got were some
automated signals using some kind of code that was way too
fast for me to decipher. I think those are airports
broadcasting some kind of homing signal. All automated,
though. Too regular to be humans sending out that kind of
rhythmic signal. There, that's right, turn the tuning knob
really slowly..." he said encouragingly.
    For that moment, they were both entirely engaged in the
sound of static that erupted, hissed and whispered from the
small speaker in front of them. Kaileigh turned the knob
more slowly than the minute hand on a clock might creep
towards tomorrow. They didn't speak or make eye contact.

                          230

Both of them stared intently at the position of the needle on the frequency bar. Minute by minute they listened, telling themselves not to expect anything.

Kaileigh could have sworn she heard a voice through the ether saying, "*We're out here. Keep looking.*"

They turned the knob for over forty minutes in near total silence before it was time to crank it again, the static fading away quickly as the last vestige of electricity in the rechargeable battery was spent. Kaileigh put the radio on the table and began to crank the generator handle. Their hearts were sinking as they realized that they had just wasted time on a hopeless quest that would never answer their anticipation. Kaileigh was cranking the handle carelessly and the radio slipped from her grip, crashing to the floor. Brady hurried to pick it up and as he did, his finger slipped on the dial.

Then the words from a world away began speaking from the edge of the ionosphere. The radio sang forth a stream of words! They didn't recognize the language at first, but they listened all the more intently as the signal kept fading and growing in strength. Brady quickly found a pen and wrote down the exact frequency on the small pad he always carried in his leg pocket.

"What language is it?" asked Brady. "Do you recognize it?"

Kaileigh held up her hand, gesturing him to be silent. She listened for another minute or so and then said, "Russian? No. It's Ukrainian. They've said 'Ukraine' a few times."

The woman continued speaking for several moments with brief interruptions from large bursts of static as the signal continued its erratic behavior. Then, a moment of silence that lasted all of twenty seconds but might have been an hour in the minds of the two listeners. Then, the voice from beyond began to speak in heavily accented English.

"This is Radio Ukraine International broadcasting on Band 41 at 7440 megahertz to North America, coming to you from the Lviv Krasne transmitter in the heart of Ukraine. This is Tetiana Savycheva calling to all people in

231

North America who might be listening to this broadcast. We are, as far as we can determine, the only remaining broadcaster in the world with full power to transmit a signal. We are broadcasting for only brief periods of time to save on fuel. Our diesel generators have enough fuel to continue to transmit and receive on a limited basis for three to four months, we estimate."

Brady and Kaileigh were staring at the little lighted dial, but Brady glanced at Kaileigh. He could see that she was rapt with attention.

Tetiana Savycheva continued. "Here is the situation as we understand it. The world has suffered a mass extinction event in the form of a viral pandemic of unknown origin. If you are listening to this, you should consider yourself one of the few people left on earth. Governments have all fallen, including our own Ukrainian government. It is only because there is no one left to govern. The people of earth are nearly gone.

"This is why we are broadcasting. We are acting as a clearinghouse of information and we want to hear from you. Details of how to transmit a signal to us over the shortwave radio will follow. For your information, we have heard from small groups of people all over the world. There are currently groups of surviving people in Australia, China, Japan, Argentina, Mexico, islands in the Pacific, Svalbard, and the east and west coasts of the United States and Canada. None of these groups are very large, with ten to fifteen people in the largest groups. Some of these contacts are only single people. We know that there are more of you out there, so we will continue to broadcast on this frequency every day at this time and we will be listening for your signal.

You will need access to a World Band radio. If you do not know how to use a HAM radio transmitter, you should seek out a local library and find a book that explains how to do so. Many people have receivers like the ones you are using right now, but transmitters are less common. You will need to find one that also has a source of power so that you can contact us."

232

The speaker began to list the cities and the frequencies at which the people living there could be contacted. Canberra, Australia, Christchurch New Zealand, Hong Kong China, and the list continued, including a contact in Vancouver, British Columbia and another in Baja California. The closest one to Brady and Kaileigh was Washington, D.C. For each site, she listed the number of people in the group and finished the list by giving them the frequency that they could use to contact her. By the time she was done speaking, she had listed fifteen different cities scattered across the planet with survivors like them. Brady had written all of them on his pad.

"Radio Ukraine International urges anyone who can hear this signal to tune in every day at this time to hear updates. The situation is troubling for us all. We are all that remains of almost seven billion people. If Humanity is going to survive, we must each of us consider that we are now family. There are no more countries, borders, or wars.

"If you have not already done so, seek protection from wild animals which are now growing more bold. Find medical supplies, antibiotics, and as much food and clean water as you can. Do not drink unpurified water unless you live in the country, as city water supplies will probably be poisoned with sewage. We are now in summer in the northern hemisphere, but prepare for winter weather now by securing some method to stay warm. You can eat canned food safely for up to five years or more.

We are now readying to sign off for the day. Please keep your radio tuned to this frequency and tune in tomorrow at this time for another update. Repeat, please find a world band radio transmitter and contact us as soon as possible. If we can contact each other, we will not have to be alone. This is Tetiana Savycheva speaking for the four technicians at Radio Ukraine International. Be safe. Good night..."

Kaileigh put the radio gently down on the table and looked at Brady, a smile widening on her face, her eyes as wide as half-dollars, tears beginning to form. Wordlessly, she threw herself at him, grappling on to him with a hug that knocked his breath away. They both screamed with excitement and unity. It was a shout that rattled rafters and rang up through the heavens. It awoke the minions of the lost and echoed down long hallways where dwelled those used to long silences.

Grendel heard it and it dug into him like a dagger of the mind. He felt the change in both of them. For some reason the monster did not understand, the girl was now twice as strong as she had previously been. Somehow, she had found and fed upon the food of power –She had found her hope and with it, he knew she would be a juggernaut.

Chapter 16
Road Trip

"I found it!"

"No way!" shouted Brady from the other end of the Reference Room as he leaped from the chair and ran to Kaileigh's side.

"Look, it says right here: *Joseph Belanger, Cider Hill Road, Route Forty-three, East Corinth, Maine. President of the Penobscot RagChewers Ham Radio Society. K1KJV. It says here that he has a transmitter with a pretty big vertical antenna - 80 meters. He's equipped with a generator backup. He worked with the Penobscot County Emergency Management Agency, advanced license.*"

Brady didn't say a word in response. Instead, he rushed to the shelves with the atlas and local area maps. He found the DeLorme Atlas of Maine, secured the proper page and with a hundred heartbeats he had his finger on the road tracing it from Bangor to East Corinth.

"Kaileigh, it's about a half-hour drive in the Lifeseeker. We can do this."

She met his gaze and a strange silence fell between them that said, "Yes, we can. If we want it badly enough, we can make this happen. Brady, this is how we survive – by contacting and meeting the others!"

For the past three days they had scoured the library's reference room looking for any information they could find about the location of a local transmitter. The frenzied search for information came only after they had failed in their attempt to set up their own transmitter. Brady had found one the size of a shoe box at a local electronics distributor and brought it to the library. With the library's generator to provide electrical power, the pair thought that all they needed was to string a long wire as an antenna, but three nights of experimentation brought them nothing but frustration and failure. They were talking but no one was listening. What they needed, they decided, was to find a transmitter that was already in working condition with a local power source and a high antenna. With all the information available to them, it was a daunting task. They both needed a crash course in HAM Radio. They had found a book, *All About HAM Radio* that was dog-eared and worn. Kaileigh chose it, suggesting that books that look like they've been run over by a truck through a mud puddle are usually the best ones simply because so many people had already used them. When Brady started to read it, he took a chance and asked it a question aloud just to see if, like *The Autobiography of Benjamin Franklin*, it could talk. To his chagrin, it couldn't. He'd have to read this thing the old-fashioned way.

A road trip was in order. Neither Brady nor Kaileigh had ever driven thirty miles in one shot. They had no idea what they would need or how long they would be away from the city. They didn't even know if they would ever return.

They listened to Tetiana Savycheva every night at precisely eight o'clock. Although the broadcast was no longer than a few minutes. The truth she spoke was bleak. Only a few people had been able to reach her receiving station during the past few days. What was troubling to Brady and Kaileigh was that no one closer than Washington,

D.C. had contacted the Ukrainians and at that distance, they might as well be on the moon. Ultimately, the idea was to meet each other in person, somehow, some way. There was safety in numbers and the future of the species would depend upon it. Kaileigh reasoned that if they could contact the Ukraine, they ought to be able to contact whoever was in Washington, D.C. Contact meant uniting. Contact meant that the species could begin again.

They carefully considered their trip. It was possible that they might never return to the city and the library. Kaileigh took several books and manuals with them in the Lifeseeker, kitting out a survival library of sorts. In it were books on the repair of electric generators, code books for Ham Radio Operators and maps. Brady was in charge of making sure the Lifeseeker was in good running order. He attached the small trailer and rolled the two four-wheelers onto it, securing them firmly. There were extra cans of gasoline bungeed to the Lifeseeker's back bumper and on the trailer, as well. He stowed nonperishable supplies on the top of the motor home and covered it all with a blue tarp and bungee cords. He filled the water tank and checked the coolants, oil and tire pressure. He even made sure to check the spare.

If a motor home was normally made for comfort and attractiveness, the inside of the Lifeseeker looked more like the inside of the original lunar module of Apollo 11. Except for the two chairs, the table and the bunk above the driver's area, the vehicle was positively crammed with items, boxes, and sundry needs. They were traveling not only into the distance, but into the unknowable future. Like the pioneers in their Conestoga wagons, they both knew that it was entirely possible that they would never see the cities of Bangor or Brewer again. They had to prepare for all contingencies and this meant that they would have to carry a lot of supplies. To make sure that they would have enough fuel to travel, Brady had three siphon pumps. He had read about 'redundant systems' and thought that they seemed like a good idea. They would probably have to take gasoline from whatever cars and trucks they came across, as well as gasoline stored in tanks in the ground at stations. The only way to be prepared was to be over-prepared.

Brady left Kaileigh at the library in the afternoon while he went to visit the General. She was double-checking all the things he had already double-checked.

When he arrived at the General's statue, Hugin was already on Chamberlain's shoulder. Brady ambled over to the general and looked at the view that he always faced.

"Beautiful day, General," he said casually.

"Yes, it is, Brady."

"I did it, just like you said," Brady explained.

"Yes, you did."

"You're not very talkative today," Brady observed.

"No sir," answered the General.

"We're leaving, for East Corinth. We need to find a transmitter."

"So I've gathered from our friend here," and the general motioned at Hugin with his eyes.

"Sir, are you upset with me for leaving?"

The General said nothing in reply.

"We'll return, I promise."

The General slowly lowered his gaze and his eyes met Brady's.

"How can you know this? You don't know what lies in store. It is possible, indeed, probable, that you shall not return. Once your journey starts, its end is often a mystery. No, don't make promises you cannot keep, Brady. I'll admit that I am a little shaken by your decision, but I am proud of it, too. I just seem to be growing less...*statuesque* lately. I do more than just stare ahead, you know. I have been thinking more. I think I have been feeling *emotions*. Imagine that? I ask myself who I am. I wonder if I am condemned to stand here for eternity. I long to move about. Behind me is the farm I knew as a boy. How would it be to walk among the back field again where my father taught me to use my hands. Oh, to use these hands again, to wander where my wanderlust allows me to go! I am growing into the person I represent, whose semblance covers my face. How can this be a good thing, rooted to the spot as I am?"

The awkward moment passed slowly while Brady

considered the General's point. If the statue was indeed taking on the echoes and ideas of life each day, soon he could be truly alive in every sense of the word, a paralyzed piece of metal forever looking over the distance he could never set foot upon.

"I don't know how you'll get up and walk around, but I have a good idea that when the time comes, you'll just do it," Brady said simply.

The face of the old general took on a distant look and he said nearly beneath his breath, "What did you say?"

"I said you'll just do it, that's how."

A smile almost broke the face of the old warrior and his demeanor changed suddenly and for the best.

"Thank you, Brady."

"What for?"

"When I was a boy, my father told me to plow that field, right there behind me. It was full of rocks and stones and I was just a boy, mind you. I asked him, "How am I do to this thing?" and he answered, "You'll just do it, that's how." You know what? I did. I did the same thing when I taught myself Greek. I just did it, without anyone's help. You're correct, Brady. I shouldn't waste any more time wondering how. It will happen, that's all. Until then, I must simply wait."

Brady walked over and put his hand on the General's boots and said, "Sir, these boot's were made for walking, and that's just what they'll do."

General Joshua Chamberlain then did something he had not done before. He raised his hand and patted the boy on the head.

Both of them were stunned and delighted. Brady's laughter filled the air and the old general himself gave a small chuckle. There was a hopeful sign.

"I will keep watch for you while you are away. Are you taking your friend here with you?" asked the general, indicating Hugin.

"If he wants to go. He's not mine. He's his own boss."

"I think he will follow you. He can follow a trail better than most creatures."

239

"What do you say, Hugin? Are you coming with us?"

"RAGnarok," he said, accenting the first syllable.

"That's a yes!" Brady said.

"Good. You're beginning to listen to him. Remarkable bird, this one."

Brady told the General about the radio broadcasts they had been listening to from the Ukraine. The general understood the idea of radio for it had been in existence before he died, so it was within his mind. Brady found that other, newer inventions were impossible to explain to the statue.

"So, there are others. This is promising. Yes, I concur. By all means you need to secure a communication with the other survivors, if you can. It is your only hope. How is the young lady...Kaileigh?"

"She's fine. She's great. Really, she's smart, tough,

funny. I'm pretty lucky."

"Does she like you?"

Brady paused and thought a moment. "I think so. It's hard to tell. I'm kind of a strange guy at the moment. Sometimes *I* think I'm a little crazy."

"You are who you are. If you pretend to be something other than you are, she will soon discover your lie, especially if she is as smart as you claim. Better by far to think you a little crazy than a liar. You might be surprised. Remember, she's all alone in this world, just like you. All you really have is each other."

"Thanks, General. I'll take your advice under serious consideration."

"See that you do, Brady. See that you do..."

The night before leaving for the transmitter in East Corinth, Kaileigh busied herself reading the book, *All About Ham Radio*. Brady knew how intelligent she really was. In school she had received the President's Award for Academic Excellence and she was always a high honor student, known for her mind as well as for her acerbic, sometimes cutting wit. She questioned everything and everyone. No one could deny that she was a scholar with the gift of being able to teach herself from books. Knowledge wasn't hard for her. People were. They always caused her frustration. She couldn't understand why people didn't just do as she expected. Brady had to learn the hard way most of the time, through trial and error and much bad judgment. He admired her focus. Kaileigh looked up in frustration at Brady at one point and muttered, "I'd give my left leg for an hour on the Internet to figure this thing out. I miss the Internet."

"Yeah, me too," replied Brady, longingly.

Silence fell for a few long moments.

"I miss fast food," Brady said.

"I miss iTunes," Kaileigh countered, quickly.

"Well, I miss the Weather Channel," he said.

"You do?" she asked.

"There's this weather caster, she was really hot..."

"Yeah, I bet," Kaileigh laughed.

241

She looked off into the corner of the room for a moment and said, "I miss chocolate ice cream."

"*Any* ice cream, really," agreed Brady.

"A hot soak in the tub and a blow dryer. I really miss those."

"Yup."

"You know what I don't miss?" asked Kaileigh.

"No, what?"

"Some of the people. I know that sounds awful because, you know, everyone is gone, but I only miss *some* of them. There are some people I don't miss at all. I feel badly about saying this, but there are some people that this world feels better off without."

Brady shook his head in agreement and said, "I know what you mean. Mean guys, for one. I don't miss them."

"Mean girls, too. They were the worst."

"And my mean old neighbor who always told my mother lies about what I'd done during the day," added Brady. "I don't miss Cable TV like I thought I would. I don't miss video games that much either."

"At least we still have music, for now."

"Yeah, I'm really thankful for music."

"And books."

"And sleep."

"And you," added Brady without thinking.

A tender smile broadened across Kaileigh's face as she watched Brady's turn red with embarrassment.

"Right back at you," Kaileigh said.

"I miss my Mom," Brady said, as a way of avoiding any further conversation about his previous comment.

"Where did your mom work in the hospital?" asked Kaileigh, "What's her name?" She was careful to speak in the present tense.

"Her name is Anne Smith and she's a nurse in the emergency room. Here," he said, pulling out a wallet from his back pocket. "I don't really know why I carry a wallet anymore except for the photos."

He pulled a small photograph from one of the plastic sleeves and handed it to her carefully.

"That's her. That's my mom."

Kaileigh looked at the photo for a long time trying to hold back the words, the thoughts and the sense of duty she was feeling. How could such coincidences be, she wondered?

"I remember her," she said after a time.

Brady's face took on a serious edge and he sat down on one of heavy old benches. He didn't say a word but his face pleaded for information, a word, anything that might help him in his search for her.

"When my mom got really sick, in her office, she told to me to stay with her, but she was slipping in and out of consciousness. I was really worried. I left her there and went out to get some cold packs, a washcloth, some fever reducer, anything that might help her. Still, everywhere I went, people were either already dead or dying. Even the caregivers were sick. I made it all the way down to the first floor. It was the headquarters for the Centers for Disease Control and the doors were guarded by soldiers, but I didn't care. Anyway, when I got there, there weren't any soldiers anymore because they were sick, too. The only two people I could see who weren't visibly ill besides me were Dr. Grindle," Kaileigh flipped the photo back so that Brady could see it and she pointed at his mother's face, "and your mom."

Brady was frozen, his bones were steel, his mind was ice. More, he thought, say more.

"She was moving from person to person, but no matter what she did, she couldn't stop them from dying. When she saw me, she came to me and asked me what I was doing there. I told her that my mom was sick. She gave me some pills and told me to get her to swallow them. Then she told me to prepare for the worst.

"Any other person probably would have lied to me, Brady, but your mom told me to prepare for the worst. So I went back upstairs to my mother's office where she lay on her couch and closed the door. I made her drink a little Gatorade and I gave her the pills. She smiled. I remember that. And then she held my hand."

243

Kaileigh was visibly biting back her tears. She had the ability to turn to stone, to seek the rigid and unbendable ways deep within herself so that she could make decisions without emotion, but recalling her mother's final moments was beginning to eat away at her deepest center.

"I was with my mom when she died. I sat with her a long time. I might have even fallen asleep. When I decided to leave the room I found myself going back downstairs, seeking out the only other living people I knew of in the building, but when I got to the first floor, your mother was...dead. I'm sorry, Brady. I'm really sorry."

Observation Mode, Brady ordered himself, nodding his head affirmatively. "Anything else?"

"She died helping other people. She was the last one."

"Did she die of the virus?" Brady waited on the edge of the question like it was a precipice.

Kaileigh looked away from him and then, after considering her answer, she said, "I don't think so, Brady. Right after I saw her, Dr. Grindle attacked me for the first time. I was stunned, but I fought back. I was so freaked out, I didn't know what to do, but I saw your mom and I know that she was untouched by the virus, like you. Like me. Like Dr. Grindle."

They sat in the silence for a long time. Brady stared at the floor, holding his head between his hands and shaking in silence. Kaileigh moved next to him on the bench and put her arm around his shoulder and leaned her head against his. He moved his head a little to touch hers and they shared a long quiet, desperate hurt. They were both orphans. Their souls had both been shattered.

Had the monster killed his mother? Almost certainly she was murdered by him. This was too much to bear. Why did Brady feel that in some small way, this was *his* fault?

They said nothing else. Kaileigh went back to her book and Brady went down to the children's section where he kept *The Autobiography of Benjamin Franklin*. He needed wise counsel. He needed to fall apart.

Grendel stood in the center of the roof of the hospital. It

was the deepest part of night and the moon had already retreated to the edge of the world, revealing the varied and numberless points of light dancing heel to toe overhead. The great spiral arm of the Milky Way spread out over him as though welcoming him. He had waited long for the strength to endure the bonding that would now take place.

All around him in the air were forming shreds and sheets of evanescent white. He spread his arms in an open posture and began to turn, following the forms as they increased in number and turned about him like an insane tornado. They increased their speed and with it, a series of high-pitched moans and dark confessions began to be told as one by one each of the now corporeal forms began to dive into the body of Grendel like swimmers in a black and oily sea.

As each ghostly form entered his body, his physical form took on a new appendage, an arm here, a horn there. His fingers grew back, as did a tail and a second mouth above his own original orifice.

Grendel's face was wracked with pain and pleasure, as though he was dying and being born all in the same moment in space and time and that somehow, they were both the same action. Once the first few forms melded with him, the others on the periphery began to act in like fashion and an onrush of ancient enemies abandoned their uniqueness to the creature that was Grendel. His body burgeoning with anti-life, his mind a maelstrom of spite and malice, the monster approached his saturation point. He had calculated this partnership with the precision of a scientist. If he had made even the slightest miscalculation, his own personality could be lost and the body that housed him would be unable to continue its biological processes, so perverse were the forms that now dwelt within him. It took all his strength of arm and heart and brain to control their competing desires within his mind. One of them wanted to kill another, one of them acting as infection against a third. Under a veritable sea of pain, the creature known as Grendel merged with the final form from the dimensions that swirled about him.

Falling to the his monstrous knees, he regarded himself

through a mask of agony. He was bent but not broken. It had taken hours for the process to complete and his resources were nearly spent, but he had transformed.

It had happened. All the nightmares and terrors, demons and dark imaginings that had once haunted the dreams of billions came from the darkness next to the Nothing and coalesced into the form of Grendel. No longer needed, their hosts all gone down to the earth and death, these imagined monsters had made the decision to throw in their lot with Grendel, prolonging their power and existence even as they were about to be extinguished forever. With no one left to be haunted, terrified, or appalled by them, the nightmares of Humanity became a single walking form in a last attempt at survival. As long as there was a single soul to torment, they could survive.

Grendel felt the power surging within him. No longer would he afraid to leave the confines of the hospital. The new world was his and he would finally claim it, cleansing it of the remnants of the past and with it, usher in his own new world.

The body beneath it all was stretched to the breaking point and even now, with the strength of ageless, timeless malevolence lurking like a demon in his veins, he could hear the faint whisper of a woman and the crystal laughter of a child. Was it his child? Was she his love? Who was he?

No, stop it! A woman's voice that sounded impossibly familiar pleaded with him to stop the conversion.

It's not your fault, honey. The research was solid. The virus must have mutated. We had no way of knowing this would happen. You can't blame yourself. Even worse, you can't continue the devastation. What you're doing is unforgivable. The world needs them. Leave them alone. Stop what you're doing and come back to me...

Even as he listened, he hardened his heart against this woman's words. Oh yes, he knew who she was. She was that pathetic doctor's wife, speaking from beyond the river, past the line that separated the living from the dead. She had perished but he could hear her pleading with her husband to rise up and put a stop to his machinations. It wasn't going to happen! Not after he had made the deal with all the devils in the world. No! He willed her to stop talking. He willed himself to stop listening.

From somewhere deep underneath, Dr. Grindle heard the voice of his wife.

When Grendel awoke it was well past morning. He made his way down to the ground no longer through the labyrinth of the hospital but down the side of the building, using steel-strong retractable claws. These limbs so lithe, these muscles to taut, how could this lead to anything but ultimately ridding himself of the two who plagued his dreams? He hated them even more, powered now by the collective hate of nightmares and fallen dreams. The world frightened him no longer. He would wander it freely and at will.

He loped towards the library, not even afraid of the knowledge housed inside any longer. His front arms were longer now and his hind legs were toned and muscled like a leopard. For his size, he was amazingly fast. Onward he sped, past the houses of the dead, over the charred and barren streets, over wrecks and beyond the beaten paths of the inglorious dead, a Lovecraftian monster, a horror-movie lover's dream.

There it was: the library. He pounced up the granite steps to the front door and screamed, "Renamer! Conduit!" His voice was thunder, the first sound of an atomic bomb just before it erases everything in its path. Then he roared out a warning and, grabbing the doors with taloned paws, he ripped the heavy oaken portals apart sending splinters and debris crashing inward and outwards. He thundered into the edifice and sought them out, throwing shelves full of books down upon the floors, hurling plaster busts of long dead poets and presidents against the wall. Where were they? Why weren't they here?

"Where are you?" he bellowed to the empty building. "Where are you?"

The only reply to his question was the voice of a stone gargoyle from Hoboken, New Jersey. The beast could not discern from whence it came, but it clearly said in a Jersey

247

lilt, "Too late, ya mook. Get outta my library before I whack you, jeesh! They left hours ago. What is it wich you, eh? Always a day late and a dollar short...Clod!" Then Gregoire slipped back into his French accent and like a demented Maurice Chevalier said, "I 'ave 'ad enough of 'zis. Go away or I will bite your ankles off, filthy scum!"

From the Tartarus of his soul, from the Hell of his mind, Grendel let loose a scream.

He had failed, again.

Chapter 17

Waking the Wizard

Brady dropped the transmission into drive and began their quest for a functioning radio transmitter. The road out of the city was fairly clear, but when they passed Three Mile Falls on the outskirts of Bangor, they were in new, unexplored territory. These were new lands in many ways. They had anticipated that the drive to East Corinth would take no more than forty minutes, but it soon became apparent that their estimate was wrong. The roads in the country were littered with more debris and refuse than the city streets. The animals had also been using the roads as highways. They encountered an abundance of deer, some cattle, several crows and turkey vultures picking at the edges of wrecked cars and trucks, both in the ditch and against the trunks of trees.

Brady wove the Lifeseeker through three automobile collisions, the wrinkled, blackened hulks that used to be subcompacts nearly filling the road and blocking their progress. Near Kenduskeag an eighteen-wheeler had tipped over, its trailer pointing like an outstretched arm at the blue cloud-laden sky. Kaileigh and Brady had to get out and inspected the shoulder of the road before determining that it was safe to continue but they nearly found their own vehicle in the ditch. After that close call, they realized that this simple trip could easily turn into their final journey. In the peopled past, such a journey was incidental, a common enough event, but in the nearly empty world, they could become stranded or injured without any medical help.

They had an uneventful five miles, the clearest stretch of road they had encountered since leaving Bangor. It didn't last long. Ahead of them in the distance was the biggest bull moose that either of them had ever seen. Brady slowed the Lifeseeker down to a crawl until they were perhaps five hundred feet from the massive animal.

Kaileigh reached for her .45 and withdrew it, releasing the safety.

"Looks like moose meat for dinner," she said.

They waited for the moose to move, but he had his hooves firmly planted where he stood. He wasn't going anywhere and he seemed to have no fear of the Lifeseeker.

Brady said, "We don't have time to slaughter it. We've got to keep moving. Besides, there might be another way."

Before Kaileigh could respond, he opened the driver's door and stepped onto the asphalt, walking slowly toward the bull moose. He must have stood eight feet at the shoulders and weigh 700 pounds or more, Kaileigh calculated. What was Brady doing?

"Brady. No. They're dangerous!" she called as quietly as she could from the Lifeseeker while still being heard.

Brady didn't even look back at her, but he did raise his hand, motioning Kaileigh to stay back. With every step he took toward the beast, her heart skipped a beat.

About two yards from the creature, he stopped and put his hands in his pockets and looked upward to make eye contact with the towering moose. Then Brady began to speak. In turn, the moose cantered a little when he first heard Brady's words. Kaileigh couldn't tell what he was saying at the distance from which she observed, but if she had been able to hear, she wouldn't have been able to comprehend. The sounds that came from Brady's mouth weren't words in any sense a human would understand.

For his part, Brady didn't realize that he was speaking anything but normal, everyday English. He wasn't. He was speaking a language very few humans had ever spoken except for long dead shamans and wise men from the prehistoric past.

"We seek to pass you and continue on our journey," he said.

Kaileigh heard the moose snort and whinny, but Brady heard, "Where are the people?"

"The people are all dead, except for a very few."

"Dead? So many? How did this happen?"

"A sickness."

The moose was shaken, his eyes wide. Such a strange turn of events.

"The animals in the forest know this. We all know it. The world is changing for us. Dog packs are forming, large beasts from the west and the north are entering our forests. All of creation is stirring, like the world is being reborn."

Brady shook his head in affirmation. "I believe it. In a way, the world is being reborn."

The moose shuffled forward toward Brady, bringing his snout with inches of Brady's face, snorting. Then the moose said, "Your kind hunted my kind. Why should I let you pass? I should trample you to death, and that one," the moose waved its massive head toward Kaileigh.

"How many of my people have you ever spoken with?" Brady asked.

The moose lowered his head and stepped a little closer to Brady. Brady didn't shift his stance, not even one inch.

"You are the first and only," answered the moose.

"And if we befriend each other, we can't hurt each other. We could help each other. We could leave each other alone."

The moose turned its long mule-like snout down to within inches of Brady's head and began sniffing. His massive brown eye met Brady's and there was a moment of understanding.

"I am Brady. I come from the city. I mean you and your kind no harm, ever, for as long as I live."

"And her? Is she your mate?" the moose asked of Kaileigh.

"She is...not really...we're friends. We travel together."

"I will trust you. If the world is changing, perhaps a truce between us is a good thing."

The moose walked away from the road, ambled its knock-kneed way into the reeds and departed, leaving Brady alone.

When he got back into the Lifeseeker, Kaileigh was wide-eyed and stunned.

"What just happened?"

"What? That? I asked him to move."

"You what?"

"I asked him to move. It was easier than shooting him and then having to move the body. That would have slowed us down."

"Well, what did he say?" she asked.

"He asked me if you were my mate," Brady said simply.

Kaileigh's face reddened and she immediately replied, "And you said what?"

"I told him you weren't, that we were just friends."

"Good," she muttered.

"Because that's all we are...friends," Brady quickly added.

"Right," was her curt reply.

"He thought you were too scrawny, anyway. He told me I needed a big, strong female." Brady said, chuckling.

"He could have killed you, you know," she said.

"I know, but one of us had to make the first move and I wanted it to be a friendly one."

She crossed her arms and laughed. "Next time you're going to do something like that, let me know first."

"Okay, but I might have to do a lot of things you don't expect. We're not on the old ride at the amusement park anymore. That place closed down. We're out here on our own and I'm kind of making it up as I go along, so stick with me. Sometimes I don't even know what I'm going to do until I do it."

"Great," was her reply.

From his vest pocket, the small voice of *The Autobiography of Benjamin Franklin* added knowingly, "Being ignorant is not so much a shame as being unwilling to learn. This journey itself is a teacher. Pay attention to the lessons. There will be a quiz later."

With that, Brady started the Lifeseeker and continued winding their way toward East Corinth, Maine, pre-pandemic population 3,000, post-virus population – impossible to tell.

They entered the town of East Corinth an hour later. Pulling off in the parking lot of the town's only pizza restaurant, they took their bearings.

"It's down that road, there, to the left," Kaileigh indicated.

"How far?"

"Don't know, but all we need to do is look for a really tall antenna. It should be nearly impossible to miss."

They drove down the Exeter Road toward MacGregor Hill. Less than two miles down the road, they saw towering in a field next to a stone house a massive steel spire: the antenna. There was also a large outbuilding behind the house as well as a few vehicles of different vintage and make in the yard and nearby field.

"This place is a mess," Kaileigh observed as they pulled into the driveway.

"Yeah, I guess they forgot to mow the lawn," Brady wryly said.

There, sitting on the mailbox, was Hugin.

"What the...? Brady, is that your Raven?"

"I think so. Yup, that's him," replied Brady simply.

"How did he know where we were going?"

"Maybe he just followed us. We weren't driving all that fast."

Kaileigh almost agreed with Brady's assessment of the situation, but she knew better.

As they approached the front door. Brady tapped

Kaileigh on the shoulder, handing her a gas mask.

"Better safe than sorry," he said, already donning his own. "It might smell bad."

"No thanks," Kaileigh replied. "It doesn't even phase me anymore."

Brady considered what she said and not wanting her to think he was weak in any way, shape or form, he quietly tucked the mask and hose back into its pack on his hip.

They opened the door of the small two-story stone house and entered. The front room was light and airy, and to their surprise, smelled fine: this wasn't a tomb. This was a safe house. Brady had developed a method of investigating any house he entered. He always made as much noise as he could, in the off-chance that someone was inside. Then, he went straight to the cupboards and drawers in the kitchen, since food was his main concern. When that was done, he would check the garage or work shed for tools he might need. He never liked going into cellars or attics. He rarely checked bedrooms anymore. He might pass by and take a quick look through the doorway, but there was never anything in a bedroom of any interest to him. Most of them were like shrines with pictures of strangers on the wall, or posters of favorite bands or actors. They always had mirrors in them, too, and Brady had grown unused to seeing his own face. This house was full of such family pictures as he had seen in a hundred other homes, of children growing up from babies to adults, the same eyes looking out from ever-lengthening faces, the same smiles.

"Brady!" called Kaileigh from down the hallway. "Come quick!"

He turned and ran down the hallway. She was standing in the doorway of a bedroom staring.

"It's a body," she said.

"Wait a minute," Brady replied. He pushed past her and went to the bed, taking in a deep breath. "How come this place doesn't smell like death?"

Kaileigh pushed past Brady and went directly to the body in the bed. She put her hand on the man's forehead. It was warm.

Nearly breathless, she said, "Brady, he's alive!"

from the Journal of Brady Smith
"There he was just lying in his bed. He didn't look like he was alive. In fact, his color was like ashes and it didn't look like his chest was rising or falling so I thought maybe Kaileigh was just wishing, but when I told her I thought she was wrong, she made me put my hand on his head. It was cold and clammy, but not cold enough for death.

Like an idiot I tried to wake him up by saying kind of loudly next to his ear, "Hey, Mister! Wake up!" But it didn't do any good. While I was busy looking stupid, Kaileigh was busy figuring everything out. She does that better than I do, most of the time.

"He's in a diabetic coma," she said.

"How do you know?" I asked.

She pointed to the table next to his bed. There was a blood sugar monitor, a syringe and a full bottle of insulin. There were also some glucose tablets and a journal. She opened it.

"He's failed to take his last insulin shot. His numbers are crazy high, too, especially in the last week. I think he's been lying like this for awhile."

I didn't think things looked good and I have to admit, I was a little more than eager to have a living HAM Radio operator on my hands than a dead one. Besides, how many people have I seen dead in their beds? It would be nice, for a change, to find a living person.

Kaileigh is the bomb! You know what she did? She talked me through it, like I knew anything about what was happening, but I think she did it kind of as a checklist thing. She took his blood sugar meter and inserted a new lancet, you know, a thing that punctures his skin so a drop of blood would form. Then she poked it in his arm. A tiny red bubble appeared and the meter absorbed it. In a few seconds, she knew.

"He's still high. If his blood sugar is high, that's bad, but maybe he hasn't been in a coma all that long."

"That's bad, isn't it?" I said, "a coma?"

255

"Well, at least we know how to treat it," she replied.

"What do we do?" I asked.

"Easy. If he was low sugar we'd have to find a way to get some carbohydrates into him, but since he's high, we need to give him insulin."

"That's it. That's easy," I said, not knowing what the heck I was talking about.

"Not so easy," she said, "we don't want to give him too much. That could lead to insulin shock or low blood sugar. We need to give him just enough."

"Well, how much is just enough?" I worried out loud, but Kaileigh said, "I'll give him half his normal dose and check his blood sugar again in a little while."

That's what she did. I was amazed at how sure she was of herself, but I didn't say anything. Kaileigh is the smartest, coolest person I've ever met. She knows all about this stuff. How? I don't know. She was a candy-striper and her mother did work in the hospital, so go figure for yourself. She's a got a way with things. She just figures things out. I really admire her, especially now.

We waited there, me on one side of the bed and Kaileigh on the other side, for an hour. She took his reading again and said he was improving. His blood sugar was still high, but lower than it had been. The minutes seemed like hours. Strange, really, that we didn't talk to each other much, like we didn't want to wake him when that was exactly what we were trying to do. I couldn't believe our luck! If this was Joe Belanger, President of the Rag Chewers Club, HAM Base Station owner and operator, then we had stumbled onto the very best person who could help us contact Radio Ukraine and the other survivors. Looking at him, though, it made me wonder because he looked pretty bad. I'd say he was in his mid to late seventies, a guy who used to weigh a lot more than he did now, like a well-worn tire that had outworn its usefulness, but whose owner couldn't afford another Firestone. There was a walker and a cane next to his bed, and he had some pretty thick glasses on the sideboard. Plus, there must have been fifteen different pill bottles there, as well. This guy had a lot wrong with him, but, thank God, he wasn't dead yet.

When he finally woke up, he was pretty surprised. Kaileigh put her hand on his to calm him down because he was pretty excited to see us. He could barely find the words to say, but I think that was because he was thirsty. I flipped open my canteen and poured some Poland Spring into a small tumbler and brought it to his lips. He sipped it slowly and as the moisture made its way down his throat, he found his voice.

"Where in Hell did you come from?" he asked in a gravelly voice. Don't get me wrong. He was pretty happy to see us.

Kaileigh said, "I'm Kaileigh and this is Brady. We come from Bangor. Can you tell me what other medications you 're taking?" She was so on top of this.

"I take so many pills I'm like a walking pharmacy. You name it, I take it." Then he grunted and said, "All of my meds are written in the back of that diary," he said, indicating the journal on the sideboard.

"How did you two survive?" he asked as he raised himself up to a sitting position, searching for his glasses.

I looked at Kaileigh and she looked at me. There wasn't an easy answer to that question. Sometimes you can look back down the road of your life and see how you got from there to here, but you have no idea how it happened.

Eventually Kaileigh said, "I survived because of my advanced intellect and he survived," indicating me, "from dumb luck, I think."

The old man looked at me and smiled. Then he asked what his numbers were and Kaileigh explained.

"Did you take insulin before you fell into the coma?"

"Coma? I wasn't in a coma. I was sleeping," he insisted.

"No. You were definitely in a coma."

He stopped and considered her words and he wasn't pleased.

Quietly he said, "Damn it. I was in a coma, wasn't I? It's just that since everything happened, I'm postponing my own death. I'm low on insulin and when it runs out, I'm a dead man, anyway. My diabetes is so out of control, its pitiful. I *guess that black cloud that keeps following me around is finally going to go into cloudburst."*

"How much insulin do you have?" asked Kaileigh.

"About a three week's supply and I've had a hell of a time keeping it cool. Lucky for me the cellar is a lot cooler than up here. I have a little igloo cooler I've been keeping it in. The stuff goes bad if it gets too warm."

Kaileigh shot me a look that told me the level of her concern. I was swift enough to understand our problem. Joe Belanger was a severe diabetic who relied on insulin to stay alive and if that magic substance ran out, so did the days of his life."

The scene was complete.Two teenagers were ministering to an old, ill man in his seventies who had fought a different dilemma than the Pandemic that killed everyone else. Kaileigh spoke with Brady quietly in Joe's kitchen while she made him something proper to eat.

"If he runs out of insulin, he'll die, Brady. We don't have much time."

"How much?"

"You heard him. A few weeks, unless we can get some more."

Neither of them had a solution to the problem. It would have to wait until later, after Joe was better. They had concerns about contacting other people but their main concern now was to help Joe. Even if they never contacted anyone else, they had *him* now. In a way, he was their shared responsibility.

"I've got a question," Joe asked, "Why me? How did you know I was here?"

"We...well, we didn't know if you'd be alive or dead. Actually, we were looking for your world band transmitter."

Joe nodded in comprehension. "You've been listening to Tetiana on Radio Ukraine, haven't you?"

Kaileigh and Brady both burst out the answer, "Yes! Have you? Well, yes, of course you have! Wow, isn't it great!"

Their fervor was short-lived.

"Oh, yes, it's just dandy. I've been listening to her. It's about all I've been doing. Spend all day waiting to hear another human voice for five minutes a night. It's a helluva way to live but you take what you can get."

Brady explained how they had found his name, how they had been living in the Bangor Public Library, how Kaileigh had survived in the worst place on earth for weeks on end while being pursued by a monster who was trying to kill her. As he spoke, Joe listened intently, seriously considering every word from Brady's lips.

"So you drove all the way from Bangor to find an old man dying in his bed and you showed up just in time to save his life. I'd say that means I've got more work to do before I'm gone, or should I say, *we* have work to do?"

"Work?" asked Brady.

"My receiver works just fine but my transmitter's been giving me problems and my generator only works for five to ten minutes before kicking off. I don't know what the hell is wrong with it. Everything falls apart, in the end. God hates me."

Brady and Kaileigh assessed the situation quickly and wordlessly.

"Well, we'll need to make it work again. We can work together, get another generator if we have to, even find another transmitter," said Brady. "There's the whole world we can scavenge and take from. We own everything, now."

Joe's bloodshot and tired eyes brightened for a moment of realization. Perhaps these two were sent to him for a reason. There was no way of knowing, but from somewhere within his heart and mind, Joe Belanger, mechanical engineer, master electrician, world traveler and jack of all trades was a necessary element in the new scheme of things. If these two had been sent to him, he wouldn't waste whatever time he had left.

"You're right," Joe said, sitting up on the edge of the bed. "I'm hungry, too. You two got any food?"

Kaileigh smiled and Joe smiled back at her as she brought in the tray with canned pudding, slices of apple and a diet Coke. In the coming weeks she would manage every bit of food Joe put in his mouth.It was a beginning.

Back in the darkness of a burned and blackened cinder that used to be his heart, Grendel sat brooding. In his great taloned paw he held an old photograph gingerly between claws. He had transformed, become stronger, able to wander the world and seek out the remaining few, but the ones he hunted were gone. He knew now that so long as even one human being survived, he could not rest. His fate was now clear. He would need to be a traveler, to hunt them down, to destroy them.

All of them, all over the world.

His massive body, larger now because of the augmentation caused by the merging of personalities and abilities, sat hunched like a small child hovering over the body of a sick pet, crouching in his own emptiness. The photograph seemed to overwhelm him, consume him, and cause him to fall into a melancholy as deep as Tartarus. Like some ancient gargoyle on a tall cathedral, no one was there to witness his longing, held down fast by bonds of hatred. Was it regret that whispered to his heart? Was it despair that lingered on the edge of his own personal and endless night? She was waiting for him to complete his task before he could rest. The only thing that mattered anymore was to complete the task they had started together.

"Get down!" Grendel shouted to the presence within him that held the photograph longingly and remembered the beautiful face it held.

Let me go! whispered the mind of the man within him, from the depths of Grendel's prison.

"No! Back down!" Grendel shouted.

Fenris studied the new, frightening form of his master. Why was he shouting and to whom?

Chapter 18
The Bearserker

from the Journal of Brady Smith

"We've been here for four days and things are looking better. Kaileigh and I have helped Joe get back on his feet, but the diabetes has given him some problems with his legs and he needs a cane most of the time. He can only walk short distances before needing to sit down. Even though I think he used to be a strong man, he's kind of fragile now. We've been in his radio room and we've spent some time troubleshooting his transmitter. If he wasn't here, in his own words, we 'wouldn't stand an ice cube's chance in Hell,' getting the transmitter working again. He said something about capacitors and circuit boards being fried by power

spikes from the electrical power going on and off so often out here in the country.

I spent three hours servicing the generator, using the manuals he had in his filing cabinet. He was pretty impressed that a fourteen year old could do such a thing, but the world is full of surprises these days. We've all been pretty focused on getting the transmitter ready, but it's been nice to be out here, away from the city, away from Grendel. Joe insists that we call him Joe, and that's kind of cool, anyway. I kind of like his attitude. He swears a lot. I mean he can string together a line of obscenities better than anyone I've ever met, and he thinks God is against him. Whenever something goes a little wrong, like when we tried to find the fried capacitor on the circuit board, he needed a magnifying glass because his vision has been nearly destroyed by what Kaileigh calls diabetic retinopathy. He said, "God doesn't want me to see. He's taken away my sight and I'm nearly blind. I can barely walk, I can't eat without risking death. Why has he done this to me?"

Crazy, right? But he's wicked smart and that's what we need right now. If he's angry with God, that's his business. The transmitter should be ready to try tonight.

We talk a lot once work is done and the sun goes down. Joe has a back deck with a fire pit next to it and we light a big fire and hang out for hours. He's been telling us that if we're going to survive, we've got to become hunter-gatherers and farmers, live like the pioneers did when people first came to this land. When we're not working on the transmitter or generator and he's not taking a nap, he goes through his library finding books he says we're going to need, how-to books and manuals, farming almanacs and living off the land books.

"You can't live on the remains of civilization. You've got to live closer to nature or you'll get soft and die young. You have to survive. Oh, and have a lot of babies. Can't forget them."

Then, in the next breath he'll say something like, "The world's probably better off without all the people. There were too damned many of us anyway - billions. This world is

262

a better place without 'em . People were like a virus to the planet, polluting it, poisoning the water and air, burning every fossil fuel they could. Seven billion people - think about it. Maybe the mass die-off is Mother Nature's answer to global warming. Hell, who knows? Who cares, anyway? "

So he hates people but he likes persons - if that makes sense. He wants us to survive, says we can 'make a better world this time.' I hope he's right.

There's something I need to write about really because I can't tell anyone - at least not yet. Two nights ago I wasn't able to get to sleep. We've all been sleeping in Joe's house. Max sleeps with Kaileigh in a small bedroom at the top of the stairs and Joe has his bedroom, but I sleep on the couch. I think Max has pretty much adopted Kaileigh and abandoned me, but that's okay. I couldn't sleep and when I looked at my watch it was two o'clock in the morning. Since I couldn't sleep, I thought I'd go out to the Lifeseeker and find my mp3 player. I haven't listened to it now awhile now, but it usually helps me drift off to lala-land. I quietly slipped out of the house and found myself under a roof of stars brighter and deeper than any night sky I'd ever seen before in my life. It was cold out and I was shivering, but the northern lights were on fire above me in great wavering sheets of greens and blues. It was like every star was set to extra-twinkle and was putting on a show just for me. For a minute, I forgot that I was standing with both of my feet planted firmly on the earth. I was up there, if that doesn't sound too crazy, like I was being lifted up somehow by some unseen hands. It lasted for just a minute, but I think about that minute a lot now, like it was a sample of things to come that was being shown to me for some reason. I don't know.

Anyway, I got my into the Lifeseeker and found my music player. As I closed the door to leave, I saw that I was face to face with a big creature. It was dark except for the light the universe showered down on me. My eyes were adjusted enough to the darkness to tell that this was a huge black bear.

He was standing on his two hind legs, his front legs hanging loose by his sides like arms. I nearly soiled myself

263

right then and there. I had no weapons and no idea what I should do, so I did the best thing I knew how - I didn't do anything. I just stood there and looked away, hoping the bear didn't take a swipe at me with those massive paws.

That's when the weird thing happened. I 'heard' the bear in my head, kind of like when I used to hear the Whisperers. It wasn't like he had human words, nothing like that. But I could sense that he was curious and that he meant no harm to me. I felt and understood at the same time, so in my heart I felt and in my mind I thought, "Please don't hurt me."

He sent this thought to me, "No hurt. Curious. Wondering. Things are different, now."

I opened my mind to him, thinking and feeling, "What do you want to know?"

He answered with an emotion and a direction, "You."

"I am Brady," I thought.

"Brady? You are human, not Brady."

"Brady is my name," I thought.

"Name? What is a name?"

"What others call me," I thought. "What is your name," I thought again.

"No name. Just me. Where are all the people?"

"Gone. Dead. Sickness."

He sniffed the air around me, shoving his great head to one side of mine and then to the other.

"You do not mean to harm me?" he asked.

"No. You do not wish to harm me?" I asked.

"People are like bears now. Few."

"Yes." I answered.

"Things...not like before. You...me...same..."

"Yes," I thought.

"Good," the bear answered and I could sense he was very pleased with this idea.

"Animals in forest...changing. People go...animals change to something else. I change to something else. Used to just eat, drink, sleep. Now I think...much. Now I think even when I sleep."

"Dreams," I thought. "You dream when you sleep. Thinking when you sleep is called 'dreaming.'"

264

"Dreams?" he questioned, "I dream when I sleep. Are dreams real?" he asked.

"No," I answered, "except you can sometimes remember them."

"But I remember dreams. If I remember something, it is real," the bear reasoned.

I was becoming very tired. Thinking and feeling as a way of communication is exhausting. The bear lowered itself to all fours and walked to the house door.

"Den...wooden cave?" he asked.

"Yes, with my people inside."

"I watch you all at night, by the hot light. So few people. Sad for you."

"Thanks."

"Four-footers, growlers, growing in numbers in the forests and fields. Growl and prowl, snap and snip. Used to live with people. Now live together and hunt. Even hunt me. Kill just to kill, not to eat. Danger everywhere. World changes."

I wondered what he meant and then it was clear. Dogs. Weredogs.

"These creatures...they are called dogs...weredogs. They used to be dogs, but they have changed and hunt together in packs. They are dangerous, even to you."

The bear snorted and thought to me, "I am strong! I kill them if they bite and growl at me. I kill them! I am strong...bear!"

As he thought this, I swear he grew three or four inches. It was like when he was angry or excited, he got bigger. I was afraid he'd grow into the size of a grizzly. As I watched him expand, I thought to myself, make sure he knows you're on his side.

"Good," I thought. "You are a great bear! You are a bearserker!"

He questioned with a deep burst of puzzlement. "Bearserker?"

"You are a warrior. You fight until they are all dead. You never give up. You fight."

If a bear can smile, this one did. He stood on his hind

265

legs again and approached me. Then he laid one massive paw on my quivering shoulder and thought, "Brother."

Immediately I put my hand on his shoulder and it was as far as I could reach. I replied in thought and strong emotion, "Friend."

"Name?" he asked.

"Name? You want to know your name?"

The bear thought," Yes! You name me," in no uncertain terms.

So I had to give him a name and I wondered what to call a bear you meet in the middle of the night after civilization has taken a nosedive and I remembered one of my favorite books, _The Hobbit_. There was a cool bear in that book - Beorn. He was a man sometimes and other times he could shift shape into a bear.

"You are Beorn!"

"Beorn Bearserker!" he thought and pleasure was in his mind. I could tell that he wasn't quite sure who he was. It was like he had been just an animal before and now he had awakened a part of his mind that he had never used and maybe a lot of the animals were beginning to fill in the blanks that people had left. Maybe when one species falls, another rises to take its place, somehow. Isn't that a natural law or something? Now he had a name and he could look at himself as a person, an individual.

As the stars began to fall down around us and the northern lights lessened in intensity, I thought to him, "Friend. Beorn. The weredogs want to kill us. They follow a monstrous master. We are in danger if they find us, and I think they will find us soon."

The great bear threw his head into the air and opened his gaping maw wide, exposing rows of huge white teeth, visible even in the near darkness. Then he thought with intensity, "I watch. I wait. I fight them...brother."

"I can't ask you to fight them for me, but if you see them coming near, you could warn me, if you are still in this place."

"I watch. I guard. I see. I warn. I fight!"

He was stumbling with this newly found form of

266

communication and I wasn't able to speak with him on any higher, more sophisticated manner, but it was enough. He was my friend now. I don't know what I ever did to earn the friendship of an expanding Maine black bear, but I was pleased to have it. We need all the friends we can get.

"Sleep now. Dream. Remember," he thought.

With that, he dropped down on all fours and walked away into the darkness, his own form like a small patch of midnight making him disappear instantly. I went back inside and strangely enough, I slept more deeply than I've slept since before the Abandonment. I don't even know if all this really happened. It all presents itself as a dream, but as the Bearserker said to me, 'If I can remember something, then it must be real."

Chapter 19
The Wizard's Tale

Tonight was the night they would attempt to contact Radio Ukraine. They needed the generator running at full capacity and Joe hoped that the atmospheric conditions would be ripe for generating skip, the ability of waves to bounce from the high atmosphere back down to the curved surface of the earth, enabling communication that would otherwise be impossible in a straight line. This only happened at night when the earth was facing away from the sun and the ionosphere lowered significantly. They would broadcast their message over and over every two minutes, hoping for a response.

Until then, though, they had time to imagine the ramifications of their actions. If they could make contact, they would no longer be alone. Each one of them had experienced the singular exclusion from all others, feeling totally isolated in the world, and each of them had also experienced the surprising joy of being with other living, breathing people again. To each of the them, the idea of reconnecting with other humans seemed the zenith of their hopes. To know that others knew of your existence was as necessary as food, water, shelter, and warmth. It was an affirmation of life.

Brady and Kaileigh had already discovered that Joe was disabled by his diabetes and that he had been an engineer at the paper mill in Old Town. Before that he had been in the Air Force during the Korean conflict where he had been a flight engineer on a B-29. He had been married and was the father of three grown children. His diabetes wasn't his only problem: he had already had two mild heart attacks and diabetes was slowly making his legs useless and his eyes blind. Even with insulin, his blood sugar spiked and fell wildly. Now that there was no medical care, Joe knew his days were numbered. He was waiting to expire, to lay down at night and never awake, but since the arrival of Kaileigh and Brady, he had found a new purpose. His workshop was full of electronic and mechanical projects that were in various states of completion. He had a full metal shop and enough supplies to last a year. The radio room was also the living room, and he had a large flat screen television that acted as his computer monitor. When the generator was running, Joe started his system and the room began to glow with the faint light of electronics. His computer was attached to the HAM radio which showed up on the large screen. There was a large array of hard drives and Joe showed them all the data he had saved.

"I backed up all the databases I could when I knew that the virus was a pandemic. The Internet was sketchy at best during the final days, but I managed to download a terabyte of data. I have frequency charts and call signs from all over the world. I can translate almost any language and I have the whole planet here in mapping software."

"In the last days, after my wife passed away, I was depressed, but I kept myself busy. I've always kept supplies, living out in the country like I do. I always bought six month's supply of toilet paper from the warehouse stores and then, I started buying everything in big lots. I don't like going to the town more than a few times a year, except for essentials. All of my medicine came to me in the mail, four months worth at a time. I had high speed Internet and satellite television. That was good, because the satellite channels were sporadic, but from time to time I got the live CNN feed. Day by day the sound of the outside world grew increasingly quiet. Then the last official news report came on the radio, of all places. It was a National Public Radio broadcast, after the Internet went down. I recorded it. Do you want to hear it?"

Joe turned on an old reel-to-reel recorder and rewound the tape until the numbers on the counter read '0000.' Then he flicked the play knob and both reels began to turn. A voice burst from the speakers, crisp and clear.

"This is National Public Radio. I'm Lee Ann Hanson. If you are hearing this, you should be aware that this will be the final broadcast from our studios. There are only a few engineers left who are able to keep the system up and running and the power is failing all around us. The worldwide pandemic has reached a critical point. The last reports received at this agency from various points around the globe indicate that the earth has suffered a new extinction event, this time only affecting Humanity. All other life seems to be immune to the virus that has been ravaging the population of all continents, including the high arctic and Antarctic research stations. No place on the planet has escaped the effects of the virus, originally thought to have been spread by birds. In fact, we now know that a U.S. government sponsored program to help immunize human populations against such a contagion seems to be the actual cause of the pandemic, although we don't know precisely why or how. What began as a simple test spreading of an airborne vaccine has resulted in the fall of our species.

All major metropolitan areas are effectively shut down. Yesterday morning, the United States Government issued a statement on the few remaining emergency broadcast networks effectively dissolving the federal government and releasing all power to any local agencies still functioning. Governments around the world have followed suit.

The situation is grim. With electrical power beginning

to fail, people are urged to assess their situations carefully. Food and safe drinking water are your most important concerns....."

The announcer continued to perform her final task with efficiency and courage. She outlined what people would need to do to survive, but she had to be quick. Already the signal was fading. She ended with the following words.

"While there is little reason for hope, we do know that the Centers for Disease Control have set up emergency headquarters in the last part of North America to be affected by the virus: eastern Maine and the Canadian Maritimes. With the last remaining experts focusing on ways to combat this killer virus, we can only hope that they discover a way for humans to survive. I have been looking for a way to end this broadcast. I can only cite the words of the poet T.S. Eliot, when he writes, *"This is the way the world ends, this is the way the world ends, not with a bang, but a whimper."* Let us hope that the poet was wrong. This is Lee Ann Hanson. Goodbye and good luck."

The tape kept turning but no sound issued from the speakers.

"We were the last place on earth to be infected. We survived longer than the rest," said Brady.

"That brings little comfort," Kaileigh said. "I was there, while they fought to solve the puzzle. All the scientists and soldiers died, except for Dr. Grindle."

"Dr. Grindle? Isn't he the scientist whose program started the whole damned thing?" Joe inquired.

"I guess," answered Kaileigh. "All I know is, he was a fairly decent guy and then he went insane. He tried to kill me, over and over again."

Joe commented, "He must have been under a lot of pressure. I mean, he's responsible for all of it. It was a mistake, a program meant to save millions of lives, even in parts of the world with no roads or hospitals. It was a good idea. Hell, it was a great idea. I wish I knew what went wrong. Poor bastard. Imagine knowing that you murdered the world. It must have driven him over the edge."

"He's a monster," said Brady. "A real monster."

271

"No doubt," answered Joe.

"Yes, he was a monster," she quietly agreed. "He wasn't, to begin with, but he turned into something...else. Something changed him."

"No, really, he was a monster with claws and fangs and spikes coming out of his back," Brady insisted.

They did not pay him any heed.

Joe asked them a thousand questions about their recent past. He was amazed when he hobbled out to the Lifeseeker and saw the collection of tools, supplies and modifications that Brady had previously made to the vehicle. He was especially excited about the four-wheelers on the trailer, claiming that he would love to "take a spin on one of those." After prolonged discussion around the back deck and lots of tea, Joe began to speak of his past and how his journey had brought him here.

Where Kaileigh and Brady had battled elemental forces, Joe had spent quiet hours pondering his short future. He had spent hours and days on the radio trying to find anyone on the receiving end. It was his only method of contact with the rest of the world. How many hours did he spend going from one frequency to another, seeking anyone at all? Meanwhile, his supply of insulin grew smaller every day. He felt lightheaded followed by chills and hot flashes and he knew his sugar level was spiraling out of control. He lay for long hours in bed in the morning, sleeping deeply and falling farther into his own illness.

"Funny," he told them, "I didn't die from the virus. Was it because I hadn't been exposed to it or because I was immune? If I was immune, then how?"

As he sat there talking to them, he pondered the weight of his own mortality. If they were going to survive, Brady and Kaileigh had a lot to learn. They had to do more than live off the detritus of civilization. They had to do more than survive – they had to thrive!

"Kaileigh, When I went to bed, just before you found me, I didn't expect to wake up. I took a small injection of insulin and said my prayers in the darkness and passed out. When you woke me, I thought I was waking up in other world and you were some kind of angel."

"Can I call you *Angel*, Kaileigh?" asked Brady

"Do that and *you'll* be waking up in another world," she said.

Joe let go a laugh. Night was falling and soon they would speak through the darkness to the other side of the world, reaching out an invisible hand into the ether, hoping someone, somewhere would grasp it.

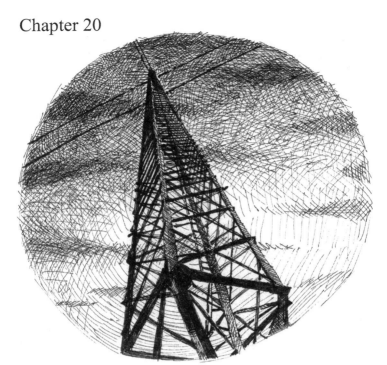

Chapter 20

First Contact

They sat in front of the Kenwood transceiver with the dull humming of the diesel generator outside in the darkness. Awash in the yellowish glow from the transceiver's interface, Brady and Kaileigh were rapt with attention as the wizard began to move his hands over buttons and dials and readied himself for the proper incantation.

Few broadcasts in the history of Humanity held so much hope and promise, thought Joe as he worked on setting the broadcast properly, except perhaps the signal sent by Marconi over the Atlantic, or the signal sent from the Lunar Module of Apollo 11 to the satellite dish in Australia to be beamed around the planet. Joe stole a glance over his shoulder at the two young people who now shared his life and was astounded. Here he was, a man nearing the final days of his own life, presented with a peculiar conundrum. He knew that if these two were to survive, they would need all the help they could get. To be sure the girl was brilliant and intuitive and he was certain the boy was not unlike himself: a problem-solver with a good attitude. Such beings might be able to survive and help the species back onto its feet. But they were young and there was so much for them to know, so much for them to do. Facing the end of his life, he had given up any reason to go on. Then Fate intervened, beyond all hope. Hope...

Now, he had one final task to complete and it was, he judged, the most important one of his life. He needed to prepare them for all the possibilities that lay ahead of them. For now, though, the simplest thing seemed to be the most difficult. If they could reach Radio Ukraine, they would no longer be disconnected. People need food, water, and shelter but more than anything else, they need a reason to keep going, a reason to believe, a reason to go on.

Joe pressed the button at the base of his microphone and leaned forward, saying "This is K1KJV broadcasting 100 watts at HF to any station that can copy. Specifically seeking Radio Ukraine International Station seeking contact. Does anyone copy?"

Joe turned a knob gently and the numbers on the LED display moved slightly. They heard the crackling whisper of the universe in the form of static, that white noise from which an answer would come. It had to come. After a moment there was still no response. Joe could see the crestfallen look on their faces.

"Nothing to worry about. We have to keep saying it over and over. If they hear us, they'll have to tune us in. The signal we're broadcasting is strong and because its night, it's going all the way up to the ionosphere, where it bounces down to them. Sometimes you have to repeat yourself over and over again before you get an answer. The damned northern lights have been playing hell with the upper atmosphere lately, so that's likely to mask our broadcast a little. We can try other frequencies, try to narrow down the signal and boosting its power. They ought to be monitoring all frequencies."

The hope that had quickly retreated from their faces returned. Joe continued to speak into the microphone, sending their lone message upwards towards the cold void of space. As he dutifully spoke into the microphone every thirty seconds or so, Joe's mind wandered to his own reason for connecting with others. He would never travel to meet other humans. He was too sick, too frail, too near the end. If the insulin ran out, he'd be dead in a week. He was ready to accept this and he had enough of religion in him to believe in the afterlife and was, in his own way, looking forward to reconnecting with beloved others. Then he would wonder if there was an afterlife after all and that led him to doubt, which made him despair, but from the apocalypse came forth these two young people and right now, the next world, if it even existed at all, didn't seem to matter. His work here seemed mighty in comparison to all else he had accomplished in his life.

Grendel stood in the middle of an open field some distance from the city, on top of Copeland Hill on the Eddington side of the Great River. He made the journey out to the highest point with the guidance of the others, those ancient enemies of Humanity that had melded themselves to his body and his spirit so that they might survive after their food supply had been exhausted. Grendel's hatred and purpose fed them now and when he suffered, they suffered. Since the departure of the two humans, Grendel had sought other means of discovering their whereabouts, methods he had never known of, taught him by his own version of Whisperers.

On the edge of the field a very large number of weredogs sat on their haunches, awaiting his command. Even those who had not fed submissively waited for their master's voice. Perhaps four hundred of the creatures, the first army of the changed world, sat at attention, watching. Around the perimeter strolled Fenris, the largest and most cunning of them all. Every so often he rose on his hind legs and walked like a man for several feet and whenever he did this, the weredogs nearest to him cowered back in fear. If one of the creatures made even the slightest noise, his keen hearing caught it and he would rush to the creature and silently stare it at the ground.

Grendel stood a hundred feet away from them, alone except for the voices whispering in his head. One, in particular, spoke most clearly.

"They are using the air to communicate with the others over vast distances. They are using technology from the human world to speak with each other."

Another voice whispered in the background, "Clever, they think they are."

Grendel asked quietly, "Yes, but where are they? Which direction? How far?"

The voices were arguing, but the first voice broke in. "They are to the northeast, I think. They are a day's run away, at least. We cannot reach them this night."

Grendel paced back and forth across the field, stamping down the grass.

"If they contact other humans, they increase their chances of survival. Together they are strong. Together they are better able to fight us," he said as calmly as he could manage.

"Disrupt their speaking," said the first voice. "You can summon the thunder. You can speak to the elements. We saw you do this, when the city burned. You must do this again."

Grendel grunted and lowered his chin to his chest. What the voice suggested was tiring and wore him away like a blade on a grindstone, but there seemed to be no other alternative. They could not physically reach them until sometime tomorrow night.

"How do they speak over such distances? The world has gone silent."

"They use the pulses of the spectrum, lord. They speak with charged particles. They throw them up to the sky and they fall toward earth again. In this manner, they speak," whispered a sniveling voice from the crowd of voices in his head.

A flash of understanding could be seen on Grendel's

face. "*Radio.* They are using *radio.* I see. Yes, I had not thought of that. Clever little...Well, there is a way to stop them, at least for now."

The voices surged with excitement. "How? How?" they inquired.

"It will take all of my strength of mind and spirit. I will be weak when I am done and will need some time to grow strong again. Some of you will perish in the attempt."

At once the enemies of Humanity that had joined Grendel began to protest vociferously. They had not agreed to sacrifice themselves so that he could live. They were not expendable.They had agreed to the bonding so that they might survive, not perish. There were some voices asking, "Which ones will die? As long as it's not me, that's fine." Grendel laughed in the deepest abyss of his heart at these voices, for they would be the first to expire. Their frustration and despair fell on deaf ears. Grendel had made up his mind and there would be no changing it.

Then, the voice of the Hag filled his mind, one of the enemies of humanity that had chosen not to meld with him, the one he called *mother.*

"You are a fool, little boy. You are a fool to even try. Why destroy them when they could rebuild and fill the world with people upon which we could feed?"

"Shut up, toothless one!" he growled, "Be still."

The voice of the Hag said, "From the edge of the abyss, I will fight you, little boy. I will help them, if I can, if only to feed upon their children in years to come. I was here before you and I will survive!"

"Oh, shut up! I hope you die!" he muttered under his breath, having no power over this elderly, powerful enemy.

"I will hover at the edge of midnight and when you fall, I will warm my hands over your funeral pyre, little boy..." she cackled. She said no more.

He called Fenris to his side.

"Yess, Maaastaa?" Fenris was now on all fours again. Grendel did not like it when he walked like a man in front of him. He preferred submission.

"Soon I am going to call forth a force from within me

and send it skyward. I may collapse and seem to be dead, but I will be alive. You will protect this body until it awakens. It may take some time while I regain my strength and during that time, you shall be my co-regent, in charge of the world."

Fenris felt the urge to please his master sink into his mind like an incisor into a slab of meat and he lowered himself, crouching.

"Yesss. I will protect you from them," he said, indicating the weredog pack.

"With your very life, if you must," urged Grendel.

"To the death," replied Fenris.

"Good. It is settled. So it begins..."

With that Grendel did something he rarely did. He dropped to his knees and curled his massive body into a ball, making himself smaller, concentrating all of his energies on the task at hand. In his mind he chose the enemies who would be sacrificed so that their life forces might be converted to the necessary overload of power needed to amplify things. In this way, he fought an internal battle, conquering the enemies of humanity within before he could use their power without.

When the wrestling was accomplished and the beings within him acquiesced to his will, he formed two fists and arose, legs outstretched to firmly plant himself on the grassy ground. He raised his two arms in defiance of nature to the sky and sent one massive and uninterrupted thought skyward. A visible pillar to light could be seen forming from his fists reaching upward to the inky blackness. This he continued for many minutes with little effect and Fenris wondered at the actions of his master. Soon the sky began to fill with colors; sheets of red, blue and green cascading like waves over the ocean. They oscillated and wavered, growing and then falling in intensity, over all creation, nearly blocking out all the stars in the sky.

With each breath he drew into his lungs, the aurora reacted by expanding. With every exhalation, they retreated. The Aurora Borealis, the Northern Lights, were now an extension of the mind and body of Grendel, bringer of Death, harbinger of a new world without humans. He had hundreds of beings within him, some stronger than others. They lined up within his mind to burn into the sky and be depleted, destroyed forever. How many would he sacrifice tonight so that the humans would not contact each other? The despair of centuries thundered in his mind, but he paid it little attention. The aurora glowed magnificently.

"This is K1KJV broadcasting 100 watts at HF to any station that can copy. Specifically seeking Radio Ukraine International Station seeking contact. Does anyone copy?"

Joe had been repeating himself for the last hour with little success. He knew what the problem was. The aurora was active tonight. There must have been a disturbance on the sun, because the aurora was an electrical storm in the earth's upper atmosphere caused by solar particles. They often knocked out satellites and shut down power grids if they were strong enough. As much as he did not want to admit it, the growing borealis was a bad sign. He didn't want to lie to Brady and Kaileigh, but he gleaned that they might already be sensing his mind.

"It's not going to work," Kaileigh said. "There's too much interference in the upper atmosphere."

"Let's go take a good look," Joe said and he reached for his cane. They went off the back porch and looked at the sky.

They were speechless for several moments. How could nature paint such a canvas? What were the pigments and from where did these colors arise? Brady thought that he had not even seen some of these colors before in his life, like they were entirely new to the spectrum of nature.

Kaileigh was stunned by their beauty, haunted by the movement of the particles, but she was also surprised by what she thought she heard. She could swear she could hear screaming coming from the sky, from the northern lights themselves. It was as though the lights were the dying cries....of what? She tried to force herself to think she was imagining these sounds, but she failed. It was Brady who finally spoke.

"I can hear them screaming," he said.

Joe nodded and said, "Me, too. What the hell is that?"

280

Kaileigh said simply, "Death. I hear it too. Something that wails like that is dying as it screams."

They watched and listened as the northern lights covered the entire night sky like a funeral pall, like a death shroud, like a winding sheet.

"We can't give up," Brady said. "This is Grendel's doing. He's causing this."

Both Kaileigh and Joe looked at him with wonder.

"How do you know?" asked Joe, who tended to believe Brady even when he sounded like he was saying utterly impossible and fantastic things.

"I just do. I can tell. He doesn't want us to contact anyone. If we contact the others, it'll make us all stronger. He wants us separated and weak, so he can hunt us down and kill us, one by one."

Joe glanced at Kaileigh and then back at Brady. There was a lot of diesel fuel. The repairs on the generator seemed to be holding and the transceiver was functioning. Was there any way he could think of to boost the power of the transmitter?

"Maybe we can ramp up the wattage. It might be possible to give this broadcast a boost!"

Never give up. Never give in. Say nothing if the world is against you. Just act casual and act as though there was nothing wrong in the world, thought Brady as they went back into the house.

Joe shut down the transceiver. He fished around under his desk and had Brady withdraw an old grey steel box that weighed at least fifteen pounds.

"What's this?" asked Brady.

"It's my Hallicrafters. It was my first transmitter. It's old, like me, but the damned thing has more power than you can imagine. I spent years tinkering with it. I talked all around the world with this, but it kept getting harder and harder to find the vacuum tubes. The world went digital and so did I, but this old puppy might be just the thing to reach the Ukraine. I bet this thing could broadcast halfway to Heaven!"

Kaileigh and Brady repositioned the old Hallicrafters

model on the desktop next to another Hallicrafters receiver from beneath the desk and began making the connections, instructed by Joe. It didn't take very long before they were ready to switch it on. Joe made his way to the closet and found a tall silver microphone with a sidebar switch. It was about a foot high and stood atop a silver base. At the top was a circular wire-mesh microphone. Joe plugged it into the transmitter and switched the whole unit on.

A pinkish glow slowly arose inside the vintage machine as the tubes began to warm.

"It takes about a minute before she's ready."

Kaileigh studied the old man's face. Joe was happy. It was like meeting an old friend from long ago, except he had grown old and this friend had remained a little boy. The old Hallicrafters spoke to him of days gone by, of friends now dead, of family and teaching his own children the craft, and he was at once filled with remorse and longing. As he readied to speak out to the sky, he longed for a real Heaven.

There was no digital LED readout on this machine. Instead, cotton thread covered with beeswax connected to small springs which in turn were connected to wheels and tuning knobs all working together to move a red needle across a dial lit by a small incandescent lamp. He found the frequency given to him by Radio Ukraine every night for the last two weeks and turned up the gain as high as he could.

"This is K1KJV broadcasting 150 watts at HF to any station that can copy. Specifically seeking Radio Ukraine International Station seeking contact. Does anyone copy?"

There, from the crystal darkness and through the barrier of the Aurora Borealis, came the faint voice of Tatiana, sole spokesperson for Radio Ukraine and the entire human race.

"K1KJV, I read you. Coordinates, please?"

"East Corinth, Maine, United States of America. There are three of us here."

After a moment of silence in which they feared they had lost contact, Joe repeated, "This is K1KJV broadcasting 150 watts at HF to any station that can copy. Specifically seeking Radio Ukraine International Station seeking contact. Does anyone copy?"

"K1KJV, your signal is breaking up. Please keep trying."

Her voice was fading fast. Through the interference they heard, "Repeat, please transmit coordinates. Where are you?"

She hadn't heard them.

For the next frantic hour, the three small voices in the night called out to the oscillating, variegated sky, in all of its terrible awesomeness. They couldn't hear the screaming from inside the house. Instead they heard Tatiana's voice in her precisely practiced English, over and over.

"K1KJV, this is Radio Ukraine, please come in."

Their reply was always the same and as Joe calmly kept manipulating the dials and gain, the squelch and volume, Brady found himself losing focus, little by little. He was fatigued. Something was happening to him. He sat down on the lounge chair and closed his eyes, his two companions oblivious to his collapse. As he shut his eyes, he began to feel weightless, his body no longer bound to the earth. Was he being overwhelmed by fatigue? Was he falling asleep?

Then, he heard her voice. Who was that? It was a Whisperer. He hadn't heard a whisperer since the night of the fire and Kaileigh's rescue. Susan had told him they would all leave him alone now. Still, he knew he was in their presence of a Whisperer. Perhaps the aurora opened the doorway again and helped the Whisperers make contact.

"Brady," he heard her say.

"Who is this," he asked quietly, so that neither of his companions heard.

"Brady, It's me. *It's your mom.*"

He couldn't find words. He could barely find his breath. His heart jumped into his mouth and his mind was reeling.

No God, no, please no. No....

If she was a Whisperer, then she was dead, but she was speaking to him, which meant that there really wasn't any such thing as death, just a transition, like birth, from one unseen place to this place and back again.

"Mom," he said, "I've missed you." Tears rolled down his cheeks while over the corner, hunched over the equipment, sat Kaileigh and Joe desperately trying to regain

283

contact.

"You are in terrible danger, again, Brady. You must listen to me. You need to make contact with the other people. They need you. There are people in the Americas, right now, who are lost and lonely. You need to make contact with them. You need to find them, go to them."

"But how?" he asked, a smile crisscrossing his face with a frown of confusion.

"The Creature is blocking your transmission, but you have the power to break into the Aurora, to divide it and create a window for your transmission to pass through."

"I do? What? How?" he pleaded.

She whispered from a well a million miles away, "Simply join with the equipment."

"What? How can I do that?" He was confused. Could this be his mother? Wasn't she supposed to comfort him?

Her window was beginning to close and she began to grow fainter and fainter, a whisper of a memory of an echo long past, against a vast static sea.

"You must join with the machine. You can be the ghost in the machine. You can boost the signal."

"Mom," he whispered desperately, "will I see you again?"

She was leaving now. The message she was tiding to him was essential and important. She may have crossed distances unmeasurable to deliver it. Why? To ask him a riddle? How could he join with the machine? She was the second Whisperer to tell him that he was needed by the rest of the world and he still didn't know why. Susan told him it was because he saw things as they truly are. Now his mother sounded like he was needed to bring hope to others? How? He was only fourteen and he barely had any hope within him at all. How could he give what he didn't have?

"Love you...will see you again...work to do yet...make contact..."

She was gone.

It was like waking from a seizure. He was exhausted, barely able to get up from the chair. He rose awkwardly and walked over to the old Hallicrafters transmitter, gently pushing Kaileigh aside and moving Joe's wheeled office chair out of the way. Then, without thinking, he turned the transmitter around and stuck both his hands into the back among the capacitors, vacuum tubes and wiring. Sparks began to fly as Joe and Kaileigh began to panic, but surprisingly, Brady was not being electrocuted. He seemed to be in full control of his mind and body and he felt no pain, just the smallest tickle against his skin.

"Talk to her now," he said in a strange, calm voice.

Joe shot Kaileigh a look of terror, but something told him to listen to the boy who should be on the floor with his eyes rolling into the back of his head and his tongue extending from his mouth. Kaileigh's expression was one of shock, but she said boldly, "Joe, talk!"

"This is K1KJV broadcasting 150 watts at HF to any station that can copy. Specifically seeking Radio Ukraine International Station seeking contact. Does anyone copy?"

"Radio Ukraine copies you. Please identify."

"Three of us, Brady, Kaileigh, Joe. In East Corinth, Maine, Eastern United States. Do you copy."

Another moment of silence and then, "Copied, K1KJV. Three of you. East Corinth, Maine, United States. What is your situation?"

They were shocked with elation, surprised by happiness. Success! Kaileigh found herself bending down to hug the seated figure of Joe as a smile spread across his face. They had done it and this strange, surprising boy had made it possible.

However, instead of hearing Tatiana from Radio Ukraine, another voice filtered down more clearly through the ether, a voice from beyond the world.

"Renamer! I hear you!"

Kaileigh and Joe looked at each other stunned, not comprehending who this could be.

Brady knew, recognizing his growl and spite.

"Grendel," said Brady to the open air, without a need for a microphone. "You lost. We escaped."

"You are pathetic if you think you've escaped me for long. Even now I track your whereabouts. Even now I know

where you are. I smell you on the wind, I taste you in the very wavelengths through which we speak."

"You can't stop us. We've made contact...You're too late."

A deep, guttural laugh spewed from the speakers as Grendel said in Tatiana's voice, *"This is Radio Ukraine. Copied K1KVJ. Three of you. East Corinth, Maine, United States. What is your situation?"*

Reverting to his own voice, he said, *"Sound familiar, Renamer? You and the girl need to know that no matter where you run, you cannot hide. I have eyes in the air. I have powers now beyond those when last we grappled and struggled. When we meet again, you will see."*

"Talk is cheap," said Brady, his eyes still closed as he pictured the beast in his mind's eye.

"I will do more than talk. I will act. Even now my forces are readying for the final assault."

Brady could see the beast clearly in his mind. His face still shifted from one form to another, first one thing - a human, and then into Jason and Freddie and the Alien, a Predator, Medusa and Scylla, from all the hated faces he had ever seen and Brady wondered if the monster could see him.

"You don't scare me, Grendel. I know you for what you are. I see you as you really are and I know that you are more afraid of me than I could ever be of you. We've survived. We're smart. We're strong. We'll fight you."

"Renamer, you will fail. You are doomed to fail. You think you know me? You have no idea. All you see is the outward manifestation of your own subconscious fears. I am all things to all people. What they hide from, worry about, panic over. These are my masks. Beneath that, I have a face even you have not suspected and because I am more than you could ever know, you cannot win. Our destinies are linked.

"Oh," Brady said, "I know. Beneath it all, you're a person. Doctor Grindle's in there. Somewhere deep below, there's a human *in you* and as long as you're partly human, a *human* will walk the earth. As long as *you* live, *Humanity* lives. You can't win!"

286

A scream filled the airwaves and a bolt of electricity moved with the speed of anger up Brady's arm and to his head, throwing him away from the radio unit, through the air as Brady fell limp against the wall and all the power from the generator failed.

Chapter 21
Revelations

The first thing that Brady saw when he awoke was Kaileigh looking down on him with ominous concern. As her face slowly came into focus, he could see Joe behind her and he heard him saying, "Check his eyes. Here, use this," as he passed her a small penlight from the myriad of pens and pencils in his pocket protector. She shone it directly into each of his eyes, waiting for them to dilate.

"Normal," she said.

"Can he move?" asked Joe.

"I don't know," said Kaileigh as she put her hand on his cheek and asked him gently, "Brady? Can you hear me?"

Brady smiled and said, "You have the most beautiful eyes, Athena." His mind was swimming, but he couldn't help thinking how positively radiant she seemed. It was as though her whole face was surrounded by a glowing halo.

She looked up at Joe and said, "He may have brain

damage."

They heard Brady begin to laugh.

"I'm okay," he said. "I just had the wind knocked out of me."

"Boy, you have some explaining to do," Joe said.

"Come on," she said, "Can you get up?"

He arose from the floor with her help and she led him to the chair.

"Brady, it's hard for us to understand what happened here."

"I know. I guess it's time to set the record straight. I'm not afraid anymore, anyway."

"What do you mean?" asked Joe.

"I mean I can tell you what I know without caring if you believe me, because if we're going to survive, you've *got* to believe me. The world has changed, and we've all changed with it, a little. I seem to have experienced the most change, but Kaileigh is different now, too. I'm not sure about you, Joe, but I'd bet even you have experienced the world a little differently since everybody else died."

Both Kaileigh and Joe remained silent to this assertion. She was open to almost anything, now that she had heard the sky screaming and had heard a disembodied voice speak with enough force to hurl Brady across the room.

"Brady, is Grendel the same Dr. Grindle I've been speaking to you about?" asked Kaileigh.

"Yes...and no. He's in there, this Dr. Grindle. But there's more to Grendel the monster than the doctor. It's like Dr. Grindle is possessed by some kind of spirit. I don't know where the monster Grendel came from, but he seems to know me."

"He keeps calling Dr. Grindle 'Grendel,' like the monster in the Beowulf story. Only he's just a man. I should know, I spent a lot of time with him."

"That's because you don't see him as he really is, not yet anyway, but I do. I don't know why I can see him and you can't, but I swear to you, the thing I fought was more than a man, way more."

"Possessed?" asked Joe. "Like demonic possession? Are

289

you saying Dr. Grindle, the head of the CDC's response unit and the originator of this plague is actually possessed by a...demon?"

"No, I didn't say he was possessed by a demon," Brady countered. "I said it was *like* he was possessed. But he isn't a demon, not like from Hell. This thing that has power over him is using him mostly as a vehicle, riding around on top of him, using his mouth, his eyes, and his hands and feet."

"A parasite?" asked Kaileigh. "Are you saying he is being controlled by a parasitic being?"

"Sort of. It's hard to put into words. Would it make any more sense if I said that to you, he looks just like a man, but when I look at him, I see a huge, monstrous body with a face that keeps changing shape?"

"Oh, that would make a lot of sense," she replied sarcastically.

"Well, it's true. I see things differently than I used to. I don't know why, but its like I'm more in tune with the world than I ever was before the Abandonment. I can sense things sometimes before they happen. I interact with things that are impossible to interact with. I thought I was going crazy, but after tonight, there's no going back. This is who I am. This is me. I'm his enemy."

Joe took a chair and brought it close to Brady so that they were sitting knee to knee. Intent upon discovering the solution to this mystery, he said, "Give me some specifics. What do you interact with?"

"I talk to statues and books. They talk back."

"It's true" muttered Kaileigh.

"I can understand Hugin when I ask him yes or no questions, and he understands everything I say."

"That doesn't make sense," said Joe, wanting to believe but needing more proof.

"Um, Joe? I don't know how to say this, but...I saw him talk a five hundred pound moose off the highway. He walked right up to it and just had a conversation. I didn't understand what I was looking at, but now, well, I just don't know. I've also personally seen a stone gargoyle and a bronze statue come to life and talk to me."

Brady continued, "I have a personal relationship with the *Autobiography of Benjamin Franklin*, and the statue of General Joshua Chamberlain in Freedom Park in Brewer. I've watched the spirits of the dead walking through Mount Hope Cemetery and I have been haunted by voices that tell me things. One of the voices was Susan, a girl I knew in school. She told me where you were, Kaileigh, and that I had to help you escape. I listened to her and that's how I found you. "

"Is the boy schizophrenic?" asked Joe in disbelief.

"What do *you* think, Joe?" asked Kaileigh.

They sat in a heavy silence fraught with worry as both Kaileigh and Joe weighed his seemingly disturbing revelations in silence.

"No," said Joe slowly in a nearly inaudible voice, "I think he's alright. We all heard the sky screaming. We both saw him control the electrical current and let me tell you, as a master electrician, that's just impossible. He's like one of the X-Men."

Kaileigh added, "He has a point. The world feels different to me. It's more than just the big empty space left by all the people. Maybe it's changed *because* of the big empty space left by all the people."

Brady continued, "Oh, and the dogs we've seen. They're not really dogs. I mean, they used to be, before the Abandonment. Since then, they've been slowly changing into creatures more and more like the humans who used to be their masters. I think they're under Grendel's influence. It's like he's their alpha dog. Anyway, Kaileigh and I together were strong enough to beat him the first time."

"You should have let me kill him when I had the chance," muttered Kaileigh.

"Don't you see," said Brady leaning forward, "If you had, you would have killed Dr. Grindle,too. He's not the problem. He's not the monster. The monster is the exoskeleton controlling the body. When you first told me about Dr. Grindle, Kaileigh, I thought *you* were crazy. How could you *not* see this monster, this grotesque beast that was attacking me? Then I thought about it and I knew you were

291

different from me, that the world changing had affected you differently. Maybe every survivor of the Abandonment is affected personally, in their own way."

"How so?" asked Joe.

"When we went to the water tower," she said, suddenly remembering.

"Yes! That was when you had this weird idea that the water was talking to you. You liked the sound of the water. It moved *towards you.* You were that way then, and now I'd bet whenever you go near water, like a river or stream, a lake or a pond, it'll affect you the same way. Maybe you're sensitive to water now. Maybe you can use it, like a tool."

She looked off into a corner of the room and said nothing, pondering his words.

Joe spoke next. "Grendel instead of Dr. Grindle. Monster instead of Man? There's another thing - the aurora. That was impossible, unless the Sun just experienced a flare so big it would have enveloped the earth, and since we're still here and not fried to a crisp, I'll take your words at face value."

"Thanks," said Brady, relieved.

"Just one thing: what is Grendel? Who is he and what is his nature? That's what we've got to discover," said Joe.

"I'm not sure where he comes from or who he is. Sometimes I think I've even met him before, like he's somehow familiar. He's a lot stronger than the last time I wrestled with him. Something has made him more powerful than when we fought with him. I mean, come on, he was able to control the Northern Lights!"

They sat in consternation for long moments until Brady reminded them, "We still haven't made contact with Radio Ukraine. We failed. He knew we were trying to contact them and he stopped us."

"He must be mastering immense power to block our transmission by generating some sort of electrical or magnetic field ," said Joe. "I wonder how he knew?"

"What does it matter? What we need to do now is try again," answered Brady.

"Not with this equipment," Joe said, rising slowly to

painful knees. He walked over to the radio bench and picked up the flashlight he always kept clipped beneath.

After examining the equipment he concluded, "Busted, fried, magnetized. This is just a pile of junk."

She hadn't said anything for a few moments, but now she stood up firmly and said, "Then we start over. We try again, with a bigger antenna, with a more powerful transmitter. We have time. We can do this. We're smarter than he is, even if he is strong."

Joe nodded and agreed. "We don't have a choice, but that poses a problem. How are we going to stop him from interfering with the signal again?"

"We can't stop him, but we can fight him, can't we? Is there a way to construct a really powerful transmitter that can break through his blocking?"

Joe cradled his chin with his hand in thought and said, "There is a way, maybe, but it'll mean traveling and scavenging a lot of equipment. I've got to ruminate over it."

They all knew without speaking that their primary mission was still to make contact with Radio Ukraine and the other survivors. It was paramount.

Brady didn't tell them about his contact with his mother. That knowledge was his alone. He didn't explain to them that since speaking with her, even for a moment, he felt even more in tune with things. The knowledge of her death broke his heart, but somehow knowing that his mother still existed and was waiting for him somewhere, calmed his mind. She had given him direction, a reason to go on, a purpose. He needed to make contact, above all. He didn't want to share her visitation with them for another reason: they had both lost loved ones, too. It would be cruel, he thought, to mention his own relief when they had no way of gaining it for themselves.

They were sitting in near total darkness now, a single candle permeating the dark. Their faces were waxing moons in the darkness, half-lit, half-shadow.

"I don't believe in demons," said Kaileigh.

"Do you believe in evil?" asked Joe paternally.

"Evil, sure, I guess," she answered.

Joe replied, "If you can, think of Grendel as a personification of evil. I've seen many bad people doing a lot of mean things in my day. I've been a soldier and I have seen man's blind indifference to his fellow man, again and again. Man is capable of almost any despicable act. After what's happened to the world, you have to believe that evil is real. Think of Grendel as a living thing, a walking manifestation of evil itself. If he is alive, he can be hurt."

"The question is, how?"

"I don't know," Joe said, "but I know that there are two languages that every living thing understands: *fear and pain.* He uses both, so he understands both."

Brady spoke up, "He fears us. He fears the people who survived. Apparently, we weren't supposed to do that, but we did. Why would he fear survivors?"

"Because we didn't die? The virus didn't kill us," responded Kaileigh.

"Precisely," answered Joe, "We're immune to it, somehow. Divided and separated, we're easy targets. We're weak. If we stay together, we present a more difficult conquest."

"That's it," Brady said quietly. "We need to gather together. Every one of us has to meet."

Joe looked up and asked, "Are either of you students of Greek mythology?"

Brady nodded eagerly. It was one of his passions. Kaileigh knew enough to win at Jeopardy, but she had filed Greek mythology into a cardboard box and shoved it under the eaves of her mind, way, way back.

"Then you know about Pandora's Box."

"Yes!" said Brady, beginning to understand Joe's reference already.

"Zeus wanted to punish mankind after Prometheus stole fire from Olympus, so he ordered Hephaestus to create woman," Joe explained.

"Nice. Women as punishment. Men were pigs, even in the ancient world. Not fair," protested Kaileigh.

"Right. Not fair, but a common conception in the West." Joe added. "Anyway, Pandora was made the first woman. To her the gods all gave something wonderful and unique, but they also contributed something to balance their gifts. They gave beauty to her, but also jealousy. They gave wisdom to her, but also recklessness. She was perfect. When all the gods had given their gifts to her, Zeus gave his last. He gave her a jar, not a box, as most people think, and was told never to open it."

"Let me," Brady said, wanting to finish the story. "So Pandora was given to Epimethius the titan as a wife and Epimethius, whose name means 'afterthought,' was told by his brother, Prometheus, whose name means 'forethought' never to trust Zeus. But Epimethius didn't listen. He told his new wife simply not to open the jar and forgot about the whole thing."

Joe was letting Brady continue the tale while he hobbled over to a bookshelf on the far wall, flashlight in hand, in search of a particular volume.

"But what happens," he asked Kaileigh, "whenever you tell someone *not* to do something?"

She considered it and said casually, "They *do* it, of course. It's classic."

"Right. One day when Epimethius wasn't around, so the story goes, she crept into the closet and took out the jar and opened it."

"I remember," said Kaileigh. "She let out all the evils into the world. It's the same old story, like Eve in the Garden of Eden. It's just another way of keeping the women in their place by blaming them for all the evils of the world!"

"Maybe," Joe said, walking back to the office chair with a small volume marked *Encyclopedia of Mythology* in his hands, "but accepted as the gospel truth for many centuries. Now I'm not saying that any of this is true, but bear with me. It may help us to imagine it as truth, to complete the metaphor."

He sat down and flipped through the pages until he found "K" and then "*Keres*." He began to read from the text.

"The death spirits of the ancient Greek world. Children of Night. Siblings of Fate, Doom, Death and Sleep, hateful of Humankind. In Latin they were known as *Tenebrae*, or the

Darknesses."

"What do they have to do with Grendel?" asked Kaileigh.

"It's in here," Joe said, finding the page he was looking for and handing the tome to Kaileigh. "Read this aloud," he asked.

She took the book in her hands while Brady moved next to her and focused the beam of his flashlight on the pages.

She began, "Nyx, the primeval night, gave birth to Moro,Thanatos, Hypnos, and the tribe of the Oneiroi. These we know as Doom, Violent Death, and Death. Then, though she lay with no one, she bore Momos, Oizys, and the Hesperides. She then bore the Fates and the Keres, whom we know as the Death-Fates. Then she bore Nemesis to afflict mortal men and Apate, or Deceit, hateful old-age that the Greeks called "Geras" and hardhearted Eris, known as Strife."

"These are the ancient enemies of Humanity, according to the Greeks. These are what was put into Pandora's Jar. When she opened it, she let them out. Were they...alive?" asked Kaileigh.

"The Greeks thought as much. We replaced these myths with science, examining nature and methodically categorizing them, but essentially it's the same. Think about the Keres. The Greeks were intuitive, weren't they, to think that illnesses and diseases were actually caused by unseen, invisible creatures: germs. We call them bacteria and viruses. They called them Keres. Human existence was plagued with them."

Brady broke in. "What did they look like? How did they act?"

Kaileigh read a little more, following the text with her finger as she searched.

"It says here that they were fanged, grim-eyed, bloody, had large claws that they used to catch men as they fell in battle to take their souls to Hades. They drank the blood of human hearts and then, like empty cups, would throw the empty hearts behind them, and run back into the battle until their thirst was quenched."

"Jeesh, I could have done without that last bit," Brady said.

"The original vampires," Joe added.

Kaileigh continued, "These creatures were often more than the cause of diseases. They were the disease itself, a different Keres for each sickness. They were cruel and relentless and since they were spirits, they went where they wanted, when they wanted, especially into the bodies of their victims. They brought death wherever they went."

"The stuff of nightmares..."

"So we found ways to fight them, with medicine, cleanliness and knowledge," Joe observed.

"Sounds like Grendel to me," added Brady. "Mean son of a gun, that one. Big and ugly, full of spit and vinegar."

"How did they fight these things in Greece? I mean, if we postulate that were dealing with such a thing, which I can't believe we are, then we might as well go all the way and figure out how they fought back," said Kaileigh.

"I imagine they prayed and sacrificed animals," answered Joe.

"I can't believe we're even considering this," Kaileigh said. "It seems kind of ignorant..."

"It is a theory, at least," interjected Joe. "A theory that we can work with."

"If he's the manifestation of all these evils, then he can be destroyed by......antibodies?" Kaileigh asked.

"The virus killed so many people because there weren't any antibodies," said Joe, stating the obvious.

"Well, maybe," Brady said, "Just maybe...*we're* his antibodies. We're nature's immune response to Grendel and what he represents."

"From the microscopic to the macroscopic, huh? He's the disease and we're the antibodies?" Kaileigh mused.

They sat in silence for a moment, considering his words. Joe, in particular, seemed to be deep in thought. Then he said, "I see. Perhaps that's why we survived, to make the right decisions, to stand when everyone else has fallen."

"But how are we supposed to destroy this thing? Antibodies in our bloodstreams have their own intelligence, in a way. They keep attacking until they destroy the virus."

"Yes, and sometimes they attack so much that they destroy the host. I bet that's what happened with the virus that caused the Pandemic. Immune systems kicked into overdrive. People were killed mostly because their own bodies, in effect, murdered them. That's what Dr. Grindle told us in the hospital before he changed into a murdering bastard," Kaileigh explained.

"This virus was so successful at killing us, but after there were no people left to infect, it had nowhere to go. It killed its hosts, which is a stupid thing for a virus to do," Joe continued.

Joe wondered aloud, "I don't get it. With the entire world at his feet, Grendel chooses to spend all of his time trying to kill us. If we were his antibodies, his natural enemies, then it begins to make sense. Where the hell did he come from?"

"I don't understand that, either. I was there in the hospital before Dr. Grindle went insane. Actually, he was a good guy, one of the best. But then he changed, suddenly, near the end of things. Maybe that's when he turned into the monster that Brady sees," Kaileigh said.

"I'm telling you, he's not Dr. Grindle. He's what Joe said, a personification of Evil in the world. It's like this," Brady explained calmly and carefully, "there was evil in people, spread out through them, a little bit in everyone, just like there was good in everyone, too. When all the people died, the evil needed someplace to go. It gathered itself together and *formed* into Grendel."

They didn't speak for a long moment while considering the idea.

"Nature abhors a vacuum. Hell, anything's possible," mused Joe, "Now, someone tell me how to kill it."

"Strictly speaking, it's not alive. It is only alive when it is in contact with its host. It needs a host to live. Remember, every virus, or in this case, every evil, needs a host," Kaileigh explained.

"Man, you must have got straight A's in biology class," observed Brady.

"Well, duh," she replied.

"We can kill Dr. Grindle. That will deprive it of its host," Joe said, a plan already developing in his mind.

"No!" Brady shouted. "I'm not killing Dr. Grindle. He's in there, somewhere. He's not so different from us. And there aren't many of us left. We need to get him out."

"Yes, of course you're right," interjected Joe, "Dr. Grindle has to be saved, somehow."

"So, how do you kill the parasite without killing its host?" asked Kaileigh.

She picked up the book and continued following the line of text for some time before she broke the silence.

"We'd better hurry if we're going to figure out how to save Dr. Grindle. It says here that the person whose body the wicked Keres possessed should beware, because they would create Envy, Hatred and Jealousy to rule their hearts, eat away their body and waste away their soul."

"You know," Brady said with a hopeful smile forming on his face, "the myth of Pandora's Box does say that she didn't let everything out of the box. There was one thing left inside. Something really important."

"What's that?" asked Kaileigh.

Joe interjected the answer. "Hope. In the bottom of the box was Hope. As long as there's Hope, we keep fighting."

Grendel awoke to terrible pain in his mind and body. The act of exciting electrons in the upper atmosphere had been akin to having his body plugged into a transformer for a prolonged time. Cell damage had occurred, but he had been able to reverse it while he slept. There had been an unexpected problem: the host had begun to rebel, to fight back. It had been a feeble attempt, but it was a new thing to consider. In a weakened state, the host might even be able to put up a reasonable resistance to his presence. This wasn't something he needed, not now. He had already found himself drawn to the photograph of the woman and child and he had even spoken to them, seeking their forgiveness. Foolish, weak human emotions. He could do without those. All of nature could do without those. So many species destroyed, so many landscapes flattened, so much pollution and desecration caused by human emotion. In the new world order, without human intervention, nature on earth would continue on the path it had started upon millions of years before humans ever existed.

It had been delicious. He ate the nightmares like candy, he burned the spirits of ancient hatred like so much gasoline in a tank. Gone from the world forever were Epiales, Lamia, Stygere and Akhlys, as well as a hundred other lesser ills and spirits. Their energy, converted and governed by his own internal engine, were transformed into the spectral pulses that covered the heavens, disrupting the signal of the humans. Mass and energy could not be lost or gained, merely changed and transferred.

There was a downside. No more could he rely on their aid, for he had betrayed them to further his own plans. The multitude of enemies that remained within him whispered quietly among themselves of the betrayal, but then they remembered that they were still alive, still vital, even though they were now part of the greater being and had lost their own free will in the process. Some wondered why they had agreed to submit to this bargain with Grendel and longed to be among those of their kind who chose to take their chances in the free world now that Humankind had been nearly erased from creation. Given time, they wondered in their black hearts, might not Humans rise again? Was the Hag right about this? Might not they survive to haunt the dreams of millions yet to be born? In the distance, just beyond his reach, Grendel could hear his mother cursing him.

There was much ground to cover and he needed rest, but he could not pretend that he didn't see the truth of the boy's observation last night. He was bonded to a human, tied irrevocably to one. Even if he could track the others all down and kill them, there would always be one more human. Him.

Chapter 22
Hope

The dream was long and exhausting, leading down pathways unmeasurable in real-world dimensions, through the farthest reaches of her imagination. She had been traveling for what seemed a very long time, at night, through dark landscapes, toward no known destination. In the dream, Kaileigh was alone and moved ever onward, inexorably toward more confusion, more unfamiliar and untrodden ground. Wherever she was going, she had a feeling in the pit of her stomach that it was not going to lead her back into the light.

She was alone, driving a truck, navigating through dark lanes that cut through mountain passes, through dark tunnels and under starless skies. Everything was gray and no color tinted her dream world. From all appearances, the truck was a troop carrier, the kind she had seen arrive at the hospital when the soldiers had taken control, the back covered in canvas and tied down with ropes. The cab showed two lit dials on the dashboard and, interestingly enough, there was a long stick shift and a clutch she had to operate with her left foot. In her waking hours, Kaileigh would not have had the slightest idea how to drive stick, but in her dreams, she was a seasoned trucker.

She had the idea that in the truck's bed behind her,

something of immense importance waited, so necessary to someone, somewhere that she could not afford to dally. Twice she had driven through villages in the darkness. In each one there was a single bulb burning in a single street lamp, revealing shadows and just enough of what lay beneath to ignite her imagination. It was a falling-down world through which she drove, devoid of people or any movement other than her own. She was immersed in a deep depression, a vast sea of darkness through which she piloted the truck. A sense of urgency pervaded her mind as she pressed the pedal down to the floor and double-clutched up the hills, over the forested mountains.

In her dream, Kaileigh was alone. She wore army fatigues and was unwashed, offending her own sensibilities with soot and grime, but it was inherent with her dream occupation and her dream world. A low drone came to her ears like a didgeridoo, the dull drone of the trucks tires on the cracked and potholed pavement. From time to time she had the feeling that she was driving past people as they stood by the sides of the dark road, just out of range of her headlights. She could imagine unblinking eyes staring back at her, watching her, even judging her. As long as she was moving, she sensed that these invisible watchers were content to stay where they were, but she felt that if she stopped, they might emerge from the shadowlands of this eternal night and move toward her with dire purpose.

Onward she drove in the dreamworld, seeking something and feeling increasingly desperate. As the miles crawled away beneath her, the feeling that the creatures in the darkness wanted to interrupt her journey now took precedence in her mind. She kept glancing more deeply into the depths of the ditches and beyond, expecting their advance.

Like something seen from the corner of her eye, she saw the form but only after her truck had slammed into it and sent it flying ahead of her. She stopped the truck and emerged from it like an insect from its chrysalis. Begrudgingly she made her way toward the thing in the road. What was it? Was it a human? Was it an animal? She

302

had nothing but her truck's headlights to illuminate the scene, but from what she could see, she had hit something that was neither human nor animal but both. It had been standing on two feet when she struck it, but it was hyper-muscular for a human. Hair covered its body and its face was something that could only truly exist in a dream. It wasn't a single face but several, like the bones beneath the flesh was alive, maggoty and writhing with mealworms. It was in constant motion and was anything but human. Had she killed it? It wasn't moving. She poked it with her foot, but the massive form did not move. She did not dare go any closer and she was filled with disgust and loathing for the thing in the road. Was this...Grendel? Was this the monster that Brady claimed to have fought?

Time was burning in her dream and she turned around to go back to the truck but was halted when the great claw of the creature suddenly clamped around her ankle, twisting her back to its form and drawing her down to the ground.

"You are not going to escape this time," it spat from broken teeth and bloody mouth.

She struggled enough to break free and found that she could barely move, as though paralysis had painted her body with a thick coat of pain. Every movement required the highest amount of effort she could muster, but she made her way back to the cab of the truck.

Once inside, she started driving, moving in madness through the darkness toward uncertainty. She left the creature behind, still alive on the road but with the dreadful premonition that he was loping behind her, just beyond her sight, getting closer with every leap. Even in her dreams, he hunted her. That would mean that he was more than Dr. Grindle, after all. Had she just seen in her dream what Brady had faced on the top floor of the hospital when he rescued her? Was this Grendel? She drove at breakneck speed, careening around curves, never using the brake, only able to think of forward motion.

She saw the lake in the distance as the moon, which heretofore had been absent, peeked out from behind a palling cloud.

Water. For some reason, she knew she needed to get to water, so she found the dirt track that veered from the main road and led down to the gravel shore of a lake set deep in the woods. Leaving the truck running, she parked as close to the shore as she could.

Before she made her way to the water's edge, she found herself wracked with curiosity and went to the back of the troop carrier, untying a strap, looking inside. At first, it was too dark to see her cargo but upon closer inspection, she could see it was a person, a young boy or girl curled up in a fetal position near the front of the bed, unmoving. The youngster was wearing army fatigues and it was clear that this poor child was somehow wounded or sick. As she climbed into the bed of the truck to investigate further, she found herself up against an invisible wall that bounded the child's edges and made it impossible for her to touch it. She could barely discern the rise and fall of the child's chest, but she could not clearly see the child's face. Finding no success, she could feel the rising frustration and anger grunting in the background and then, she heard it.

Water! The lake was *singing* to her. It sounded like crystal rubbed across the rim in a myriad of notes and octaves. She left the truck bed and found her way to the lakeside, falling to her knees. She plunged both hands into the water and suddenly the world exploded.

What had been night was suddenly day. What had been gray was multicolored and bright. What had been depressing was suddenly delightful. It was like the Land of Oz after the death of Wicked Witch of the West. Around her the trees and bushes swayed gently back and forth in the breeze. The truck was still running behind her and she could see that its lights were still on, but she was no longer dressed in army fatigues. She was dressed in a lovely formfitting dress with finely laced sandals. When she looked into the water, she saw elegance and beauty gazing back at her. Who was this person? Was that her reflection in the water? She had transformed into a vision of loveliness. What was this dream or a nightmare within a vision?

Then the water sang to her. It did not speak. It was a

thousand sitars being picked and strummed, a timeless raga, a hammered dulcimer weaving its melody with the humming of the very earth itself.

"You are safe here, in this place," it sang to her.

"Where am I?" she asked aloud, speaking to the water, and it heard her.

"You are in the world as it was meant to be from the beginning of all things. You are in the world as it truly is, beneath the mask of vision. In the time of people and their doings, so few found their way here. We are pleased that you have made it so far. We know the dream journey is difficult."

"Why am I here?" she inquired.

"We have tried to speak to you in the waking world, but the dreamworld is closer to our own home. It is easier to speak to you in dreams."

"Who are you?"

"We are *Of the Waters*, that flow among, betwixt and between the worlds. We girdle the world of Humanity. We are Styx, Lethe and a thousand other names for water that humans have invented to label us. We are the ocean sea and are known by many names."

"I don't understand," she said simply.

"All of life is born of water and borne to the world on water. Before you were born, you traveled on the water toward the world and when your body eventually dies and all that was physical does perish, what is left will travel upon the waters again, toward...toward."

In her dream mind, she thought of the boundary between the world of life and world of death in so many ancient cultures, embodied most recently in her imagination by the River Styx, the first of the seven rivers of the Underworld in Greek mythology.

"I can hear your voice in the waking world, can't I?" she inquired.

The voices sang, "You are the Conduit to all the remaining humans; our way in. We chose you at the beginning of things, when first we glimpsed the future."

"You can see the future?" she asked.

"We were of the Water before Eden fell. We have

lingered here since Time began. All water is connected to all other water. All water is the same, throughout time. All water is one. We were created deep within and have circulated throughout the Universes. We are the matrix and life cannot exist without us. The rain on the dinosaur's back, the snow on Beethoven's shoulder, the water at the wedding at Cana turned into wine, it is the same water, not new or different. We see the future, the beginning, the now and we see that today is forever."

"What do you want of me?"

"We have a message."

"What message?" she wondered, not fearful but curious, so strong was the sense of peace this lake emanated.

"First, you must learn to listen to the waters of the world when you awaken. To speak to you in dreams is difficult. So many things interfere. Some of what you see is real but some is your imagination. In the waking world, you will know the difference. We will speak to you, but you must *learn to listen.*

You are the companion of the Renamer. He is a boy now, but he will become something much more powerful. He sees the world as it is, even now, when his ability to see is newly awakened. Doubt him no longer and see to this: you alone can save him. You alone are destined for this task. If he does not survive the harrowings that follow, humans will cease to exist forever, on this plane, in this moment. So we have called you, to sing you your name."

"My name is Kaileigh," she said.

They made such music then in reply that she knew her name was not only Kaileigh, but something else, something from before her birth, from a time before the foundations of the Earth were laid, stone by stone. It was not a name she could pronounce or even imagine, but she knew that they spoke to her. When she knew that the sounds falling upon her ears were a name and not simply a melody, she was seized and surprised by a joy she had not felt in her entire life. Her soul jumped up. She swam in laughter. She was immersed in the light of the truth of it: her real name.

The music slowed and eventually returned to the tinkling

306

of bells and the harp sounds of water.

"We have named you. Now you will understand."

"What will I understand?"

"The way things truly are and your relationship with all the life of the earth," they answered.

She was confused, flooded as she was by the emotions so strong in this dreamworld, so strong that if they had been felt in the waking world, they would have utterly overwhelmed her.

"You must return. It is not long before you will be tested. Both of you must go through the fire to obtain the hardness of stone and the tenacity of time."

She knew what she must do. In the dream, she had to deliver the child in the back of the truck to its final destination. Only then could she awaken.

"Where do I take the child?" she asked *Those Of the Waters.*

"Take him to the very end of the road. Do not abandon him. Safeguard him when he is weak. Feed him when he is hungry. Cover him when he is cold."

"But I can't even touch him," she replied.

"Yet, you must care for him."

She withdrew her hands from the lake and immediately was thrust back into the depressing darkness of the twilight world. She arose and made her way to the truck and again climbed into its dark bed. She crouched down next to the child in the back, but this time, she put her hand softly to its shoulder and found that if she didn't push, but simply rested her hand there gently, it penetrated the invisible field that encased it.

The child stirred and turned as though in sleep, but she saw its face and understood what *Those of the Waters* had meant. For there, in the back of the dingy, grimy truck lay the sick and twisted form of the child whose name she knew well. For some strange reason, in a bone-deep way, she understood that she was now his guardian and that his final destination was her final destination. Just before she woke up from this strangest of dreams and thrust back into the Abandonment and all that it required of her, she ran her fingers through the child's hair and whispered the child's name. Funny, she thought, but simply saying his name brought her relief, even comfort. It was what was left in the bottom of the box after Pandora opened it. He was a dream child but he was also a child yet to be born, a child she would raise. In a language only she and *Those of the Waters* understood, she whispered his name.

Chapter 23
Flight

As they ate their evening meal on Joe's back deck, Kaileigh noticed a form coming from the rim of the forest's edge toward them, loping on all fours: a black bear. She immediately reached for her .45 automatic and withdrew it, switching the safety to the 'off' position.

When her two companions saw what she was doing, they both sent her questioning looks but she only nodded toward the form that was getting closer by the second.

"No, Kaileigh. Put the gun away," Brady whispered, his mouth still half-full of canned ravioli.

"What? No way. It's a big black bear," she whispered back.

"He's a friend," Brady said.

She lowered the gun, but did not put the safety back on.

Brady jumped down off the edge of the deck and walked towards the animal. In a moment, the boy and the bear were face to face. They stood that way for many moments while Kaileigh and Joe looked on in stunned silence.

"What the hell is he doing? I've never seen the like of it."

"I have," said Kaileigh, still fingering the trigger of the

pistol.

"Are they...talking?" asked Joe.

"I think so, but I don't know what would they have to say to each other."

The bear raised both paws and placed them on Brady's shoulders and as he did this, Kaileigh raised the pistol and took careful aim, but Joe's hand fell upon her arm and made her lower her aim.

"Look, it's not a threat," he said.

Sure enough, Brady had put his hands on the bear's shoulders. Then, the bear fell to all fours, turned around and began loping away, back to the forest while Brady ran back to the porch, a deep look of concern painted on his face.

"We have to get ready. We don't have much time!" he said firmly.

"What is it?" asked Kaileigh.

"Weredogs. They're almost here!"

"Did you just speak to that bear?" asked Joe incredulously.

"Yeah, and his name is Beorn. He just learned how to speak so his words are simple, but he told me enough. A large band of weredogs from the city is almost here. He's been watching them. They've gathered a mile or so away from us in the center of the town. Come on!"

Brady and Kaileigh ran to the Lifeseeker to retrieve their weaponry but Joe found himself barely able to move, his legs stiff and nearly unresponsive. He found his cane and moved with slow purpose toward the stone house.

"We need to protect him," said Brady.

"I know," Kaileigh replied, fitting the bandoleer over her shoulders and sliding her katana into its sheath over her back. Criss-crossed over both shoulders were various full clips of bullets for her pistol. She was a Ninja princess, the image of danger and righteous indignation, grim and determined.

Brady said, "There are too many of them for us to handle here and now. We have to split up. I'll take Rocinante and draw them away while you and Joe get the heck out of here. I'll send Hugin when I'm clear of them. He'll lead you back to me," Brady said urgently, his plan already solidifying.

"Brady," she said, holding back her fear, "I don't want to leave. I want to fight them...with you."

Brady said nothing in reply and simply looked at her, smiling.

"You may have your chance if you don't get out of here, and soon. They're only minutes away. With the Lifeseeker and Rocinante, we can easily outrun them. They're not a threat if we hit the road, soon."

She stopped him, reaching out and taking both of his hands into hers. He was rapt with attention. She wanted to say something, but she just could not grab the words from the whirlwind of thoughts now churning through her mind.

He spoke, breaking the silence at last. "I know. I know, but Joe needs to survive. We need to build the big transmitter. It's our only chance. Take Max and Joe and get out of here."

"Okay," she said, nervously letting go of his hands, "but promise me you'll make contact, soon!"

"I promise," he answered. There was no doubt in his voice.

They had lingered too long. There, from the edge of the woods, the creatures came, perhaps thirty varied forms of weredogs thrusting towards them.

"Get in the Lifeseeker!" Brady yelled, but Kaileigh was standing by his side, her pistol drawn and aimed. Squeezing her finger, she let go three shots. One of the weredogs in the lead fell in mid-stride to the ground, its tumbling form tripping the weredogs behind it.

Brady pulled his sword from behind his back and held it in both hands, legs spread wide in a firm sideways stance. These were not the same kinds of weredogs he had faced in the parking lot when they had attacked Max. These creatures did not stop their advance when Kaileigh shot at them. Brady recognized the lead animal, huge and manlike: Fenris. He was the only one of the advancing troop that walked upright. Brady was grateful for one thing: they still had no way to hold weapons. They still had the paws of dogs, which

311

meant that their only weapons were claws and teeth, though with this many of them, those might be enough.

They were almost upon them when, from the side of the deep grass in the unmown hay, the great form of a black bear threw itself at Fenris, taking him by complete surprise. He slammed at the dog with both claws and clamped his jaws down upon the dog's shoulders. It was Beorn, placing himself in the midst of the field so that the humans might escape. With every motion, Brady could have sworn the bear grew a little, as though fighting caused him to become more massive.

"Run," transmitted the bear to Brady in thought. "There are too many!"

With their leader down, the weredogs ceased their advance. The bear and the dog grappled, their thrashing amidst the tall grass only partially visible while the troop circled them, waiting to make their next moves upon the outcome of this encounter.

Joe came out of the house with a shotgun in one hand and Max in the other. He made his way to the Lifeseeker and opened the door, putting the struggling dog inside. It was all that he could do to close the door.

Kaileigh took careful aim and shot down three more of the circled weredogs, felling them where they stood. She backed away to the Lifeseeker, never taking her eyes from the throng watching the bear and dog grapple. In a moment she was inside, turning the key, putting the Lifeseeker in reverse, and shooting a longing look at the lone form of Brady, who was now on Rocinante, driving in the opposite direction. Reluctantly, she pointed the nose of the vehicle to the west and stepped on the gas, wondering if she would ever see him again.

They drove forever, deeper and deeper into the country. She was in higher country, now. She found a hilltop with an open field and a small barn and parked the Lifeseeker in front of it, wondering what to do next. She hung her head, her chin resting on her chest. She did not want Joe to see her tears.

"We're supposed to wait until Hugin sees us. He'll fly

back to Brady and then Brady will come to us," she said.

Joe was troubled. This last turn of events made him reassess everything.

"That bear fought to protect us," he said.

"Yes, he did."

"Why?" Joe asked.

"Brady said they were friends."

She glanced at the clock on the dash. It was just past ten o'clock in the evening. They stared out of the windshield at the darkness, the overcast sky threatening rain, perhaps even a thunderstorm.

"He'll be alright," Joe said. "He's remarkably resourceful."

"Yes. Brady was right. Those weren't dogs. They were something new. Everything is new."

"Yes, without a doubt."

"And we're new, too, in our own way," she continued.

"So it seems. I have been thinking about this for a little while now, since I first saw you two. You want to know what I think?"

"Yes."

He seemed to be looking out into the distance, toward the forest edge perhaps a half-mile away, but his thoughts were of other times, other places, and other people.

He said, "I think that there, at the very edge of the world," here he pointed to the forest, "magic just sits and waits. It mixes into our ordinary world in a thousand different ways. It always has, but we were too busy to notice, with our busy lives, our schedules, our television shows, and our gadgets."

"You're saying all this stuff that's been happening, the stuff that would have been impossible before the plague, has always been there?" she asked.

"The ancients knew about it...them...whatever. You know, we always liked to think that we were smarter, wiser, and better looking than the people of the past. That might not have been the case. Maybe we were just better at building machines. Maybe they were better at *seeing* the world. We didn't see nature as anything except something that we could

313

use. The ancients respected nature as something that was always trying to kill them, but if they watched her carefully, they might be able to survive because if they behaved properly, she would help them."

"It sure feels like nature has been trying to kill us," she agreed.

"What would explain our new abilities, then? How come Brady can talk to animals? How come he sees things differently than we do? Me? I'm beginning to sense things differently, too."

"My theory? I don't think any of us has changed at all, not one little bit. I think the new way of things is just bringing out abilities we already had deep within us. We just never needed them before and as I said, we were too busy following all of our trivial pursuits to truly see anything clearly. I'm as guilty of it as the next guy."

"Have you changed in some way?" she wondered.

"No, I don't think *I've* changed at all. I've always had the ability see how things are put together and how they work. I could always picture it in my mind. I'm too old and in the way for any last minute changing, I guess."

"Old is a state of mind," she answered.

"Tell that to my knees," he answered.

Joe yawned and pushed the chair back to a semi-reclining position. Max came over and put his head on the old man's leg, and Joe reassuringly put his hand on the dog's head.

In a moment, the old man was deeply asleep. Kaileigh reminded herself to check his blood sugar and then realized that unless he had brought his glucose monitor with him, they had no way to do that. As he dozed, it began to rain, first very gently and then a strong, steady downpour beat out its marching tattoo on the metal roof of the Lifeseeker. She sat there in the darkness as the rain pattered down and she couldn't stop her mind from racing. Where was Brady? Was he okay? We're they ever going to see him again? How long could Joe go without proper insulin injections? What would she do if Brady didn't come back.

As the minutes rolled into hours, the rain became

slightly more than just background noise. Try as she might, she couldn't get the idea out of her head that this was more than just a rain shower. What had Joe said, "Magic at the edge of the world, mixing with the ordinary?"

Then the rain became more than rain and she quietly opened the door and stepped into the dark, moist downfall, letting the water drench her. She walked a small distance and stood just in front of the Lifeseeker. Closing her eyes, she lifted her head to the sky and outstretched her hands and waited, thinking only one thought.

Brady, Brady, Brady...

Those of the Waters spoke to her in a whisper, no louder than a raindrop falling upon the grass, but she heard it clearly, so tuned was she to their vibrations. In brief splashes like snapshots projected on a screen for just a second and then taken away, they revealed Brady's predicament. Through pursed lips and clenched fists she watched and shuddered. No, this was not happening, had not happened, but the voices whispered back to her, yes.

In her mind a movie was pieced together from the still images and she saw Brady turning Rocinante down another path, away from the road that she had driven down immediately after they left him there. Brady had driven into the thick tangle of the weredogs, steering the four-wheeler just to their side and slashing at them with his sword as he drove by like a cavalry officer from the Civil War. The remaining dogs gathered their wits and started chasing him, leaving Fenris and Beorn alone on their field to finish the fray. Gunning Rocinante full-throttle, he replaced the sword into its scabbard on his back and began to drive down field roads and over ground he had never seen before.

That was when it happened.

He was driving fast, attempting to draw the throng of weredogs away from the house and Kaileigh and Joe, that he did not see the small ravine in front of him until it was too late. He steered Rocinante to the left, but the two front wheels pitched into the ditch and the whole contrivance, Brady included, flipped over onto its back throwing him some distance from the wreck, landing against the trunk of a tree.

As she watched her mind movie, she cried and her tears mixed with the rain upon her face and became part of *Those of the Waters*. She protested, "No!" when she saw the weredogs catch up, running past the ruined, twisted hulk of Rocinante and to the quiet form of Brady against the tree. They nipped, scratched and bit at him. Brady was in too much pain to fight back. He managed to withdraw the pepper spray from his trouser pocket and brandished it, sending a number of the beasts back into the darkness and away from him. They regathered and circled him, growling. How long did Brady sit like that until the limping and battered form of Fenris stalked into the scene and spoke? She could hear the weredog speak in this vision using human words.

"You thought to escape us, eh? You thought to throw your bear-beast at me, eh? Well, too late!"

"He should've killed you," Brady said through clenched teeth.

"He nearly did, but he ran off in the end. He knew better than to fight with me any longer. Now, we will take you back to Grendel."

"You've had some speech lessons," Brady said mockingly.

"Yes, I grow more human every day."

"You're a dog. You were born a dog and you'll die a dog," Brady spat. He was about to withdraw the taser when Fenris shouted orders to the throng of onlooking weredogs and as one they pounced on his prone form, ripping and tearing the weaponry from him, gnawing and pulling on leather and canvas, cotton and plastic until Brady was a bleeding, nearly naked wreck on the ground, bereft of all of weapons. He was shirtless and only his trousers and black boots remained. Blood streaked upon him here and there like an insane painter might paint a scene for Halloween. He was still conscious while Fenris lay his body over the back of a rather large weredog that may have once been a Great Dane, and the whole troop disappeared into the forest.

Then the rain was just rain, only rain. The vision was

done. Kaileigh was soaked to the skin, her world shaken more horribly than she would have imagined. After losing her mother and being surrounded by death like it was a palpable thing, she thought that nothing could ever phase her again, but she was beaten down in her soul from the vision she had just witnessed.

For all of this, she knew where to find him. *Those of the Waters* had given her that much, perhaps as recompense for what she had just endured. The weredog troop was moving back, toward Bangor and monster known as Grendel.

She ran back to the Lifeseeker and started the engine, Max yapping loudly. Kaileigh pressed the accelerator to the floor, pushing the Lifeseeker's eight cylinders for all they were worth. In the seat next to her with a furrowed brow and white knuckles that held onto the armrests with all of his might sat Joe. They were barreling down the highway with the needle just touching eighty-five miles per hour. Although she knew there would be animals and barriers, she also knew that what they had all just experienced in the last few hours would spell their end if she didn't act quickly.

"If we die in an accident, we'll never be able to help Brady," Joe commented grimly.

With both hands widely gripping the wheel, she didn't even blink or let a second pass before replying, "Time is against us! I don't even want to imagine what they've done to him. He could be dead already."

They were halfway back to Bangor with only a vague idea how they were to discover and rescue Brady Smith from the fell clutches of Grendel, self-proclaimed Enemy of Humanity. Since she made her defiant decision this morning, there was no arguing with her. She was adamant: he had little choice but to follow. In his heart, Joe was with her, but he was physically drained and knew that the insulin he had just taken was no longer as effective as it should be: it had deteriorated with the heat and the passage of time...like he had. He was so tired.

These two young people were in a fight for their lives, perhaps for the future vitality of an entire species, and he was a tired man who could barely walk or see. Still, from

317

somewhere deep within him, he knew he had a purpose. If the insulin wouldn't keep him alive, perhaps purpose would. He needed to construct a powerful radio transmitter and he had a plan.

"Kaileigh," he asked, "how do you plan on finding him?"

She said nothing as she let a half-mile pass underneath the tires of the Lifeseeker. "I don't know. I think," and here she wondered if she was the crazy one now for saying it, but she ventured forward anyway, "I think that the water *showed* me."

"Excuse me," he replied incredulously, "but what the hell does that mean?"

She didn't want to take the time to explain. There was too much else to think of, plan and carry out, but there was no getting around it. Although he was an engineer and a man of science, he had wanted to believe in Brady when she hadn't. Perhaps he might also believe in her.

"Since Brady rescued me, I've had some new things happening. It's all pretty weird, and I don't know why or how, but I can use water to...see things."

"See things?" he asked.

"Yeah, sounds pretty stupid, doesn't it?"

"A little," he said.

She was surprised. The engineer in him should be chiding her for this lapse into the supernatural. "People have been sensitive to water for eons. We're made of water. I even hired a dowser to help me find my well in East Corinth."

"A dowser? What the heck is a dowser?" she asked.

"A person who is sensitive to water. They walk along the earth and use their skills to tell you where to dig for a well. Most of the time, they're right, too. I went down two hundred feet and found a great spring. So no, I don't think it sounds foolish," he said.

"You don't? Because I gotta tell you, I think it does."

"I don't care. All that matters now is finding Brady," he said.

"First, we need to take care of you. I think I know where we can find some viable insulin."

318

"Where?"

"Where else? At the hospital.They have pharmaceuticals stored in the deep basement. Some of the cooling there is done with the liquid oxygen tanks. Maybe some vials of insulin are still viable."

Joe felt terrible, knowing that with every passing second that young man could be suffering at the hands of a monster and her first concern was a dying old man.

"No, we need to find Brady," he said.

"I don't think so," she muttered resolutely. "You need to build a transmitter. You have to survive. Without you, we'll never make contact."

"You would both survive. You'd both make a world of it, together."

She nearly spat out her next words, "I don't want to make a world of it together with only Brady. We need all the people, every survivor, and we need to make contact. If we make a world if it, we make it with you!"

"I'm just an old man that God wants dead," he muttered.

"Tough! God will have to wait. He's got plenty of company already. I want you alive, and right now, I'd say my game plan is the one we're following."

"You'd be better off without me. I'm not doing anything but slowing you down."

"No! We need to find insulin to keep you alive!" she exclaimed. "You're the engineer. You can build the transmitter. Don't you get it?"

"Get what?" he asked.

"You're the Wizard!"

Then, choking back an angry tear, her voice wavered as she added, "You're our Hope and it's my job to protect you."

He studied this strong, resolute and powerful girl. Brady had called her Athena. Was there any way of winning an argument with her, so steely eyed and grim?

"Brady would agree with me. I'm going to get you some good insulin, somehow, somewhere, and then we'll free him from Grendel."

"Or die trying?" Joe added in a question.

She looked over at him and let her foot rise slowly off

319

the pedal, bringing the Lifeseeker's speed down to a more survivable rate. Then, she smiled a smile made to smash walls and break down doors.

"I hope not," she replied.

Chapter 24
The King of Pain

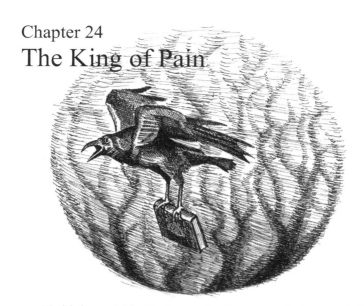

"I think you'd better brace for the worst,"whispered *The Autobiography of Benjamin Franklin*. Somehow the old paperback had remained in Brady's pocket when he had lost everything else to the machinations of the weredogs' assault the previous night. He was glad that he had pocketed Joe's dog-eared copy of the book. At least he knew that it didn't matter which actual book he held, as long as it was a faithful copy of Ben's actual writing.

"I think my arm is broken," Brady replied in a nearly silent voice. He knew that he was in a frightfully bad situation that promised little hope of escape.

"If you are going through hell, keep going," said Franklin. "Winston Churchill told me that once when they shelved me in the wrong place. It is always darkest before the dawn, Brady."

"It's pretty dark," Brady said, describing his situation.

His body was chained to a small stone tower near the back entrance of Mount Hope Cemetery. The chains were long and ponderous and wrapped around the entire structure three times, securing Brady quite soundly against the stone in a crisscross pattern. Above him on the small battlement was a defunct cannon pointing toward the sky and under it, in stone, where chiseled the numbers "1861--1865".

He had barely been conscious when Grendel and Fenris chained him just before full daybreak. Now that the sun was rising, he was roused by the light and its warmth, only to find himself held captive. He was Prometheus bound on the rocky mountain, waiting for the eagle.

"It must have been quite a journey last night. You fought bravely. Sorry I couldn't be of any assistance," said Ben quietly.

"It's okay," grunted Brady, struggling against his bonds.

"What do you see? Where are we?" asked the Autobiography.

Brady knew where they were, although why Grendel chose this place was a mystery to him.

"We're in Mount Hope Cemetery, chained to the Civil War Memorial tower. I can't move."

"Don't struggle. You'll only do more damage to yourself. Are we alone?"

Brady looked around as far as he could see.

"I think so. All alone. Not a weredog or monster to be seen."

"They won't be until darkness falls. Grendel might come during the daylight, but those foul creatures do most of their dealings after nightfall. They'll wait until twilight."

"Why didn't he kill me last night?" wondered Brady aloud.

"Perhaps he wants you to be conscious when he destroys you" ventured Ben.

"Or he wants Kaileigh and Joe to find their way to me and kill us all in one shot."

"Yes, that's a possibility," replied Ben. "Actually, it's not a bad plan."

The great black form of Hugin appeared in the air in front of them and landed at Brady's feet.

"RAGnarok!" he croaked.

"Oh, Hugin!" exclaimed Brady as the bird walked in his gunslinger crouch, assessing the situation. He sauntered over to the chains and began testing them with his beak, fiddling with them, manipulating and testing them. After a few moments, he waddled back to Brady and cawed again.

"RAGNAROK!"

"Yeah, I know," Brady said. "Hugin, buddy, you've got to find Kaileigh and Joe. Tell them not to come here."

"How is he going to do that?" questioned Ben, "Can they understand the Raven as you can?"

"No!" said Brady in exasperation. He knew in his heart that Kaileigh and Joe would seek him out and that Grendel would be watching for them. He might even be luring them into his trap at this moment and there was no way to get a message to them.

"Perhaps there is a way," Ben ventured. "There is *always* an alternative, Brady."

"What? Would you mind telling me?" Brady said as he twisted his good arm under the chain.

"I'd rather not. If I told you, you might object and then we'd have to enter into negotiations and that would simply take up too much time. The time is right for action! The idea I have would mean abandoning you for a while. Hugin would need to take me somewhere."

"Where?"

"No time for explanations, Brady. Time is of the essence. Hugin, can you hear me?" called *The Autobiography of Benjamin Franklin.*

"RAGnarok!" replied the bird.

Brady wasn't at all surprised that the bird and the book could communicate.

"Come on, over here, in this trouser pocket. Just lift the flap and take me."

Hugin walked over to Brady and deftly placed his beak under the flap and lifted it. Then, fishing within the pocket, he withdrew the old paperback, held it firmly in his beak and took to the air.

In a moment, they were both gone, leaving Brady alone with his anger, pain, and worry.

Kaileigh walked carefully through the darkened

hallways of the hospital, moving ever downward toward the lowest level. They had arrived there this morning just after sunrise, entering through the very door through which she and Brady had fled from Grendel on the night the city had been consumed by the fire. Joe had insisted on following her in, but said he would wait in the main entrance hall.

"There's a pharmacy storeroom in the basement. They've got a cold room and a freezer room. They use liquid nitrogen to keep things cool, so if the seals are still tight, we might get lucky."

"How do you know this?" asked Joe.

"I lived in this place for a month, remember? I used to crawl through duct work and service tunnels to get around, looking for a way out."

He looked at her like a father might scrutinize a wayward daughter. "Please be careful."

"I will," she said, "and I'll find some good, viable insulin. I'll fix you right up."

"I know you will," he said firmly. He hoped she hadn't heard the lingering doubt in his voice. Now that he had purpose, living was something he planned on continuing, at least until the boy and the girl were safe.

She had taken a walkie-talkie and given the other to Joe so they could remain in touch. Now, as she slowly sought her way through the labyrinth left by the confusion and madness of the final days of the pandemic, Joe busied himself by investigating the remains of the papers left by the Centers for Disease Control.

There was so much clutter and catastrophe in this room and he still had many unanswered questions. Piles of papers lay strewn on the floor, laptops hurled against the wall, monitors staring blankly at him: no doubt the work of an angry Grendel. What had transpired during the final days of Humanity in this last of strongholds? What efforts were expended, he wondered, to save the species? How had the disease beaten the vital mind of *homo sapiens*? What final domino fell to exacerbate the fall of all the others?

As he searched, he began to stitch together a loose idea of what had transpired before the end. There was a table in the rear with a sign clipped on a pole that read, "Incident Reports." A pile of papers spiraled out on the floor. Joe began to pick up the incident reports, one after the other, studying them carefully. The story they told was one of almost superhuman effort and focus. The team from Atlanta had been in Washington. When it became clear that they had lost the battle in that city, they moved north to Princeton, New Jersey. Again, they moved, first to Boston and finally to Bangor, last bastion of hope. One by one the nation's cities succumbed to the plague, devastating entire metropolitan areas. Each move took more effort as their own numbers diminished.

From what he could deduce, Joe saw the same story told over and over again. First, there were mass deaths of birds reported from the United States, Mexico and Canada. Tens of thousands of birds, entire flocks died in flight. Then humans began to succumb to the illness. The first cases presented themselves to local doctors' offices and hospital emergency rooms and within seventy-two hours entire populations, even shut-ins, were infected. It was the most virulent, contagious agent ever seen by the investigators. The virus caused a massive immune response from the body, turning it against itself. In the end, it was the body and not the virus that finally caused death, or so the reports speculated.

City after city fell. After the federal government released its powers to local authorities, it became clear that the end was very near because there were no real local authorities left to take charge. Joe mused that everything came to Maine last because Maine was the end of the line. The virus choose this place as North America's final battleground. Within seventy-two hours, anyone who caught it was dead, except for Brady, Kaileigh, Dr. Grindle and for some strange reason, him.

Kaileigh called on the radio, "Joe, I found some! It's still cool enough down here, I think the insulin is good."

He breathed a sigh of relief. "How much did you find?"

"At least a three month supply, if we can keep it cool."

"The Lifeseeker has a propane refrigerator," he replied.

"I'm on my way. I'll be back up there in a few minutes. Any sign of Grendel?"

Joe looked around warily and replied, "No. Nothing yet."

He arose from the floor slowly with a great deal of effort, his knees stabbing at his mind with knives of pain. They were almost done here. That was when his eyes were drawn to a photograph on the floor along with a printed sheet of paper. They were well-worn and dog-eared, looking like some animal had been handling them. Strange, he thought. After he read the writing, he spent a long moment studying the faces in the photograph.

When Kaileigh returned from her mission with a cooler full of insulin and syringes, a blood glucose monitor and other supplies, he showed her the letter with the photograph.

"What's this?" she asked.

"Here," he said, offering it to her.

"What is it?" she asked.

"It's a printed email," he replied.

She set the cooler down upon a desk, took the paper and began to read aloud.

"Dear Peter,

I know how swamped with work you must be, so I'll keep this brief. Things here are bad. The power and the Net are spotty, and it won't be long before the Net fails. The end has come and that is that. I'm so sorry that things didn't work out, but I don't want you to go on blaming yourself for what's happened.

It isn't your fault. No one could have foreseen the consequences of our actions. We had the best of intentions and the plan should have worked. Imagine, immunizing whole populations of people at a time through an airborne inhalant! We could have saved millions of lives and stopped so much suffering. All of the trials were successful. We never would have received permission from the CDC if our work hadn't been rock solid. The ramifications of our work would have earned us both a Nobel prize, I'm certain. To immunize entire populations nearly at once from a myriad of diseases: this was our life's work and I stand by it, even now. Whatever happened, it wasn't our fault. All I can say is that I suspect involvement from other sources who would put our technology to other deadly and evil use.

I don't know how to tell you this except to come right out and say it. Our boy is dead. It happened last night of complications from the virus. Our little Phil is gone, honey. He's not suffering anymore and I don't expect that I'll be far behind him. We'll both be waiting for you there, in a little while. I just wanted to tell you that I'm not afraid. It's the way of things. It's not anybody's fault. It just is. I accept that. I just wanted you to know that we both love you, more than words can say.

You are still everyone's greatest hope. The survivors of this Pandemic, and there will be some, will remember that you worked until the very end to find a way to stop it. I know you well enough to understand that you would never give up. Find the answers. If you survive this, do not regret. Instead, remember us. I love you, always. -Diana."

The email had an electronic signature, but they both had already read the name of the addressee "Diana Grindle, Research Assistant, Airborne Inoculation Program, CDC."

"Dr. Grindle's wife," said Kaileigh.

"And son," said Joe, handing her the photograph.

They seemed to both understand at that moment that there might be something down deep in the darkness of the monster known as Grendel that could be saved. There was a husband and a father in there – a good man who meant to save the world.

Brady was parched beyond any thirst he had ever known. Time slowed for him as the sun beat down inexorably from the high heavens, the temperature rising quickly. He ceased to struggle at midmorning and by noon, he was only barely conscious. His shoulders ached like someone had driven a knife between them. His body was chained in the shape of an X, a position that elicited nothing but torment as the minutes turned to hours and his mind swam in delirium.

He remembered the events of the past few hours only vaguely. Kaileigh and Joe thankfully still hadn't arrived. He dreaded their arrival as a harbinger of their own doom, unwittingly falling into Grendel's clutches. Then again, how would they know where to look, unless Grendel had given them the proper clues to lead them here? Beorn was wounded, having limped off into the forest after Fenris left him fallen in the grass to lavish his attention on Brady. Rocinante was dead, a twisted heap of metal off the forest path. *The Autobiography of Benjamin Franklin* had told him of a plan, but what good could a book possibly do? He was only a book, after all, and there was nobody who would read him, Brady thought. Hugin was gone to do the book's bidding, whatever that might be.

Of course, there was nothing else to do but think and he imagined that this was part of the torment that Grendel had planned. There was no worse torture than to leave him alone with his thoughts. Brady wondered if he had survived the worst pandemic in the history of his species only to be destroyed by a monster.

Who is he, really? he asked himself. Was Grendel the Antichrist, as described in the Bible? Was he some sort of Dark Lord, like Sauron from *The Lord of the Rings*? Was he the Devil himself, finally walking the empty earth, claiming his domain? He wasn't human, was he, underneath it all? The monster wanted no humans remaining – his hatred was complete. Brady wondered: who else but a human could hate other humans so well?

As Apollo's fiery chariot began its downward ascent from the heavens into the west, Brady's mind swam in thought slowly moving from one memory and possibility to the next. Time was viscous and thick, slowly dripping away. The monster would return shortly and Brady had no weapon other than his words and will. Any other boy might have despaired as helpless as a baby, but Brady knew that words were also weapons, used wisely. As long as he had his senses, we was not totally unarmed.

Twilight began to fall as the air began to cool,

mercifully. Brady's head nodded, his chin resting on his chest, his mouth was dry cotton. Swallowing was sandpaper scraping against stone, rough and pointless. Yet even in his quiet, painful state of suffering, he noticed a change in the atmosphere, a subtle shift among things. He heard sounds. Was that Grendel and the weredogs, come to witness his end?

No, he thought, slowly lifting his head and opening salt-caked eyes, it was something else.

Coming into focus as the sun had all but vanished from the sky, leaving purple and red bands around the edge of the horizon and a color that had no name, was a nearly transparent form of the little boy, the orphan with the red ball. He stood a few feet from Brady and gazed at him, saying nothing. He seemed to wait in a place between the worlds, in a time apart from time. He was the ghost of the orphan boy Brady had met weeks ago, the only shade in Mount Hope who had interacted with him. Now the boy moved his lips, but the sound produced from this ethereal child did not come at the moment of utterance. There was a time delay and reverberation that indicated vast distances and long pathways to reach him.

Brady heard the boy ask, "Why are you here, like this? We would like to know."

Barely able to speak, Brady muttered in response, "I've been captured by the monster. He's using me to draw other survivors here so that he can destroy us all."

The boy moved closer to look into Brady's bloodshot and tired eyes.

"You are not dead. Yet I can see you. We can see you. How can his be?"

"We?" asked Brady through dry lips.

He raised his head again and in the twilight he could see amassing around him in a vast semicircle the shapes of the ghosts of Mount Hope. They stood in lines, one behind the other, all dressed in the funeral attire they wore when they were laid to rest. When he had first glimpsed this shadow world weeks ago, most of the shades he saw were happy, pleased to be meeting each other again, pleased to have

329

arisen. Now they were a solemn assemblage, a Greek chorus standing to the side, watching the suffering of the hero, sharing it in suffering silence. They seemed to sense that this was a critical moment in the world and though none but the boy spoke, he knew they all could hear him.

"Am I going to join you? Are you my welcoming committee?" Brady asked, half smiling through pain.

The boy said, "We don't know. We have been waiting to move on, but we just stay here. We hope there's more to come, but for now, we've come to stand beside you."

For the first time in hours, Brady's mind ignited like the smallest of flames in the darkness. Had the boy said they had come to stand beside him? What did that mean?

"I don't understand," Brady said.

The shade of an elderly, professorial man came forth from the silent throng and knelt one knee on the ground, whispering to the boy gently. The boy nodded to the professor and then relayed the words to Brady.

"We are only Watchers. We cannot act to help you. The only thing we can do is stand beside you. The only thing we can do to help you is stand by you, so that you aren't alone. No matter what happens, you aren't alone. You're never alone."

Brady surveyed the shadows, phantoms, and shades of the departed that surrounded him. They were a strange mixture of time and place, but all of them looked back at him with eyes that bore into his mind, some nodding, some smiling, some looking at him with grave concern. How odd, Brady wondered.

"Am I going to die?" Brady asked.

"Someday," said the boy. "Everybody dies. Everybody. Everything. It's just the way it works."

Brady rephrased his question, "Am I going to die tonight?"

The boy seemed puzzled, but the professorial gentleman knelt next to him and whispered something into his ear.

Then he responded to Brady, "We don't know, because Time is gone from us. You are in the River of Time, where only the living can dwell. We don't want you to die. If we could, we would help you beat your monster. We can only watch. You have to fight him alone. Our days of doing are done. Only your actions can change the way of things. Ours can't, so we'll stand by you, so that you won't be alone."

Brady understood. They felt concern for him, both in this world and the next. He repeated the boy's words aloud, causing a smile to come to the boy's face, "My actions can change the way of things. I can still make a difference."

A ripple, like a wave of understanding, fanned out through the throng of the Watchers. Their demeanor changed. Though he could only hear the little orphan boy, he knew that their changed aspect was a *'message received,'* in their collective mind: don't give up, no matter the pain or the cost. Though you die a thousand deaths, never give in, never give up, never ease up on your throttle. It is always darkest before the dawn.

As the last light of the setting sun shot like a spectral sword from the West, darkness fell, and the stars began to come out one by one. The moon was full and the shades all began to fade and then disappear from his eyes. Brady's head sank onto his chest once more in pain, but not entirely in despair.

The next time Brady raised his head it was because he felt the lash of a whip's tip against his chest, snapping and ripping at his flesh. His head jerked upright and the back of his skull slammed against the stone of the tower. Opening his eyes, suddenly wide awake, he saw something nightmarish and unnatural. Fenris, the alpha weredog, was standing in front of him and in his hand was a long rawhide whip. Then realization came thundering into his mind. His hand! The weredog no longer had a right paw. In its place was a *human* hand, complete with opposable thumb, holding the whip. When the weredog saw the look on Brady's face, he snarled, curling his lip and let go another snap. The tip of the whip carved a gash in Brady's left cheek, the blood flowing in a line punctuated by minuscule red drops.

"Awake now, little boy? Did you get enough sleep?" asked the weredog. Around the stone tower in the darkness sat a mass of weredogs and at Fenris' words, they barked and howled their pleasure. Fenris seemed more human than dog now, but the others were still more canine in their frames.

"He wants you awake, my master does," continued Fenris.

"You know what's sad?" asked Brady of Fenris. "You probably used to be a good dog. I bet some little boy or girl really loved you, took you on walks, played with you in the park. I bet you fetched balls and caught Frisbees. You peed on fire hydrants and car tires. When you were a little puppy you pooped on the floor and that was okay because you were so cute. I bet you even stuck your head out the window when your owners took you for a drive in the car. Look at you now. It's sad, really. Now you're nothing but a *bad dog*."

The weredog snarled and let three lashes of the whip fall haphazardly across Brady's body. Brady lurched as much as he could under the bondage of the chains, but he didn't let the weredog have the satisfaction of a cry in the night. Instead, Brady laughed.

"I was never a dog. I am a man! I have always been a man!" the weredog insisted.

"A man? Ha! You? You were never a man. You're only *man's best friend*," said Brady, sarcasm clearly flowing in his voice.

"No!" shouted Fenris, but then his shout turned into a wolf-like howl, the ancient call of the wild through the nights of the world. When he heard that, the weredog stopped altogether, embarrassed by his own betraying utterance.

"See? It's no shame. Better a good dog than a bad man, wouldn't you say?" asked Brady.

But the alpha weredog could not reply because there was a disturbance in the throng of weredogs behind him and they parted like the Red Sea as from their midst came the form of Grendel, emerging from the darkness. Brady heard his stomping and felt the ground shiver and quake before the form of the monster emerged. He was larger than ever. He towered over them and they drew back, many of them whining as they backed away from the sheer force of his presence.

Brady thought, *Dragon, Ymir, Balrog, Cthulu, Mephistopheles.*

Even though the only light that shone down upon them was that from the moon and stars, Brady could easily discern the beast. He had never had the time to truly look at him before, but now he found himself calmly examining his adversary. How strange, he thought, that I can turn on my *Observation mode*, even now, at the end of things. How comforting...

His body was much larger than when he had first fought with him in the hospital. Though he wore no clothing, he was obviously neither male nor female. Muscles rippled from legs the thickness of cinder blocks. A massive chest the size of several men expanded to gargantuan proportions and reminded Brady, of all things, of the trolls from Tolkien's *The Hobbit* or the giants that Don Quixote fought, but turned out to be only windmills. He was at least sixteen feet tall with arms like stone columns and hands like Thor's hammer. The blades that thrust out from the spine of his back were larger now, saurian in their appearance. A monstrous, humanoid creature stood there, as though in mockery of the human form, a walking cartoon of malice, taking the form of that which it sought to destroy.

Still, Brady couldn't capture an image from the continuously changing putty of Grendel's face. Instead of one face, there were tens, hundreds, thousands. He walked ponderously, like a great pendulum or battering ram, and when he spoke, it sounded like the sinking of great ships into the deep or the thundering toppling of tall buildings suddenly into the ground. He was malevolence incarnate and though his unnatural form seemed unstoppable, Brady made a decision: no matter the pain, the torment, or the likely outcome of the struggle, he would not give in.

Pay attention! He told himself. What was that? Brady asked himself. Imagined? Imagination? Everything I imagined evil to be? His musings were cut short by the words of the monster.

"Renamer! I have you at last!" laughed Grendel. "How does it feel, boy, to know you have failed?"

333

Brady looked up and beyond all hope of rescue or protection, smiled a crooked, wry grin and said in a relaxed voice, "Talk, talk, talk. It's all you ever do. I think you like the sound of your own voice."

The bite of the whip found a purchase on Brady's abdomen and he winched, yet he did not scream. Again, he raised his head in defiance and gave a single, relaxed laugh.

Grendel walked to within a foot of Brady and said in a low tone, "I can kill you anytime I wish. I can, with a single deed. I can be the cause of your prolonged and painful death and yet you mock me?"

"You're beginning to understand. I'm not afraid of you," Brady said, simply. "You might be able to hurt me, kill me even, but I'm not afraid of you."

Imagination? Brady thought of that word over and over, an echo machine-gunning in his mind. Why was he thinking that word? Why now? The monster's fetid breath was so strong that Brady thought it might even serve to melt human flesh, yet the word *Imagination* ricocheted in his mind like a super ball from a grocery store vending machine.

He looked down at his feet and he could see the outline of the little boy. Neither Grendel nor the weredogs could see him.He could view two worlds at once. They could only see one. The little orphan looked up at Brady and in his mind, Brady heard his voice.

"We understand! The monster! You did this. You...You..." he thought.

"I did? What do you mean?" thought Brady to the child.

"You were so angry, when the world fell. You didn't know how powerful you had become since everyone else passed over to the other side of the River to the Far Shore. You were so angry..."

Brady tried to remember what he was talking about, but he still heard the chanting of the word in his mind, this time not from the Whisperers but from the invisible Watchers, the inhabitants of this graveyard: *Imagine.*

"What did I do?" asked Brady in his mind as Grendel tugged at his chains and cursed him with foul epithets.

The boy rose in the air and whispered in Brady's ear,

"*You made the monster. You imagined him into the world. The scream that woke us from our slumber also called him forth. You did this...*"

Scream? What scream?

Then he remembered. How could he ever forget? Noah's house – the realization that he was all alone – the Whisperers maddening cacophony in his mind – his mother missing – all those dead bodies in various states of decay – the sudden painful realization that he was all alone – all of this came back to him as the monster moved malevolently around him. Brady had screamed a scream from the depths of a darkness where no light ever entered. The loss of his father nearly destroyed everything that made him who he was and left only a shell of a child who needed his father more than ever. The loss of all the other people on earth left him devastated, depressed and then *angry – so angry!*

A wave of nausea flooded over him. *Imagination* had brought Grendel into the world – *his* imagination! Could it be? Was imagination a force that could be used to bring thoughts, even emotions, into reality? He remembered exactly what he was feeling at that moment in Noah's house. He wanted, he *required*, someone to blame. Someone to blame, an individual, would make the bearing of this weight possible. Having someone to blame was *easy*. Blaming a person rather than a virus made sense to a boy whose entire inner life was a series of imagined battles between Sith and Jedi, Monsters and Heroes, knight errants and giants. He sat on Noah's doorstep and let forth a scream that tore at the fabric of the new reality – the reality devoid of people except the ragtag survivors wandering a quiet land. He needed a monster to slay!

One came forth.

From the depths of his own emptiness he had called forth the only thing that his imagination could create that could have caused such an extinction – a compilation of demons, every single monster he had ever read about, dreamt of, seen on screen or imagined, all rolled into one.

Grendel was *his* monster.

Grendel seethed at him, lingering at the edge of the

circle with acid spittle and flamethrower eyes. He seemed to be waiting for something.

Brady smiled. "I know your secret..."

"What?" he growled.

"You heard me. I know where you came from. I know how you came to this place."

The creature looked at the boy with stern disapproval and then turned his head up to the sky and began to laugh a deep, rolling chuckle that could topple mountains or split the heavens. As he did this, the weredogs in the circle began to look at each other, troubled. Even Fenris backed away, letting the whip drop to his side, nearly falling back down to earth to retake the stance of his former canine self.

"So, you know my secret. My origin. What of it? Soon the girl and the old man will be here, and I will destroy you all at once and be done with you."

"What will you do, after we're dead?" Brady inquired.

"I will dance about on your graves and bones! I shall sing songs of hatred," said the monster. "Then, I shall travel the world, gathering forces, altering nature, mutating and destroying life. I will hunt down humans to the last and send them all down to their doom and then, when that is done and only then, I will suffer nature on this miserable world to take her original course, before the rise of human life, so long ago. Some other species will rise and I will be there to taunt it."

Brady smiled a crooked grin. "Nice plan, but you have one flaw in your reasoning. You're Grendel, but you're also Dr. Grindle, underneath. As long as you need a host, there will always be one human left."

Grendel roared in anger, "He is nothing to me. He is a pathetic creature who happened to be present at my summoning. You should see how he cowers beneath the surface while I walk about in his body, growing stronger than his weak human flesh could ever become. He will disappear soon enough and become like the rest of you – a memory. I will assimilate him, as well."

"I made you and I can destroy you," Brady said, his words a challenge.

"You think you made me, but I existed in other forms, on other planes, long before you were ever born. With every injustice, with each act of hatred ever committed by humans, I became more and more aware. Each time a father hit his son, I grew a little. Each time a woman broke her lover's heart, I took on more weight. Each time a war was fought, my mind took on a new dimension. I have been forming in the womb of Humanity's hatred, indifference and anger since the first step your species ever took. The *idea* of me is ancient. I am the sum of your human equation – I am your final answer. You think you called me forth, but you were merely finishing the project. You laid the last stone. You merely solved the equation."

Brady tried to take in the significance of Grendel's assertion. Humans had ravaged the earth, nearly destroyed the atmosphere, trashed the oceans, ripped up the land, toppled the timber, and always because they could, because it was so easy to do. Humans always seemed to solve their problems by repeating the mistakes from their past. War, famine, deprivation – these had never been eliminated. At the end, just before the advent of the Pandemic, Brady had read that fully one-third of the human race was at war somewhere on the planet. A fifth of the world starved to death while in many nations, obesity was an epidemic. In a stunning realization, Grendel's words had the ring of truth, and that truly saddened Brady, stunning him more than any whip could. The monster was not his alone. He was the child of a lost race. Brady had summoned him, but he was the creation of all humanity.

"You're the sum of all our mistakes...of all of our sins," said Brady.

Grendel stopped his gloating and momentarily was taken aback.

"You understand?"

"People were destroying the world. Maybe it's time for our rule to end," muttered Brady.

Grendel hadn't anticipated this. The boy was not supposed to agree with him. The boy was supposed to frustrate and bedevil him so that in the end, smiting him

337

would be as easy as swatting a fly. Oh, Grendel thought greedily, how wondrous it would to kill your own creator! This boy seemed to grow in the eyes of the monster and he stepped back a pace, wondering. There was humility here, in the end. There was acknowledgment of past deeds and the wrongs committed by the species from the last, best example of it. For a moment, the bewildered form succumbed to confusion.

That was when it happened. A fleeting emergence from below the surface arose in the form of a face finally emerging from the malleable putty face of the monster. Brady didn't recognize the face, but he understood who was speaking to him.

"*Fight him! Concentrate! Now! Use all your strength of arm and heart and brain!*"

Brady had never seen him before, but he knew who was speaking to him in Grendel's moment of indecision. The face of Dr. Grindle emerged from beneath the surface and was as quickly forced down again by the ambient life force of the monster. Brady was surprised to see that Grendel seemed to have little knowledge of the doctor's brief appearance and he continued as before, unaware.

"I would show you things before you die. I would have you hear the words from the lips of those who spoke them."

His face formed into that of Brady's mother. Her face was twisted and full of pain when she muttered through Grendel's lips, "No! I have a son! He needs me! Don't do this..." and then her face twisted into a tormented grimace.

Brady tried to look away from his mother's face, but he couldn't. Kaileigh claimed his mother had been murdered by Dr. Grindle. Was Brady watching her face as an actual rendering of her final moments, a kind of macabre recording? A million knives jabbed into his heart, a thousand needles pierced his eyes and still he watched as the life drained from the face of his mother. Then she was gone.

The face morphed again. This time it was his best friend Noah, then his neighbor, his aunt, the priest from the church, and a hundred other faces, all in their death throes, all muttering last words, some simply expiring their last breaths in a death rattle, some raging against the end like fire in the face of a tidal wave. Grendel seemed to have knowledge of all who had succumbed to the virus, a library of recorded death.

"Stop it!" Brady screamed.

The fluid face of the monster rejoined and asked, "Had enough? Ready to die?"

Then from the deepest pit of his anguish and determination, Brady lifted his head high and met the monster's gaze so fiercely that the creature's face finally took on a solidity that he knew was its true form. It was a twisted, double-mouthed visage with tiny appendages near its nasal slit and yellowish eyes straining to see through a catlike slit in the pupil.

"I swear," said Brady, "that no matter how long it takes, or how far I have to go, I will kill you."

His words hit the beast with so much force that Grendel staggered backwards a step before regaining his footing.

"Is that so?" asked the monster, a sneer forming on his lips. "Then I'll help you," he finished.

He walked over to Brady and reworked the chains so that the boy's arms were now free. Then the monster stepped back and gave Brady a curious look.

"Not enough? Let me see? Yes, that's the ticket!" he said in a feigned comedian's voice.

Madness mispronounced itself in the mind of the creature as the malleable face took on a twisting manner once again. This time when the features settled, the face was one Brady hadn't seen for a very long time.

Oh, no, please no, not him. Not now...

"Dad..." whispered Brady, his heart in his throat, a broken and pitiable thing.

In his father's voice, Grendel said, "I have a present for you, son. This is something fun. You're gonna love this!" and with that, he gave the signal to Fenris, who fetched an object from behind a tombstone. He grasped it with his one human hand and warily approached the chained boy, placing the object in Brady's hands, scurrying away as quickly as he could.

339

It was a hunting rifle.

"There you go, boy. Now, you've got the weapon and you made the promise. Just point it at me and pull the trigger. That's it. You can do it! Come on," he said with all the encouragement that a young father might offer his child just learning to ride his bike.

Brady knew in his heart that this monster wasn't his father, but longing is a lonely child within every human heart that seeks and seeks and seldom finds. How much would anyone give just to see their loved one's face, one more time, to hear their voice, to converse with them, even for a minute? Brady understood the monster's intent, but he was tired, thirsty and weak. The hunting rifle in his hands was heavy and handling it felt awkward. Part of his mind insisted – *shoot him!* Another part of his mind said – *this is a trick!* Neither of these little voices would compare with the face of his father looking back at him, encouraging him.

"What'sa matter, Brady boy? You afraid? Aw...come on, now. It's not your Dad. It's a big, bad monster."

Brady lowered the gun and remained quiet, looking away as a single tear appeared in his eye.

The monster began to laugh and the weredogs began to howl in syncopation. Beyond all measure of cruel intentions, Grendel knew he had won. It had not been enough to kill the boy – he wanted to break him first. He wanted to hear the invisible bones of the mind snap and crackle, to rip the veins of hope and desire from the structure of the boy's soul.

Brady dropped the rifle on the ground in despair. The last time he had seen his father was at the funeral home in his coffin where everyone cried and marveled at how lifelike a dead man could look. Brady's first real encounter with death wasn't a slight one. It had been a train wreck of an encounter and had dug a deep trench within him, deep enough to crawl into and hide away from the world when necessary, deep enough to delve a cave of silence from the rock of Time.

He found that dark furrow deep inside his mind and thought to himself, "It's hopeless. I'm sorry Kaileigh. I'm sorry Joe. Max, I'm sorry. For everything, for the whole world, I'm so, so, sorry..."

Grendel added insult to injury. "The other two will come and find you and we will be waiting. It might take a day, or a week, but that infernal bird of yours will surely lead them here, and when it does, is there anything that you'd like us to tell them, before we conclude our business?"

Brady was already too far within himself to answer, especially to the face and voice of his dead father. He would have liked to say something, anything, but no words came.

"Enough chatter!" shouted the monster.

With that, Grendel laid his hands upon Brady's head, cupping massive hammer-like hands over each of Brady's ears. Brady tried to close his eyes, but he couldn't help but see his father's face next to his, murder present in the furrowed brow. Brady felt the pressure begin to build on his cranium. The idea that his own father was murdering him predominated his mind, captured his reason and made any rational thought unbearable.

Then, a small voice whispered from the darkness, and relit the flame that was Brady. It was barely audible, but it was enough to throw just a guiding spark of light against the vast sea of darkness that was the truth.

The orphan boy gently whispered, "*We are with you. You are not alone...*"

The weredogs gathered closer into a tight circle. Fenris rose on his haunches and held the whip in his one human hand, ready to strike. Grendel's monstrous hands began to squeeze more and more tightly like a vise, causing Brady more physical pain that he had ever endured in his life.

"*You are not alone,*" the orphan boy whispered to him, and Brady opened his thoughts to the world, the universe - everything. His mother and father were dead. His friends were, too, but he was not alone because in this world of uncertainly and danger, he had found new friends. Grendel claimed that humans were a blight upon the world, but Brady knew the words to a different song. People were a part of nature, not something separate. He had every right to be here, now. Things were unfolding and he was part of the plan. As he concentrated, he could feel the thoughts of all the shades of the cemetery adding their force of will toward his own, bending back Grendel's hands, pushing back against his onslaught on Brady's skull. The force against Grendel continued to grow until, in a moment of exasperation, the monster's hands flew away from Brady's head and he stepped back several paces, stumbling before regaining his balance.

Grendel looked at Brady in anger and surprise, not sure of his next move. Was this possible from such a frail thing as this pitiful human boy? It couldn't be. He hadn't foreseen this. The weredogs were in turmoil. Fenris was stepping backward, confused. Even Grendel hesitated as Brady looked at him and said, "I'll fight you from above and Dr. Grindle will fight you from below and together, we'll defeat you. The world will rise up against you."

At that moment, from beyond the fringe of darkness, navigating through the gravestones and tombs of Mount Hope came a roaring and a thundering never heard before in all the dark nights of the world. From the darkness and beyond all hope, leading a charge of statues and human forms with his sword brandished high, ran the bronze form of General Joshua Chamberlain, answering Brady's call.

Chapter 25

The Battle of the Stone Tower

They came from all over the city, these strange, implacable forms, thundering over the ground like titans or frost giants of old. They emerged from the thick darkness with weapons brandished, alive and mobile for the first time since they were molded in the furnace, some at least a hundred years old. Who were these warriors coming to the aid of Brady Smith, still helplessly chained to the stone tower in the graveyard?

Leading the charge with his saber brandished high in front of him, a look of grim determination on his face, General Joshua Lawrence Chamberlain of the Twentieth Maine entered the fray. Behind him followed the ranks of statues from the parks and monuments of the two cities - the three loggers from the Pierce Memorial next to the Bangor

Public Library, each one of them nine feet tall carrying ax and peavey. Following close behind was Hannibal Hamlin, first vice-president under Abraham Lincoln, his long bronze cape flowing in the wind, his walking cane brandished like a cudgel. Then there was the winged statue of victory, her flame a bright torch whose fire lit the night. There were others, as well, most of which were known to Brady, including the fiberglass astronaut from the military supply store. These sculptures stood like timeless sentinels for years against the onslaught of frost, snow, hurricane and worst of all, time, but here they were, alive and mobile, detached from their bases, walking and running into the open area in front of the stone tower to come between Brady and the monster known as Grendel. The earth shook with their advance.

General Joshua Chamberlain stood between the monster and the boy, firm as a boulder against Grendel's approach. It was clear that the monster was confused, caught off his guard. The personification of Brady's concept of evil was facing a personified person. How singularly strange the comparison, thought the General as he said, "Stay back! Keep your distance. You'll harm this boy no more."

The monster drew in a breath and seemed to grow in size as he took a step forward toward the talking statue. This was not flesh and bone. This was not anything but metal, even down to the lowest molecular level. For Grendel, there was no way in, no doorway for intimidation because he was anathema to life and these statues were something other than alive. He was not their polar opposite. All he had against a walking metal man was sheer, brute strength. His massive hammer hand reached forward to clutch the warrior's arm, in hopes of ripping and snapping it from the brittle bronze that formed him. However, he found that the stiff metal felt like flesh, did not snap but bent and then reformed. The General wasted no time in hacking at Grendel with the dull bronze sword which, for all of its poor quality as a blade, still caused the monster to reel backwards, howling out his pain to the skies.

Grendel stepped back a few paces and the General used

that moment to turn and cut the chains that bound Brady to the stone tower.

"There you go, Prometheus," he said calmly, turning back to face the monster, like he had already read Brady's mind.

Brady was reborn. All the self-pity and loathing that he felt inside that was for him the true Abandonment, was gone. Because someone moved heaven and earth to come to his aid, he was renewed. "Thanks, Hercules," he replied. At this point, if anyone could have seen, they would have noticed a wry smile forming on the face of the general underneath that massive Civil War era mustache.

"Rout 'em out, boys! Attack! Attack!"called the General.

The army of bronze moved forward with all the lithe grace of seasoned warriors toward the darkness and the weredogs. What ensued, if anyone could have filmed it, could best be described as flashes of light and color, sounds of wounding, a vignette of a lumberjack against the walking, angry Fenris as axes fell and metal arms met with all too weak flesh.

The Battle of the Stone Tower had begun.

In strobe-light staccato they grappled, the personas of men and the myths of their imagination in hand to hand combat. Brady found himself looking for a weapon but still could not bring himself to pick up the rifle at his feet. He stood behind the General and waited for...what? Time here was frozen in the moment as he discerned the various statues fighting the weredogs. Time in a battle is not like time in any other situation. It is a long and winding thing, a tenacious insect that claws its way forward toward its end. Time on a battlefield does not flow like normal time. It climbs, backtracks, and stands still as one opponent meets the other in combat. So it was here, the only light visible coming from the torches of the statue Brady referred to as *Victory*. Her torches worked as flamethrowers in the darkness, burning away the night and the weredogs in their path. With blast after blast, fire spewed from her torch and cut at the edges of the weredog pack and at Grendel himself.

Grendel understood what was happening. If this new

world had such beings from within, he would meet them from within. Deep down inside the prison that held them like Cronus held his own swallowed children from Greek mythology, the monster opened his throat and vomited out the nightmares and fears of old that he had absorbed many nights ago. They came out of him in ectoplasmic sheets and ribbons, white and ethereal, flowing like nearly frozen water into the darkness and the night sky. Brady watched behind the form of the General as the sound filled the sky and the battle effectively stopped. Everyone waited to see how this would effect the outcome of the fray.

The whirling tornado of forms turned in the air about them for a moment and a hundred or a thousand, perhaps a million voices could be heard shouting and swearing, screaming and crying. These were the enemies of Humanity, the *Keres* that Joe referred to, all personified diseases and ailments, dreads, horrors, terrors, hatreds, loathings and fears. They had agreed to the joining with Grendel for their very survival and now they had been released to fight for him. Useless in this form and only powerful when infecting the bodies of humans, they were Cancer and AIDS, Anthrax, Typhoid and Cholera and a hundred other ailments that had claimed millions of victims over the centuries. They flew from form to form, seemingly sniffing the air, tasting the statues and finding nothing there to fight. They were useless against the statues as mere diseases. No, they needed hosts. They needed humans to worry and bother, taunt and infect but all they had was Brady and he seemed impervious to their onslaught. They arose again into the blackness, each one of them a ribbon of nearly transparent white and then they flew upward into the dark night sky and out of sight. Everyone on the battlefield looked up, wondering where they had gone as the form of Grendel, now smaller and more like the original monster Brady had first encountered in the hospital while rescuing Kaileigh, stood weakened.

From above them they heard a screaming in the sky as the white ribboned worms of disease sought new living tissue in the form of the weredogs. They entered the bodies of the weredogs violently, knocking the creatures down to the ground and pushing the air out of their lungs.

It became clear to Brady why Grendel had purged himself of his assimilated strength as the affected weredogs began to shiver and quake on the ground. Their whole bodies took on the semblance of Grendel's ever-morphing face as though the bones beneath their skin were being rearranged in some evil and malevolent way to create new forms. Their flesh quavered as though dancing to some discordant music and they grew taller, more muscular, and more dire in their obvious purpose. As the transformations continued, Brady realized that Grendel had unleashed his army of titans, had opened his Pandora's box. Around him began to form an opponent for every statue that had come to his aid under General Chamberlain's command. Brady had to stop himself from vomiting as he viewed them. One had flesh that appeared to melt off in sheets, one had growths of reddish-black all over its form and they appeared to writhe and twist of their own accord. Still another had yellow weeping pores from which issued foul-smelling and acidic pus. For each of the new monsters being created, Brady felt the pit of his stomach fall more deeply. Now, instead of one monster in the form of Grendel, there were seven new ones, each one formidable.

The statues under the command of General Chamberlain awaited their orders. Each of them stood resolute, unafraid and this brightened Brady's wavering hopes. He wondered if they felt fear. He wondered how their 'life' was different from his own. He could die, but could they? He imagined that they could be destroyed, torn apart, or melted down.

"Looks like the battle just got more interesting," said the General to Brady, shielding him.

"How did you know I was here?" shouted Brady.

"Your amazing raven and Dr. Franklin informed me this morning," he answered calmly in the quiet before the next round of fighting.

"Of course!" Brady exclaimed.

"Benjamin Franklin can be very persuasive when he wants to be," answered the General. "He talked my feet right off of that pedestal. Then we went from park to park, statue to statue, awakening them together. Seems these good fellows," he said, indicating the statues waiting for the next wave of fighting to commence, "had been watching and wondering, too. When I explained your predicament, they all agreed to come to your aid, each and every one of them."

The statue of Hannibal Hamlin strode up to Brady and said, "We've met before, son, in the library. A pleasure to meet you in the...well, I was going to say the flesh, but that isn't right, is it? Anyway, I am pleased to meet you here, like this."

"Me too, Mr. Vice-president," responded Brady. "Where are Hugin and Ben?"

"They've gone to find Kaileigh and your Wizard. We'll need all the help we can get," answered Hamlin.

"They're going to bring them here?" asked Brady, obviously concerned. "They shouldn't do that. They need to survive."

"Survive? Are you worried you're going to die, Brady?" asked Chamberlain.

"Well, yeah," replied the boy.

Looking at Hamlin, they both shook their heads and smiled, "You have to survive, Brady. You're...well, you're *essential*. You're frightened, and you'd be foolish not to be, but see this through. Stand with us. Fight with us. Together, with you leading us, nothing can stop us, so long as we stand together."

Brady weighed the General's statement in his mind and heart. Anyway, standing and fighting seemed better to him than hiding behind the General like a child.

"I need a weapon," he said simply.

"Here," said Hamlin, "take this cane. As a club, it does wonderfully. I can use my own bare hands against these fellows," he said with resolve.

Brady hefted Hamlin's cane and found it to be heavy and therefore, deadly. He tested it against the air and smiled.

"Thank you, sir."

"Brady, my boy, I am proud to stand with you against the Powers of Darkness. Our union must stand!"

From the darkness, the unaffected weredogs were

growing restless. Grendel was with the six monstrous forms that had mutated from weredog to mythic beast. There was the Lernean Hydra, the Erymanthean Boar. There was Cerberus and the Balrog, the Rancor from Star Wars and the Jabberwock from Wonderland. They huddled together and gathered their strength as Grendel communicated with them in a wordless, cellular way, sending chemical messages to them through physical contact, communicating on a primitive level. A simple command was issued, "Kill, kill, kill."

They burst forth together but each took a different direction as they sought the statue they had been created to battle. One chose Victory, while another chose the Logger with the peavey, as one by one each of these forces collided in the cemetery. Brady watched as the other two loggers were each engaged in battle by Cerberus. Ancient foes grappled on the cemetery ground in close and deadly combat. The monsters were stronger than they appeared. Brady was trying to help, but it was clear that Grendel would be *his* opponent.

Into the fray the monsters swarmed, their own various appendages flailing at the moving sculptures like sledgehammers, pounding down a rain of destruction. Each statue fought valiantly. The General, in particular, found himself hacking and slashing at the beast he knew to be the Hydra. For most of his adult life the real Chamberlain had lived with a wound that most surgeons would have judged mortal. At the Siege of Petersburg in 1864, a mini-ball pierced his right hip and groin. Chamberlain fought on during that battle, even though he lost a copious amount of blood. They pronounced him dead. The newspapers even reported his death. But he survived, received Lee's sword at Appomattox, and became the Governor of Maine and the President of Bowdoin College. Not even the Hydra of legend could stop such a man.

"I didn't have six horses shot out from under me and survive six wounds, one of them mortal, just to allow you to even so much as lay a finger on me, you minion of Hades!"

His foe slashed at him with heads full of hundreds of

large, spiny teeth jabbing at the General over and over again. In his turn, the General simply used his sword to slice them off, falling like icicles from a spring roof line. They regrew the needles and he kept cutting, mowing them like so much hay. At the last moment, Victory arrived and began cauterizing the wounds as Chamberlain decapitated each repulsive head, Iolaus to Brady's Hercules.

The others were fighting with all of their might. Vice-president Hannibal Hamlin was engaged in battle with a small, corpulent creature, red-faced and foul-breathed. His weapons were long snake-like tendrils that emerged from his sides like Shiva. They wove their way though the Vice-president's thundering pounding trying to squeeze him around his neck, his arms and his legs. Brady watched as, in the blink of an eye, the muscular form of Hamlin fought back, ripping tendrils from the creature's side. Too late, Brady realized, the Vice-president was caught off his balance and he tumbled to the ground, his head snapping off and rolling away like a pumpkin thrown by a teenager on Halloween. He watched the head and he could have sworn that he heard the decapitated head of Hannibal Hamlin shout, *"It's only a flesh wound, you baby! Come back here and I'll bite your legs off..."*

Victory's flamethrowers were growing weaker as she spent what she had left on the Balrog. Never once did she fail to move forward toward it, advancing ever to make the creature stagger backward. Its unnatural abomination of weaponry consisted mostly of its own fire and internal flame, ever seeping and weeping onto the statue, eating away at the bronze like strong, sulfuric acid. Victory grappled with the thing and it nearly covered her in its ooze, a blob of foul excrement draped over the symbol of achievement. Victory's left arm was eaten away by the dribbling mass that was the Balrog's weapon until finally, the statue's left arm cracked and then fell to the ground with a resounding thud.

Everywhere he looked, the statues fought bravely, but seemingly in vain. Advancing toward him was the form of the beast Grendel, the Sauron of his epic, the Alien that

Ripley faced alone, the Candyman, Freddie, Darth Vader, Chucky, and Bloody Mary all poured together and stirred until this thing arose from the muck and mire. He was no longer as tall or muscular as he had been since shedding himself of the Keres that now tore the shreds of peace and laid waste to his only allies. Brady thought as hard as he could, 'Please Kaileigh, stay away! Stay away! Don't come for me! Run!' hoping that she might hear, or see, or know.

Brady didn't immediately grapple with the beast. He had no weapons except for his fists and his brain and he certainly didn't have a plan. Grendel could crush him with one fist, with one simple, fluid movement, so the only thing he could think of to do was run. He had been chained all day to a rock and he had been wounded, but when he looked down to see his broken arm he discovered that he was healed.

No, he thought. No, that can't be. Last time this happened, it was because Kaileigh had been near me, kind to me, caring. *That means she's near.*

No! he screamed in his mind as he turned his back on the advancing giant and sprinted away into the darkness of the ever-deepening night. Jumping over gravestones like they were hurdles, he made much faster progress than Grendel, who simply found himself knocking them down and often falling, an arrogant, lumbering creature at best. The dead were helping him as they appeared throughout the cemetery pointing with faintly glowing hands which direction Brady should run, leading him, showing him by seeing through his own eyes the path which he should take. Brady remembered their faces looking at him, heard the

351

orphan boy say, "You are not alone," and took courage from the memory.   All of the dead wanted him to live and though they couldn't directly interact with the world, they could influence Brady, a boy who walked between the worlds.   Down a steep incline Brady bounded while behind him the monster shouted epithets and curses.   Although he was unsure of his final destination, what mattered most to Brady was movement.   The beast was now so far behind him that he was a dot in the moonlit distance, fumbling towards him awkwardly.   Brady ran past the orphans' graves and the graves of the elder ladies home until he saw the Angel.

There near the entrance of the cemetery was the form of an Angel, made of metal, holding the dead body of a fallen soldier from the Great War, World War One.   It was a loving, protective thing, a beauty to behold even in the grim shadows of this night.   Brady had seen it before and never given it a second thought, but now he felt as though he was in the presence of something divine, something elegant and perfect: love for a fallen soldier, pathos for Humankind in the form of a divine being.

"I have seen them all fall," whispered the Angel in bells and chimes.

"I'm not ready to die," Brady managed to say from his heaving chest.

"You are not meant to die, not this night," whispered the Angel.

"Then please, Spirit, tell me what I have to do," pleaded Brady, looking over his shoulder at the advancing form of Grendel, whose obvious anger was mounting. He would be sure to visit every ounce of anger upon the weaponless boy when he finally caught up with him.

The Angel looked skyward, holding the dead soldier even more closely, tenderly like a small child.   Even though Brady had just witnessed the most macabre and frightening scene of his entire life in the last few moments, and even though he faced nearly certain death from the hammer-hands of Grendel, he found himself suddenly visited by utter peace. The Angel raised its loose arm and pointed to the Great River, less than five hundred yard away.

352

"Sometimes the best thing you can do is nothing at all. Sometimes the best thing you can say is...nothing." Then the Angel looked back to the heavens and settled into its quiet, solid, metallic repose.

The Penobscot River. Brady didn't stop to think or wonder. Instead, he bolted out the front gate of the cemetery, across U.S. Route Two and down the hill to the railroad tracks. Behind him, thrusting himself forward now unhindered by tombstones, rumbled Grendel. But where Brady was lithe and fleet of foot, the monster was ever ponderous and clumsy. Brady was past the railroad tracks and then down to the riverside. He didn't know how deep the water was. He hadn't set foot in it, not even once since the Abandonment had settled down upon the world. Now, without reason or cause, he flung himself into the water. It was deep, for he felt no ground beneath his feet. Brady was a tremendous swimmer and moved easily, swimming to within a few feet from the shore. Then, quietly, he floated, trying to move as little as possible.

Grendel made it to the edge of the water and stopped. He searched the riverbank with his eyes, turned around and looked behind him up the hill, and Brady could tell that the monster could not see him in the water.

"Ahhhhh! Where are you! Show yourself you little lickspittle!"

Brady thought to himself, 'Say nothing, act casual.' For a long moment, he did little but slowly move his hands and feet, just enough to tread water as it flowed downstream, carrying him away from the monster. Brady watched the frustrated movements of Grendel and marveled at his own ability to call forth such a monster from the depth of his darkness. If he could summon Grendel, perhaps he could summon something else. He thought very hard. He imagined very hard, losing all the world except for the thought that was preeminent in his mind.

With all of his might he called forth a titan to battle a titan.

Kaileigh and Joe didn't know where Brady was and as the hours ticked past, they both were becoming more and more irritable. They knew that he had been captured, but they didn't know where he was being kept. Even now, it might be too late. It was all Kaileigh could do not to imagine Brady's limp body dumped into some ravine, bereft of life and nothing more than a shell.

They were driving down the road near the Bangor Mall when Joe saw the flashes of light down Mount Hope Avenue. Immediately Kaileigh steered the Lifeseeker down the road, past Evergreen Woods and the Bangor Humane Society, down into the gully and up to the rear entrance of the cemetery near the Korean War Memorial. It was there that they saw the battle in all of its strange, unworldly fury, flashes of light emanating from the Keres each time one of them either gave or received a blow. Both of them sat in the Lifeseeker, its headlights bathing the scene in white halogen light as metal people fought incomprehensibly horrific shapes.

"What the hell are we looking at?" asked Joe.

"I've no idea," she said, her mouth hanging open.

"Well, whatever the hell it is, Brady can't be too far away," said Joe as he reached into the back seat with his left hand and withdrew his shotgun.

"Are you thinking what I'm thinking?" asked Kaileigh.

Joe's face gave little trace of anything but focus and determination. "If that boy is out there, we have to help him."

Kaileigh reached for the .45 in her shoulder holster and withdrew it. She was already wearing the bandoleer with the extra clips, her sword and various other weapons she had accumulated during her time with Brady. Joe reached into the pocket of his vest and took out a box of shells.

He shot her a glance that would have melted glass and said, "Be careful." He might have said, "Please don't get killed because I don't want to deal with that and I don't want to die alone, either. I've grown awfully fond of you both." He might have said that, but he didn't.

Kaileigh walked into the fray first, with Joe having to

hobble as best as could with his aching knees. Where she walked, he barely could even stay upright. Still, both of them studied the battle for a moment before making the determination about which side they were on.

"The statues! There!" pointed Kaileigh, "That's General Chamberlain!"

"Right," said Joe, raising the shotgun to his shoulders, taking a stance and letting go a blast of shot into the gruesome form that was nearly subduing the bronze general. Surprisingly, the blast had a definite effect. The monstrous form turned in surprise to face his new attacker and then, as much surprised by the thing that was happening to it as it was by the reinforcements, it began to quiver and shake. The form fighting Chamberlain fell to the ground, it's face contorting in confusion instead of pain. The blast had not killed the Kere, but it had clearly wounded the weredog beneath, upon which this parasitic being fed.

Kaileigh took careful aim and let two shots from her .45 go into the monster. It was clear to the other Keres that they had reason for concern. The Keres inhabiting the wounded weredogs began to vibrate and shift, appearing to melt like ice in the summer sun. They were not simply shedding themselves of the body of the wounded animal: they were also weakening. There was a screaming in the air. It was glass scraping against glass, it was a world being rent, it was a simple cry of pain and then, the only thing left on the ground was a dead dog.

When the remaining Keres saw what had transpired, it became clear to them that they could no longer continue in this manner. They were angry, to be sure, because they had nearly triumphed against the metal forms. They had no choice now. They had to flee. The screaming multiplied as the Keres each detached themselves from the weredogs they had been secured to and took to the sky, back into the darkness from which they came, back into the netherworld where they were undoubtedly fated to go.

Kaileigh heard the sound of an old woman cackling into the ether. She did not know it, but it was the Hag who had refused to join Grendel in the first place. She shrieked, "Just

as I thought, you fools! He has betrayed." They heard her cackling laughter fade away into nothingness.

In a moment, all that remained were the weakened forms of the weredogs, except that they were only dogs now.

Kaileigh walked over to one that had been attacking Hannibal Hamlin and pointed her pistol at it. The dog, obviously once someone's pet and enamored of human girls, reached its muzzle up to Kaileigh and licked her hand. She lowered the gun, clicking the safety back into position.

"Well met, Kaileigh!" exclaimed General Chamberlain.

"My goodness," said Hannibal Hamlin, holding his severed head under his arm, "Why, you don't know it, young lady, but I have been watching over you as you slept, in the library."

She looked at him with confusion and distrust, thinking, *Creepy. How weird is that? A statue stalker.* Introductions were given and Kaileigh was surprised by how easy it seemed to shift realities and speak to statues as though they were alive.

"Where is Brady?" asked Joe.

"He was here, but instead of fighting Grendel, he ran. The monster followed him," answered the logger with the peavey.

"We must find him, and quickly," urged Chamberlain.

356

"He went that way," said the logger with the ax resting on his shoulder.

"Let's go," urged Victory, now beaming a bright flame from her remaining torch.

"I can't," said Joe under his breath," I haven't got it in me," he said.

"I can drive us. There are roads through this place," said Kaileigh.

"I will track him" said the General, "and it should be easy enough. The monster knocked down gravestones as he blundered through. The shame of it, such hallowed resting ground disturbed," said Chamberlain.

It was Hannibal Hamlin who said clearly, "Look, General, I'm buried in this place and let me tell you, it's been good to have a little life in a world that's known so much death. This is life! Doesn't it taste good! I wish I had lungs so I could light up a big old cigar and breathe it in! Oh, that would be truly living!"

They all looked at him with doubt, but the old statesman walked off into the darkness with an obvious smile on his face under his arm, following the trail of broken tombstones.

The Keres that had detached themselves from the weredogs sought out the form of Grendel. They threw their spectral noses into the air and sniffed and found his scent, down near the river, which made them wince, though they continued trekking towards it nonetheless.

Sure enough, they found him near the riverside, angry and frustrated at having lost the boy again to the river. Without permission they alighted upon him and he felt them there in the darkness. He breathed in and focused, ready for the re-bonding. They were tired from their exertions so the fusion took place more slowly than the last time, but the result was tremendous. The creature that could not see in the dark now had night vision, heat vision, cold vision, infrared and ultraviolet vision. He was exhausted from the melding process but there was the boy, floating in the water not fifty feet from him.

Through gritted teeth he said, "Finally, I see you..."

Brady could see Grendel from his place in the stream. The monster now took on greater shape. He was that mighty monster that he saw while chained to the stone tower once again. He did not seem diminished; in fact, he seemed somehow larger and more belligerent, perhaps grown fat on his anger and the food of battle.

The monster put one foot in the water and shuddered, a long gasp emitting from what must have been a throat. He stepped backwards like a child at the local pool, too frightened to move forward, to jump right in and let the waters surround him. If Brady could have peered into the mind of the monster he would have seen the truth of things: the water was a solvent to Grendel. When it touched him, it dissolved the bonds that held fear to fear and anger to hate. If he stepped into the water, he would ever-so-slowly be diminished until there was nothing left. The river was water and water was more than water, as Kaileigh had lately discovered. Water held the worlds apart and connected them all at once.

Chapter 26
The Colossus of the Ruined City

Kaileigh saw Grendel as Brady had originally seen him for the first time and it was enough to cause her to loose her breath and stop the Lifeseeker askew on the road. Nothing she had experienced gave her such pause, caused her so much terror. If Brady had willingly walked into the hospital with only a few meager weapons to take on that *monstrosity,* she thought, he is a bravest person she ever met. The Keres that had fled from the weredogs had re-bonded to the mainframe of Grendel, grafted like skin onto a wound. In that moment, her respect for Brady took a manifold step forward.

Brady? Where was he? As the General and his metal entourage met them near the river's edge, they paused to assess the situation. Brady was nowhere to be seen and Grendel, reinvigorated, stood at the shore shouting in anger.

"Where's the boy?" asked the General with concern.

"I think he's in the water," Joe replied. "If my memory serves, ghosts and supernatural beings can't cross or enter running water."

"Like in *The Legend of Sleepy Hollow* and the Headless Horseman?" asked Kaileigh, scanning the dark river for any sign of her friend.

"Right. Ichabod Crane had to reach the bridge and cross it before the horseman caught up with him. Washington Irving didn't make that up. It's folklore," answered Hannibal Hamlin in reply. His head had been replaced on his shoulders and in some manner unknown to any but the statues, it had reattached itself, only now it was slightly cocked to the left, as though he was the victim of a stroke.

"And if that's the case, as long as Brady's in the river, he's safe," said Joe.

"As long as he can swim," was Kaileigh's concern. She was worried that since she couldn't lay her eyes on him, he might already be drowned in the depths of the Great River.

"Troops, I'm not going to lie to you," the General said plainly, "the enemy stands by the banks of the river and we linger here, for no good purpose. The heat of battle is still upon us! We must gather our strength and rally once more. This creature cannot be allowed to stand and take down the last few humans on earth."

There was agreement among the metal throng as they took to the path that led down to the water. Grendel had lost control of his temper and was raging against the loss of the boy. While he railed and shouted to the darkness, the six metal warriors took their positions near him, the General with his sword at the ready, Victory with her torch. The loggers from the Waldo Pierce Memorial had an ax and a peavey, leaving the third logger empty-handed, but being a meaty-fisted fellow, it seemed like a foregone conclusion that five-fingered Mary would be his weapon of choice. That left the old statesman weaponless, but being ever-resourceful, he searched the ground near him and found a length of railroad iron. Wielding it like a hickory-wood baseball bat, Hannibal Hamlin was ready to engage in battle.

"If they kill the monster, they'll kill Dr. Grindle," Joe said quietly. Neither he nor Kaileigh wished Dr. Grindle to perish, but they *needed* Brady alive. How could they have one of them survive without the other's death?

They watched as the metal squad cautiously made its way down the embankment, towards the distracted beast. It seemed like a hopeless assault, knowing that they couldn't

360

actually end this struggle tonight.

The river called to her in its melodious rhythmic song. "Joe, I've got to leave you here for a few minutes. I need to get down to the water."

"The water?" he asked simply.

"I have an idea," she replied. "The other weredogs; I don't know where they went, but I have the feeling that they're lurking in the dark, just beyond. Keep the doors locked and the windows closed."

"Don't worry about me," he answered confidently, "I'm as tough as nails. I've been taking care of myself for a long time and I don't plan stopping any time soon! Do what you have to do. Oh, and Kaileigh," he asked.

"Yes?"

"Be careful."

"I will," she replied.

The metal troop was upon Grendel before he had time to react. Hamlin swung the railroad iron hard into the creature's back, knocking him off balance and sending him tumbling toward the water. To Grendel's relief, he didn't fall into the river, only near it. Victory thrust her torch toward the monster and sent a plume of yellow and red-tongued fire over Grendel's head and shoulders. He screamed in pain and anger, but this didn't deter him from moving forward, toward the stand of fighters. The Ax-Logger swung mightily and let the blade fall into the beast's side, but it rebounded back like he had just struck stone. Stunned, the Ax-Logger fell backward and onto the ground from the recoil of his own strike. With his fists, the meat-fisted logger began hammering into the torso of Grendel, but the monster seemed to grow stronger with each hit. Grendel appeared to be getting physically larger with each attack that he successfully fended off.

Kaileigh found her way to the water and thrust both hands into it. The world changed, like it did in her dream. White light filled her vision and she was no longer only on the banks of the river near the ruined city but in some other place, as well.

"You've returned," she heard the musical voices sing.

"Brady. I need to find Brady!" she said as quickly as she could.

The voices took their time in responding, finishing one musical movement before allowing themselves to utter, "He is safe. We guard him."

"Can you bring him to me, here on the shore?" she asked urgently.

"That would mean reversing the flow of the river," they began in a minor key.

"I don't care!" she insisted, "He's my friend and I'm supposed to protect him! Bring him to me!"

She heard the voices began to disband and whisper among themselves. She heard them say, "*Does she know? Can she know?*" and then, "*We cannot deny her. She has answered the call. She is the Conduit.*" She didn't know to what the voices referred and she didn't care.

A stronger tone answered her, not a bell or a cymbal but perhaps a bass drum, deep and sonorous, it's voice rang and lingered.

"Yes! As you command, so it is done!"

Kaileigh kept her hands in the water, her mind in the bright white world where the fluid transported her, and she watched as they began to flow backward. The air took on a blue aspect. *Time* shifted itself into reverse, if such a thing was possible. She could see a small speck drifting towards her, getting larger in aspect as the speck became a person and the person became a man.

She was stunned. Where was Brady? This was a grown man, very tall and muscular and singularly handsome. As the waters brought him nearly close enough to touch, their eyes met and she couldn't believe what she was seeing. Was this possible? Could this man be....no, it couldn't be. But his eyes! Did she know this man?

"Hey, Kaileigh!" said the man in a deep tone, obviously pleased to see her.

He reached his hand out to her and she took it, rising from her knees and helping him out of the water. The second her hands left the water she was back in the night world with the metal men and monster in battle in the distance and holding her hand was Brady Smith, fourteen year old genius of the Abandonment.

"That was weird," he said, "it was like the river just brought me to you," he said in amazement.

"Yeah, weird," she replied, not explaining that her own bewilderment and surprise was for another reason entirely. Had that handsome young man been an older version of Brady?

"Are you okay?" she asked.

"Yes, I think so. A bit waterlogged, but I'll survive."

She looked at him with serious eyes for a long moment and then hugged him tightly, nearly pushing all of the air out of his lungs.

"Wow!" he said when she let go of her grip.

"Don't you ever leave like that again!" she implored.

"Sorry. I thought it was a good idea at the time," he replied.

"You're not playing at survival as the last boy on earth anymore. We're a unit. All of us. We act like a family and we stay together! Got it!" she demanded.

He nodded in agreement. Even if he didn't agree with her, it would not do to further anger gray-eyed Athena.

A shotgun blast filled the air, even causing the monstrous battle near the riverside to halt momentarily to see what had happened.

"Joe!" said Kaileigh, grabbing Brady by the hand and running back up the slope towards the Lifeseeker.

When they got there they saw Joe standing outside of the motor home, his shotgun squarely aimed at a group of weredogs that were circling ever closer to him. At his feet lay the form of Fenris, still breathing but riddled with bird shot. The animal wasn't dead but it was wounded, his brothers growing more nervous as the moments ticked past.

"Come on, give me another target," said Joe calmly, his aged face full of vigor. Max was at his side, his lips curled in a sneer and a low growl tumbling from his throat.

One of the weredogs jumped forward, lunging high.

Max was ready to pounce and land his own jaws around the weredog's throat, but it was too late. Joe aimed and shot quickly and efficiently. At his feet, near the still-breathing body of Fenris, it fell lifeless.

"Any more?" Joe asked as he quickly reloaded his shotgun.

The weredogs fell back into the night. Leaderless, they had to determine which of the remaining pack would become their new leader.

Kaileigh and Brady were at his side within a moment.

"I told you I could take care of myself, little girl," he said, smiling.

"I guess you're right," she said, pleased that Joe was in once piece.

Brady was at the Lifeseeker and in a moment, still soaking wet from his river experience, he brought out a first aid kit from the back.

"What are you doing," asked Kaileigh.

"I think he's going to tend to the big weredog," Joe replied.

It never occurred to Kaileigh to even give the creature another thought, but there was Brady, on his knees in front of Fenris, looking over his broken body for the puncture wounds inflicted by the shotgun blast. It didn't take him long to back away in frustration.

"There are too many," he said. "I can't treat them all. He's going to die."

"Good riddance," muttered Kaileigh.

"No," Brady explained, "don't you see? This is just somebody's dog, someone's pet. He's not a bad dog, not really. It's just that Grendel was making him into something else, something he didn't want to be. In a way, he's just like Dr. Grindle."

Both Kaileigh and Joe understood and realized that Brady was right. Something akin to compassion even flared in Kaileigh, whose heart could be steel and whose aspect could be stone.

Fenris' breathing was shallow and getting weaker with each breath. From several small wounds, rivulets of blood slowly seeped into the spongy ground. Brady put his hand on the weredog's head and began to stroke his fur. For an instant, he felt Fenris respond and move toward his touch.

"I bet he was a good dog," said Brady simply, as Max found his way to his side. Brady reassuringly began to pet him with his other hand.

They remained in silence for a few moments until it was broken by a cawing coming from the sky. Brady looked up into the darkness, but instead of the raven Hugin appearing from the blackness, a paperback book held together with an elastic fell at his feet.

It was *The Autobiography of Benjamin Franklin*.

"Ben!" said Brady.

"Hello, my boy. Are you well?" asked Ben Franklin in his avuncular fashion.

"So far, so good," replied Brady, seeing the initial confusion on the faces of Joe and Kaileigh.

"I've formed an alliance that should stand against this monster long enough for you folks to determine how to bring it down," informed the book.

"I can see that. Well done, Mr. Ambassador," Brady replied.

"That marvelous bird! He understands everything I say! You know, when the Congress made the eagle our national bird, I protested, saying that the Wild Turkey was a better choice. Now I would change my vote to the Raven. I think if we gave him enough time, he'd learn how to read, write and play chess!"

Everyone heard the book now, as clear as a bell. The world had changed again.

"What happened? Where did you go? What did you do?" asked Kaileigh.

"I contacted the General. I convinced him, with mere words, to simply step right off of that platform. When he knew that you were in trouble, he did a brave thing and once he knew he could perambulate about the world, he accompanied me on my mission. We found every statue that this fine city has and awoke them. Seems they'd been waiting for someone to talk to, as well. How fares the battle?"

Brady looked up and watched as the monster seemed to be growing larger and larger as the statues continued their onslaught. Because they were not made of flesh and bone, they could take a hit and arise to continue their assault. Still, even though they may be mighty, they did not seem to be weakening or slowing down Grendel.

"Not well, I'm afraid," Brady answered.

"Well, then. I daresay it's time for some reinforcements!" answered Ben Franklin with not a small amount of satisfaction seething from his voice.

The General watched with a look of grave concern on his face. He glanced at Victory, who looked down to the ground in worry.

"I am concerned about the outcome of this event," stated the General simply.

"Don't worry. Something's coming to help us," Brady said, smiling. "Something big..."

They felt the approach of their new ally before they saw it. It rumbled through the ground sending seismic shocks through their feet. Whatever it was, it was huge. The moon cast down enough silver light upon the landscape to give a hint of what was coming. There in the distance, a slight image formed. Closer and closer it tromped until they could all clearly see Brady's handiwork.

"No way!" said a stunned Kaileigh, her eyes nearly popping from their sockets. "Oh, that is so freakin' cool!"

"I don't believe it," said Joe, thunderstruck at the size of the approaching colossus.

"You didn't" the General said to Brady..

"He's the only one big enough to get the job done," answered Brady in smug self-satisfaction. He had summoned this behemoth as surely as he had summoned forth Grendel.

The city of Bangor had a few claims to notoriety throughout its history. Among other things, it was once the lumber capital of the entire planet, shipping out more wood from its riverside warehouses than any other city. In fact, the lumber that shipped from this place helped build cities all over the world, especially eastern seaboard cities and those in Europe. It was pride in that accomplishment that led the city fathers to erect a monument to their city's past glory along Main Street in front of the Bangor Auditorium. A monument to the era in which it was built, it was oversized, optimistic and garish. It was the largest of its kind in the world and it stood on a tall stone pedestal, a long threaded iron rod connecting it's head to the rest of its body. Some might claim him for Minnesota or Wisconsin, even Oregon, but Bangor had him first.

There, clearly approaching them from the burned and ruined city of Bangor, was the giant statue of Paul Bunyan., striding as a colossus through the world. He strode toward them, over thirty feet tall and weighing almost four thousand pounds. In one hand he carried a giant peavey and on his shoulder rested a gigantic ax. He was the tallest statue of Paul Bunyan on earth. With green wool pants, a red and black checkered wool coat and a red toque on his head, he sported an enormous and somewhat idiotic smile frozen onto his red-cheeked face. He strode in mightily, with sweeping steps making his way to them, the raven Hugin settling proudly on the giant's ax-head. He stopped in front of Brady and waited.

"I think he's waiting for you to tell him what to do," Joe insisted to Brady. "He's big and goodhearted, but he's not the sharpest tool in the shed."

Brady nodded, his mouth still agape from the sheer bulk of the creature towering over them.

"Mr. Bunyan, sir?"

The grinning colossus looked down at the small group and said nothing.

"Mind of a child, Brady, mind of a child. You're going to have to give him some very specific, simple instructions. Speak slowly and use small words," offered Joe.

"Paul, you see those people fighting over there?"

The giant turned to the direction in which Brady pointed. When he saw the fighting, he smiled and nodded affirmatively.

"Well, the little metal people are trying to stop the big

white glowing monster from getting to us. You've got to help us. You've got to help them," Brady slowly explained. "Do you understand?"

Paul Bunyan nodded, his grin beginning to disturb all of them, especially Kaileigh, who found she couldn't look at his face for long before averting her gaze.

"Okay. Good. What I want you to do is go over there and grab hold of the monster with your strong arms. Just hold onto him so he can't move, okay?"

The giant nodded and turned his body toward the fight by the riverbank, treading down the hill in only a few steps. They watched with rapt attention at the reaction of the combatants as this Goliath suddenly entered their midst. The general understood immediately that this was the turning point and ordered his soldiers to fall back and get out of

Bunyan's way as he moved into the fray and closed in upon Grendel.

For his part, Grendel saw the huge statue and did something truly unexpected. Brady's breath escaped him as he saw the monster double in size with seconds, expanding like a supernova in front of their eyes. It was obvious that Grendel was using all his strength, expending the Keres within him to enable him to respond to this new, gargantuan threat. With mighty arms, the giants began to battle.

"All we need now is a giant gorilla and a flying robot," Kaileigh said.

"I hope this works," Joe replied.

"It will," Brady answered.

The two behemoths wrestled and fought, hand to hand, shaking the ground. Paul Bunyan swung his ax but it seemed to have little effect against Grendel. Lightning could be seen in the distance as Grendel summoned every fell power to his aid. Thunder rolled closer and closer. Grendel countered every move that Paul Bunyan could throw at him and it quickly became clear that Grendel was the more cunning of the two combatants because every time he was caught in the grip of Bunyan's mighty fiberglass and steel hands, he simply changed form slightly and slipped away, a wraith, a greased pig, a wisp. The earth shook and the water rippled until it became obvious that this was a stalemate. There was no clear winner. Even though Grendel was smarter, Bunyan was stronger.

"We can't just stand here!" Kaileigh said.

"What can we do?" asked Joe.

"He's afraid of the water. It burns him like fire," Brady answered. "When I went in, he wouldn't follow."

"You mean...you want the lumberjack to throw him into the river?" asked Kaileigh.

"If you do that, you risk Dr. Grindle's life. He might not be strong enough to survive such a shock," Joe reminded them.

"I don't think the water will kill Grendel, but it might get him to abandon the body of Dr. Grindle, don't you think?" asked Brady.

"I don't know. I say we do it," said Joe.

Said Franklin, "We all need to hang together or we shall indeed hang separately..."

Kaileigh wondered silently if she might not be of some assistance in this plan, for she had used the waters to bring Brady back to her. Perhaps she could use them to save the good doctor from drowning. Besides, since they had made their way to the riverbank, she couldn't get the sound of singing from ringing in her ears. It was like the water was summoning her, seeking her for company, as though it needed her.

"Do it!" she said firmly. "If that fiberglass skyscraper can manage to throw Grendel into the river, this is a no-brainer! Do it!"

Brady put his two pinkies into the side of his mouth and whistled a loud sharp report to the wind. Within a minute, Hugin was on his shoulder. "Tell Paul Bunyan to throw Grendel into the river, as far as he can. Can you do that, Hugin?"

"RAGnarok!" croaked the raven as he took to the air, pumping his black silken wings. He made his way to the fighting giants and wove a circle in the air around Paul Bunyan, cawing and screeching his pleas. The giant was slow to notice and even more slowly did he respond, but he eventually changed his tactics according to Hugin's order, no longer seeking to restrain Grendel. Instead, he picked up the beast and with Herculean effort, he threw him far out into the main stream of the Great River.

What happened in the next moment burned itself into the minds of all who witnessed it upon that fateful night. Long years would pass before anything as violent and climactic ever happened again in this quiet, forested part of the world. However, on this night, with the moon now directly overhead and the stars waltzing slowly, the form of Grendel hit the surface of the water with an explosion that knocked all the onlookers flat on the ground, a shock wave blasting like a tsunami pounding anything itn its path. A mushroom spout arose from the water and Kaileigh, who was now down by the shore, saw the river shrink back from its banks as the fountain of water thrown into the air continued to rise. Within the spout of water was the glowing form of Grendel, personified anger and hatred of all Humankind, struggling like a panic-driven, drowning man. Sparks and electrical tongues of static shot out from the water and upwards to the sky as Grendel began his death-throes. Except he wasn't drowning. He was being shredded, burned, flayed and ripped all at the same time. The water churned and bubbled, boiled and rolled.

Kaileigh alone knew that there were beings in the water, *Those of the Waters* and she dove into the water and allowed her entire body to go beneath the waves. Submerging, she entered the ghost world again.

She was surrounded by music and she wasn't swimming but flying through what seemed to be air. She was surrounded by forms in the water, female forms that swam next to her and around her and with unseen hands held her up and propelled her along. Were these the bodies whose voices she had spoken with before? How strange, she thought, how real this feels, how familiar. Were these nereids? What were nereids doing in the Penobscot River? Except this wasn't the Penobscot River. It was another kind of river entirely.

"She has returned," she heard an indistinct voice sing.

"*Welcome, welcome, welcome...*" a thousand voices chimed.

She didn't know how to respond. All she wanted was to find the form of Dr. Grindle. If the plan went as she hoped, Grendel would abandon his body to the waters as he desperately tried to escape, and she was bound and determined not to let the doctor drown. She understood now. He had not been the one hunting her. He was a victim as much as her.

"What's happening?" she asked aloud.

Voices answered, "The inhuman anthropomorph is shedding its host," and "Ancient treaties are being honored," and finally, "What is your bidding? What do you wish?"

"There is a man within that monster, held against his will. Find him and, please, bring him to me alive!" she

371

ordered, suddenly feeling foolish for speaking in the imperative. Still, somehow, it felt natural and the voices responded favorably.

"*Yes, yes, yes*," was being whispered and sung as she found herself lifted to the surface and guided toward the shore. For a moment, Kaileigh saw something that none of the others would ever see, for she saw it while between the worlds, while in the water. She watched in the Light of the Waters as Grendel writhed and moaned. He was different in this world, as everything seemed different. Instead of a large and monstrous excuse for a human, he was smaller, more vulnerable. As every second ticked by, if time even existed here, she watched him diminish into what he must have been before the Abandonment and the great dying. She saw into the heart of things and there, nearly empty, was a boy who looked a little like...Brady.

She could hear it calling, "Not now, so close, nearly finished! Leave me be, get thee hence! Begone! I am meant to cleanse this world! No!"

She watched as it rose from the river. *Those of the Waters* had erased all but a mote of what had been Grendel. He diminished and grew ever smaller. She observed with more than human sight as the mote, the cell, arose from the waters and floated into the sky like some drunk bumblebee, like Tinkerbell in the land of lost boys. She followed it as it rose over the riverbank and up toward her friends and the Lifeseeker. It dove down amongst them and was no longer visible to her.

The voices continued and spoke to her, saying, "*We have him. We are moving him to you. Does this please you?*"

Kaileigh answered, "Yes, very much. Thank you."

"*She thanks us? Oh, she is the One.*" A hundred other echoes of similar import came to her as she saw the form floating toward her on the water. She recognized him. Floating towards her, looking like a dead man, was the inert and sodden form of Dr. Grindle. Invisible hands guided his body toward her and handed him off with silent respect. She could feel that he was nearly spent of life, but she knew he was alive. *How do I know this?* How long had he been a tool of a thing so full of spite and malice? The monster had detached himself from the doctor at last leaving little more than an empty husk.

As she arose from the waters, the dark night of the world returned again, but this time, Brady was there, helping her tug the body from the water. He knelt down and checked for a pulse, his finger pressed firmly against the doctor's carotid artery. Weak, but there was definitely a pulse. He put his head down to hear if the man was breathing. He was. Brady brought a blanket from the Lifeseeker and covered Dr. Grindle. Only then, after he was fairly certain that they were out of danger, did he stop and marvel at Kaileigh.

"You're amazing!" he declared. "How did you do that?"

"Do what?" she feigned, smiling nervously.

What none of them noticed was that the small dot of light that was still Grendel floated purposefully through the night air, over to the side of the Lifeseeker. Since all the assembled were looking down at the river and the great commotion that was playing itself out, they didn't see the nearly dead form of Fenris begin to quiver as the small speck of hatred, envy and pain entered the weredog's body through one of his open, seeping wounds. They didn't see the human hand begin to shake, quiver and move once more. Like a virus, Grendel infected humans, not other animals. This creature he entered now would have to do, even if the only human part of Fenris was its hand. He could survive in this body, even if he couldn't thrive. He could hold on and if he was able, further stab at those humans who remained, some other time and some other place.

The hand of Fenris obeyed its master and very quietly, while no one noticed, it pulled at the ground, grasping at whatever it could to pull itself away and into the cover of darkness. As it did, if one could have peered at the damage done to the animal by Joe's shotgun, one would have watched as holes ripped open by lead shot began to push out the round pellets and close of their own volition. With every passing moment, Fenris began to heal as, with each passing moment, the inexorable force known as Grendel began to

373

take hold of his newest host.

Chapter 27

The Doctor's Tale

from the Journal of Brady Smith

I know two things now that I didn't know before. First, I think that I'm responsible for calling the monster Grendel into the world. I remember how I felt when I found everyone dead and how freaked out I was. I remember wishing so hard that I had someone to blame for all the death and I think that it was at that very moment that Grendel appeared in this world. He didn't have a body, so he took the closest, easiest host he could find – that of poor Doctor Peter Grindle.

I also know that I was able to summon the giant statue of Paul Bunyan to the river by 'imagining' him there. I thought of him at the river and for a second or two, I demanded that he was there, in my mind. And then he was. That's two for two. But once I discovered that I had the power of converting my thoughts to reality, I was frozen in fear. My nightmare could come true. How do you stop yourself from imagining terrible things, anyway? Then I thought, why not try to imagine Grendel as dead. I tried it, but it didn't work. So, as powerful a wizard as I am, I'm no Harry Potter. If I'm going to beat the monster I created, I'm going to have to beat him some other way, without magic or telepathy or whatever the heck it is I have now.

I was on the riverbank as the giant statue of Paul Bunyan lifted Grendel's expanded form above his head and threw him, like a watermelon, into the Great River. It bubbled and boiled and gave off the best light show I've ever seen–even better than the fourth of July fireworks! Whatever Grendel was, the water seemed to erase him. He disappeared, leaving only the nearly dead form of Dr. Grindle floating in the water. I never thought, in my wildest dreams, that I'd be back in the Bangor Public Library sitting with a cold Coke next to me writing in this journal again!

<u>The Autobiography of Benjamin Franklin</u> has told me that it's always darkest before the dawn and I think that's really true. Just before sunrise, Grendel was defeated. The weredogs slipped back into the forest. Their leader, who I named Fenris, was nearly dead but while our backs were turned trying to rescue Dr. Grindle, he must have had enough life in him to wander off and die. There's no way he could have survived Joe's shotgun blast. Still, I'll write it down here so I don't ever forget: that animal had a human hand! How did that happen? I wonder sometimes how things are changing, by what strange process can a dog change into something human?

Originally I thought it must have all come from Grendel, but Joe insists that the old world of the ancients was real and that science came on board and eventually dismissed most of what they believed as superstition, or religion claimed it was false. Magic, he says, may have been a real thing. It might even be explainable someday, when our knowledge of the world improves. He thinks that the world's reset button has been pressed. What matters now is that we have to learn to live in this new, changed world - even if we don't understand it. We have to learn to live within this world, or it will kill us.

As the sun rose, the General gathered his troops around us and said goodbye, for now.

"We are weary from our battle and must retire to regain our strength," he said.

I asked what that meant and he explained that they needed to return to their pedestals, to recharge their powers. It's like plugging in your cell phone or ipod to recharge the batteries, I guess.

"How long will that take?" I asked.

"We don't know," he answered, "We've never done this before. It might take a day, a week, a year or a century. Do not be surprised if, when you visit us, we appear to be nothing but statues. We will be sleeping."

It made sense to me. Everything living thing has to sleep, so why not this metal band of warriors? They were so awesome!

Now, to be honest, that giant statue of Paul Bunyan was still freaking all of us out. He was one of the good guys but he had that stupid grin wiped across his face and like the other statues, he never blinked. Still, because he was so large, he was a little frightening, even to us. That's when Kaileigh walked over to Joe who was standing quite near the giant, looking up at him.

Joe says,"Did you know that his head is attached to his body by a long metal road that connects to his butt?"

Kaileigh answered in her usual serious tone, "Really? I wondered why Brady walks that way."

After they both had a good laugh on me, Joe continued, "How all of this manages to bend without cracking or breaking makes no sense. The tolerances shouldn't allow it. Cast bronze is just as brittle. I've studied science and engineering all of my life and I'm here to tell you, this doesn't make any sense. At all. None."

"Well," answered the General, "how do you explain a bag of water and various assorted trace minerals being able to write Hamlet or a symphony? We're all moving, and we like to think we know why, but the life spark that animates anything must be something elusive, don't you think? Who knows why we can move and think, eat and sleep? What

377

matters, in the end, is that we've been given the gift. We should never forget that."

"Well said," agreed Joe, but I could still sense the engineer in him swimming in confusion and he didn't find any comfort talking to a statue.

We said our goodbyes and off they went, leaving Kaileigh, Joe, Hugin, Max and me to tend to Dr. Grindle.

He was alive, but he wasn't conscious. We managed to get him into the Lifeseeker and made for the closest place that had all of the provisions we needed -the Bangor Public Library. I was never so happy to see home as I was when that grand old building came into my view.

The doors had been ripped off, broken into a thousand pieces. Grendel must have been here. This was going to take some time to repair. I was met by none other than Gregoire, the gargoyle.

"Oh, now you come home, eh? Don't expect any parties or anyzing, eh? 'Dis place 'as been too damned quiet – like a library, eh? Come on, come on," he insisted. This was even more bizarre than watching Paul Bunyan walking around the city. Gregoire stood about two feet tall and waddled like a duck with a hernia. He didn't speak so much as he grunted things, but when Kaileigh came to the door, his whole demeanor changed.

"Oh, my lady. Let me help you. I am not worzy of your gaze, but let me serve you, eh? Lets me carry your zings, eh?" and then to me he said in a very loud attempt at a whisper, "Oh, she is beautiful, eh? You leave her alone, you...you boy! She is mine! Mine, I say!"

Then he took Kaileigh's weapon belts and waddled off into the building.

"What the...?" she said, flabbergasted.

"He thinks you're beautiful. I think he's claimed you for his own," I told her.

If looks could kill, I'd be a dead man. Then she said, in a way that only she could utter, "Like hell, he has..."

I thought I'd write this down before I passed out from fatigue. I've made two beds out of the chair cushions in the magazine room - one for Dr. Grindle and one for Joe. We've had some cold rations to eat and we're pretty tired. We're taking shifts sitting at Dr. Grindle's side with Kaileigh taking the first one. She's sitting on the floor next to him and every so often she puts some Gatorade between his lips and down his throat. Max is right next to her and I guess he's not just my dog anymore. In fact, I think he's adopted her, if you know what I mean. Gregoire is next to them, squatting on the floor like he's ready to take a stone dump. He's as quiet as a rock, and since he's made from poured cement, that makes sense, but he's looking over at Kaileigh longingly and every so often she asks, "What are you looking at?" and he answers, "OH, I am looking at zee most beautiful girl on earth!"

Then she rolls her eyes and ignores him."

"Brady, Brady!" said Kaileigh and she shook him back into the world and out of what he considered to be the best night's sleep he had since the Abandonment. It had been perfect with no interference from Whisperers or screaming auroras or monsters trying to kill him.

"Wake up!" she said and when his eyes began to open into tiny slits, Brady saw her hand raised, ready to slap him if he didn't comply.

"What?" he asked sleepily.

"Dr. Grindle's awake, and he's pretty freaked out. Come on. We need your help!" she urged, taking him by the hand. Brady was still in his underwear and when he arose from the sleeping bag she let go of his hand, looked at him, paused as she scanned his frame and said, "Jeesh, will you put on some pants!"

He put one leg into his jeans only to be tugged onward by her, nearly falling to the floor. On the way to the magazine room, he managed to get into the other leg of his jeans while she spoke quickly, "Joe and I have been trying to calm him down, but he's been saying something over and over. Maybe you can help him."

"Is he okay in the head, or what? Maybe being bonded with Grendel drove him insane?" Brady hesitantly asked.

"Maybe," she answered.

Dr. Peter Grindle, chief investigator of the viral outbreak, creator of the airborne inhalant vaccine program that had inadvertently caused the fall of Humanity by acting as a dispersal agent for the virus, sat incoherent on a chair in the magazine room, sweating profusely, babbling beneath his breath. Brady could barely understand him, but he could tell that the doctor wasn't quite with them.

Joe sat in the chair next to him and Gregoire was around the corner behind a bookshelf, having been sent out of the room so his strange presence would not distract the poor doctor anymore. He was peeking in like Kilroy around the corner.

"She's gone. He's gone. End of times. Everyone dead. Long time, forever is...my fault. All my fault. Don't understand how...took precautions. Makes no sense."

He went on and on with barely distinct phrases all obviously connected to the end of things and his final struggle to find a cure. He was as pale as a ghost and he rocked back and forth slightly in the chair, his hands clutching his own shoulders. His gaze didn't focus on anything in the room, for whatever he saw in his far sight, it wasn't the library. What distant place he gazed upon, one could only guess. Brady could tell that Kaileigh and Joe were concerned that they had a madman on their hands.

Brady walked slowly up to Dr. Grindle and got down on one knee so that their gazes could meet. Then, he leaned over and whispered, "Dr. Grindle...Peter, are you there?"

The babbling continued. Brady tried another tactic. "We haven't *all* died, Dr. Grindle. Some of us have survived. Look at me," Brady said, taking the doctor's chin in his hand and turning the doctor's gaze directly into his. "See, we're still here and we need you to come back to us, please," Brady said simply. "Dr. Grindle, are you still in there?"

The doctor stopped babbling for a moment and his gaze shifted from something just slightly over Brady's shoulder to Brady's eyes and then a moment of re-imagining came and he said in a whisper, "Where am I? You? I know you. He wanted to kill you..."

"I'm Brady Smith. This is Kaileigh and this is Joe.

We're alive, Dr. Grindle, and so are you."

"Alive?" he said, a look of confusion washing over his pale face, lips trembling. "Alive? No, that's not possible."

"Yes, it is. We survived. You survived."

"How?" he asked "I need to know. How?" He asked as a desperate man whose only purpose in life was encased in the answer to his question.

Brady shook his head and looked down at the floor, finding it hard to the meet the intensity of the doctor's gaze. "We...we don't know how. But we're alive and so are you. There's a lot for us to tell you, but we need you to relax. Here," said Brady, handing a bottle of water to the doctor, "Drink this. You need some food, too," he said, nodding to Kaileigh, who complied by rushing down to the small kitchen to make some broth on the small butane camping stove.

"Then..." he began in a stutter, "then I'm not in...Hell? I'm not in Hell?"

Joe shot Brady a look of worry, but Brady understood. Dr. Grindle had spent the last weeks being controlled by something so foul that it must have seemed to him like a demon straight of out the pit.

"No, sir, you're not. You're not in heaven, either. You're on earth, alive, with the rest of us."

"Angels and ministers of grace, thank you! Rest of us? How many?" he inquired shakily.

Brady hesitated to answer but found the truth when he said, "In this part of the world, three of us. There are a few more across the planet. Just a handful."

Dr. Grindle's bloodshot eyes fell on Kaileigh and the light of recognition dawned in them. He looked at her for a moment and then moved a little closer, obviously agitated by what he beheld.

"Kaileigh? Is that..can it be that you...survived?"

She was conflicted. Part of her distinctly remembered having been held captive by this man for many weeks, but she also knew that he had been an unwilling participant in the events that befell them all. Could she hold anger at bay and work with this unfortunate shell of a man?

381

"Yes, I survived," she said coldly.

"And..." he counted, "there are three of you?"

Kaileigh shook her head, her gray eyes boring into his, and said, "Three. That's it."

"Three? So few? Too few. My fault..."

"Dr. Grindle, you need to rest."

The doctor settled back into the chair, "I thought I'd died and gone to Hell. It was torturous. I was chained and beaten. I was held prisoner and no one could see me but...him! The Devil!"

"It wasn't the Devil. It was," and here Brady hesitated before simply saying, "It was something else."

The long hours passed and Doctor Grindle found himself eating, sleeping, talking and sleeping again. He was as weak but he found enough strength in small fits to give the trio a good picture of what had happened to him and how the monster had taken over the last of his will and then, his body.

They were sitting in the magazine room well past nightfall on their second day back in the library. The light came from two strong twelve volt lanterns Brady had discovered at a local RV center. Joe and he had gone on a scavenger hunt of their own to the local automobile parts store where they took as many deep cell twelve volt batteries as they could find, as well as a plethora of wiring and connectors. The plan was to charge the batteries for now with the library's generator but Joe envisioned a small windmill or two on the hill behind the building that would charge the batteries and give them ample lighting and power for other appliances. That would be in the future, which for now looked plausible, even positive. Joe had lists of tools, parts and devices that would be necessary to build the transmitter he hoped would place them in touch with the people of Radio Ukraine. In fact, as they sat around the warm light of the lanterns, Brady reached down and clicked the wind-up radio off, the nightly broadcast over after only five minutes.

"They aren't saying so, but they're running out of time. The broadcasts are shorter and the signal needs constant readjustment," said Joe with obvious concern.

"She sounds less positive about things, if that makes any sense."

"It does. I felt it too," Kaileigh said. "We need to get in touch with them as soon as possible."

"I'm working on it," Joe answered as he checked his watch. "Today is August 17. We'll need at least a week, maybe two."

"What's the plan, Joe?" insisted Kaileigh.

"When I have the plan I'll let you know," he replied.

"You don't have a plan?" asked Brady.

Joe gave all of them a stern look and said, "Only part of one. I need to see if all the components can be found or possibly, made. Brady and I will keep looking tomorrow. Tonight, we need to rest and stay positive. All of you. I don't want that black cloud that followed me for the last ten years to figure out where I am now. It just might come back, attracted by your negativity. Besides, I said I'd built you a transmitter and I damn well mean to do just that. Don't rush me. I'm old."

They didn't say anything for a long moment until Kaileigh said in her own precise and serious way, "I don't doubt it at all."

It was only then that Dr. Grindle had gained enough strength to tell some of his story. He was still exhausted and he wore fatigue like a shawl, yet he carefully considered his words.

"I want to thank you all for what you've done for me. I don't deserve it. I'm ashamed of myself, more than you can imagine," he began. "I came north to Bangor as it became glaringly clear that this would be our last battleground. Everywhere else the virus took hold, it utterly destroyed the population. I had been the mastermind. It was my idea to test the dispersal process with a killed virus – nothing out of the ordinary, really. I was in charge of the process of dispersal, not the design of the virus itself. Something happened. The killed virus caused the opposite response in humans than what was intended. Instead of giving the body the blueprint with which to fight the virus, it turned on the immune system and wouldn't allow it to shut down. How? It was so carefully planned.

I was one of many put in charge of regional response units, but within a week, I was the only one still reporting in. We had to use satellite phones in the end. They were the only thing that worked. We had uplinks using military satellites and the military Internet, but it became apparent that there was no one on the other end of things. No one was receiving our messages.

"We managed to treat the sick, but our main mission was to further investigate the virus itself and try to discover some way of attacking it on a smaller scale. We needed to get into it, somehow and change its coding so it would elicit a more benign response from the human immune system. Every time I got close to the answer I was led down pathways that ended up in failure.

"I don't know what happened. I think I...I killed someone. Who? I can't remember," he said dismally, looking off into dark corners that none of the others in the room even knew were there. No one in the room knew how to answer his claim.

"No," Brady finally replied, "It wasn't your fault. In the end, you were absorbed by Grendel. He used your body as his own. If anyone was killed, he was the force behind it, not you."

The doctor looked at Brady like he was speaking another language, like he had three eyes, like his hair was on fire.

"Who is Grendel?"

Joe, Kaileigh and Brady glanced at each other, wondering who would eventually stop and explain to this nearly broken man of science how things had changed while he had been in the belly of the beast.

"We think that Grendel is a monster, created by Brady's force of imagination," answered Joe slowly. "We're not sure how, or why, but we believe it to be true."

Gradually, Dr. Grindle's face began to take on a different look than one of simple confusion.

"I thought I was in Hell. When you woke me, I thought that perhaps I'd just gone mad. I had nothing with which to fight. I had lost everything, my wife and boy," he said.

"Anne?" asked Joe.

Stunned, the doctor said, "Yes. How do you know her name?"

Joe took the email he had found in the hospital from his shirt pocket and gently unfolded it, handing it to Peter Grindle, who read it slowly. He read it and reread it in silence, tears forming in his eyes and staining his rough cheeks as they made their way down.

"I killed them," he said, mired in guilt.

"No. You can't think like that, Dr. Grindle. We've all lost our families, friends, neighbors, people we love. You're not alone. You didn't create the virus. No one knows where it came from," answered Brady.

Kaileigh sat down and took Dr. Grindle's hand. Her silence spoke volumes.

"I...I tried to kill you?" he asked, still trembling.

"No, The monster did. He possessed your body, took over. I don't blame you, Dr. Grindle. I understand. Can you remember anything?"

"I remember bits and pieces. I think I remember meeting you, Brady, but that's...impossible. It can't have happened."

"It did," answered Brady. "You tried to save me, when I was chained to the stone tower. You spoke to me."

The doctor was considering his words carefully. "I think I remember moments of...well, I can only call them moments of torment. There was the time in the operations center, when almost everyone was gone. I was there...."

They waited for him to continue, but he stopped as though trying to recall something from the gray edges of his mind. He was having trouble remembering things in their proper order and many of his memories had been erased or corrupted by his parasitic bond with Grendel. He was trying to remember and when he made eye contact with Kaileigh, he stared intently at her, unblinking. For her part, she made no effort to look away, keeping her firm expression, her eyes boring a hole into his head.

"I...I remember being there when the last patient died. He was a soldier sent to protect us, to protect me. The nurse, the only one left besides me, was unaffected by the virus. I didn't know why we weren't affected, but it was the only thing I had. I asked her for some of her blood. She agreed, but when I analyzed it, there was nothing apparent that would explain her immunity to the disease. I tested my own blood, as well, with no success.

"I kept looking at the picture of my family, reading and rereading the last communication I would ever have with them. I remember a little more, but it's vague at best. She came over to me and tried to console me, and I remember wishing...oh my God...wishing that I would die, too. I didn't want to live. I think that's when I gave up. Then everything went blank. Maybe that's how the monster was able to possess me so easily. I had no fight left."

While Brady listened, his heart sank as he tried to conjure up the image of his mother's visitation and the sound of her voice. He could only imagine what happened next, but he stopped himself. There were some things, he decided, best left behind, unremembered. He didn't want to hear any more about his mother – not now.

"You went blank because at that moment, Grendel logged on and booted up. He took control of your conscious mind and your body, which he needed to possess, in a parasitic fashion. He used you as a mode of transportation, as a house in which to live while he did his business," explained Joe, postulating.

"In a way, he consumed you," Kaileigh said. "I know. I fought him, tooth and nail. I know that *you* aren't *him*. You were broken and he took advantage of you at your worst moment. That's when he entered you and began to dominate you. Maybe he never caught me because you fought against him, underneath."

They were quiet while the weight of things settled upon Peter Grindle's shoulders. Every now and then they could hear him mouth a word or two, but it was clear to them that he was recalling things, remembering, digging deeply into the black coal mine of his memory. Somewhere down there, it must still be waiting.

"I remember a ceremony. I remember creatures in the

night. I can recall the corridors of the hospital and hunting something...perhaps you, Kaileigh. I remember a great fight, and I remember...the northern lights?"

"Yes, that's right," Brady explained. "Grendel had some kind of power over nature. He could summon the lightning. That's how he burned down the city, with a lightning storm."

"Yes, I remember lightning! Is this true? Can it be true?" he asked again, pleasing for a different answer.

"It's true," Kaileigh answered, "cross my heart and hope to die."

"Oh, no, don't say that," he said gravely.

"Why not?" she asked innocently.

"Because," he managed to utter, "I remember the battle with the giant. He threw me into the water. That's when Grendel unhooked his claws from my mind and soul and flew away. I watched him fly away like a firefly, like a will o' the wisp. I watched him, a small ball of light against the night sky. You don't think you destroyed him, do you? He made it to the shore and chose another host. I saw him rise up and lope away on all fours – was it a dog?"

"I know," said Kaileigh, "I saw it, too."

They sat in stoney silence until Brady said quietly, "He's still alive."

The Wizard's Den

In the dark recesses of a burned out basement, a lone figure lay panting, nearly dying of thirst. He was ragged and dirty, surfing on the edge of death while deep inside him, another force was at work. Fenris lay in pain in the cinders and smoky earth while within him the minuscule piece of Grendel multiplied and grew in consciousness, knitting the wounds back together into solid flesh. Grendel worked on a cellular level, sending out tendrils and chemical messages to the weredog's body. He had been reduced to this pitiful state by the actions of the boy and his people, the newly awakened metal and fiberglass men of the Ruined City. Bent but not beaten, the tenacity of his sinews and the hunger of his mind vowed never to bow down, never to give up, never to die.

As he rebuilt the weredog's body from the inside, he had

to draw upon his own vital energy, drain his own essence to the point of near nonexistence, but only just. The long nights passed and gave him time to think. Now that he was rid of Dr. Grindle, he realized that over time, he had been influenced away from his original purpose. As hard as he worked, he couldn't rid himself of the idea that the form he occupied was human and if he succeeded in his bid to rid the world of these viral creatures who killed the oceans and polluted the skies and made the earth infertile, the boy would be right: he would still have within him the last human being. A reckoning would still come and the boy would die. Ironic, he ruminated, that the battle in the river helped him solve his final problem. The form of this weredog was perfect as a host. Although the creature was beginning to morph some human characteristics, he was still essentially a dog, longing to please his master.

He would give him a master, now! The world had never seen such a master! He would dominate this dog. Certainly the creature had a human hand, a result of some still mysterious genetic manipulation deep within the strands of DNA, shuffling the nucleotides and ester bonds to create something nature had never seen before – abomination. Why this was happening was unclear to Grendel but he supposed it didn't matter as long as he had the advantage.

"Fenris?" he whispered to the internal world of the weredog. There was a universe in there. "Fenris, can you hear me?"

The weredog's mind began to hear as in a dream and like a good dog, he responded, "Master?"

"Yes, Fenris. I have saved you. The humans shot you. They destroyed my body, but I am still here, within you. I am glad to be here."

"Master, master," was all the weredog could muster from his reserves.

"I am here to heal you, to make you strong. I will be different, now that you and I are together. We will help each other, cooperate, and grow strong. Will you help me?"

"Master, master," was the poor dog's only response. It was enough.

Like a long note plaintively struck against the immutable silence, sleep descended upon Fenris while Grendel gave all his focus to the reworking of the physical body of the dog.

"Yes. I believe he's still alive," agreed Dr. Grindle.

Kaileigh and Dr. Grindle's revelation was treated with suspicion by the trio. They wanted to believe that this strange episode in their lives was over. There was much to consider and even more to do before their next step. Thinking about the possibility of Grendel's survival only distracted them from what Joe said was their primary purpose.

"There's only one task for us now. Anything else is extra. We need to build the transmitter and antenna and make contact with other survivors. It's our primary mission. Nothing else matters." Joe spoke from an internal sense of time. He did not speak of it to them, but he thought of his own death far too often. How long before the new batch of insulin ran out? It would be soon. Heat and insulin do not get along well. He marveled that he wasn't so much afraid of his own death as of the death of these other three. He knew he was their last best hope at connecting with the others, somewhere out there.

"You know what? I don't care about Grendel, even if he did somehow manage to survive. If he did manage to manifest into another host, we have a window of opportunity before he gains enough strength to attack us again," Joe explained.

The Autobiography of Benjamin Franklin urged "Time is of the essence. We must work and forget any relaxation and leisure. The grave waits for no man!"

"Really? Well, good thing I'm not a man," Kaileigh interjected.

"I don't understand. Do I offend?" asked Ben.

"Never mind," Brady answered, "she's just pulling your leg.

The next three days were a whirlwind of activity at the Bangor Public Library. Joe sat with the others at one of the

390

large oak tables in the Reference Room and explained his plans in detail, writing them on pads of graph paper he had scrounged from behind the main desk.

"I expect we can build this thing within a week, perhaps two, but Brady and I will need to go exploring. We'll need to go back to my workshop in East Corinth."

"Why?" asked Kaileigh, "Can't you just build the transmitter? There must be a lot of tools in the city."

"Yes, but we'd have to spend valuable time searching for them. Besides, I don't need just any tools. I need *my* tools. I spent sixty years amassing a very specific collection of them and they will make the construction of this thing much easier. Don't argue with me. I know what I'm doing."

"Why do we have to build it? Why can't we just get a transmitter from someone's house, like we did when we found you?" asked Kaileigh.

"We have to put this thing together because any transmitter that's bigger than two hundred watts is going to be fairly rare," he said.

"How big do you want it to be? How powerful?" asked Brady.

"*Very* powerful. I want at least 2,000 watts, hopefully more. We ought to be blasting out a signal almost as strong as Tatiana's," answered Joe.

"Well, how powerful is the Radio Ukraine transmitter?"

"I'm not sure, but I'd guess about 10,000 watts."

"Is that a lot?"

"It's too much. That's why they can only transmit for short bursts. A standard SSB HAM radio that you'd find in a ship at sea can send out messages as far as 6000 miles with only 150 watts. Our transmitter is going to be much stronger than that."

"Won't that mean we'll need a lot of power?" asked Brady.

"Yes, it will," answered Joe.

"Where are we going to get that kind of power?" asked Brady.

Joe looked up from his rummaging and said, "Oh, you leave that to me, boy. I've got that one covered, I think."

Brady began to sense urgency in Joe's tone, something underlying every word. He didn't say anything to Kaileigh because he wasn't sure what he was sensing and he didn't have a relationship with Dr. Grindle, yet. The poor man spent most of his time sleeping and when he was awake, he often babbled incoherent thoughts, rambling about things that none of them could understand. Brady began to wonder if Dr. Grindle would be of any use to them. Perhaps he would be more of a burden in the long run, but he was one of them, human, and they would care for him. His union with Grendel had stripped him of something essential. It was like he had been put back together but with some parts missing, a jigsaw puzzle completed by an impatient child with some of the pieces jammed in the wrong places. Brady worried that if things didn't improve for him, all of them would have some tough decisions to make. Still, even one more broken human made the world a better place, considering the alternative.

As he had done with everything else, Brady gave the transmitter a name, *The Great Device*, even though Joe was the only one who understood what he was building. Kaileigh lingered over the plans and asked enough questions of the old wizard for him to take her on as his helper, reducing Brady to the role of gopher. They scoured the local environs for the proper equipment, finding themselves in the hospital and in emergency response vehicles brought by the CDC and the military when they made their final journey north. Of great interest to Joe was the discovery of two satellite phones and solar chargers.

"Here," he said to Brady after examining the devices carefully, "hold this and see what happens."

"Okay."

Joe dialed a number on the phone he was holding. Within seconds, Brady's phone began to emit a ringing tone! Amazed, Brady pressed the 'answer' button and said, "Hello?"

"Sweet Lord Almighty!" said a stunned Joe, a smile gracing his face, "The military satellite phone system still works! I wonder for how long? You know, if the other survivors had one of these and we had their number, we

392

wouldn't have to build the transmitter! Still, of all the luck!"

"Are you going to use these to help you build the transmitter?" asked Brady.

"No, but these are our connection to each other, don't you see? We can be thousands of miles apart, even on the other side of the world and still communicate with each other. As long as the satellite system keeps functioning and these batteries are charged, we can communicate."

"Yeah, but how long before the satellites eventually fail?" asked Brady.

"The satellites up there act like cell phone towers down here, as relays to each other. I bet these even tap into the GPS satellites, so as long as even a few are functioning, these should work, but you're right. Nothing lasts forever. Everything we build fails in the end. It's the Second Law of Thermodynamics, boy. Entropy enters everything. A closed system always breaks down. It's one of the laws of the universe," explained Joe.

"Doesn't make me feel any better," Brady said.

"Relax, kid. Things usually work for awhile before they break. We're all electrochemical machines. Our bodies work, then they begin to fail and then, they stop working. Can't be avoided. That's the way the world goes round."

They covered much ground, entering the homes of fellow HAM radio operators Joe knew from the Rag Chewers Society, gathering as many items of use as he deemed necessary. Brady began to appreciate just how much of a wizard the old man was because he understood things that they didn't; he was a wizard because what was science to him was magic to Brady and Kaileigh. After successfully raiding two labs at the Engineering Department of the University of Maine at Orono, Joe said all that they needed now was to make a trip to his own shop in East Corinth for the final items and tools.

With Dr. Grindle too fatigued to travel, Kaileigh volunteered to stay with him at the library to help him recover. Brady was convinced that the trip to East Corinth shouldn't take as long as it did the first time. Joe insisted that they could be back to the library before sunset. After an uneventful journey, Joe pulled into his own driveway.

Even though the fate of the species was resting on his actions, Joe lingered in front of the doors of his shop and time suddenly froze. He put his hand on the old brass doorknob and let it rest there for a moment before turning it and opening the door. Like any wizard entering his den, perhaps he was recalling other projects. Perhaps he was saying a quiet incantation for protection or success, or perhaps, like most people, he was remembering, a magic with a mighty power all its own. Brady noticed that hesitation, but said nothing, concluding that all of them had been shattered by the Abandonment and that Joe was bearing whatever weight it had given him upon unsteady shoulders.

His demeanor had changed the minute he walked into his workshop. This was his domain and he did not politely ask in this realm. He proclaimed and spoke in the imperative. He had created this world over many years, knew where everything was because he had placed it there. This was his Sanctum Sanctorum, his growlery, the Wizard's Den and he was its master. He was suddenly impatient with everything at his fingertips. sometimes throwing a part or a tool when things didn't work out to his pleasure or when something wasn't where he remembered it to be. Brady was stunned by the change in Joe's personality, but he knew that somehow, this was just part of his creative process.

"Where the hell is that voltmeter? I left it right here! Now its gone. It figures!" he thundered at the silence and clutter. Similar outbursts would occur from time to time as he delved into the wide array of items, seeking out the necessary tools.

The main room of the shop was large. Everywhere they looked were tables and workbenches covered with tools and arcane devices. In that corner was an arc welder and acetylene torch. In this corner was a metal lathe and band saw. A large wood stove sat hunkered down in that corner and in the final corner was a doorway that led to a back room that was full of bins and cabinets. There was really no good place to set down any of the equipment and supplies because every surface and workbench was literally covered

394

with piles of tools and materials, cardboard boxes of bits of metal and coffee cans of nuts and bolts.

"Get that box over there," Joe directed, "and that green one under the bench. We'll need that too."

While Joe lingered and thrashed over his workbench and the many shelves and piles, seeking the tools and supplies he would need to build the device, Brady let his eyes wander, soaking in the residual energy. There were hundreds of unusual things, wrenches, sockets, blades for various power saws, lengths of pipe, wood and wire, many suspended from hooks in pegboards that covered all the walls. There were hundreds of little plastic and metal drawers, perhaps fifteen metal tool boxes and cardboard boxes whose contents remained a mystery. The whole place had a layer of dust and oily grime and the odor that lingered in the air was one of ozone, welded metal and paint thinner. The collateral effect was one of a latter-day Tesla whose various batteries and motors, clamps and collections of nuts and bolts held the world together.

This was more than a building to Joe. This place, with all of its boxes and benches and seeming disarray was an extension of his own mind. The change that was evident in Joe now was no different from the change that might come over a master of a musical instrument when finally handed the score and asked to play. Something incorporeal emerged from the artist and for a brief while, the musician became the music. While in this workshop, each tool was an appendage, linked to his body with invisible tendrils. Every part that rested on a shelf was part of him, and he could call upon each part at will.

"There, that ought to do it," said Joe finally as he handed the last toolbox to Brady to take to the Lifeseeker. As he left the workshop, Brady noticed Joe carefully closing the door. He stood there a little longer and then turned to Brady.

"I'm going into the house for a few things," he said quietly. "You stay out here and secure the gear inside the Lifeseeker, okay?"

"Okay," Brady assented. He understood that Joe didn't want him inside and he wasn't one to question why. He had a Treasury of his own, back in Brewer.

After putting the gear into the Lifeseeker, Brady went to the back porch and sat in one of the lawn chairs on Joe's back deck. He liked it back here, overlooking the field and then the forest in the distance. This was where the attack of the weredogs occurred, although there was no sign left of the struggle. As he sat there and the afternoon's breeze cooled him, he saw a black figure advancing toward him from the forest.

It was the Maine black bear, Beorn.

Brady descended the porch and met him on the back lawn. The bear bore a great scar across his face, but beyond that he did not seem any worse for the wear.

"Thank you," Brady thought, and the bear rose on his hind legs, his front paws raised in what looked to Brady like a high-five signal.

"You are alive!" the bear's thought reached Brady's mind.

"Yes, but we might all be dead if you hadn't acted as you did on that night," Brady explained.

"I am happy," the bear said. "Were do you dwell?" asked the bear.

"In the Ruined City, down the long road and to the east," Brady thought.

"I wish to dwell with you," the bear thought strongly.

"Why? You're a bear. The whole forest is your home. Without people, you're the master in there," explained Brady. He was surprised that Beorn could understand these more complex thoughts. He had apparently become more aware in the past days.

"I am not a bear any longer. I am *other*. The other bears avoid me. I cannot speak to them. They cannot speak to me. I am away from them, now. You can understand me. You are my *not alone...*"

Brady thought he understood what had happened. "You were affected in the battle with the Weredogs. Fenris clawed your face. Maybe you've been altered, somehow. I'm sorry," Brady answered.

"I am not man, I am not animal – I am *other*."

Brady put his hand on the bear's shoulder and noticed how much he had grown.

"You are bigger," he said simply.

"I became more when I fought the creatures. I grew."

"Strange..." Brady said under his breath.

"I wish to stay with you and the others," Beorn insisted, "I am alone. I am your friend."

Brady knew what his answer had to be. For some reason, the fight with the weredogs had changed him into something else, something other. Beorn was not recognized as a bear by the other animals and was now separate from them. Perhaps that was the most human thing about him – his understanding of what it means to be alone. Life's good friends are very hard to find, especially when most of the species has perished. So what if he was a bear? Brady thought. Big deal. Max is a dog. Hugin is a raven. A friend is a friend.

"Will you ride with me, in that?" Brady pointed to the Lifeseeker.

The bear looked over and snorted. "Oh, yes!" Brady could sense Beorn's obvious excitement, like a child at the fair.

When Joe closed the door to his home, it was a bittersweet moment. He and his wife had raised three children in this house. He had rebuilt most of it and spent the best portion of his life within its rooms. How strange to leave a place for the final time, he thought. He went from room to room, locking windows and closing curtains, emptying the trash and even went so far as to descend to the basement and turn off the main circuit breaker to the house, knowing that it was unlikely electricity would ever run through the wires again. He found a few things to throw into a suitcase: pictures, videos of his family, along with the video player. Of the thousands and thousands of items collected over his span of years, in the end it didn't seem to matter what he took, only *that* he took. Undoubtedly time and weather would tumble this place to the ground and all would turn to dust, rust and ruin, but he needed to take what he could carry and leave all the rest, no matter how precious or fine. He grimaced as his knees' stabbing pain told him how old he was and he knew the house and all of its contents would last much longer than he would. Still, a person doesn't live in one place for so many years and then just walk away. A small portion remains until the timbers rot and the roof caves in, and even then, an echo lingers. He let his hand rest on the doorknob a moment before he pulled it closed for the final time. What mattered wasn't yesterday. What mattered was today.

They pulled out of the driveway and back onto the road towards Bangor. Joe still hadn't told the others about the enormity of his plan and had purposefully been evasive and vague. It would all become obvious the moment he flipped the final switch. What he had in mind would be much better than anything they had imagined, his final gizmo, his ultimate machine – his legacy to the human race.

He nearly had a heart attack when he glanced in the rear view mirror and saw the furry figure of Beorn sitting on one of the seats in the rear of the Lifeseeker, the bear's mouth open to catch the cool stream of air coming from the open window.

"Brady! There's a bear in here!" he said nervously under his breath.

"I know," Brady answered quietly. "Joe, meet Beorn."

Shaking his head and grinning, Joe could only say, "Well, I'll be damned..."

Chapter 29
The Ghost in the Machine

Kaileigh walked freely underneath a blue sky for the first time since the Abandonment and the pandemic that wreaked devastation on her species. The sky was a shade of cerulean blue; it might have been the sky over Sebago Lake the last time her family was together. A faint cool breeze tussled her black hair and twisted it in fairy rings about its fingers while in the trees, she saw small birds connecting the dots from branch to branch. She breathed deeply, taking in great lungfuls of air, holding it within while her body absorbed the freshness of a new world. She felt safe for the first time in a long time.

Joe and Brady were scarce, busy gathering materials for building the transmitter while Dr. Grindle slept most of the time. He was a shell of his former self when he was the chief epidemiologist for the Centers for Disease Control. Grendel had settled upon him, taken over his body, and pushed his mind down into a dark and frightening place, like a son of Cronus before Zeus's liberation. How the monster had altered his body to become the amalgam of beasts and nightmares that had threatened them, they didn't fully understand. Brady believed that somehow, he had created the monster from his anger, frustration and pain, but when she asked him how he did this, he wouldn't answer. A monster born of anger and spite might raze the world to its bedrock but Brady Smith would rescue kittens from trees and help elderly women with their groceries. Anyone who had survived the Abandonment would have some residual issues with which to deal. Most people, she thought, would have simply gone mad. Why their little ragtag band hadn't gone insane was perhaps the biggest mystery of all. Why had *they* survived? *How* had they survived?

Sitting in the library only held her interest for so long. Books written by dead people about dead people seemed pointless to her, their meaning diminished in the light of the new world. No, what she needed was to walk among the green and growing things. It was the height of summer. She needed some time to clear her head. Once she started, she felt like she could walk to the other end of the continent and not even need to rest so while Dr. Grindle slept and the wizards conjured, she took the time to explore the city.

She avoided the burned-out basements and tumbled brick structures, their blackened bones of splintered wood defiling the sky. She kept to open land and found herself walking by the Great River where the fire had been more merciful. Trees and bushes were variegated and seemed newly sprung from the primordial morning. Max was next to her, trotting along happily and every so often she threw a tennis ball and he would bound off into the distance, returning with eager anticipation of yet another "Go fetch, boy." Max had adopted her long before she adopted him. In fact, he rarely left her side. It was difficult to determine if Max was Brady's dog or if he had pledged his allegiance to this new and steely eyed mistress.

How was she going to survive on this empty, quiet earth? Though she may have three human companions, she was the only girl and this posed some interesting problems. She knew there were other survivors somewhere out there and that, if their plans came to fruition, she would eventually have a wider circle of companions, but even then she knew that never again would she stand in line, go to a large party, or be a member of a bustling crowd, noticing that cute boy standing in the corner and wondering wistfully. Those days were long gone and if they ever came again, she would be long, long gone.

As she walked, she thought of her mother and of the last words they exchanged. She didn't always like thinking about her mother but she was always there, resting quietly in the back of her mind like she was watching her daughter, waiting for her to do something. Her mother? How much she would have given to speak with her for even five minutes? Even stranger, why was it that she felt that her mother was still lingering somewhere nearby? Was her mom's spirit watching over her? No, that wasn't it, she decided. She felt the presence of something *motherly*, something *maternal* in nature, but it wasn't the woman who raised her. It was something *other*.

Her brother? What of him? She knew from the Ukrainian broadcast that a small group of humans survived near Washington, D.C. Was it possible that he was one of them? She had survived so perhaps he might have, as well? Perhaps her ability to survive the great falling was genetic and, if so, he might have made it. If they could make contact, she could find out. Then, if he was alive, she could travel, even if she had to go alone because there would be continuity. Something from before would have survived to this place that was forever 'after.' For now, there was only the not knowing, only the lonely wondering of 'if'.

She was past downtown and near the Bangor waterfront next to the Great River. Max was adamant about fetching today. They were always so busy trying to destroy the monster, to survive in this post-human world that he often went ignored. He looked up at her with big wet eyes as though to say, "Please, please, throw me the ball. Throw me the ball..."

"You want a good throw, don't you, boy? Huh? Yeah? Okay, go for this one!"

She threw the tennis ball as hard as she could and Max bounded off into the distance and then, to her horror, followed the ball right into the river.

She ran to the shore and shouted, "Max! Come back here! Max! Back to me, boy!"

He paddled out a little further into the waters and clamped his jaws around the yellow tennis ball, turned

401

around and eagerly paddled back to the shore. He didn't appear to be having very much trouble moving through the water, much to Kaileigh's relief. As he neared the shore, the shoreline sloped up quite sharply and Max found himself unable to find a purchase on the ground. He kept attempting to jump on to the shore but every time he tried, he failed and Kaileigh could see that he was quickly tiring.

She found herself on the edge of the shore reaching out her hand to grab Max and help him make it safely up the bank which she eventually did. However, in lifting him to the shore, the awkward stance she took caused her to stumble and she fell headfirst into the cold waters of the Great River. Max was safe, but she was suddenly gone, thrust into another world.

"*She has returned,*" the voices seemed to sing. A thousand small bells rang and tinkled as she found herself immersed in something, but it certainly didn't feel like water. Again, as before, she felt herself lifted and held in place by unseen hands, surrounding her like a blanket, caressing her like a mother might to calm a nervous child. She had been here before, in the rainstorm and during the battle when Grendel was defeated.

This was someplace *other.* This was somewhere *else.* All sense of time immediately ceased and she felt the presence of a plethora of others, and she knew they were *Those of the Waters. S*he was surprised that she wasn't afraid.

"You have returned to us! She will be pleased. We welcome you, Charon."

Kaileigh didn't know what they meant. Wherever she was, it was as serene as silent, still waters just before dawn. Whoever they were, they seemed pleased to see her.

"How do you know me?" she asked.

"We have known you since before you were named. We would know you in another life, in all the universes."

They spoke in riddle and metaphors.

"Where am I?" she asked.

"In the waters between the worlds, in your place, made for you since the Fall."

402

"I don't understand," she replied.

She floated for moments past long tributaries, rivers within rivers, streams within streams. There were colors here mixing with shades of gray. There was a long, low sound just barely audible to her ears. Were those forms in the water? Was she seeing people in her midst, floating around her? Were they human or spirit? They swirled about her and as she floated she was amazed that she was breathing and still quite comfortable, even though she assumed she was now deeply under water. Invisible hands moved her along, passing her from one to the next in a long succession of handlers until she found herself in what must be the center of the waters, the exact spot between the banks of whatever river in which she was now immersed.

"You are the Conduit," a voice whispered to her.

"I'm sorry. I'm the...what does that mean?"

The voice began to sound somehow vaguely familiar, like one she had heard for the first time but which must surely have been a sweet sound in her ears for years and years before.

"The channel, the connection between one world and the next through which we may communicate."

"If you're going to talk to me, could you at least show yourself?"

There was a muttering of voices, some murmuring agreement, some opposed to this idea. Finally, through a myriad chorus of discord and syncopation, a figure began to emerge from the shades and forms that flowed around her like ectoplasm.

All in shades of blue and white, she formed from the spectral nebula of water, the medium of their universe. It occurred to Kaileigh that the water surrounding her was warm to the touch, and soothing, enriching, even amniotic. As Kaileigh watched, she could see a tall, coldly beautiful woman of indeterminate age, neither old nor young but both,simultaneously. She was a sister of Time. Her face was a child's on Christmas Day layered against an aged mother's face upon a bed of pain. She was long upon this world and well-beyond it.

403

"I am the River," she said in the most beautiful, sonorous voice that Kaileigh had ever heard. It was the first laugh from a baby, an echo from a song composed before Eden fell. Kaileigh heard her and felt the import of her words. Had she heard this voice before? She thought she recognized the intonation, even though the woman had barely spoken.

"I'm Kaileigh," she replied.

"Yes, of course, But you are also Charon, as you ever have been and shall be," replied the woman.

Kaileigh didn't try to reason with her, because she felt that in a way, she was not wholly with her. She was a hologram, a phantom, and a dream. She inquired further, as though this moment spent in absolute beauty might burst like a bubble on the wind.

"Your name is *River*?" she clarified.

"I *am* the River. I am as you can understand me in your present form."

"But I *don't* understand. You're the Penobscot River?" Kaileigh asked, still confused.

"No. I am *the* River, the water that separates the worlds. As such, I touch all worlds simultaneously, seeing all possibilities. This world is one of countless worlds that I touch."

"I'm sorry," Kaileigh replied, mystified but still enchanted, a smile broadening on her face. She imagined white castles and tall mountains, fields of green and gold under a sky as blue as this woman's eyes. She remembered long meadows and sunsets that lasted forever above a twilight sea and then marveled that she remembered. Was that a melody sweetly played in tune from some immeasurable distance lightly falling upon her now? How could she remember something that she had never seen? Was she within a dream?

"No, you are not within a dream," said the woman, reading her thoughts, "The land you were in, like all the other worlds, are the dreams. This place, the River, is that which is *real*. *Nothing* is real but the river. In a way, *you* are a dream, as well."

Kaileigh's heart weighed as light as a feather.

The woman put her insubstantial arm around Kaileigh, a mother being reunited with her long-lost child. "I am sorry you have borne so much pain. I am afraid there is much more for you to bear before you can make your way home," she explained.

Kaileigh spoke quietly. "Home? My home is gone. I'm an orphan in an empty world. Except for my friends, everyone else is dead."

"The dead?" The beautiful woman paused and smiled

before continuing, "No, you do not yet comprehend. You are the Conduit through which one world may speak with another, and that means you are powerful in ways you do not remember. You are unique, out of all the humans from your world. To them, time is a river in which they are inexorably immersed. You are different, although your powers are only newly awakened. You will see."

"My powers? You mean these visions I have when I'm in water?"

The woman nodded with smiling eyes as understanding began to take root in Kaileigh's mind.

"You can stand upon the banks and watch the River of Time flow past. You can stand apart from the passage of Time. Because of this, I know you are truly my daughter - River-Daughter."

So this must be a nightmare, thought Kaileigh.

Kaileigh apologized, "I'm sorry. You're not my mother. My mother died in the hospital from the virus weeks ago."

The woman's face saddened and eyes with the depths of the abyss expressed such recognition of loss and pain that Kaileigh wanted to look away but found she couldn't.

"I know. I was there."

"How? I was alone with her," Kaileigh said.

"Oh,but you weren't alone. You are never alone. No one ever is. I was there. I am the River, and I flow between the worlds."

Kaileigh drew back and brushed the woman's hand from her shoulder.

"The only thing in that room with my mom and me was Death," Kaileigh said plainly, as though stating a simple, obvious fact to a child.

The woman smiled and tilted her lovely head so that her chestnut hair fell about her shoulders in a cascade. She didn't speak, but her smile bored into Kaileigh's heart and awakened ideas and suspicions.

"Most people suspect I will be wearing a black cloak and carrying a scythe."

Kaileigh's heart would have raced if she had a heart in this place, wherever it was. She tried to take a deep breath but found that she didn't need to breathe. She wasn't afraid. How could she be afraid of such a warm, welcoming, beautiful person? It would be like being frightened of a flower, of a gentle breeze, of a glass of ice-cold water on a scalding day. She was relief and release. She was the River.

She was Death.

"If you're Death, how I am your daughter?" asked Kaileigh.

"Because you are here, speaking with me. Do you think beings from the Multiverse simply enter my waters and converse with me without having to die first? You are my daughter, born from the depths of Time. You have been moving in an endless cycle of coming towards me and leaving me again for eons. You live, enjoy the passage of time, fall in love, struggle to survive. You are born to a living woman whom I chose for you. I only chose the best, strongest, and wisest of women to help me raise you and yes, Charon, she is your mother, too. You are graced with two mothers – one immortal and one mortal and both full of love for you. When I need you the most, and those from a world are ready to pass away in great numbers, you have always returned to me, to aid in the transition. This time it is the Earth's turn. You are born an earthling because you would be needed to help your people in their transition."

"But I remember growing up here. I have *seen* my baby pictures. I have video!" Kaileigh protested, not understanding what this vision was explaining, not wanting to.

"Yes, yes and so you grew. Of course your past is real, but now you will learn to see things *differently*. So you have dreamed. So all beings dream of their lives. "

"You mean like "Row, Row, Row Your Boat? Life is but a dream"?

The River smiled at Kaileigh and nodded affirmatively.

"You understand. Life *is* but a dream," she answered with laughter ringing in her voice.

"Am I dead?" asked Kaileigh, "Drowned in the river?"

The woman let go a laugh that would have woken fields of blossoms and caused the rain to crystallize. Her eyes smiled.

"You are not dead, and how can a daughter drown in her own mother's womb?"

Kaileigh was overwhelmed. She couldn't fathom the ideas and words this woman was uttering because to her, they were nonsense.

"I don't believe you," she said flatly.

"Oh Charon, you never do," laughed the River.

"If I'm truly your daughter, what happens now. Do I stay here with you?" she asked.

The River woman shook her head and for the first time, a look of loss and pain, of regret and remembrance melted over her beautiful, finely chiseled features. "No. You never remain, and that is my reason for flowing ever onward, hoping for the moment when I will meet the endless sea and all will be reunited. I have something to show you that will help you understand. Here," she said, "take my hand."

They flowed through dark caverns and down to a sunless place where no light could penetrate. There were no echoes, no colors, no sense of Time or place or life. Kaileigh was not even sure if she was truly moving at all. She wondered if they were standing still and the world was moving past *them*. The River Woman, who claimed to be her mother, did not look back at her but instead reached her free arm in front of her, steering with it through a pathless ocean of darkness that she knew intimately.

"Imagine being alone," she said to Kaileigh as they moved onwards, "Always alone in your thoughts, never another to speak with or worse, to love. This would be true desolation, true death. No love, no understanding, no knowledge, no wisdom – only you. This would be true darkness."

"Yes," Kaileigh answered, "I think I understand the *alone* thing."

"Mortal beings think of Death as an end of things," the River Woman continued, "but Rivers all flow to the sea and one journey leads to the next. In life, beings are all alone in their thoughts and minds, always imprisoned with that singularity that is their aloneness. People are all drops of rain in a storm while they live, but when they die, they gather into pools, then rivulets, streams and all of these come back to the river that is the sea. When they die, they gather together and no longer are they alone. No one is forever parted from another. It is the way of things for souls to meet again, as sure as it is that raindrops form the ocean."

There was a shore in the distance, a place where the River flowed against a land mass. They moved toward it, and Kaileigh's feeling of well-being was disturbed. As they drew closer, she could see thousands upon thousands of gray shades standing in a dark land that stretched farther than any far horizon she had ever seen on Earth. They were of all ages, dressed in clothing from different time periods and places, all in shades of gray.

None of them wore a look of peace and contentment, much less grace.

"What is this place?" she asked her guide.

The River Woman replied, "This is the Far Shore, the Land of After and Before, the place between the worlds where the dreams return once they have been dreamed."

Kaileigh weighed the idea in her mind.

"Is this Heaven?" she asked.

"This is the Far Shore, the Land of After and Before. Call it what you will. Dreams begin here. Dreams return here, as well. In between, dreams are dreamed. That is the way of things, but you are more than they are, Charon. You are the Conduit."

"What does that *mean*?" she asked urgently, suddenly feeling trapped and confused.

The River Woman squeezed Kaileigh's hand in concern and met her eyes. Kaileigh could see the steel blue-gray were the same color as her own eyes, and her face seemed like...her own? Could this be? And her voice? Why did it sound so familiar?

"You alone can move between the two shores, of the living and dead. You can journey to and from this place. You can speak with the Dead."

Kaileigh's eyes were beginning to burn. She was tearing up, angry and frightened. This was cruel and tiring. Was she being tricked by Grendel, after all? Was Dr. Grindle right? Had part of him survived to torture her?

"You need to speak to the people on the shore. I cannot speak to them as I speak to you now. I am merely the River. I have seen the fall of millions before, on different worlds, in different planes than this. You have, too, though you cannot yet remember. These humans are different and I am...troubled."

"Why? Why are you troubled?" asked Kaileigh.

"Because they cannot rest. They were awakened from their dreaming too quickly, all of their dreams unfinished, at once. It was an unnatural summoning from life. They cannot rest. With all of my strength, I can barely hold them back on their shore. They swell and burgeon until bursting. I have never experienced anything like this before in all of my flowing and ebbing. It is as though they were all awakened at once by some unnatural, skewed energy. They would cross the depths to go back to Earth, if they could. They linger here when they should move on, billions of them. They suffer. You must help set these poor souls to rest, help them find their peace. This is the River Daughter's task. It is *your* task, the task for which you were created in the first place."

"You want me to speak to the dead?" she asked, not believing her own words.

"You are the only one who can," replied the River Woman."They need your help, as much as you need theirs," she added. She looked long and deeply into the River Woman's eyes and wondered why she had ever been afraid of Death before.

Then the River Woman was gone and Kaileigh was on the shore with thousands, millions, billions of gray shades. From the distance they had seemed restless and she could see the concern in their faces and from this close place, the fear in their eyes. They saw her there and began to move toward her like moths to a flame, crowding in upon her, minions of the dead. She wanted to panic, but as they moved ever closer, she was surprised that she couldn't feel their weight against her. They flowed through her. They were tissue paper and soap bubbles. They were insubstantial phantoms.

"What do you want?" she shouted. Though they all opened their mouths to talk, no sound came from them. They were entombed by the silence of the grave.

As they swarmed closer and closer, she began to walk among them, letting them pass through her. What was agitating them so? What could possibly cause such anxiety?

Then she saw her.

'NO!' she shrieked in her mind, but her legs moved her closer and closer and her arms attempted to wrap around the personage, but only cut through the air and clasped themselves. A ghost! Her mother's ghost!

Like a dagger to her heart and a balm to her mind, she heard something she had never thought to hear ever again - the sound of her own mother's voice, her human mother, the mother she loved.

"Kaileigh," she said, but her lips did not move in cadence with her speech. Like some badly dubbed foreign film, it became apparent to Kaileigh that the voices of the dead are out of step and out of tune, and especially, out of time.

Her mother's voice continued, "We were all taken at once, moving away from the earth, with years and years left to finish our dreaming, to finish our living. So many things left undone and we don't yet understand why."

Tears streamed down Kaileigh's cheeks as she put her hand up to touch her mother's beloved face. Her hand simply flowed through.

Her mother continued, "We don't want our deaths to be worthless. We want our deaths to mean something. We weren't allowed to live our normal spans, taken against our will into this place by the virus. So few of you remain, Kaileigh."

"Mother!" was all Kaileigh could manage to whisper through tears and sobs that wracked her frame. "Mother..." she whispered through a stream of conflicted feelings.

"I know who you are. She told me, the woman in the water. I am supposed to tell you that none of us will move on *until we know that we will not be forgotten* and that those

411

few humans left on earth *will survive*. Right now, that is not certain. In order for it to happen, for Humanity to continue, you must connect with the other humans. So few remain. You must, you must, you *must* survive.

"We can see the world as it is, only from a long distance away. Everything is out of focus. Everything is out of tune. We can see the world and know that it has been altered. The world is wrong, altered by the monster created accidentally by the boy. He did not understand his power when he created the monster and now, he cannot destroy it alone. If the monster is not destroyed, then all humans will perish and all of us will have lived and died in vain.

"We would help you but we cannot interact with the world any longer. All we can do is watch. *You* can act for us. You must return from this place and tell those who travel with you our message. You must relay it. You are the Conduit. Speak with them so that we can move on."

"I love you, mum. I'm sorry I couldn't save you," Kaileigh said through tears.

"The message, Kaileigh, the *message*," her mother said urgently.

Through her tears, Kaileigh bit her bottom lip and replied, "We're working on a transmitter powerful enough to reach the other side of the world."

"We know of your work," her mother said, "but this will fail unless you transmit over running water, for water is the medium and you are the Conduit."

"What?" Kaileigh asked through her confusion.

Her mother's shade pointed off into the distance. Row upon endless row of human shades began to move to one side. There, off in the distance, she could see something real, something from her world. Yes, she knew this place. A look of recognition lit her face, followed by a wave of confusion.

"You took me there, once."

"This is the place," her mother said, "from which to broadcast your signal, but the generators won't fully power the transmitter, not without *your* help. You must follow your friend's actions in the farm house, when the monster called to you on the night of the aurora. Unless you act as the

Conduit during the transmission, you will never reach the others and you will be doomed to wander the wide world over without ever meeting another human soul for all of your days. You and the boy have special places in the new world. If you act together, the beast will be sent back to the place made for him and the world will continue moving in the direction set down at the beginning. We will be able to move on, then. We will be remembered. Humans will rise again."

"Right," Kaileigh said, beginning to understand.

Her mother began to fade, the last minutes of the film in a theater, after all the lights have been lit so that the tired audience might go. Kaileigh watched and began to panic. There was so much left to say.

"I love you, Mom!" she said between and within her tears.

"Love....." was all her mother said before she dissolved like a spider web in the rain and Kaileigh found herself clinging to the bank of the Penobscot River, Max barking anxiously at her. She was soaked to the bone, but she had received the message.

"I've had a vision," she explained to Brady, Joe and Dr. Grindle as they ate their evening meal.

"What kind of vision?" asked Dr. Grindle, whose own ability to maintain a clear head had slightly improved over the past few days.

"I don't know. Call it a *visitation*. I have some information that could help us."

Joe and Brady stopped chewing and perked up, listening intently to Kaileigh's words.

"We have to build our transmitter at the Penobscot Narrows Bridge, between Bucksport and Verona Island," she explained.

Joe stared at her blankly for a moment, considering her words.

Then he said excitedly, "We could use the entire bridge, the superstructure, as the antenna. A transceiver that big would require a massive amount of power, but if we had the

413

electrical energy, that bridge is already in the shape of a transmitter. It has towers and miles of cable. It wouldn't be that hard to adapt our equipment."

They could all see the flash in Joe's eyes as he grew increasingly interested in the idea.

"I was planning on using a cellphone tower, but this – it's amazing!"

"I'm sorry," asked Brady, "but how did you know about this?"

She shook her head in confusion. It had all been so unclear, so rushed and above all, so real that she didn't bother to ask questions. She only knew enough to concentrate every bit of herself to experience the meeting with *Those of the Waters.*

"I met someone today," she began.

Chapter 30
The Narrows

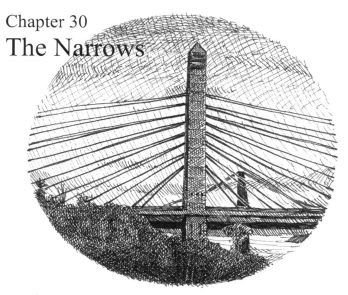

They neared the doorway to the Penobscot Narrows Bridge, a stone portal built to last the ages at the base of the tallest obelisk in the state. To anyone who had ever seen the bridge, it stood out as an anomaly. In the midst of the northern boreal forest stood two Egyptian-style obelisks four hundred and twenty feet high, the tallest bridge observatory on Earth. What a strange sight this might be in centuries to come, if they were successful and those few straggling communities of people who might somehow survive the Pandemic Age saw these again, rising out of the trees or at a distance from their canoes in the bay. How out of place they would seem, how magisterial, how impossibly wondrous. The gods themselves must have built these, or people whose knowledge was so great as to be like gods.

They had driven to the parking lot at the base of the structure and were now walking towards it, inspecting it for the first time. To the right of the bridge stood the Civil War era Fort Knox, a holdfast of stone dug into the granite, squatting like a tomb. Like explorers in some newly discovered country, they all felt as though this bridge and in particular, this tower, was more than it appeared. A bridge spanned the distance between two shores, connecting them. If this structure could serve as a giant transmitter, it would become a bridge in a different way, connecting them with the few groups of humans still walking the earth.

At its base, they were lost in a meander of time. Was this an entryway into a tower that led to an observation deck at the top, or was this the portal to another place, built for another reason entirely? From his imaginative perspective, he was entering an impossible place. Brady knew that the structure was less than seven years old, but it felt ancient to him, even timeless. He had the distinct feeling that this tower had always been here and would always be, constructed by giants for the use of the gods. This was the dark tower to which they came, the last citadel, the foundational spire that began in ancient Egypt and thrust itself into the stars. Brady's imagination was alert with possibilities.

The entrance was a decorated metal double door inset into a massive granite lintel. The entire lower part of the structure had been constructed from Maine stone, the very bones of the Earth. Looking up, it appeared to Brady as though this structure was even taller than he remembered, as though another nearly invisible section projected from the top of the visible structure, reaching through the sky and clouds towards the void of space, a spire continuing like a mathematical line into infinity.

"It's just your imagination," Kaileigh muttered as she took up a place next to him, both of them looking skyward.

"You see it too?" he asked.

"Just keeps going and going, doesn't it? All the way to Heaven," she said.

He couldn't deny his vision, of a tower stretching upwards into infinity. "That's impossible."

She smiled at him and said, "Yes. I know. That's why it's not real. Can't be real if it's impossible, can it?"

They both stared long at each other, wondering what the other would say. Brady didn't know how she would react. He loved the fact that she was anything but predictable. She smiled and gave him a wink, "Come on. We've got a bridge to break into," she said simply.

Joe was already at the lock. He had two power drills, spare batteries and a pocket full of titanium-tipped drill bits. He was leaning heavily into the lock, drilling it out for all he was worth. Dr. Grindle stood by, another drill in his hand, ready to take his turn when Joe's turn was over. This was a secure facility and it would take them the better part of two hours to drill the door lock out and open the great doors.

Brady and Kaileigh began to unload the Lifeseeker. Hugin took to the sky the moment they arrived and flew to the top of the bridge, landing on one of the long cables that held the bridge's deck high above the Penobscot River. Beorn left them to reconnoiter the vicinity for any trace of Fenris or the weredogs, but Brady could sense him on the very keen edge of his mind and they maintained contact. If Beorn sensed anything at all, a single thought would join their minds in an instant.

"This is going to work," Brady said. "Joe's excited. He knows what he's doing. Tonight, we'll make contact with the others, finally!"

"I hope so," she said, not imparting to her companion the doubt she kept hidden beneath the surface.

She knew that Brady's brilliance was that he saw the world two ways at the same time: the way that it was and the way that it should be. He could sense things unavailable to the senses of others, but Kaileigh had been given direct visions of the afterlife and had been subject to startling revelations about her own nature. She had even been given a task by the vast assemblage of the dead. If this failed, she couldn't give up, but what would be the next step?

"Grendel's biggest fear is that we'll contact others," Brady continued as they walked. "I think he knows something. If we can contact others, we can rebuild things, start over, do it right this time," he said.

"You two," Joe said as he stopped the drill, sweat rolling down his brow and into his glasses, "Get to the trailer and unload the generators. Start unpacking the Lifeseeker."

Joe knew the secret of getting things done. It was called 'work'.

She was waiting for this moment to arrive. Finally she was alone with Brady and she needed to explain things to him. They started to unpack and she didn't say what she was thinking. She didn't say, *'The Dead are waiting on the edge of the river that separates the land of the living from the land of the dead and they refuse to continue their journey until we make contact because if we don't, all the humans who have ever lived will have done so for nothing. It will be like we were just a mistake. Humans will be like dodo birds or dinosaurs, just a memory in the fossil record. The virus changed the course of things, but Grendel can erase any chance of human beings rising again.'*

"Brady, we need to talk."

"Okay, Kai. Whatever you say. What's up?"

"I have something to tell you and I want you to think about it before you laugh at me."

"I won't laugh at you, promise."

"You won't?"

"Course not. You're Kaileigh Tremble, monster-slayer. We're friends."

Friends. She smiled, nodded and continued. "Alright. Brace yourself. This is going to sound crazy. I've been having visions, whenever I'm in the water. I see things that don't make any sense, except that they are all beginning to make sense, sort of."

"As if anything makes sense anymore," he interjected.

"Anyway, I've seen another world in the water. Whenever I touch it, I leave this world and go into another, a world that doesn't experience time in the same way ours does. I go there and meet a woman who is the personification of...this is where it gets really weird...*Death.*"

He considered her words and nodded patiently. She was pleased that he smiled.

"Go on," he said.

"She claims that I'm her daughter and that I am supposed to convey to the few living people left on earth the final words of the dead."

"Please continue," Brady nodded patiently and waited.

"You don't think that I should be locked up in a padded room, do you?" For once she wasn't defensive when she asked.

"No, unless I'm in there with you. I believe you," he answered.

"She took me to the land of the dead. I don't really know how to name it or describe it. It wasn't Heaven or Hell, just a quiet, colorless, dark place where there were millions of people just standing around."

"The Asphodel Fields, from Greek mythology," Brady added.

"Greek myth? How did you...? Anyway, I spoke to my mother there. She told me what we need to do."

"What did she tell you?"

"She told me that all the dead who perished in the pandemic, billions of people, are waiting on what they call the 'Far Shore' and won't continue their journey to wherever it is they are supposed to go until we set things right in this world. In order to do that, we have to destroy Grendel or he'll hunt down and destroy all the remaining humans on earth. They can't move on knowing they'll all be forgotten, that people will simply cease to exist. Humanity needs to rise again and we need to make it happen."

"Makes sense," Brady said. "It's like in all those ghost stories. It's their unfinished business."

"Well, I wonder," she asked with more than a little trepidation, "Have you ever thought about where Grendel came from?"

He blinked and looked away for a moment before responding. He knew the answer, but to speak it aloud meant acknowledging responsibility for all the damage that Grendel had done, possibly including the death of his own mother. He knew he had somehow summoned forth what people would easily call a 'demon' and this creature had possessed the weakest vessel it could find. Dr. Grindle was simply a man, broken because he had helped unwittingly by creating a device that could rapidly spread the most contagious, deadliest virus ever known to Humanity, a man who could not find a cure, a man who had just lost his own wife and child. Once inside his body, the creature even twisted the good doctor's name: Grendel.

"You know what I think. I've said it before. I created him," he said.

She paused before adding, "I think so, too."

"I didn't mean to call him forth, or whatever it is that I did. I was angry. I didn't know that the world had changed. I didn't know that *I'd* changed. I still don't know what that means, but when I freaked out and began smashing things and screaming, breaking windows and losing control, I think I opened a doorway and he came into the world. I let him in.Noah was dead, the world left me there all alone and I didn't know what else to do."

"I think that doorway," Kaileigh added, "was a doorway *inside* of you. He's *your* monster. He's your anger and pain, frustration and loss. He's every fear you ever had, all balled up into one being."

"I know," he answered, looking away towards Penobscot Bay and the ocean.

"You have to beat him. You have to destroy him. Only you can beat this devil," Kaileigh said plainly, as though she was saying that the sky was blue and that snow was white.

""How? He grows every time I see him. I can only imagine what he looks like now, what creature he's possessing. We've got another monster on our hands who could show up any minute to stop us."

"It doesn't matter what he looks like on the outside. What does matter is this: you have to face the monster in his own lair. You have to lure him into the place he came from. Come on! Think about the hero stories you love so damned much! If you have to kill the monster, you have to go in after him instead of waiting for him to come after you. Only in the monster's lair can the hero destroy the dragon."

"His lair? I have to go in after him. He came from me. How do I do that?"

"Don't worry. I have a plan," she said.

420

Chapter 31

He Doesn't Think-He Feels

Joe successfully broke into the lower chamber of the bridge tower after nearly three hours of drilling. They swung the two massive doors inward and entered, the echoes of every little sound they made flying in a cacophony throughout the structure. He was Howard Carter breaking into Tutankhamen's tomb. He was Indiana Jones discovering the Ark of the Covenant. They all turned on their flashlights and entered the chamber. There was an elevator shaft that ran up the very center into the spire's dark heights and large, empty spaces surrounding it. There were some informative plaques on the wall along with pipe and conduits that ran to steel boxes mounted on the walls. This was the control center of the building. Joe had the biggest flashlight and he directed its beam up the shaft that led to the observation deck. The light ended in the darkness, revealing nothing but mystery.

"Folks," Joe began, "you are now in the tallest public bridge observatory in the world and the first bridge observatory in what *was* the United States of America, truly one of the seven wonders of the Abandoned World. It's 490 feet up that Stanley elevator shaft before we make it to the top, or we can take the stairs."

"Stairs? I thought we were going to get the power going?" asked Brady, not happy at the prospect of climbing that endless spire.

"That's the next order of business. I'm going to need your eyes, Dr. Grindle. Mine aren't so sharp anymore. Can't see a thing – diabetes has nearly blinded me. We're going to see about the generator. Hopefully it still works and there's a supply of diesel."

Beorn sent a message to Brady. His manner of expression was still somewhat limited, his grammar childish and awkward, but the mind behind it was keen and clever.

'Something here,' Beorn sent, 'Smell it. A dog and not a dog. More. Fanged. Clawed before. Different. Bigger. Stronger."

Brady put the toolbox he was carrying down and went out into the sunlight, looking for the direction of the thought.

"Where are you?" sent Brady.

"Edge of water. Look to wide water."

"You mean the bay, Penobscot Bay, you're down river near the bay?"

A confused thought was all the bear could send.

'Is he alone or with others?' send Brady.

'Alone.'

The last time Brady had seen Fenris was at the destruction of Grendel, at the riverside near Mount Hope. Dr. Grindle insisted that the monster hadn't perished, only diminished and was still able to infect a host and possess it. Where had the body of Fenris gone on that fateful night, he wondered? Perhaps the weredog hadn't simply crawled off to lick his wounds and die. Perhaps his old master took advantage of his weakened state and possessed him now.

'Come back to the bridge,' Brady sent to Beorn.

'No,' was the bearserker's reply.

'He might attack you. You'll be safer with us," Brady sent in the imperative.

'Guard you all,' was Beorn's only reply.

Brady put two and two together and *Observation Mode* kicked in again. He was going to have to do something soon. He needed to speak with Dr. Grindle. Brady approached the doctor quietly from the back and when he spoke, he frightened him.

"I'm sorry," Brady offered, "I didn't mean to scare you."

"Oh, yes. Sorry. It's just that, well, I'm always worried that he'll, you know, come back," muttered the doctor in frustration.

"Yeah, I feel the same way," he replied and then with a firmness to his voice, he said, "Dr. Grindle, we need to talk."

The doctor looked at him askance and turned his gaze back to the river emptying into the bay.

"About what?"

"About Grendel. About what it was like to be possessed."

The doctor turned and gave Brady a horrified look.

"Whatever for? Why do you need to know what it was like? I don't like to talk about it."

"If Grendel comes back, I intend to fight him and I need to know everything I can about him, how he thinks."

The good doctor was shaken by this request and his face was ribboned with the pain of recall that Brady suggested. He remained tightlipped and silent.

"Look, I know you've suffered. Dr. Grindle. We all have, but we have to make contact with other humans and if Grendel comes back, he won't stop until we're all dead. Every last human on the planet."

"What do you want to know?" the doctor asked quietly with a tremor in his voice.

"What was it like in there? What was it like to be possessed?"

The doctor began to pace back and forth from one edge of the rampart to the other, making Brady nervous, lest he took one too many steps and vaulted himself over the side.

"It was like being in a deep, dark prison. I was in the blackness and could hear echoes. I was often very tired. I could catch glimpses of things. If I concentrated, I could break through and see the world again, even talk."

"I know," Brady said, "you spoke to me in the cemetery."

"Yes, I remember," he said.

"Did you fight him, while you were in there?" asked Brady.

Dr. Grindle shook his weary head. "Not exactly. I was in a place, wandering, lost. I didn't know where I was. I thought I'd died and gone to, you know, some other place. How could that be? I wasn't aware of my body's movements. It was a dream world, Brady, a nightmare world. There were things in there."

"Things?"

"Oh, I don't know. Items, artifacts, like a museum or warehouse. I couldn't tell if I was imagining it all or if it was real."

"So, you were free to wander around in there, like you were in a place?"

"Yes, but it was a labyrinth. There was no way out. The only thing I could do, after a while, was just sit down and forget. Do nothing. Cease to think or feel or care and start to die inside. So, that's what I did."

"Can you think of anything that I should know about if I have to face him again?"

The troubled man looked out over the water and stood awhile in thought before he said, "I know that he's frightened. I could feel it like I can feel this breeze, right now. He's frightened and angry. He's not rational. He doesn't think. He *feels*."

from the Journal of Brady Smith

"This might be my last entry, so I'll try to put it down as I remember it. It was a long, slow ride to the Obelisks, otherwise known as the Penobscot Narrows Bridge. If anyone ever reads this in years to come, it occurs to me that I ought to take a second and explain what I know about the bridge. It connects Bucksport on the mainland with Verona Island in the middle of Penobscot Bay. Its not the longest bridge in the state, but it's unique because it's so different.

See, it's the highest structure in Maine, with two tall towers like ancient Egyptian obelisks with long cables that suspend the bed of the bridge really high over the bay and the Penobscot River. There are only three of these bridges in the world and to be honest, they all look like they come from some futuristic science fiction movie. It looks like something the Time Traveler from H.G. Well's <u>The Time Machine</u> would have seen in the distance when he first stepped into the future. Honestly, I think it is the coolest building I've ever been in. To think that Maine has something like this has always seemed a little out of place, like having a skyscraper in the middle of the forest, a tall tower like Orthanc from <u>The Two Towers</u>.

There's an elevator that goes all the way up to the top and a stairway, as well. I knew that if we couldn't get the elevator going, it was going to be some hard trudging up those stairs to get the equipment up to the Observation Deck. But our wizard did it! It requires a lot of power to pull something that far up, but he hooked a large generator to it that we found at an equipment rental place. All he had to do was connect to the main panel and it kicked into action. I wouldn't want to get stuck on that thing!

Joe put together the mother of all transmitters, but man, it's heavy. In the end, we took the radio equipment from the Coast Guard ship at the dock and broke into the tower at Bangor International Airport for the rest. We've got two portable rolling generators. Kaileigh keeps telling us that we'll need more than two generators and that we'll need more power. When we ask why, she just says that she has a way to get it.

The Observation Deck is a glassed area at the top of one of the two towers that supports the bridge. From up there, you can see for miles and miles, the highest building where humans can walk around and see all four directions in the state. From up here, you can see the whole world, or at least enough of it to satisfy a traveler's mind. Joe says that Kaileigh's idea of using the entire bridge as the antenna was genius. All we had to do was tap into the cabling and turn it on! But nothing is ever that easy. I sure hope Kaileigh's

425

secret answer to powering this works, whatever that is. The two generators, Joe tells me, will do nicely, but she just shakes her head and walks off, quiet. I don't know what's come over her."

Kaileigh was only beginning to understand the words of the River Woman. She remembered being Kaileigh, being a child and growing up in Brewer. She had photographs to prove it, along with all the paraphernalia that accompanied a normal childhood: a closet full of toys and albums full of photos. Still, she was beginning to think about what she was *before* she had been born and that was just weird and perhaps even wrong. Could there even be a time and a place before a person is born, she wondered? The River Woman had called her daughter, and by another name, a name that sounded familiar to her. Charon? Wasn't Charon the name of the ferryman of the dead over the River Styx in Greek mythology?

She understood that all the dead of the Abandonment were waiting on the Far Shore, their unblinking eyes staring over the River towards them, single-minded, longing and true. They would wait forever, if they had to, or at least until Brady and Kaileigh joined them. They wouldn't move on past the shore and towards the undiscovered country that lay beyond until Brady and she had set things right. Apparently that was her job and somehow, she knew it in a bone-deep way. Kaileigh walked the world with a new understanding of the way of things.

There was the nagging sense that Grendel was nearby, crouching in the shadows and growing stronger every minute. If she could be both a human teenager and an immortal daughter of Death, with all that it entailed, then Brady could be more than he appeared. So could Grendel. How had she managed to avoid the monster so long in the hospital? How had she known what his next move would be every time? The world had changed. She began to comprehend her place in it and how her own transformation figured into the final equation.

From the edge of the forest, a wolf-like form hunkered down and watched with keen eye the doings of a small band of humans on the bridge in the distance. If anyone had bothered to look skyward, they might have seen a black shape take wing and travel back inland, towards Brewer and the seemingly sleeping statue of General Joshua Chamberlain and the Library of Alexandria.

Chapter 32
The Last Message

"It's faint, I tell you, but she's definitely there!" said Joe sternly, putting his finger to his lips to silence the others. They were all standing around the radio transceiver in the Observation Deck at the top of the tower of the Penobscot Narrows Bridge. Night had fallen nearly an hour ago as the crimson sun painted the sky a feathery maroon with dusk. They had spent many hours readying the bridge as a massive radio transmitter using the suspension cables as huge antennae, but they were frustrated. They had been broadcasting on low power for twenty minutes with no response from anyone, anywhere. All of their hopes and aspirations for the future were wrapped up in this one event. It was paramount that they succeed, for each of them knew the dilemma of isolation. People needed to contact each other or else they would be like blue whales, wandering the wide oceans for decades, never seeing another one of their species.

"Tatyana's been broadcasting every night for over a month! Why now? Why would her signal disappear now?" asked Brady.

"I'm telling you, she hasn't disappeared. She's there, but the signal is weak. Now all of you, be quiet!" Joe grunted while his right hand slowly turned the knob as red LEDs numbered themselves up and down the dial. The white noise of the universe filled the air with static while each of them held their breaths, waiting.

"....our last broadcast," came the voice of Radio Ukraine over the air in a tinny whine, barely audible against the background static. Joe maneuvered the dials and pressed a button that seemed to eliminate most of the static. She continued.

"...only one left...am broadcasting from smaller backup transmitter. Our main transmitter...destroyed by fire. All my engineers died in fire."

The gathered eyes of the company were all focused on the one glowing dial on the transmitter. Joe was recording the transmission on a small battery-powered digital recorder for later review, but it was clear already that they would never forget the words they were hearing. It was too unbearable, like listening to a dying woman's last words.

"This is final broadcast. Repeat. This is final broadcast. I am alone now. I have been contacted by just over one hundred and twenty people, spread over the world. Only continent I have not been contacted is Antarctica, but is winter there and many may have survived in isolation from people. Europe has approximately twenty survivors, Australia as many, Africa and South America much the same. Asia has another thirty to forty. North America, where virus is believed to have originated, has twenty-five. I have instructed all to broadcast on this frequency. If you are listening, you might still be able to contact these people. Keep trying. Do not stop. Increase your signal strength. Make contact.

I am sorry to tell you our problems. We have been bothered many nights now by strange happenings, by things we cannot explain. We hear voices from radio even when radio is off. The voices threaten us to stop. Some of those who have contacted us have told similar circumstances all over world, of things that do not make sense happening around them, like the old world of our grandfathers is waking up from long sleep. Last night lightning struck transmitter and it began to burn, trapping engineers inside building. I could not help them escape. Today I am alone and reach out to you one last time before back-up generator runs out of fuel. Please to relay this message all around world -we live. We are still alive. While we live, the world continues. We must survive and build again."

The Observatory filled with an eerie silence as Tatyana's voice ceased. There was nothing but a palpable silence, thick enough to cut with a knife, filling their minds with sorrow and loss. If losing everyone you ever loved wasn't enough to drag a heart through the gutter, the loss of this one voice alone felt like an end to all things and sounded like the way the world ended, with a whisper followed by the white noise of static.

"Damn it," Joe said quietly. No one spoke for a long moment, letting the silence overwhelm them. "That's a shame. At least we know how many people are out there and in a larger sense, where they are. She gave us some cities from earlier broadcasts, New York, Washington, D.C. We also know that if they'd heard her before, they'll still be listening to this frequency. Imagine how many other survivors there might be out there who never once thought of tuning her in on a world band radio. There could be thousands. If we act quickly, we can transmit our own message out to the world while a few of them are still listening."

Each of the faces in the group quietly affirmed their agreement with a quick and silent nod. There was no time to waste. What Radio Ukraine had started, they must continue. They had the transmitter, the power and more than that, the will to contact other survivors. Tatyana's final words haunted them while giving them a purpose: contact others or die trying.

It was the only thing left on earth.

In a moment Joe was rehearsing the actions they would all need to take to bring the transmitter to life. Dr. Grindle would monitor the signal strength while Joe would operate the transmitter. Brady and Kaileigh would take the elevator down several stories to the base of the tower and stand by the generator, just in case there was any problem. From his work at the library, Brady had become fairly handy with a diesel generator. For his own comfort, Brady took *The Autobiography of Benjamin Franklin* with him.

"We'll start the auxiliary generator at 8:55 exactly. That, along with the power from the bridge's built-in emergency generator ought to be enough for a short, but very powerful broadcast."

"It won't be enough," Kaileigh said quietly.

Joe looked at her askance and frowned, continuing, "We go live on the air at 9:00 PM. Everyone to their stations," Joe spoke without making eye contact, his hands a blur over the various switches and buttons on the mountain of equipment piled on the white folding tables they had brought with them.

"Have you thought about what you're going to say?" asked Dr. Grindle.

Joe turned to him for a quick moment and said, "No, not really. I guess I ought to say something simple and easy to understand, in case anyone who is listening doesn't speak English very well."

"How about, "We are here! We are here! We are here!" It worked for the Who's in *Horton Hears a Who*," said Kaileigh without missing a beat.

"Nice!" Brady said in approval.

Joe grunted. "We've got a radio station to run. Everyone to their stations, now!"

Brady and Kaileigh took the elevator down to the deck of the bridge and the generators. Once they were out of earshot of Joe and Dr. Grindle, she spoke.

"Brady, I need to get to the river and make contact with those on the Far Shore. I'm not sure how, but I believe they can help boost the power of the broadcast."

431

"I did what you asked. I've rigged a cord long enough to reach the shore of the river down below. The other end is already connected to the electrical service box. We'll just need to flip this circuit breaker," said Brady as he pointed out the black switch box on the panel. "Now, tell me exactly what it is you hope to do."

"I'm going down by the shore. I'll take hold of the cord and I'll step into the water when Joe tells you to flip the switch. If I'm right, we'll get a little power boost from, well, from *them*."

"But if you do that, you'll electrocute yourself!" Brady exclaimed.

"Death and I are on very agreeable terms, Brady."

"What?"

She took his hand and held it tightly and for a long moment she gazed quietly into his eyes. Then she smiled.

"I wouldn't do anything to leave you. Ever. Not after what we've been through, but you have to trust me. Got it?"

Brady smiled and nodded his head. Such power, such purpose.

"Got it," he replied.

As Kaileigh started to walk away so she could position herself at the base of the bridge at the river's edge, Brady said, "Hey!"

"Yes?"

"Be careful."

"I will."

Brady tried to brush it off, knowing that the entire future of the human race depended on the broadcast and hopefully, the eventual contact from other survivors. Joe's idea was to continue Radio Ukraine's work and to broadcast nightly as long as possible. Radio would bring the world back together and link the far-flung groups of survivors into one collective human group - a civilization, for lack of a better term, connected by waves of the electromagnetic spectrum. This night's broadcast would be historic and Brady didn't want to be the one asleep at the wheel when nine o'clock came around. All there was to do now was wait for the ionosphere to lower and then make the call that could change the world.

"Brady, time check," Kaileigh's voice sang out from the walkie talkie clipped to his belt.

"I have eight fifty-four," he replied.

"Check. One minute to auxiliary generator start-up," she said.

"Check. One minute and counting. Don't worry. I'm on it," he said.

He was alone in the huge room at the bottom of the tower with a single light shining in the corner. He had a twelve L.E.D. headlight on his forehead and he was fully loaded with tool belts. He didn't carry any weapons, even though he suspected that his need for them was not quite over with. He knew that the kind of battle he was going to fight tonight would only need one weapon: an intangible one called courage.

"Ben, I'm nervous," he said to *The Autobiography of Benjamin Franklin* resting in his back pocket.

"Yes. You should be. A lot depends on you," answered the good man.

"Thanks for the encouragement," replied Brady.

"You don't need encouragement, Brady. You're the bravest young man I have ever had the good fortune to meet. I have no doubt that whatever happens, you will act with the good sense you've always shown and things will unfold as they should."

Brady wished that Ben was more than a voice proceeding from a book, because at that moment, at the base of the lit tower of the Penobscot Narrows Bridge, looking up at the moon, he felt very alone.

Joe's voice broke their silence and Brady put his hand on the switch, ready to start it. "Throw the switch," came the order.

Brady moved the switch on the circuit breaker and the generator they had hauled from the construction company's lot roared into life, a deep guttural, throaty sound, suddenly awakened into action.

"How's that?" Brady radioed to Joe.

"We're pushing twenty-thousand watts," Joe said calmly.

Brady smiled and waited. Then, at the appointed moment, the broadcast began.

Then Joe's voice said to the quiet earth, "This is Civilization Radio broadcasting from Bucksport, Maine at twenty-thousand watts to the entire planet. If anyone can hear......"

From out of nowhere, a bolt of lightning struck the tower, its white arc of frenzied light dancing upon the cables and down to the deck of the bridge where Brady stood next to the auxiliary generator. At that same moment, the tower went dark and the signal failed. Then another sound of thunder cracked above them and Brady felt Beorn's powerful message reverberate throughout his frame, but Brady knew what he was going to say before he understood the bear's message. He could feel his presence behind him.

Grendel.

Brady slowly turned to look at the spot behind him where the second lightning bolt had struck. Fenris-Grendel stood there, different from before and because he had occupied the body of a dog rather than that of a human, he looked more like a werewolf from the movies than anything else that Brady could imagine. His snout was massive and full of teeth, a snarl bending his lips. Hair covered his eight foot tall body and he walked on the strange and awkward hind legs of a dog, yet his arms were fully human and muscular, ending in the disastrous claws of a feral creature, still retaining the human hand shape. Brady could smell his fetid odor and nearly swooned from its effect. He understood Grendel's ability to summon the forces of the storm and knew that it had been his doing to call the lightning down upon their enterprise and stop them from making contact.

"I knew you'd come back," Brady said.

"From the ends of the earth and the first syllable of time, I would find my way here to end your days. Humanity has spent itself and is finished," spat out the monster as he advanced slowly toward Brady who seemed to grow smaller each second.

From the last place he expected to draw upon, Brady began to laugh. At first, it was no more than a smirk on his face, but soon a giggle turned into a guffawing, belly-shaking, air-gasping laugh, one that could melt all the walls of the world and send dictators and politicians down to their final doom.

With every passing second of laughter, Fenris-Grendel grew more irate beyond even the small amount of reason he possessed. Brady calmed himself, holding a hand to his belly, putting one hand up in the air to hold the monster back while he regained control and his breath.

"I'm not afraid of you. Don't you see? I'm your match, Grendel, old buddy. I know you better than anyone. Ben Franklin told me all about it - I'm positive and you're negative. If we fight, we'll only cancel each other out. Don't you get it? If I die, so do you. We're matter and antimatter. We're a perfect match! Ha!"

Grendel paused for a moment to ponder the words from this enigmatic boy who stood in front of him as though he was some sort of ancient unstoppable warrior returning from a nether region to face his eternal opponent again in their endless cycle. Fenris-Grendel knew fear and hated himself for it and somewhere deep inside, he cowered in a corner.

Brady knew what was about to happen and surrendered himself to it. He felt at peace with the solution he had chosen. Kaileigh needed the time to complete her job; she knew that Joe needed her power to augment the generators, even if he didn't suspect a thing. If Brady did this, what little of Humanity that remained could regroup and this hateful enemy would be destroyed. He thought of Dr. Grindle and his words, "He doesn't think. He *feels*." He knew what he had to do.

He reached into his shirt and grasped his grandfather's medal, the one he had carried for so long. Like Frodo grasping the One Ring, he felt it's power surging. It gave him strength.

"I'm ready ," Brady said, standing tall and proud.

"In the words of your girlfriend in the hospital when she cut my fingers," Fenris-Grendel snarled, "This ends here!"

"If that's the way it has to be, bring it on," said Brady, "And by the way, she's not my girlfriend!"

435

Chapter 33

Brady's Decision

Brady glanced down at Kaileigh on the shore below. She was watching in horror, a speck of hope near the water's edge. They made eye contact as the monster took a new stance and put some distance between himself and the boy. A look that lasted longer than any they had shared before transferred between them an understanding that surpassed words. She knew in a general way what he was up to and, more than that, she knew how he felt about the monster, about the world dying, and the survival of the species. What she didn't know was that as he did this final thing, Brady mostly thought about her. She looked up at him in wonder because she knew that this was *the* moment and every cell in her body called out to her to rush to his side and assist him against the monster, but she stopped herself and stayed near the river's edge.

The message must be sent, she thought. The radio must transmit tonight, right now, and nothing on the earth or heaven above should stop this broadcast. She was the River-Daughter as well as the daughter of her biological mother. Like most things on the quiet earth, she was realizing that underneath the masks that people wore all day, there was something more, much more, only people didn't want to see the truth beneath the surface and the real shape of things, so they spent their time watching TV, working, worrying and staying busy with trivial pursuits. Who was she, really, underneath the mask named Kaileigh? Tonight would tell.

Tonight, the power of the Dead would flow through her into the transmitter built by the last wizard on earth.

Had she been able to hear through the wind and thunder, she would have witnessed Brady say,"I'm ready. I won't fight it. I surrender."

The monster towered above Brady and moved closer, a troubled look of confusion painting its face, not knowing if this was yet another trick.

"You freely do this thing?" growled Fenris-Grendel doubtfully.

"I do," replied Brady, his face grim with determination.

A peal of laughter from the broken bell of Fenris-Grendel's heart rocked the air and lightning flashes lit the sky, strobe lights showing the strange motion-picture movement of the monster toward the boy. Kaileigh's heart raced and she shuddered with fear, her teeth clenching.

The monster said simply, "Fool, I accept."

The form that was Fenris-Grendel began to shed and divest itself of the body of the weredog previously known as Fenris. With a silver-white light of a twisting tendril, the demon unwrapped its ectoplasmic form from the weredog and moved through the air like a small opalescent cloud, forming reaching fingers and grasping at Brady, covering him like a funeral pall. In a moment, all Kaileigh could see of the bravest boy she had ever known was his face as Grendel started to become *Brady-Grendel.*

Just before the final possession of the boy's body, she heard Brady shout out to her, "Kaileigh! The message! Use the river!"

Had she been closer, she would have heard Brady clearly say, before he disappeared into the monster's body, "*Anything that can be imagined can be real...*"

In the split second before Grendel took possession of Brady's body and began to morph and punish it with writhing change, Brady Smith turned his body and ran. With a mighty leap, he threw himself off the edge of the bridge and into the bay below, into the River of All Things.

437

Chapter 34

In the Belly of the Beast

Brady found himself in darkness. He remembered throwing himself from the bridge in an action that would have been suicide for a boy but a mere trifle for a monster like Grendel. He was sure he had survived the fall, but he was not sure where he was now. He had imagined that to be possessed by the monster would mean cessation of consciousness and self-awareness, but he could move his body and stand up. He could smell and taste and feel and see, but only barely. In a moment he could sense that he was not immersed in total darkness. As his eyes adjusted to the light, he could see that he was in a sort of cave and that a faint bioluminescence seemed to be emanating from the walls. When he touched the walls, they were moist and warm. He thought he could detect a thrumming sound around him and feel a pulsation from underneath his feet. This was a cell, he thought, but not the kind in a prison.

"Brady, are you there?" he heard a voice say. It was...but it couldn't be. Ben?

"Ben, is that you?" he asked, searching his pockets frantically.

"Oh, it's good to hear your voice!" said *The*

Autobiography of Benjamin Franklin.

Brady found the old paperback in his pocket. He wasn't alone. Even though Ben had no body and therefore could not help him escape, there was solace in the knowledge that he had the mind of Ben Franklin at his disposal.

"Where are we?" asked the old printer.

"Inside of Grendel. I think." Brady paused, unsure how the old gentleman would react to his next statement. Then he said, "I allowed myself to be possessed by him."

Ben didn't respond for a moment but when he did, there was a wry note to his voice. "So, if one is going to beat the enemy, one does so either from without or from within, eh? You're planning on infiltrating the enemy camp and striking a death blow from inside, aren't you?"

"Something like that," Brady answered.

Brady started feeling around on the walls, like a mime trying to find a doorway, but the walls were perfectly curved and seamless. He was sealed tightly in this small chamber, away from the rest of the being that was Grendel.

"If there is no doorway, make one!" Ben suggested.

Brady stopped and considered and then began feeling around in his vest pockets and on his belt. He had many tools, but he was searching for the one that would work the best. His pocket knife! This just might be the tool needed to escape this *oubliette*. He went to one of the walls and slowly pushed the blade into it. Surely enough, it responded like flesh, more like cartilage than muscle. Once the blade was through, a simple sawing motion revealed a tight slit through which Brady could move. When he stepped through, the slit healed itself.

They were in another place, not a cell but the area in between cells: the interstitial region. It was more like a meandering hallway, with cells at regular intervals but with no straight lines evident anywhere. The faint light continued to glow from around him, from everywhere, just enough so that he could navigate. With his knife in his hand, he began the act of entering chambers by incising them with the blade, seeking out the beast. What Brady and Ben found so profoundly odd was that the chambers were not all empty

439

like the one Brady had discovered himself in moments ago. Some chambers were huge, like warehouses. They had lines of shelves that held artifacts-toys and clothing, schoolbooks and novels on the floor. There were piles and objects lying around in all the cell chambers, placed in disarray and left there for some unknown reason. In one room there was a complete set of encyclopedias. In another room there were piles of graphic novels and comic books and in yet another, what appeared to be walls and walls of video games and music CDs. Some rooms had furniture and others had boxes and bags. None of them had anything living in them and certainly there was no evidence of Grendel.

"Where did Grendel get all of this stuff?" asked Brady aloud.

" I believe we are wandering through its memories," said *The Autobiography of Benjamin Franklin.* "or should I say, *your* memories?"

The idea seemed ridiculous and plausible at the same time. How could memories be actual things that he could reach out and touch? Then again, he asked himself, how could he be a person wandering around inside a place built of fear and pain?

"This isn't real," he said to Ben.

"You mean that we aren't really here?" asked the good doctor.

The old scientist took a moment to respond. "I have had the opportunity to spend some time mistakenly shelved next to some of the writing of a fellow named Albert Einstein and I can tell you, he taught me a thing or two. Perhaps this isn't a real place, but a theoretical place and, as such, it is real enough for the moment. Call it a thought experiment."

"Theoretical?" asked Brady.

"A mental place, a place of the mind, but that doesn't mean it isn't *real*, Brady. The mind is real. You have one. I have one and my body has been dead for a very long time. So if we are somehow wandering around in the mind of the monster, then it is a fine labyrinth, indeed, but it is most certainly *real*."

Brady considered the words of the patriot carefully.

440

"Labyrinth, huh? Like the one Theseus entered in Crete to slay the Minotaur?"

"Yes! Exactly! That's the spirit! You're Theseus and the beast within this labyrinth is the Minotaur. 'Tis a good metaphor and apt. Remember, lad, *There is always a monster and he always hides in his lair. Without this, there can be no hero.*

Brady cut himself into chamber after chamber, always working his way down the hall. In one chamber he found children's toys, a Big Wheel, a red wagon and a rattle, GI Joes and Star Wars plastic light sabers. In yet another chamber a movie was playing against a cell wall. How it was projected was unclear, but it was definitely a movie in black and white, with no sound. There was a tall thin man with a bowler cap and a silly grin and a taller, fatter man, dressed in a similar fashion. They were trying to push a piano up a long set of stairs and having very little success. Brady found himself staring at it, distracted by it for a few moments before Ben asked him where they were and what they were doing.

"Oh, sorry, I was, um, well, I was watching a movie. I love this one. They're called Laurel and Hardy. They're trying to get this piano up a long set of stairs." Brady answered.

"An enemy that knows what distracts us can use that knowledge to thwart us from our first purpose," replied Ben. "He tricks you by showing you things you wish to linger over."

"I know, it's just that I remember some of these things. I lost most of them. It's just that now, I can see them, touch them again. It feels good."

"Brady, one today is worth two tomorrows..."

Brady begrudgingly moved away from the movie on the chamber wall. How could a being of hatred and enmity be made of such things as toys and old comedians, he wondered? Then he asked himself why anyone keeps anything and the answer came down to two things - necessity and memory. Were these things which seemed to have no common purpose tucked neatly away because deep within he thought he might *need* them later or were they souvenirs - memories? If they were memories, they seemed somewhat personal or even heartfelt. They were human souvenirs, he thought to himself, or at least the kinds of things something might keep if it was striving to be human. Grendel hated humans and wanted all of them gone, yet deep inside the essential part of him, Grendel clung to human wants, desires, even dreams.

They wandered the endless serpentine hallway through the pale ghostly light and with every step, they found more of the flotsam and jetsam of Brady's memory. With every step forward, the anger and remorse he felt grew more distinct. His heart beat more quickly as he passed a hundred rooms? A thousand? Time seemed to have no meaning within this place. Instead of time there was something else. If time was a river, Brady was on the riverbank, aware of it in the distance but no longer immersed in it. Was that a woman weeping in the distance? What could cause such bereavement? Who could carry on such a demonstration of woe for so long? In a place away from time, nothing lasted at all and it continued forever, all at once.

The penknife slid deeply into one cell wall and this time the cell wall resisted. It did not easily give way to the pressure of his wrist as all the others had. This one fought back and Brady could feel the knife twist in his hand like someone on the other side was pushing it away, like the flesh itself was rebelling against him. Not easily deterred, Brady had the sense that urgency was the only thing that mattered. Somewhere outside, Kaileigh, Joe, Dr. Grindle and Beorn were probably already facing the new monster that must be Brady-Grendel. Who knew what new form the monster had taken from Brady's fears and worries, from his loves and hatreds? Brady hoped that deep down, the monster had to rely upon the physical attributes and the emotional responses of his host and he was no weak dog or beaten man.

He tried pushing the blade into the cell wall with more force, but it only fought back with equal pressure. He tried slashing at it, but to no effect as the blade bounced off the wall like rubber. Both he and Ben noticed that whenever the knife touched the cell wall, the sound of growling intensified, only to wane again when it withdrew the blade. Then Brady remembered: the password, from *Ali Baba and the Forty Thieves* and the way into all caves of wonder.

"Open Sesame," he commanded.

I always say that when I want to get in somewhere, he thought.

An open doorway appeared in front of them.

They stepped into the chamber. It was darker than all the other chambers and when the slit behind him healed shut, it was pitch black. Brady fished around in his pockets and withdrew an L.E.D. flashlight, switching it on. The chamber was cavernous and as they walked, it was the first time they could hear no thrumming at all. Instead, what pervaded the air and their senses was the sound of music. As they moved toward what Ben explained was *Bach's Toccata and Fugue in G minor*, they saw a small living room complete with a suite of comfortable furniture, a widescreen plasma television and soft lighting. In the distance they saw a window into a kitchen where the smell of roasting turkey emanated and filled their senses. A small fire was burning in the fireplace and several beautiful paintings from various time periods were displayed upon the walls.

"What is this place?" Brady asked aloud.

"I wouldn't be surprised if this was where the real Grendel spends his days. Remember Brady, he's not really alive, but he knows you better than anyone else. He will try to trick you."

Brady was now in the living room, examining the paintings. They seemed to be real and not copies but how did Van Gogh's *Starry Night* get inside the mind of a monster. Yet another painting was Rembrandt's *Night Watch*. There was the album art to Led Zeppelin's *Stairway to Heaven*, complete with the hermit holding his lantern. Upon closer inspection he could tell that these were incomplete. Faces were not fully painted and colors were wrong, less vivid than they should be. Everything about the paintings seemed like they were approximations of paintings only.

There was a large bookshelf in the middle of the two

paintings and it stretched from ceiling to floor in its walnut and cherry glory. Among the tomes on the shelves were the works of Shakespeare, Dante, Cervantes, and Dickens, all carefully alphabetized, no one volume sticking out any further than any other. Brady recognized one of his favorite books and withdrew *Don Quixote*. It was bound in leather and had gold lettering. When he opened it, it's spine cracked as though it had never been opened before. This would indeed be a tedious read, however, because all the pages were blank.

Brady put the book back on the shelf and walked over to the television, picking up the remote control. He switched it on and began to look through the channels, one after another, channel after channel. They all displayed the same program: an episode of *South Park* that kept looping back upon itself, repeating the same minute of the show over and over again. He switched it off and understood everything.

This was his home, his true abode. This was the home he would have had if his father had never died. He couldn't allow himself to imagine this in the real world, but here? Now? No one should have to experience this.

If this was his home, it was Grendel's home and therefore, the monster's lair. The other Grendel in the epic of *Beowulf* lived in a cave deep within a mountain and away from the world of men. So this monster lived in his own kind of cave and tried to create a world that approximated the one he longed to control. Our living rooms are our modern caves, he thought.

"Come on in, Honey. Supper's almost ready..."

It was his mother.

"Go wash your hands, Brady. I've made meatloaf and potatoes – your father's favorite. He'll be home in a few minutes. Go and wash your hands so we can eat together as a family."

Brady stood as still as a statue. He was in his home, the home he would have known if his father had lived. She was here, as well, and the world seemed somehow better. There was the smell of fresh food in the kitchen and photos of the family on the wall. Brady lingered near them and examined them closely. There was one of his father and him sitting in kayaks in Orrington, both of them smiling widely. There was another of the whole family walking up the trail at Mt. Cadillac on Mount Desert Island, the Porcupine Islands in the distance. Still another was of Brady and his dad working on a pinewood derby car for Cub Scouts.

Except none of these had ever happened. They should have, but they didn't.

Brady walked down the hallway toward his old room, the one he had before his father died and they had to move to an apartment because mom couldn't afford a mortgage any longer. As he entered his room he saw it not as it was then but as he would have it today, with AC/DC and Five-Finger Death Punch posters on the wall, a large LCD screen television and a laptop in the corner, along with a whole wall of music CDs and in the other corner, a full drum kit. He took a cd down from the shelf and opened it to find it empty, then another and another. All of them were empty and no music would play here. He sat on the edge of his bed to look into the mirror and found the bed was solid wood. The mirror didn't even reflect his image.

He heard the door close in the living room.

"Brady, come on in. Dad's home," he mother called.

His heart hastened and became a frightened bird cased within his ribs. Sweat began to form in small beads on his forehead. His father had been dead for years now but here he was, somehow alive again.

Each step toward the living room was torture. He emerged from the hallway to see his father sitting in his chair looking at the Bangor Daily News.

"Hey, buddy," he said, "come on over here and talk to your old man."

Brady said nothing and obeyed his father, sitting on the edge of the couch next to his father's chair. His father put the paper down and looked at him, smiling all the while. Then he reached out and lightly punched his son on the shoulder.

"That's for nothing. Now, do something!" he said jovially.

"Hi, Dad," Brady said.

445

"What did you do to change the world today?" asked his father.

"Oh...nothing," he answered.

"Well, you must have done something," he said casually, picking up his paper.

"At the moment, I'm saving the world from a monster named Grendel that I created. He wants to destroy all human life on earth."

"That's nice," his dad said, "I can see you've been reading again. What an imagination!"

His mother came into the living room. She was wearing an apron and a dress that he had never seen her wear in life.

"Dinner's ready! Let's eat, you two."

Brady sat down and cut a piece of meatloaf with his knife, bringing it to his lips. It was warm and moist and meaty. He savored it. He hadn't had meatloaf in months. His mother and father exchanged pleasantries while Brady sat quietly, taking it all in. *Observation Mode* was strictly in force.

"We need to get to bed early tonight, son, if we're going hunting in the morning," his father stated while chewing a mouthful of potatoes.

Brady froze and stared at his father. *Hunting?*

"What's the matter with you?" his father asked.

Brady didn't answer. He lost his grip on his fork and it fell to the floor. His mother told him to pick it up. He had to get down on all fours to retrieve it and as he did, he heard a voice.

"Brady? This isn't real. Your parents are dead. Wake up. Don't lose yourself in this. It isn't real."

It was the voice of the *Autobiography of Benjamin Franklin.*

The spell was broken. For a few blessed moments, Brady had forgotten about the Abandonment, about the death of his parents, about the rise of Grendel from his own anger, and about his purpose in this place. He got out from under the table and stood up.

His parents were still there, but they were no longer as he had previously seen them. His father was a skeleton with

446

a foolish, macabre grin and his mother was slumped over the plate of meatloaf, obviously dead, her face flat down on the plate.

"I'm sorry, Brady," said the book.

"It's okay. It's not really them," said Brady.

Immediately the scene changed and Brady found himself in a very familiar place: his sanctum sanctorum, his growlery, his Fortress of Solitude, his bat cave. There were the giant monitors on the wall, the rows of computer banks full of flashing lights and on the far wall, weaponry and tools of various advanced designs. A large chair that was an exact replica of Captain Kirk's from the original series of *Star Trek* sat in the middle of the room. Brady walked over and sat down. This was the place he always went in his mind when he needed to solve puzzles.

"Computer, where is Grendel?" he asked.

Clicking and clacking sounds, hums and beeps sounded and then with the sound of an old dot matrix printer running, he heard the voice of the Enterprise's computer say, "Grendel is in two places simultaneously. He is in the river and also all around us."

"Computer, show me the world through his eyes."

The large view screen in front of him turned blue and then showed a high-definition view of the river and of the form of Kaileigh at the edge of the water. She had both feet in the water at the river's edge and she was holding on to the thick electrical cord he had lowered for her. She was readying to make the connection. He could see through the monster's eyes that Grendel was approaching her with great rapidity. Soon he would be upon her. Brady completely understood his intent. If he was going to do this thing, he had better do this now.

"Computer, I am ready to face my fears. Please open the portal."

"Portal opening," said the computer.

"Brady," said the *Autobiography of Benjamin Franklin*, "be true of heart. Be brave."

On the wall opposite the view screen a round white-edged portal began to form from the center, whirling in

447

circles, widening slightly with each turn. Brady knew he was stepping out of the safe zone of his mind and into the insane part, the part that all people keep in check and hold inside. He was stepping into his own private Tartarus, taking only an old paperback and his imagination.

After he stepped through, the portal closed. Immediately he was enveloped in chaos. A thousand figures swirled around him. There was Susan, the first girl he had crushed on and she was giving him an ugly glare. There was his science teacher, Mr. Page, marking an "F" on a paper with his name on it. There was his friend Noah, shouting out, "I hate you! You stink!" He saw Hugin limping on the ground with a broken wing and Joe in his bed, his face grey and ashen, his mouth open in death. A thousand 'what-ifs' whirled past him and he was reminded of the *Wizard of Oz* and the moment when Dorothy is in the tornado and all the things in the world fly by her window. There were fears here he had forgotten, like the one where he thought his mother had left him alone in the store and he screamed and cried until a kind person brought him to the service desk. There was the fear that he had cheated on a test because he had accidentally seen an answer on another person's paper. There was the fear that he would never be good enough for anything because he was fat and short and had a high-pitched voice and that no one anywhere could ever stoop so low as to love *him*.

Swirling in a soup of anger, the fears intensified and whenever one came close to him, his heartbeat quickened and his anxiety heightened. These things were real to him. These were his fears brought to life.

"Grendel, I know who you are!" he shouted over the wind of panic.

"You are too late," shouted the monster.

Out of the chaos of swirling embodied pains and fears, the monster flew out toward him. They grappled and fell into the long, dark chasm, a bottomless hole in the Tartarus of Brady's mind.

Chapter 35

The True Battlefield

Kaileigh took hold of the cord and stepped closer to the water. She was already aware that the newly formed Brady-Grendel was stirring awake from his conversion somewhere in the water of the bay. Soon, their window of opportunity would be closed and she would have to fight him. Beorn stood at the water's edge and huffed, his snout flaring and his mouth open. She wished she could understand the bear as Brady did.

She had one task to complete and it was the future and the remainder of time. She needed to get power to the transmitter so that Joe and Dr. Grindle could complete the transmission and let the word go forth.

Her position on the shore allowed her a clear view of the tower and the Observation Deck at the top. Up there, she thought, is the power to unite all the remaining humans on earth. This was more than just a chance- this was *the last*

449

chance. She understood that if the scattered pockets of people never connected, then it would be as though people had never existed. All the music, all the books, all the dancing and loving and beauty would vanish because there would be no one to remember it. Within a thousand years, all evidence of a bipedal creature that called itself 'human' would have been erased.

She remembered the vision from her last visit - the dead waiting on the Far Shore refusing to move until they knew that they would be remembered and that someone would carry on. She suspected that it was the connection that allowed the living to move forward, but she hadn't thought about it from the other perspective. She understood that the dead needed the living to know that they had not lived in vain, so that they could continue to their final destination secure in the knowledge that they had paved the way in the world for those who followed. They had lived for a purpose. They were the people. They were Humanity. All those gathered on the Far Shore in that multitude had died too soon because of the advent of a species-killing virus and their appointed tasks would forever remain undone. If they were remembered, Kaileigh mused, it might be enough.

The bear fell to all four paws and began to walk a circle around her, each circle getting smaller and smaller. It was clear to Kaileigh that he was driving her towards the water's edge.

"Okay, I'm going, I'm going..." she said finally.

Beorn grunted, but before he could move, his body was lifted and thrown through the air, landing against the trunk of a nearby pine. Standing in his place, the form of Brady-Grendel had emerged from the river. Kaileigh recognized the part of the monster that was Brady and it frightened her more than any other incarnation that Grendel had taken. How could she fight this thing that was also her friend, somewhere deep beneath?

The boy had become monstrous. He rose to eight feet tall, his chin was square and his head had a Frankenstein quality to it, chiseled and blocky. Arms rippled with musculature and his eyes were burning red with anger. His whole frame shuddered with strength. Club-like hands formed fists of rage. The behemoth of Brady-Grendel towered over Kaileigh's diminutive form.

"Too late, Kay," snarled the beast. "I'll rip your head from off your body and shove it down your beautiful throat!"

"Brady?" she asked, detecting a hint of her friend's voice. "Is that you? Are you in there?"

"Oh, he's in here, all right. He's in a place darker than oblivion and as timeless as a black hole. You'll never see him again, Kai. Never.

Something gave her pause, something *familiar*, something *Brady*. Had the monster which had fought her and kept her prisoner just called her 'Kai'? That was what Brady had starting calling her and only recently had he felt comfortable enough to do that. Though her heart raced with adrenalin and fear, she suspended her instinct to plunge into the battle immediately.

"Brady, you have to fight back! I know you're in there, in between the words. Remember the reason we're here. Focus! If you fight him from inside and I fight him from outside, he doesn't stand a chance."

There was a strange strangling noise in Brady-Grendel's throat and he paused, confused at the sudden change in his physical state. He cleared his throat and spat out a greasy, gray wad of phlegm upon the ground in front of Kaileigh.

"Don't waste your words! He's long gone. He's lost and all alone. You can't find him in here. I'm all that remains of him. I *am* him!"

"Brady, I know you," she said calmly as she looked directly into the eyes of the monster. "I know you're good. I know you always do the right thing. If you're in there, I want you to know...how much you mean...to *me*."

The monster stopped. He blinked and shook his massive, irregularly shaped head and raised his hands to cover his own ears. Then, through a garbled, gargled voice, he said, "Kai? Is that you?"

She smiled and replied, "Brady! I knew you were in there!"

"Kai..." the voice was distant, like the last vestige of an echo in a windy day. Brady spoke from an immeasurable distance.

"All great battles are fought from within...remember?"

In one fluid moment she withdrew the katana from the scabbard over her shoulder and in the same movement let it fall upon the monster's shoulder. A wave of pain shuddered up the blade and into her hands - Brady! Still, she did not stop. Another swipe of the blade along the cap of the beast's left knee brought it down for a moment. She moved away for a moment to reposition herself for her next aggressive move, but the beast arose with all the alacrity of an athlete and turned away, letting his taloned paw slice three red lines of pain into Kaileigh's right cheek. She wondered if Brady was feeling the pain or if the monster was and then she remembered: they were both the same. Still, she needed to buy time.

The monster laughed. "I know what you're doing. I've absorbed the Renamer's every thought and memory. I know you're a Water-Witch. I know you speak to the waves and they obey, but I've mutated since then. Water no longer affects me. I'm immune to its effects, so whatever you are planning, it is a waste of your time. You see, little witch, I learn from my mistakes. I evolve into something better and stronger each time I'm attacked. Fight me and you only make me stronger! Soon, nothing will be able to stop me."

Kaileigh didn't show one single emotion. She was stone. She was ice. Her only focus was the blade and where it would strike next and even if what the monster said was true and all of their hopes and dreams were about to be smashed into oblivion, she would stand this ground until she fell, adamant. Her fear had grown to ripeness: a monster with Brady's abilities would be nearly impossible to stop.

"I'm not going to give up. You're going to have to kill me," she said stonily.

Brady-Grendel shook his head and laughed. "I don't have to kill you. I'm beyond you. All I need to do is stop the message from going through. Then, I can destroy the transceiver. The old man will die and he is the only one who understands how to built and operate the equipment. He's your wizard, probably the only human left who truly understands how things used to work. The few pathetic humans left on the face of this little world will never meet again. They'll wander the earth for the rest of their lives looking for each other, but they will never again connect. Humanity is finished! Then, when you're all gone, nature can finally take its proper course."

"Joe is your friend!" she said.

"He is the Renamer's friend. He is my enemy, like you. I have no friends. I *need* no friends."

Kaileigh's face changed and a wry smile began to form just on the corner of her mouth. She tried to hold it back, but the monster saw the change and for a moment, he wondered. There is always something you can't predict, she thought.

"You're gonna wish you had some friends," was all she said.

She knew what was coming, even if the monster didn't. From her perspective she saw the metal form of an oversized sword come crashing down upon the monster. It was a saber from the Civil War, or at least a good facsimile, oversized and made of brass. From beyond all hope, Hugin had brought him. It had taken all day, but General Joshua Chamberlain had arrived with all the simple good sense his real-life counterpart had always exhibited.

Brady-Grendel screamed in pain. The saber had sunk deep into the monster's flesh, touching Brady's form beneath. Kaileigh didn't stop to ponder the implications for her friend. She knew that the General could fight all night long and never be wounded. He was invincible. Even if he couldn't beat Brady-Grendel, he could certainly keep him busy,very busy. That would give her time. Joe and Dr. Grindle needed power to transmit to the others out there, somewhere in the dark, far away. She was the only one who could do it.

Brady-Grendel evaded the General's next thrust and slipped past the metal man and back toward Kaileigh. He lifted a taloned claw high and began to bring it down like a rake of knives against Kaileigh when a stone creature not three feet tall barreled past Kaileigh and against the monster, knocking him off center.

Gregoire turned and said to Kaileigh, "I 'ave come a long way to be 'ere. I apologize for my endless, shameless lateness, but zeze little stone wings do not fly worth a damn. I 'ad to walk ze 'ole way from ze city. Oh, my legs, zey are so 'eavy!"

"Gregoire! Thank you! Watch out!" she shouted as the monster arose and lifted the stone monster like a bowling ball in his fist.

"Do not worry about me. I am made of stone but my 'eart is full of passion! Vive la resistance! Unhand me, you putrid, sorry, ignorant ass! I swear if you lay a hand on her beautiful head, I'll kick your ass all the way to Sunday! You ain't never gonna touch her!"

The gargoyle quickly went from his ridiculous French accent to his Jersey Shore lilt in one sentence. Before the monster could hurl him away into the river where he would undoubtedly sink like a stone, Gregoire whistled and Hugin dive-bombed Grendel's face, pecking at his eyes with feverish ferocity. Gregoire managed to get free and land just at the end of the river.

"Now, while we got his attention. Do your thing! Come on! Hey, you! Doggy doo doo, are you lookin' at me? Huh! What are lookin' at? Think 'cause I'm short that I can't take you on? Try me! Try me!" shouted the Gargoyle as he charged the monster.

The General's blade slashed at Brady-Grendel as Gregoire's small but well-packed form ran into the monster's knee, sending him to the ground flailing. The two unlikely allies were buying her the time she needed. She didn't even hazard a second glance at their ensuing battle. Instead, she turned and dove into the icy coldness of the Penobscot River and the mixing salty waters of Penobscot Bay.

She was the Conduit.

Kaileigh found herself in the world of the River again. She was greeted by a thousand hands and arms that carried her like a rock star who had dived into an enthusiastic crowd. The hands carried her along and she flowed like the river. She was water, time and tide.

"You've returned, my daughter," said a voice from everyone all at once. She felt the voice deep within her bones rather than hearing it with only her ears.

"I have," she answered with thought. "I'm ready to fulfill my purpose. What do I do?"

"*Believe.*"

Kaileigh weighed the words in her mind, wondering how such things could be, but it did not matter. She was alive, suspended in another world next to her own.

"The Dead await your task. This much is clear. But your friend needs your help, too. The monster will consume him," said the River Woman. "You must help him, else he will perish."

"How can I help him?" she asked.

"By helping him remember who is really is, by standing next to him and believing in the future as strongly as he does. So many of the living believe that they are alone when all the time, we are nearby. His belief in the future of Humanity is the strongest force on Earth. He sees things as they are and how they should be, at the same time," answered Death.

"Who is he, precisely?" asked Kaileigh, feeling bold in the face of the eldritch woman.

"Ah," whispered the River Woman, "he is able to see the truth of things and give things their true names. All the old names have no meaning now. The dictionary has been erased. Creation demands a new listing of names. Here is the secret that wise ones have known since the world began: to name something is to control it. He has the power to rename the world and everything in it. He has already begun this with his map and his way of changing the old names to the new. But who will name the Renamer? Whoever can rename him has power over him, for to name is to master. Only you can tell *him* who he really is. You know him better than you think. Only you can name the Renamer."

"How do I do that? Do I just call him something like Joe or Bob?"

455

The River-Woman laughed and the stars blinked on the panoply of the night sky. "You need not do such a thing. Only tell yourself who he is to you. That is all. Who is this young man who went bravely into the beast? What does he mean to you?"

Kaileigh felt the frustration mounting on her shoulders, her face reddening and her mind reeling.

"He's...he's my friend. He's the best friend I've ever had. I'd die for him."

"There," said the River-Woman. "You've done it. Such a friendship can save the world."

Kaileigh did not know what to do next.

"What is the trouble?" asked *Those of the Waters*, though she could not see them.

"Soon, if I don't do something, the monster will make his way up to the tower and kill Joe and the doctor. I'll be the only one left, besides a bear that walks on two feet and a raven I can't even understand, and a stone gargoyle who wants to be my boyfriend. I need power for that transmitter!"

She heard the sounds of bells and the wind, the long whisper spoken ages ago and voices whose reverberations were singing, "Sins are rewarded, good deeds are denied..."

Who were they and what did they want, she wondered?

"Do not listen to them, daughter," said the River-Mother. "They are the lost. They are the damned. They do not want to see the light."

These were the voices of *Those of the Waters* who had carried her along like slaves that did her bidding, like fawning servants to her royal highness.

"*Those of the Waters*..are they dead, like those on the Far Shore?"

"They are," answered the River-Mother, "but they do not matter. They are not of the River or of the Shore. They are the Lost. They were shown the way to the shore but did not seek it. They were afraid and did not move on. They serve me in hopes that I will somehow send them forward to their own final destination, but that is not my place. They missed their chance, but they will do your bidding because they believe you, as my daughter, will one day allow them to step upon the shore they once denied. They are my servants and now they are yours, too. They are the Lost."

She thought of the billions of souls waiting for her on the Far Shore and immediately the unseen hands of the waters began to propel her toward it. Kaileigh didn't resist any longer. She gave into this reality and embraced it like an amnesiac newly awakened, letting things happen. Somehow, at the end of it all, this felt right.

"Charon," a voice said to her as she stepped upon the shore. The name echoed endlessly as it passed from one shade to another in a maddening refrain. She stepped into the throng of impatient souls as their hollow eyes followed her. They said nothing else and waited for her to speak.

"My name is Charon. I am the Daughter of the River. I am here to ask for your help."

They waited like a Greek chorus, stone still and emotionless.

"On the other side of this water, a battle is taking place. It is a battle for your memory. If those few brave people who fight for your memory and the future of our species fail, then it will be as though none of you had ever lived. No one will live long enough to remember and in a generation, all will be forgotten."

The throng began to tremble and she could feel its tenebrous motion as she concentrated. Six and half billion souls cried out in frustration and anger. If she had been on the other side of the river, she would have felt the small earthquake that ensued. The souls of a nearly lost Humanity chose a leader who stepped forward from the crowd. He wasn't in the forefront of the miles and miles of spirits and as he moved, the other spirits parted to make way for his approach. They slid to the side to allow him to pass without moving their legs. Kaileigh wondered who they had chosen to speak for them. Who would speak for the dead? Would it be some great statesman, a leader of men, a holy man or a general?

When the wave of souls parted before her, she saw who it was and was driven to bite her bottom lip in pain and

457

frustration. Why him? Not now, she thought, I need to concentrate.

It was her lost beloved, Bob.

He stood there expressionless for a long moment and a silence fell between them like a wall of lead. She didn't know what to say and she began to weep. At this sign, the souls collectively murmured a sound that seemed like pleasure.

Finally, she said, "Why do they suddenly seem happy when my heart is breaking?"

Bud answered, "Your tears. You see, no one mourned them. Everyone died and no one was left to cry or say a prayer or miss them. Except for you and Brady. Thanks, Kaileigh."

With tears still staining her cheeks, she stepped forward and opened her arms and Bob stepped forward to meet her embrace. She felt nothing as she hugged the empty air, but the shade of Bob seemed relieved and moved. In a moment he stepped away and looked into her eyes. She remembered all the times she had imagined sharing her life with him. Now he was a memory, a lost future she would never know.

"I've been asked to speak for them," he said.

Kaileigh nodded. "I've come to ask for their help," she said. "Brady has become one with the monster" she explained, "and I don't know if we can destroy Grendel without destroying him."

"Brady is known to us. He is the Renamer. He is the one chosen to begin the rebuilding of the world."

She thought of him so often as that annoying boy who sometimes seemed totally insane and quirky, who referred to stories from books like they'd actually happened. He didn't even brush his hair.

"Yes. Together, you both will guide those who survive through the Change. He is the Renamer and you are the Conduit."

"Bob...I'm just me."

He smiled and took her hand. She felt nothing but her hand rose nonetheless.

458

"None of us are what we think we are. Kaileigh, I love you. I loved you from the minute I saw you. I saw you as the amazing person you are, even when you were confused and feeling small and other people judged you poorly and because I love you, I'll tell you the truth."

"Can spirits lie?" she wondered aloud.

"Yes, they can. Especially to themselves. I could never lie to you. We're waiting here because we're uncertain. We are the first of all the people to not move on because we desperately need to know how this story ends. You see, it's our story. Everything's a story, even this. It would be like reading a book for a lifetime and then never turning that last page to see how things ended. We need to know. We understand that if you don't broadcast this message, that the few and scattered groups might never meet and all will be forgotten. We know that Joe is the last man on earth who truly understands the technology to make such a broadcast and that soon, he will be here with us."

"Then you understand why I'm here, don't you?"

Bud looked at her longingly and nodded.

"We understand you need our help and we're ready to give it."

Kaileigh looked around her, beyond her dead boyfriend's lifeless eyes and as deeply as she could into the ranks of the populace. They looked back with an intensity and fear that plainly spoke to her. They were beyond the world of humans and doings. They were the dead. As much as they longed to, they couldn't move a grain of sand upon a beach or with their breath make a leaf tremble in the wind. What did Bob say to her? She was the one who would connect the world of the past to the world of the future. Did that mean...? Could she do this thing if...?

She looked down at her hand, the one that Bob was holding without so much as a touch. That much was real: a dead boy and a living girl, holding hands and all was right with the Universe. She felt it and that was enough. If one of them could lift her hand and hold it, then how much more could a thousand, a million, or a billion hands do?

She stood on her tiptoes and spoke loudly and clearly and her voice was not that of a teenage girl from Brewer, Maine, the United States of America. It was an ancient and ever-youthful voice, the voice of Persephone, the voice of the water and the end of all things, beautiful and terrible at once.

"If you wish to be remembered, if you wish those few survivors on the other shore to have a chance, then you must do something you could never do in life. Old or young, regardless of your beliefs and views, loves and hatreds, you're equal now. You must join hands. Join hands now!"

Because she was River-Daughter from a time before the river flowed against the banks of Humanity, each and every shade that waited on that Far Shore heard her clearly. There was no need to wait for the word to be passed.

Had she commanded them? No, it didn't work that way. She had pleaded with them, offering them a way to continue on their journey. She finally understood what the term 'conduit' meant. As she stood there, she watched as a billion souls joined ethereal hands. Those who would have murdered each other for their beliefs in life joined hands here, creating one massive chain of souls. Kaileigh's hand was still being held by Bob and she began to feel something amazing. As increasingly more souls began to link together, she felt Bob's hand begin to solidify. It didn't feel warm or even alive, but it was definitely *there*. All of their longing and remembrance coalesced in the palm of her living hand, this brazen and brave girl who had journeyed to the land of the dead to save the world of the living.

"It's done," whispered Bob into her ear. He stepped back and smiled. As she looked out upon the endless throng that stretched to the dark horizon, she saw the smiles of a billion souls, all looking upon her as the last thing left in Pandora's Box.

Now she understood. It wasn't Joe and it wasn't Brady. It was her. She was the last best hope. She was the little child in the back of the army truck from her dream. Where the shades had stood without hope as the days and months passed, they now all felt that hope had returned to them and they began to move away from the shore, finally. She felt their satisfaction and longing for the future of humans. She was the hope of the dead.

"Thank you," she said to them all in her River-daughter voice. They said nothing in return. They were beyond the need for thankfulness. They were the dead.

Because the bridge stood in the river, the power that surged from the dead through Kaileigh, a frightful, dark energy from another world began to power the machinery of the transmitter. On the bridge the lights began to glow with growing intensity. On the Observation Deck, Joe and Dr. Grindle saw the power lights on the transmitter suddenly turn on. *God bless her*, thought Joe, *I don't know how, but she's done it!*

Joe worked feverishly to transmit their message. Later he would explain to Kaileigh that the wattage was off the meter and that equipment that should not have been able to tolerate such energy stood its ground and continued to function. He did not know how much power went through their equipment that night, but there was no doubt that this was the most powerful radio message ever sent in the history of the world and in far off places, small groups of humans heard a voice in the night. In times to come, they would talk about that night and they would discover that every radio on earth turned on, each of its own accord. Their broadcast was heard in every language ever spoken, over and over again on a billion radios, translated by the filter of the dead.

"This is Civilization Radio. We are broadcasting from Bucksport, Maine in the United States of America. If you are hearing this, you are not alone..."

Joe and Dr. Grindle repeated their message, along with specific coordinates and almost immediately began receiving broadcasts from small groups of humans from all over the globe. What Joe would later claim was unusual, at best. He would explain that each transmission they received was as strong as the transmission they were broadcasting. This was, of course, impossible. Within moments, Joe and Dr. Grindle had personally spoken with over twenty groups of people in

461

North America, alone. More messages kept arriving as the power from the water continued to flow into the instruments. The lights on the bridge burned brightly and from their vantage point at the top of the tower, Joe and Dr. Grindle watched the statue of General Joshua Chamberlain and the tough little gargoyle continue to lay into the monstrous form of Brady-Grendel on the river's edge below.

The monster drew back when he saw the lights begin to burn fiercely on the bridge. How was this possible? Hadn't he had destroyed their generators! They were transmitting! How? He could hear it in his mind. No! He had failed, again! No, it couldn't be happening, but they had done it. They had made contact! All the rage and ruin of the world mounted upon his shoulders and he flexed his mind towards the river just as he threw his body onto the form of the determined metal man who slashed and hacked at him with his sword.

"No!" he screamed, and from somewhere deep within him, Brady-Grendel felt a twinge that he had never felt before. What was that? A cutting of some thread that held him together and if severed would begin his unraveling? As he attempted to pay attention to such a myriad of enemies and ideas, Brady-Grendel felt his strength begin to waver.

Deep inside the maelstrom of Brady's fear, he continued to fight with Grendel, unaware of the world outside. He countered the monster's blows and offered his own in return, a thousand strikes in one, tumbling as they fell. It was clear to Brady that they were equally matched. This fight might last an eternity.

"Brady" called the book from his back pants pocket, "close your eyes. I can hear her. She's calling to you..."

Brady closed his eyes.

There was the most beautiful girl he had ever seen in his life standing next to him, just underneath his eyelids. Her own eyes were filled with sadness and...what was that? Love? She had long black hair that fell over her white-skinned cheeks so that it framed her deep, blue eyes and she wore a dress of silver and blue so pure it was almost painful to view. Brady was transfixed.

"Brady? Do you know me?" she asked.

"Kaileigh?" he answered, "How can that be you? You're older. You're different?"

"This is how I appear - my form in this world. Listen. We don't have much time. You have to listen to me. Do you understand?"

He smiled and nodded. She was so beautiful that she erased all the ugliness he had seen since the Abandonment, the death and the loss of the world. Simply standing next to her cleansed his mind and soul. She was supernatural in her energy.

"You need to stop fighting. You need to stop resisting. I know what needs to be done." She smiled and tilted her head slightly to the left, her hand cradling his chin. He smiled, not truly understanding how near death he truly was.

"What do I have to do?" he asked.

"You imagined him into the world. Once he was here, you couldn't do anything to stop him, but now you are with him in *your* world. All you have to do is *un*imagine him."

"I don't understand," he said.

She answered, "Remember your theory of quantum fiction? Anything that can be imagined is real? The multiverse runs on *imagination*. It's a natural force, like gravity. It's an energy field. Remember the laws of physics – like energy, it's never lost or destroyed. If, all of a sudden, billions die, the power of their imaginations is left to those who survive and to you, in particular. You created him out of your imagination because you were a child when you woke up to the Abandonment. You needed someone to blame. That's what children do – blame someone, even if it's not their fault. Since you had no one to blame, your imagination made someone – Grendel. If you let go of your need for blame, he'll weaken and fade away. Stop blaming, Brady. You need to *grow up*. You're not a kid anymore. You're a man now."

Grow up. Be a man. Stand tall. Be brave. He heard it said in a hundred different ways, but when Kaileigh said it to

463

him, he finally understood. He wanted it now, more than ever.

Brady looked into her eyes and found himself nearly lost within them. How could this be the girl who saved him in the hospital, so unkempt and severe, the goddess Athena? Here, in this place, she was so beautiful, so calming and knowing, ageless and timeless and yet, she was his friend and he knew that she was right. She was his best friend.

"I get it," he said, and opened his eyes.

He was no longer falling, grappling with the beast. They were near a riverbank in the country, the sunlight shining down upon them through the dancing green of the shimmering leaves above. Brady saw the form of a young boy about two years younger than himself sitting on the riverbank on a pile of field stones, throwing pebbles into the babbling brook. He looked over his shoulder as Brady approached. All was tranquil.

"I'm sorry," said Grendel in a child's sorrow-filled voice.

"I know," said Brady, as he sat down next to him. "I'm sorry, too. It must have been awful. It was all *my* fault."

The child Grendel nodded his head and then looked back toward the River, throwing another stone. Brady put his hand on Grendel's shoulders. The boy leaned into him very slightly, like a trusting little brother. For a few minutes they just sat there, watching the river run.

"I'm going to set you free," Brady said as a light breeze blew through his hair. He knew this place was also inside of his mind because he recognized it as *his* special place, the space he had created in his mind to *forget* about things. He had first constructed it on the day his father died, complete with a cool breeze, flowing water and light dancing through high birch leaves overhead. The smell of freshly mown hay permeated the air. He had almost forgotten it.

"You look just like me," the child Grendel said.

"You, too," Brady answered.

"I'm scared," said the child Grendel. "What are you going to do?"

Brady put his hand on the shoulder of his younger self and patted him on the back. "First, I'm going to tell you I'm

464

sorry for calling you into the world. Then I'm going to let you go."

The child turned his head and looked Brady in the eye and smiled.

"Really? I can go?" he asked uncertainly, a promise of happiness on the edge of his smile.

"Tell me where you want to go and I'll imagine it for you. You can go anywhere you like."

The boy smiled and thought for a long time. Then he took a big, flat stone and whipped it across the water as hard as he could. It nearly made it to the middle of the stream.

Then he said, "I know where. I want to go home, to the day before Dad's accident, except I don't want him to go hunting. I want him to stay home and live, so I can grow up and we can be a family together and he can watch me grow up and teach me. Then, when he's really old, he can pass away in his sleep and I can become a good man."

Brady understood and his heart flooded with grief and relief, all at once. Of course. This was *his* dearest private wish. Of course the child, who was really Brady, would want to go to a place where things worked out, where fathers didn't die in hunting accidents and where pandemics never occurred.

As Brady imagined, a portal to that world opened in the form of a white iris in midair. He had not *created* that universe or timeline; he had merely dialed it up in his mind and opened the passageway. It was there, nevertheless, just like the Quantum Law of Fiction said it would be. All possible universes exist, therefore all imagined universes must also exist. He could see Holyoke Street in Brewer on a sunny day, with cars driving by and people walking on the street. His house was clearly in view and there was his Dad's truck in the yard.

"This is one of the worlds where Dad didn't die," Brady explained.

Grendel, who was his spitting image from two years ago, said, "Thanks, Brady. Thank you!" The younger child turned and gave Brady a hug.

465

"No problem, buddy. Go on, now. Give 'em both a big hug. Remember, be good and read a lot of books. Remember to *imagine*."

Grendel stepped towards the round portal and then started running, shouting, "Hey Mom! Hey Dad!"

The portal closed just as his mother and father stepped out onto the porch and waved to their boy as he ran to them from the distance. The iris of the portal closed. Brady stared at it a very long time as a different life passed before his eyes, the life he might have lived if things hadn't turned out as they had, of a father who would be there when he graduated first high school and then college. He imagined meeting a certain blue-eyed, raven-haired girl a little older than himself and of finding true love, adventure, a future and a new family. He imagined everyone alive again in this other world and then he imagined himself away from his place, out into his own reality.

"Not so easy to get rid of us, though," Brady heard the voices gurgling and struggling for breath, like ancient athletes nearing the end of their marathon. "We made a bargain with him!" the voices of the remaining Keres whined.

"You made a bargain with him and I'm his lawyer. Sue me."

The voices began to gasp for breath and complain more vociferously. Ghostly forms began to emerge from the air before him and grab for him like swimmers on the edge of some high embankment, hoping for rescue.

"The world can do without you," Brady said.

They screamed their angst and rebelliously tried to push against Brady with their incorporeal forms, but in this place he was bedrock and they were a whisper on the wind. He knew they were trying to somehow merge and bond with him as they had done with the monster, desperately seeking to continue their existence. They had survived for millennia alongside humans, infecting them, driving them to commit heinous and unforgivable actions. They fed upon human weakness, fear and longing. They swirled around him in a perverse ballet but Brady stood quietly and waited for them to wear themselves out. Then he heard her voice.

"Pitiful, aren't they?" she asked, half-laughing. It was the voice of the Hag, the one who refused to bond with Grendel in the first place.

"Totally," Brady agreed, unsure of her particular evil.

"I will take them, with your permission, Renamer," she stated simply.

"What would you do with them?"

"Punish them for their desertion."

"Who are you?" he asked.

"The Hag," she answered.

"Why do you care about them?" he asked.

"Care? I don't *care*. I hate them, no more than I hate humans. Besides, I will need them in the distant and not-so-distant future."

"I can't let you just take them," he answered. "One of them might be cancer, another might be envy or war or even ignorance. The people of the world are so few now. We need a break from those things. Let them fade away and die," was Brady's response.

The Hag cackled and coughed a long while before she responded. Brady wasn't sure if she was amused or angry.

"I'll make you a deal, Renamer. For all time, you and your descendants will have power over the Keres. We will respond to your commands and do as you say. We will infect who we wish, trouble people with all manner of afflictions and trials, but in the end, if you command it, we will leave those alone who you signify.You will see that we are as much a part of being human as love and kindness and joy. Do not try to rid the world of those of us who remain. Many of us perished by the monster's greed, but no world with any good in it can pretend that evil and darkness don't exist. You can't have the light without the darkness. There are other powers out in the wide world now that you do not even know of that are far, far worse than us. You are not the only one with newfound powers. Others will task you. We can be of assistance. We can help you."

467

Brady asked, "How can I trust that you'll keep your word?"

The Hag laughed again. "You can't! There are so few of you left. It is a gamble."

The weakened Keres struggled against a tide that threatened to drown them in nothingness, less and less visible each passing second.

"I agree to your terms," replied Brady.

The forms immediately screamed in agony and began to implode upon themselves into tiny singularities. One by one they began to form small black dots that swirled around Brady's head like evil little Tinkerbells. Then they converged and like a dying ember, simply went out.

"It is a bargain, Renamer. I will be your intermediary. Simply summon me by calling my name when you wish. I will answer."

In the world outside, the General found himself watching Grendel's face again began to shift and turn, morphing from one form into another, from animal to human and back again. There were faces too deformed and ugly to even glimpse for a moment without pain. The General hoped to see one face in particular, but it was not forthcoming. Ten thousand faces came and went with ever increasing frequency as the monster's body began to thrash and twist. It was somehow shrinking into itself, imploding rather than exploding. Quivering with convulsive fury, Grendel began to change back into his original form and then shrank still further until he was nothing more than a point in space. Then he was gone.

When the General saw the truth of it, he gently sheathed his sword. He had successfully held the monster off, but he was already beginning to feel his bronze begin to stiffen and crack. He needed rest desperately. Gregoire was licking his hands like a dog as he squatted on a stone on the riverbank, swearing a blue streak beneath his breath. He had fought valiantly, as well.

"Oh, Mon Dieu! My tail! It has fallen off!"

Time began to flow again. Lights flashed. The earth formed and settled into shape. Brady was no longer in the monster. Back in *Observation Mode,* Brady took his bearings. There was the bridge above him. The lights were on, electricity was flowing. He was lying on the riverbank, soaking wet and cold.

Walking up to him slowly was the form of General Joshua Chamberlain. Brady wondered if he would ever be able to successfully convey the truth of what had happened inside of his own mind to his friends. The only thing he knew was that a small boy had somehow made it to a place where everything was as it should be. In all the years to come, through all the battles and miles, the knowledge that his younger self was happily living the good life in another place would give him the strength to go on. Kaileigh had named him a man, but somewhere inside, there was still a boy. There always is, he thought, even in the oldest warrior.

Brady looked for Kaileigh. She was still standing in the water at the very edge of the river, but she was also somewhere else, frozen still, eyes staring straight ahead. He ran down to her and waded toward her, taking her hand.

A thousand cannons fired. The world exploded. Sound took on a new dimension as the power that had been flowing through Kaileigh and into the bridge suddenly changed its pathway and coursed through their bodies. The impact threw Brady and Kaileigh through the air and back against the far bank of the river. When he regained consciousness a moment later, he saw the form of Beorn pulling her body from the water and back to the shore.

Chapter 36
The Journey South

from the Journal of Brady Smith

"The long night ended. Kaileigh reached across the river of death and darkness to bring enough power to the transmitter to send messages all over the world. She said that her last vision of that 'other world' was of billions of souls walking away, toward a bright light in the vast distance. Since the primary broadcast, we've been in touch with groups representing over a thousand people all over the world, from places like Burma and Adelaide, Australia, among others. I thought that since the dead finally moved on from the 'far shore,' we would lose the living statues, but we didn't. They're still very much with us, including Gregoire who's complaining of arthritis and bursitis, whatever that is. He claims he's in pain all the time and he grunts when he moves, but I think he's doing it more for attention than anything else. He follows Kai around like an evil, roly-poly little puppy, swearing under his breath from time to time when she doesn't pay enough attention to him. But he fought to save her from, well...me, in the form of Grendel. Who would have thought that he and the general would strike up a friendship? I can't believe all that's happened in the last weeks, but I think people on this planet at least stand a chance.

We're leaving Maine. We have heard from a small group of survivors in Washington, D.C.. They're the closest group of people to us. But there's another reason we're going to Washington. Dr. Grindle told us about his suspicions concerning the virus that nearly destroyed us. He designed the dispersal method for an aerosol vaccine, but he thinks that someone substituted a live virus for a killed one, something called "the Blood of the Gorgon." He claims it was supposed to be an airborne respiratory virus, a biological weapon. He never believed there was enough of it to be dispersed in such large quantities, but now? So we're going to look for clues and information. This kind of thing – the pandemic – can never be allowed to happen again. Because he knows Washington D.C., and all the places we're going to have to visit, Dr. Grindle is traveling with us. I caught him reading the letter, that email from his wife. I didn't really want him to come with us, thinking he's still too much of a broken man, but he handed me the letter and pointed to the final paragraph.

"Read it," he insisted.

It said, "You are still everyone's greatest hope. The survivors of this Pandemic, and there will be some, will remember that you worked until the very end to find a way to stop it. I know you well enough to understand that you would never give up. Find the answers. If you survive this, do not regret. Instead, remember us. I love you, always. -Diana."

"I have to go with you. It's all I have left. I need to find out what happened and record it forever somewhere so this never, ever happens again. It's what she would want me to do."

Remember Fenris? He's coming with us, too, along with Max. I always thought there was a good dog under there, somewhere. When Grendel left him to possess my body, Fenris turned back into a regular old dog again. I think he's half German shepherd and half collie, definitely a mutt. He was pretty sick, but seeing him like that brought out the doctor in Peter Grindle. He nursed him back to health in no time. It's awesome to see Max running around with Fenris. At night, Fenris sleeps at Dr. Grindle's feet. I think he just needed a human to care for him to turn back into a real dog. Maybe that's all the weredogs need – human companionship, to turn back into old-fashioned, lick-your-face and I-love-you-food-guy dogs. In the meantime, they're still out there.

What you see isn't always what you get. I used to look into a mirror and see this boy called Brady who was a little too short and a little too heavy who had all kinds of

471

challenges and one gigantic imagination. Now when I look in the mirror, I see a question mark. I don't know why or how to use them, but I have powers, strange, uncomfortable and surprising powers. I'm finding that a book can be a good friend and that a statue is a lot more than a hunk of metal. You might not know it when you look at me, but I have monsters deep inside of me. So do you – we all do. But we also have monster-slayers in there, too. Imagination is a power like gravity or magnetism and I've begun to figure it out. There are a million different worlds and the quantum theory of fiction holds true: there are places out there. When we imagine them, we're not really imagining them at all. We're becoming aware of them. They're already real. Infinity is an endless number.

Dr. Grindle is coming with us, but Joe insists that he's staying here to man the radio station. So I did this thing – I'll tell you about it because it's a secret and you, whoever you are, can't tell anyone about it anyway. Joe's future has been really bothering me because I know Kaileigh and I will be leaving here soon and he's too old and sick with diabetes to travel. Besides, he's got a big plan to continue broadcasting every night and pull the world together through the radio. He's got so much to teach us and we need him – the world needs him. But who knows how long he's going to live? So I did something..."

One evening about a week after the events that changed the world, Brady asked Joe how he was feeling.

"I haven't felt this good in years," he said simply.

"How's your blood sugar?"

Joe smiled and said with a twinkle in his old gray eye, "You won't believe it, but for the last two days, my blood sugar levels have been normal."

Brady smiled in return but did not betray his secret to his friend. Two nights ago he sat at the edge of the river and imagined Joe's pancreas in his mind, the organ whose malfunction leads to diabetes. He didn't know what a pancreas looked like, but he had done his research and he knew how it worked – kind of. He imagined small cells called 'islets of Langerhans', the organelles that produce insulin, and he placed them carefully within Joe's pancreas by *imagining* them there. It was a gamble. He had no way of knowing if it would work, but if it did, Joe would survive. It was his first work of wizardry since sending his younger self home. From all indications, it looked like Joe was going to be fine. Because of his act of summoning imagination into reality, diabetes never afflicted humans again.

"Are you going to be okay up here all alone?" asked Brady.

"You don't need to worry about me. I was making it in this world long before you were even a gleam in your mother's eye. I'll be all right. Besides, I won't be alone. I have the General and all those people on the other end of the airwaves to speak with. I'll talk to you daily on the satellite phones. You're the one who needs to worry. There's no telling what you're going to find out there."

"I'm going to worry about you, even if you tell me not to," Brady said.

Joe put his hand on Brady's shoulder and assured him, "And it won't do you any good."

In the long night, Kaileigh had come to an understanding: she was the daughter of the River Woman, the daughter of Death, a woman in a brown dress who lived in the water that was the matrix connecting all things. Kaileigh no longer feared her.

On the evening before their departure for the south, Kaileigh stole away from the group accompanied only by Gregoire, who would not leave her side and insisted that his sole task in the world now was to protect her. They went down to the riverbank and she sat on the rocky shore at low tide with both feet in the water. *Those of the Waters* met her there and fawned over her, giving obeisances, flattering her, hoping for release so that they too could finally reach the Far Shore. Kaileigh paid them no heed and called for her mother, who showed herself in a flash.

"I am going to travel," she told the River-Woman.

"I gathered as much. It's what the living do."

473

"Will I still be able to contact you?"

"Always and everywhere. I am wherever, always."

"Now that they have moved on, will I have any further purpose?" asked Kaileigh.

"Of course you will. You are the Conduit and you have helped the dead move on, but there will always be more of them, first a few then more. You will be able to communicate with them. It is the *living* who need you now. Keep your mind on the living and how you can help them through their passage in this world and all will be as it should be. Keep your mind on assisting the Renamer. He still has much to learn and he relies on you."

"What do you know of Brady and his purpose?"

"Only that when a world experiences such a great passing as this one, those few who remain need to reset the balance. Brady's purpose is singular. He alone can rename the world and all the things in it. Renaming is more than just giving something old a new word that will help recall it in memory or conversation. Renaming means giving things precisely the right name and no other. This is his calling and it makes him very powerful. To call something or someone by a true name is to have power over it. It is one of the most difficult tasks in the worlds."

Kaileigh hesitantly said, "Thank you for your help."

The River-Woman smiled and the universe issued a sigh. Kaileigh removed her feet from the water and reached out quietly to put her hand around Gregoire's shoulders and stony, stubby vestigial wings. The little gargoyle smiled and closed his eyes, huddling closer, like an ugly kitten getting ready to purr. Kaileigh looked up at the moon over Penobscot Bay and wondered what lay in store for them.

Before leaving, they had created a cache of supplies at the room at the bottom of the observation tower, with food, fuel and tools. Joe had become the teacher of the General, who was fascinated with all the new developments in the world around him, a world he could take part in as an equal, now. The human man and the metal man would keep each other company during the long winter months while the others journeyed south.

Brady had suggested sailing, but Kaileigh was still troubled by her experiences with water. It seemed that whenever it rained, she found herself between the worlds, in the land of the River and her mother. Instead, they would journey on horseback. It was no difficult task to find horses to carry them southward, either. The moment they called to a set of horses foraging at the edge of a field, the horses galloped over to them, eager for human contact. Beorn told the horses of the journey that the humans had in mind and Brady made sure to ask permission to ride them. In the new world, humans might do well to cultivate relationships with animals rather than try to master and subjugate them.

"What are their names?" he asked Beorn.

After a long moment, the bear thought to Brady, "Like me, they do not have any. I told them you would give them names. Name them. I will tell them."

Brady thought hard and recalled all of his reading and the names of valiant, noble steeds within the pages of those wonderful books. Names were his province, now. In the months and years to come, Brady would be required to look into the heart of things and discover the word that was the place, thing, quality or idea. He walked to the horses and touched their foreheads, caressed their manes and patted their strong backs, seeking the words.

"I will call you after an old friend," he said. "Rocinante – the noble steed of Don Quixote. And you," he said to the other, "I'll call you Sleipnir, the eight-legged mount of Odin, the All-Father himself. And I'll call you Bucephalus, the mount of Alexander the Great."

The bear wasn't sure about the meaning, but he sent the names to the horses who, forever afterward, came whenever their names were spoken by their riders.

from the Journal of Brady Smith
"Everything is set. We'll ride slowly, allowing Max and Gregoire to follow us along on the ground. The little gargoyle can move remarkably fast if he has to. Beorn has

475

agreed to scout ahead for us. We'll stick to the major highways and find food and shelter along the way. We should make about twenty or thirty miles a day if we're lucky. There's no need to rush since we plan on wintering over in Washington, where Dr. Grindle can help us discover precisely what happened to bring about the end...or should I say, this new beginning?

There's a place in another universe where Mom and Dad and I are all together and the people didn't die. The whole family is probably out driving to get an ice cream on a hot summer night and then they'll all drive back home together in the front seat of dad's truck. Then they'll watch TV and mom will fall asleep with her head on Dad's shoulder and my other self, the one who I sent back, will look at them and smile and maybe he'll even remember me like a dream he had once, a long time ago. It brings me some comfort knowing that they're going to be alright."

Hugin flew down from the bridge and took wing toward the southern road, over Verona Island and back inland because it was a more direct route. To their astonishment, another large black raven joined him in flight.

"Well, I'll be. Looks like your raven's found himself a mate," said Joe.

Brady smiled. "I think I'll call her 'Munin,'" he said.

"What's that mean?" asked Kaileigh.

"Memory," said Brady, thinking of Odin's raven pair.

They urged their mounts up the road and away from the bridge and their past. Brady made one last look back before turning down the road, toward Portland, Boston, New York and finally, Washington, D.C.. The last thing he saw were the words he had painted over the sticker on the back of the Lifeseeker. It read, "In loving memory of...everyone."

As they rode up the edge of the blacktop, heading south, Brady looked at Kaileigh and studied her for a moment. She was, as ever, in the lead. She had changed and seemed more at ease now, less worried. He sidled up to her and asked simply, "Kaileigh, if I was the last boy on earth and you were the last girl, do you think...?"

476

She interrupted him with laughter. "No way! No way, not in a million years!" she said as she kicked her horse into a gallop.

As they urged their mounts onward, Hugin gave his call of 'Ragnarok' to the road that lay before them. Brady found himself imagining voyages of great wayfarers from history and from all the books he had voraciously read before the Abandonment. He was about to travel away from everything he had ever known in search of what was just beyond. His journeys, he imagined, might be remembered years and years from now by people not yet born in lands not even settled by humans. Would he be like Odysseus setting out from Ithaca to fight the Trojan War? Was he to be remembered as Bilbo Baggins might be when he became lucky number fourteen on an uncomfortable journey that might make one late for dinner? Perhaps he would be remembered only as Brady Smith who set out one day in search of survivors from a deadly plague. He would encounter many monsters, deal with thieves upon the highway and explore lost cities, taking treasures from their ashes so civilization might one day rise again. Brady wondered if anyone in some distant future would ever take the time to write down his adventures. Memory, he thought, was almost as important as imagination.

Statues still walked the earth even though they remained on their pedestals, recharging their powers for long periods of time. With no humans to awaken them, they dreamed and remembered and slept. Some books still spoke in sandpaper whispers and the earth kept on moving around the sun. Knowing ravens, their wings as black as obsidian reflecting the stars, still winged overhead towards the morning. There was an empty world full of promise and a million deeds yet to be done to set the world back on a course in favor of human life. Every single person left on earth had an important part to play and a specific purpose to fulfill. For the world had changed in so many ways. As they urged their horses forward, one thing was clear: they were moving toward and not away.

Author's Note

I had a nightmare as a child. I grew up less than ten miles from Loring Air Force Base in a town called Caribou, Maine. The cold war was at its height. Every day, B-52 bombers would fly overhead, rumbling through the air and shaking the walls. Inside of the belly of each of those airborne behemoths could be nuclear bombs that might rain destruction upon an enemy of the United States. Like so many people in my generation, I didn't believe in the future, or at least the future that has inevitably become today. The future I believed in was a post-apocalyptic wasteland with radioactive ash falling from the sky like rain, sealing the fate of those poor wretches unlucky enough to survive the end of all things. I had dreams of Soviet warheads screaming as they fell from the sky and in a flash of light before any sound, all that I knew was erased from creation. The schools had stopped doing their air-raid drills by then, either because they didn't want to scare the dickens out of us or because they thought, what's the use? In the end, huddling under a desk or lying in a ditch wouldn't make any difference. We were all going to die. My nightmare was not something that my mind concocted while I slept. It was a waking dream. It was an accepted state of madness.

I've taught for over twenty-five years and I'm thankful that none of my students really comprehend this mindset like I did, even though the threat is still as real today as it ever was. Great powers have fallen and we make progress in the area of arms reduction, but we still have enough nuclear weapons aimed at each other to destroy the world several times over. As a boy, I created a fantasy that helped me deal with the intensely depressing prospects I held for my future and that of my species. I imagined that somehow, *I* would survive. I wasn't quite sure how this would happen and in my adolescent mind, it didn't matter. Heck, I wanted to live! I imagined that although almost everyone else died, I made it. I would be sad, to be sure, but time always passes and I would have to survive, somehow. Having been a real fan of the book and movie, My *Side of the Mountain* by Jean Craighead George, and having seen *The Omega Man* at least three times at the Polaris Drive-In, I knew people with enough ingenuity could survive almost anything. If Charleton Heston could survive a vampire plague and if a lonely boy could live in a hollow tree, I could make a life in the ruins of the world. I would have absolutely everything at my disposal: all the things of the earth, all the supplies, the tools, the weapons and the toys left over after the fall - all mine. I could do anything I wanted because peer pressure would have been blessedly eliminated. I would be lonely, but very busy...surviving. Then, after all of the time and effort spent staying alive in a world that needed rebuilding, I would miraculously discover that the cutest girl in the school had somehow survived, as well. Life held promise. Like the last item in the bottom of Pandora's Box, the fantasy gave me hope.

But I grew up and the world didn't end. So what? That's a good thing. But the fantasy never quite went away. It lingered there in the corner of my mind and every once in a while, before falling asleep, I would check in with that young teenage boy and see how he was faring in that alternate universe my imagination had created. Just to let you know, he's doing okay. He's older and has a family - other survivors of the holocaust have gathered and they make a small but growing community. Sometimes the sun even comes out from behind the nuclear winter sky.

So I wrote this book. It is a little bit like my own fantasy, but the characters are certainly different. Brady and Kaileigh have taken on a life of their own in whatever universe they reside. In the book I talk about the *Quantum Theory of Fiction*, which is my own rather innocent way of trying to prove that all fiction is somehow real. **All fiction is real - all reality is someone's fiction**. Think about it: every time you write anything down, it is a reflection of one of the infinitely possible universes that already exist out there, somewhere. Maybe books are the only way we'll ever be able to visit these other places – these other *real* places. It works for me.

In this world, as in the imagined world of the Abandonment, imagination is a force to be reckoned with, like electricity, magnetism, atomic forces or gravity. In this world, young women can wade into the River Styx and return unscathed. Young men can tackle demons and with a little perseverance, they can beat the tar out of them.

The adventures of Brady and Kaileigh in the Abandonment will continue in the next volume of the series.

For more information about this series, please visit the author's website:

http://www.thelastboyonearth.com

or follow the author's blog at

http://tomburby.blogspot.com